The Lost Boys of Prometheus City

A.J. Kirby

Published by Armley Press 2016
ISBN 0-9934811-5-4

About the Author

A.J. Kirby has lived in Leeds longer than he has lived anywhere else. The city got its hooks into him when he studied English at the university, and he's been unable to escape its clutches ever since. He began writing seriously following an appearance on a TV quiz show hosted by Les Dennis. Despite being told the answers prior to the show, Andy still managed to grab defeat from the jaws of victory and walked away with nothing. Ever since, he has been trying to prove he is not a complete imbecile, one book at a time. And thankfully, he's been recognised with regular appearances (and competition wins) at Yorkshire literary festivals, some high-profile publications (of both short fiction and full-length works), and he has also been short-listed for *The Guardian*'s Not the Booker Prize. *The Lost Boys of Prometheus City* is his tenth novel.

Acknowledgements

Copy-editing: John Lake

Layout: Ian Dobson

Production: Mick McCann

Cover design: Mick Lake

Cover art: Jack Hurley

To see more of Jack's work, visit www.loudribs.wordpress.com

The Lost Boys of Prometheus City © A.J. Kirby 2016

For Leon and Peggy

PART I

I

Looking back, the bubble burst the night Carl got the bouncers to beat seven shades of shit out of those two lads, Neanderthals really, outside The Townhouse. But actually it might have been earlier. Still, that was the night I realised there was no turning back for us and that everything had changed. It wasn't fun anymore.

Before that night it was the best of times.

This was us: every night like we were on camera; every night like we were stars of our own show and fat millions were tuning in to watch us. Everything we did was deliberate, and if it wasn't we made it look that way.

Cabs would drop us off at the bottom of Call Lane. We didn't have to take cabs; we were only coming down from City Square. But it was all about our image. How we'd *de-cab*. Everyone watching us. Business-cazh Carl in his pink contrast-collar shirt, dollar-sign cufflinks, watch as large as a sundial. Aviators. Adam, who despite the Leodian cold would have changed into a tight white tee which showed off his biceps and his tan. Me, in whatever clothes Ace had had in their window display that week. (Tonight, a nice new tan coat, black jeans, some clunky shoes which looked half Desert Boot and which I now wasn't entirely sure about, though in the shop mirrors, they'd looked all kinds of boss.)

Call Lane. Rampant with skinny jeans and complicated hairstyles. Constellations of neon shining out from the bars and vomit running down the gutters. Bouncers calling one in, one out, and Johnny Yellow, as much a Leeds institution as the football team, walking up and down the queues, strumming his guitar and singing nonsense lyrics, entertaining those unlucky enough to have to wait. Not us, of course. We knew people. Had bouncers calling us over, trying to get us in Norman or Oporto or Jake's. They were all like 'Evening, Carlo' and 'Hey, Adamski!' and 'Yo, Neal!'.

The bouncers who let on to us were, without exception, wearing black bomber jackets which, had you got the balls to spin them about a one-eighty, you'd see were all branded with the legend 'SAS'. They weren't Special Air Service, of course. They worked for a kind of bouncers' co-operative which was named Safe and Secure. (And if you *had* spun them around, they'd have knocked you into the next millennium.)

We were friendly enough with them. Maybe went over to this one or that one to share a word (acting like we were superstars on a meet-and-greet with our adoring public; actually I suppose we treated them like *roadies*) but we ignored their invitations and eventually walked on, past the Corn Exchange, round the corner and onto Assembly Street and our place: The Townhouse.

Cordons would be opened and we'd step inside like invited vampires. Catcalls and complaints from the queue outside would follow us over the threshold and up three flights of stairs. But by the time we reached the top, the air was more refined. Warmer too. Generally, we lived life closer to the sun than most. Sometimes we got blinded by it. We lived the high life. By day, we worked on the top floor of One City Square; by night, the top floors of clubs. Then back to bed at our penthouses.

We were forever looking down on everyone else. We knew it, too, deep down.

Still, despite the above-it-all atmosphere, it was always busy at the top of the stairs; girls who'd spent a week getting ready trying to talk their way inside the VIP section. Fellas pretending they knew a man who knew a man and couldn't they come in? Look, they had money, if that was what it took. Pointing at VIPs, riddling the bouncers this: *What's he got that I haven't?* And everyone who was anyone knew the answer.

Sometimes Adam or Carl – and sometimes me, who am I trying to kid? - would throw a bone (*fnar!*) to one of the girls. Link her arm and guide her past the Safe and Secure bouncer – this one was even wearing an SAS armband of the type a captain might wear in football – and into the promised land. And, of course, she'd be all kinds of grateful and, of course, if she stayed the course she'd make it up to us back at one of our penthouses.

That night, the night Carl got the bouncers to beat seven shades of shit out of those two lads outside, we took one each. They seemed to come as a threesome so what the hell? They were hanging, kind of on the outskirts of the general melée, pretending to be more interested in something on one of their phones (a crappy brick-like thing none of us would have been seen dead with). Something about them screamed trouble but they were the types Carl always went for. They looked plenty old enough, at least (some of the others in here were all kinds of underage). So what was it about them immediately made me think, *Steer clear*?

I think it was the air of bald desperation which clung to them. They were so hungry for something better that they didn't even recognise the sleaze pouring off Carl like cigar smoke. He went over and asked one of them for a light and she pulled out a cheapo lighter she must have bought from one of those ten-for-a-quid stalls on the market. Give the girl ten years and she'd probably be working one of those stalls.

Carl burst out laughing at her lighter and pulled out his own, a gold-plated Zippo which his dad, Carl Senior, had given him when he was twelve to celebrate his first lay. Carl's family was like that. Carl didn't think there was anything weird about them (though in truth he barely knew them: boarding school).

On producing the lighter, Carl adopted a stupid Aussie accent. Said: 'That's not a lighter. *This* is a lighter.' Aping fucking Paul Hogan in *Crocodile Dundee*. Sleazy bastard was forever quoting from movies. Sometimes I think films raised him more than his parents ever did. Made him the man he was.

None of the girls seemed to get the Hogan reference, which probably meant they were on the young side. But fair play to them, they none of them let Carl's stupid comment put them off. Not when they were so close to getting in to VIP.

Adam asked what they were called, and everything was OK after that. Adam could get a fucking *stone* to melt and give in, the good-looking bastard.

Their names were Natalie, Rachel and... I forget the other one.

Natalie latched herself onto me. She talked ten to the dozen and I barely listened to a word in three, but from what I could work out she called herself The Nat. Like she was a real one-off; the one and only. But she was just like every Natalie I'd ever met. Dyed blonde hair, caked-on make-up. Ridiculous spray-tan. Great figure. Terrible Leeds accent. She tried to soften this when speaking to me, but sometimes the Yorkshire just slipped out of her.

Rachel went with Adam. Practically climbed inside his already tight tee, she was on him so close. Honestly, she was like a brunette hermit crab. To be fair – and this used to be hard to admit; after all it's hardly the kind of thing you want to say about your close friends, especially in our... I suppose you'd call it a clique, which operated and balanced itself out on healthy doses of schadenfreude, piss-taking and banter – Adam *was* beautiful. I mean, he had a great big beauty spot the size of a fifty-pence piece on his cheek and on most people this would have been the worst kind of deformity, and, as soon as money happened their way the spot would have gone under the knife. But Adam wore it like a badge of honour: he'd been through rough times with it – kids can be all kinds of cruel – and come out the other end. Now women couldn't get enough of it. They thought it made him sympathetic. Mysterious. Full of hidden depths and pain. In effect, the spot kind of balanced out the effect of his bulging biceps and his cut chest and his square jaw, which was to make him a type of identikit beautiful, and elevated him to another plane: a *unique* kind of beauty. Everyone knew who Ads was.

(Hell, Rachel wasn't even put off by his clumsy chat. She was caught so off-guard by him I heard her introduce herself using her full name, like their meeting was some kind of job interview. 'Rachel Stonehouse,' she said. And Ads raised an eyebrow, like he does. Then proffered a paw. 'N'I'm Adam Penthouse. As in, I live in one. As in, d'you wanna see it later?')

The other girl, the one I never caught the name of, was the best of the bunch. She *was* stunning. Real Jewish princess type. Could have been a contender, or at least a winning contestant in *Big Brother*. She went with Carl, only as soon as we'd been shown to a table and had our drinks order taken she went off 'to powder her nose'. Never came back. Not to us. Turned out she'd had a better offer (or had sensed Carl's sleaziness). We saw her later on dripping off the arm of a kid I thought might have been a boyband singer. Of course, we gave Carl all kinds of shit for her deserting him but he took this with good grace. Least we thought he did. What happened later *might just* have never occurred had the girl not used him just to get inside the VIP section and had we not hammered him with so much banter he should have been wearing a tin-hat.

So anyway, what we did was what we usually did. We lounged. We were cool as geckos. Carl, unreadable behind his mirror-shades. Sometimes you couldn't tell whether he was asleep behind them. But then he'd flick out a tongue and lick a girl's ear or nibble on her shoulder and get her to pour him another drink. (Already another girl had come over and replaced his Jewish princess). Adam more twitchy: he was caning it on the coke. But cool as fuck whatever because he had that first-man look about him and he could have pulled off a full-on eppie in here and still everyone would have wanted to be him. Me, method acting like crazy. Trying not to grin like a loon. All the while feeling like all kinds of a fraud (but a well-dressed one).

We were princes and this was our court: The Townhouse, Assembly Street, Leeds.

We were princes and this was our court: I kept telling myself that over and over and eventually it *sort of* materialised into truth, like, to use a Carl reference, when you said 'Beetlejuice' enough times in the mirror. Well, hell, there were enough mirrors in this place. It was just about the most narcissistic bar in the world. It was all sheen and sparkle and minimalist and sterile. It bore about as much likeness to the pubs I'd grown up in that it might as well have been a spaceship. There wasn't so much as a single brass affixed to the wall (though there were a couple of speakers tucked up in the corners which always struck me as looking a lot like those buckety, pod-shaped urinals we used to have in our Gents; Dad had installed little footballs in the well of them in order to assist the pissed-up old alcies to shoot straight).

We were sat in our own booth. It was always reserved for us. Might as well have stuck a plaque on it. Just far enough away to the bar so you didn't get jostled. Just close enough so you could catch one of the barmaid's eyes and get her to whip you up a quick cocktail or whatever. Other booths were filled up with rock stars, soap starlets and footballers. We were on nodding terms with most of them. Carl had Rio Ferdinand's number in his contacts list on his Nokia, his gold Nokia which when you looked at it squint, he claimed, looked a bit like C3PO. Said he could bell him – Rio, not Threepio – anytime he wanted for comp tickets to Elland Road. Which was all kinds of funny because none of us would have been seen dead there.

Every night it was always the hard core three of us, but there'd also be the hangers on too; sometimes we didn't even know their names, just their needy faces. We'd slap their hands away from the bottles – blueberry Stoli and strawberry Stoli – chilling in the ice buckets, and once Adam gave one of them a smack for having the temerity, the stupidity, to try to wipe off his beauty spot, believing it some kind of smudge; but occasionally we'd toss them our leavings, our leftovers: a girl who'd had too much to drink and who'd gotten all maudlin; a bottle which had gotten warm.

There were a number of these malingerers that night, the night Carl got the bouncers to beat seven shades of shit out of those two lads outside. One guy who looked like Toadfish out of *Neighbours* – hell, maybe he *was* Toadfish out of *Neighbours*: a couple other Aussie soap stars had come over to guest in *Emmerdale* recently – was particularly annoying. He claimed to know Adam from the gym but by the way Adam kept looking so quizzically at him he might not have done.

Mind you, Adam often forgot faces. And names. And other things too.

Toadfish was toadying up to us in all the worst ways. He kept trying to drag Adam off to the toilets because he had the best 'Colombian marching powder' known to humanity. We kept telling him to keep his fucking voice down, Brains. He kept staring down The Nat's top, too, and, bloody hell, was that not on because *I* was the one paying for her bloody drinks so who was he to get a freeman's look-see? And he was annoying Carl just by being alive.

In the end Adam and I got rid of him by sending him over to the DJ to ask for 'Kernkraft 400' by Zombie Nation. Reason we wanted 'Kernkraft 400' was kind of an in-joke. We hated it really and no DJ worth his salt would have spun such commercial bullshit. But Toadfish was all like, *Yeah man, that's my favourite tune too!* So enthusiastic we all wanted to throw him out the window. In the end the DJ must have done our job for us because we never saw Toadfish again and we certainly never heard Zombie Nation (though we did a few rounds of the zombie-walk dance from the video just to annoy Carl all the same).

Another fella kept pestering me for my phone number (must have been how Rio Ferdinand felt before he finally relented and gave his number to Carl). I had no idea *why* he wanted my number; just saw how desperately he wanted it. Which obviously made me absolutely desperate not to give him anything. Not even an acknowledgement of his presence. When he walked away I heard him say something about me being 'a real dick', and had I been Adam I might have gone after him. But I wasn't Adam and besides, even though it was still the best of times, even I could see how dickishly we all behaved sometimes. So fair dos.

Still, it seemed the more dickish we were the more everyone else presumed we were top-drawer people. In those days most of the people on The Calls or in The Townhouse must have thought we were famous in some way or other – maybe they thought they'd seen Adam modelling smalls in *GQ* or Carl playing some kind of lawyer in *Emmerdale* (despite all his efforts, there was definitely something sleazy about him: people could sense it) or me warming the subs bench for Leeds United – and we didn't bother trying to disabuse them of this notion.

And anyway, we *were* famous. In the right circles.

And anyway, we had money (some) so that was all that mattered.

The Nat and Rachel kept trying to find out what it was Adam and I did. Just so they could be sure the next morning when they texted their mates and told them 'Slept with a *whatever* last night' that they had it right. Adam tried to spin some yarn about being a famous artist, the next Damien Hirst, but neither of the girls knew who Damien Hirst was so his story was dead in the water. Probably a good job. He was babbling all kinds of nonsense by that point – a couple of times even lapsing into Polish, which he spoke with his parents – and his legs were juddering up and down like pistons under the table, so for anyone to even consider he might be able to hold a paintbrush or a sculptor's chisel or whatever might have been a leap too far. He was drinking like a fish, too. Coke made him do that. Speed made him even faster. Even though the rest of us had barely touched our drinks, Ads was already reaching into the bucket and pulling out the bottle, ice and water slewing off it, tipping it over his own glass once again.

And again: *na zdrowie.* Down the hatch.

'So what *are* you?' The Nat was pressing me now, in more ways than one. I felt her leg hard against mine.

I just told The Nat she didn't want to know, love. If I told her what we really did, she'd want to punch me hard, right in the solar plexus. Or else her eyes would roll back in her head and she'd slip into some somnambulist state. Sleep for a hundred years. When we talked about what we did for a living (or should that have been dying?) it often had that effect.

The Nat asked me where my accent was from. I told her it was from the same place as me.

She pouted. 'Ha ha. Where are *you* from then, Mister Comedian?'

I told her I was from London. I was a spy, working for MI5.

She rolled her eyes and poured herself another drink.

I was already growing bored with her. I looked over at Carl. The girl sat with him appeared to have changed again – unless she'd done her hair different in the toilets – and he seemed to be having a bit more luck with her. He caught me looking and reached over for the ice bucket. He picked out an ice cube and he ran it all the way up her leg and then under the hem of her (very) short skirt. She squealed and Carl winked at me, sleazily.

Then The Nat squealed too, and for a moment I thought she'd done so because she'd also been watching Carl's ice-cube show and maybe she was either disgusted or turned on by it. Who knew?

But when I swung round to her, I saw she wasn't even looking in Carl's direction. Instead she was looking off to the right, where some sort of commotion was taking place at the top of the stairs. The bouncer with the captain's armband was trying to hold back two immensely angry-looking and *tough*-looking lads. You could tell from the start these lads weren't cut out for the VIP section. They'd dressed *okay* but their gear wasn't *quite* in season. Shirt, trousers and shoes were TK Maxx specials if ever I saw them. They looked the type to have *paid* for their booty by stealing tools from the backs of white vans or else raiding other people's garden sheds; selling on the loot on the black market in shitty, dead-end pubs like the one I grew up in. Their haircuts weren't right either. Frankly they looked as though they'd tried too hard when they didn't have the beans in the first place.

We saw that kind of thing all the time up here.

The Nat clearly hadn't though. All the blood ran to her orange, spray-tanned face and she began slipping down in her seat. I tried to tell her everything would be okay; the bouncer would sort this; obviously he had something about him if he was wearing that luminous armband (even if I didn't know the

16

guy personally, I knew other upper-echelon SAS and they were a cut above, truly). But she ignored me completely. She was practically kneeling on the floor now, in what Carl would have called 'optimum blowjob position'. She jabbed her finger into her friend Rachel's calf, then hissed: '*Look.*'

And Rachel looked, and Rachel said: 'Oh... shit.'

Over at the entrance, things were beginning to kick off. The TK Maxx lads were gesticulating, pointing, shaking fists. I hadn't known any fucker shook their fists anymore. Well, maybe they still did in Chapeltown or Harehills or Burmantofts or wherever these Neanderthals were from. The bouncer was facing them down, his arms crossed resolutely over his massive chest. But then the pushing started. One of the Neanderthals thrust both of his hands into the bouncer and the bouncer took a half-step backwards. The Neanderthal *bounced* off the bouncer and stumbled back about five yards. Yet already his pal was on the bouncer, pushing and pushing some more.

Rachel stood up. 'We have to do something – '

The Nat dragged her back down into her seat. 'Don't, Rach. You'll only make things worse.'

But they were worse already. One of the TK Maxx Neanderthals looked over and picked Rachel right out from the crowd and then he was yelling her name. Screaming it from the top of his lungs. Yodelling the bastard like the caveman who'd just discovered his vocal cords ('*WILMAAAAAAA!*'). And then he was running at the bouncer, attempting to dodge past his spaghetti arms. And being flung back once more.

'Who the fuck are they?' I asked The Nat. But I already knew the answer to my own question, and she didn't bother replying.

By now, the pair of TK Maxx Neanderthals were attempting to rugby tackle the bouncer onto the ground. A punch was thrown: I'm not sure by whom. But then the bouncer was right back at them, scuffling, gaining territory, scrimmaging them away from the VIP section with such aplomb the guy had to be a rugger-bugger, an egg-chaser, not a football captain. In the end he somehow managed to grab the pair of their rugby-ball heads in headlocks under his massive arms and he began to march them downstairs and away. At one point, we heard a clatter, as though one of them had fallen, and this was over and above the tunes which still pumped out The Townhouse's sound system (Cool Croc: a French electropop outfit a little like Air, who until very recently hadn't been heard of outside two nightclubs in the Fifth *arrondissement* of Paris.)

Carl lit a cigarette. Puffed out a smoke ring and contemplated: 'Well, that was fun.'

Rachel sniffed.

The Nat clambered back onto her seat in the booth. Nibbled at her fingernails. Then shifted my legs out the way so she could get past. She went to the window, looked down into the square of Assembly Street. Po Na Na opposite.

'Can you see them, Nat?' Rachel's voice was shaky.

The Nat pressed her face against the glass. 'Not yet... Wait... Yeah, I think I can. Oh God, they're looking back up here!' She jerked her head back.

A phone rang. The Nokia text message tone. So insistent: *you-got-a-message, get-it-now; you-got-a-message, get-it-now.* Everyone scrambled for their pockets or their handbags.

Another phone text alert blatted.

The Nat and Rachel both had their phones out; their faces illuminated and sick-looking in the glare from the screens.

'It's Dan,' said Rachel, at exactly the same time The Nat said: 'Rhys!'

Carl sucked hungrily at his cigarette and then leaned forward, interestedly. 'And what do those two fine upstanding citizens have to say for themselves?'

Rachel clutched her phone to her breasts, as though to stop him reading her message. The Nat cringed.

Carl grinned. 'They pissed they couldn't get in? Is that it? They should know the score: your name's not down, you're not coming in. Mind you: his name's Dan. Your name's not

Dan, you're not coming in... Hey, somebody didn't get the memo.'

Nobody laughed at his lame-ass attempt at a joke.

Another phone text alert blatted.

And another.

'Seriously,' said Adam, 'what are they saying? You know, girls, I hope you haven't gotten us in trouble here. How were we supposed to know you were *attached*?'

Rachel sniffed again as she read her message. Adam draped an arm over her shoulder and she made a cursory attempt to shrug him off, then accepted it. Then started sobbing. 'We never should have come here... It's only... We just wanted to see what it was like, and Dan and Rhys were all like, *We're not going in that poncey place*, and so we just thought we'd come here ourselves and then... It's not fair. He always spoils everything.'

Adam *there-there'd* her. Then he reached out and took her phone. Read the message. Wordlessly he pushed the phone over the table to Carl, who also read it.

'I don't know what we're going to do. Dan trains in mixed martial arts. He's... very strong.' Rachel was blubbing now. There was a snail-trail of snot on the shoulder of Adam's tee. Maybe a smudge of mascara too. Knowing Adam, he'd be more worried by this eventuality than by whatever the text said.

The phone finally found its way to me and I read Dan's threat. And I felt a twinge of fear in my gut and realised it was the first time I'd felt... well, maybe not afraid proper, but at least uneasy... in the longest time. 'Says they'll be waiting outside for us,' I said, pointlessly, seeing as though everyone else had already read the missive.

Carl narrowed his eyes. 'Yes, that's what I thought it said too. Though you can never tell with these primitive forms of communication. I mean, did you read the guy's grammar? And his spelling?'

Rachel looked as though she wanted to scoop his brains out with a silver spoon. Adam held her back, whispering some kind of sweet nothing into her ear.

The Nat showed me her phone. Nearly the exact same message from Rhys.

I tried to put a brave face on things, for her benefit as much as mine. Type of guy I was. 'Look, how long do you honestly think they're prepared to wait? Because it's half-ten now, and party animals like us will stay 'til the bitter end. And it's cold outside. That would be some staying power if they—'

The Nat put a finger on my lips, stopping me mid-flow. For some reason, I found the gesture remarkably sexy. 'Dan went on hunger strike for four days until Rachel said she'd get engaged to him.'

In the background I heard Adam gasp: 'You're engaged?' and Rachel's tearful response: 'It's not one of *those* engagements. It's not like we've set a date or owt. We're just, you know, engaged. He hasn't even got me a ring. And anyway, I found out later he was still at it with the protein shakes when he was on his hunger strike so it shouldn't have really counted.'

'What about this Rhys character?' I asked. 'You about to make an honest man out of him, too?'

The Nat looked sheepish.

'What?'

Rachel said: 'They've got a kiddie. Jake.'

The look which The Nat shot her friend could have turned her into a zombie. 'He's with his grandma,' she said, hastily. 'It's not like we've just left him. And besides, Rhys doesn't live at ours no more. Not since he got out.'

This just got worse. 'By "out" I presume you mean prison.'

The Nat nodded. 'Armley nick. But he was only in for assault.'

Only.

'He's wearing one of them tags now so he shouldn't even be out at all past curfew.'

Carl rubbed his hands together. 'So we got a mixed martial artist and a jailbird with a history of violence waiting outside for us. We got all that squared off now, have we, girls? That what we're up against?'

The Nat nodded solemnly.

Carl laughed. 'Ah, chin up, the pair of you. For Christ's sake, if this is a siege, we're at least in the right place for it.' He clicked his fingers. A barmaid appeared right on cue. 'Right,' he said, 'what's everyone having?'

Apparently Rachel couldn't even *conceive* of having a drink. Not now. She was all for following the boys outside and trying to talk some sense into them. But The Nat was more realistic. 'They won't see *any* sense now, Rach. They'll be off their heads. And if we've any sense in *us,* we'll get the same way. I'll have a voddy. Double. No, treble.'

I said I'd have a gin and tonic. I needed to keep my wits about me, I reckoned. Adam and Carl ordered up another bottle of Stoli and then sloped off to the toilets together for another line.

Then it was just me and the girls, and suddenly it was all kinds of awkward. Tense. At last the silence was broken by another text to The Nat's brick-like moby.

This one read: *STILL WAITIN 4 THEM MUPPITS.*

And that pissed me off. 'We should text them back. Here, give me your phone.'

The Nat shook her head. 'No credit. I'm on pay as you go.'

'Fucking hell. Okay, give me his number. I'll just… I'll send an apology. I'll just tell them… We were only having a bit of fun. No harm done.'

The Nat shook her head. 'I'm not giving you his number. He'll… he'll do something with your number if he gets it.'

I raised an eyebrow. 'Like what, for Christ's sake?'

She shrugged. 'I dunno.'

And so it was back to the silence again. The barmaid came back with our order and I took a large gulp of the G and T and felt it smoothing out the wrinkles in my brow (which was something my dad used to say). But I didn't want to feel loose and relaxed and off my guard, just in case. I wanted to stay with it. I needed to stay *on it.* Because Carl and Adam certainly wouldn't be. I pushed the drink to the side and attempted to make small talk all over again.

'So, this Jake,' I said.

The Nat washed her face with her hands. 'I don't want to talk about him. Not with you... Look, give me your phone and I'll try sending a message to Rhys. Maybe calm him down.'

I took out my Nokia and handed it over, warning: 'Watch out; it's on predictive text...'

She sighed. 'I know how to use predictive bloody text.'

She was remarkably quick, remarkably dextrous with her thumbs. It was almost as though she'd been born double-jointed for the very purpose of cracking out texts. She showed me what she'd written before she sent it. *DON'T GO OFF ON 1 R. WE WASN'T DOING NUTHIN WIV THEM LADS. JUST USED EM 2 GET IN VIP. THEY HV GONE NOW – OUT THE BACK WAY.*

I narrowed my eyes. I didn't like that. Not at all. It made it sound like the three of us were cowards. I held my thumb over the delete button. Erased it all. Then started again. *HELLO RHYS. THIS IS ONE OF 'THEM MUPPITS'. LOOK, NOTHING UNTOWARD HAS HAPPENED HERE. YOU'VE GOT HOLD OF THE WRONG END OF THE STICK.* I sighed. That wasn't right. Pressed 'delete' again.

I tried another tack. *MUPPIT HERE. POLICE CALLED. YOU BETTER DO 1. FAST.*

This time I pressed 'send'.

A message pinged back almost instantly, so obviously Rhys was just as adept with his thumbs as The Nat was. *ELLO CUNT. DON'T BELIVE U... DAN BEEN DOWN 2 ELBOW ROOMZ. GOT POOL BALLZ NICE N WRAPPED UP IN SOCK. ALL THE BETTER TO CLOSH U WIV.*

I returned the phone to my pocket and grabbed the G and T again, taking another nice long slug from it. From over the top of the glass I saw Ads and Carl emerging from the Gents. Adam was kind of rolling his shoulders around as though limbering up for a fight. Which wasn't a good sign.

Neither was the fact I could see – even from this distance – the snow which still clung to Carl's sweaty top lip.

I put down my glass and mimed wiping my nose. Carl was looking straight at me but he didn't bother. He simply flashed me his Colgate smile and then thrust himself into the throng of minor celebs at the bar. I lost him for a while, then saw him again, sharing a quick joke with one of the Leeds players: the Aussie striker, Mark Viduka. Perhaps they were comparing notes on Toadfish. Viduka was a broad-shouldered guy who most of the time looked as surly as an Eastern European assassin. But he roared with laughter at Carl's comment, then slapped him on the back. Another Leeds player – Harry Kewell, who was rumoured to be nobbling one of the *Emmerdale* actresses – turned around to see what all the commotion was about, and was soon giggling away too.

They were loud, brash, utterly self-satisfied and I told myself it was because they were Australians. But it wasn't just that. It was because they were *players,* like us. It was just over a year since two of their team-mates, Jonathan Woodgate and Lee Bowyer, had assaulted the student, Sarfraz Najeib, on Mill Hill after a night out at the (utterly over-rated) Majestyk night club. The trial was pending, but apparently Sarfraz still had *teethmarks* on him from the attack (he'd also suffered a broken leg, nose and cheekbone). And yet, these Leeds players were out in force. They didn't seem to care. Hell, there were rumours other players had done worse than what Woody and Bow had done, but these 'discretions' hadn't been made public. Yet. Still, the gossip flowed like great lumps of shit through the sewers of the city.

Woody and Bow were the 'unlucky' ones. They'd been too obvious in what they'd done, and the racial element made their crime impossible to ignore. But right then as I looked over at Carl, in the midst of all of *them,* I felt sick. These guys thought they were *so* above it all they could do exactly what they wanted and fuck everyone else. And most of the time they could, and did. There was a gloss of protection over all of them which couldn't be chiselled through, not easily. And they knew it. They knew the local media, who had their ears to the ground and their noses in the sewer, knew all about some of the 'great lumps of shit' bobbing around in it. And they knew the local media would say shit-all about it. Not while Leeds were riding high in the Premier League and doing well in the Champions League.

Protected. Shielded. Allowed to do what they wanted, like spoiled kids whose evil streaks sometimes caused them to do bad things but their only punishment was a pat on the head and a 'play nicer next time'.

It was easy to ignore consequence. Sometimes I felt like that too, but right then I didn't. Right then, I suppose I maybe had a premonition of what was going to happen later that night and how similar it would be to what happened on Mill Hill.

Adam came back to the booth. 'What the fuck's up with *your* face?' he demanded. His own face was twisted with the coke now and he was looking at me like we'd all looked at Toadfish.

I shrugged. Tried to play it cool. But then my moby buzzed in my pocket. It had been doing so intermittently ever since I'd fired off that (ill-advised) text to Rhys. I understood now I should have never given him my number. I pulled out the phone. Seven new messages. Seven!

Ads came over and tried to wrestle the phone out my hands.

'Leave it,' I told him.

He snarled at me like a feral cat. Hell, he *looked* feral. In the daytime, we were Olympians. Renaissance Men. We had talents. We were young, good-looking and rich. But sometimes at night, when the wildness took us, we really went west. Problem was, when Ads went west, he was so big you couldn't control him. Even Rachel – the previously besotted Rachel – started to cringe away from him then.

Eventually his sense-memory (somewhere inside him, his instincts were good; almost noble) kicked in and he slumped down into the booth. He dragged the Stoli out the ice bucket and he ran the dripping glass over his forehead. I offered him a Marlboro Light and his mouth twitched into a slight smile when he took it.

All was well again, I reckoned, until I happened to glance over to see where Carl had gotten off to, and I saw him with Captain Bouncer.

The bouncer was twice the size of Carl and had bent over so Carl could whisper in his shell-like. And though there was no chance I could hear exactly what my friend was saying, I knew it was all kinds of bad.

It was that premonition again: a coppery stink on the air of blood about to be spilled.

Carl fair bounded back to our booth. There was a terrible Joker-from-*Batman* smile on his face. His eyes were popping out his skull. Then, channelling *Gladiator,* he told us, *Watch this.* 'Watch while I unleash hell.'

Captain Bouncer had been nodding like an ornament from the back of a car all through his (one-sided) conversation with Carl. He was still nodding now as he pulled his radio out of his Action Man utility belt. He uttered some kind of, I don't know, *military code word* into the radio – *CODE RED! CODE RED!* – and then he called over one of the bar staff. Small guy. The small guy took over at the cordon and Captain Bouncer clomped down the stairs faster than a speeding bullet.

Carl winked. 'The bouncer grapevine. Every SAS bouncer in Leeds'll be passing on the message by now, and they'll all of them hot-foot it down here. *Told* you all this would be fun!'

The Nat gulped. I think by then even she was having premonitions of what was to come. 'Great,' she said. 'How bleeding nice for you. The big boys have threatened you, so you go running to the even bigger boys to sort out your problems for you. Fucking *spoiled brats* is what you are.'

I tried to remonstrate: 'Hey, *hey!*' But Carl was in there first, talking over me. He held up his hands in a surrender gesture. But there was nothing remotely placatory in what he said. 'Stupid numbskulls didn't know who they were messing with. Threatening *us?* We're *connected* guys.'

Thought we were mafia, didn't he? The silly bastard. He always got this way on coke.

'Come on,' he said to Ads, 'let's go down and take a look.'

With that, the pair of them were rumbling over to the entrance, vaulting the cordon and then clattering down the stairs after Captain Bouncer. Rachel and The Nat shared a scared look, then they too vacated the booth. I sat there a moment, wondering how things were slipping from bad to rotten so fast, then I stood too. Walked over to the window and looked down onto the square of Assembly Street. The grand white buildings contrasting so starkly with the bulky black-clad figures who were, like big roaches, swarming out of alleyways and ginnels, down the cobbled sweep of the road which ran around the Corn Exchange, and from every which way but loose.

'Oh fuck,' I said to the glass.

I drained my G and T on the way to the stairs. By the time I got down to ground level I could feel the booze spreading through my system. Felt like there was a troop of ants skittering about in my bloodstream. There was some kind of commotion at the door: one bouncer had been left to hold the fort and was clearly struggling to hold back... well, they looked like kids, really, desperately trying to get into the famous Townhouse while the coast was relatively clear. The mass of them were blurry: seemed kind of inconsequential as I tried to elbow my way through them, and I barely heard their yelps of complaint as I pushed and shoved my way past.

But *this* commotion was just a red herring, drawing the eyes of witnesses away from the main action, which was taking place in the shadow of the railway arches past the entrance to Po Na Na. A murderous assembly of bouncers – a veritable picket line of them – spread right across the mouth of the tunnel. They were eerily quiet and bristling with menace. From behind the line of them I heard shouts. A scream from one of the girls: The Nat? Rachel?

But then, as if on cue, an oncoming train – the Manchester-Leeds Trans Pennine Express maybe – honked overhead and then, *then,* the line of bouncers stepped forward *en masse.* I made it to the railway arches as the train thundered overhead; Carl and Ads in the shadows, wild, wild looks on their faces. Carl was laughing his tits off, but when he saw me, he laid off a moment and said something to me. I didn't catch it, but I saw his gesture, him clicking his fingers. He was clearly buzzing at the fact we were all here, the bouncers especially, to do his bidding.

My legs felt filled with tonic water. My knees knocked like ice-cubes. Suddenly, I wanted to be sick. Or I wanted to run; far away from here. I didn't want to have to bear witness to this. It was *too much.* Too heavy.

Most of the bouncers were solemn as monks and this was their ritual. I recognised a couple of them. Niall, who always worked Norman Bar because Norman always had the best pussy (his words). Connor from Oporto. Many, many more of them were silhouetted in the archway, watching as the Chosen Ones – Captain Bouncer from The Townhouse, Rick (I think he was called Rick) from the Hi-Fi Club – faced down the two lads.

The girls – it *was* The Nat, it *was* Rachel – were still screaming, though you couldn't hear them now, not above the rattle and hum of the train. The girls had formed a kind of strappy-topped and high-heeled shield around Rhys and Dan. Behind this cordon, the Neanderthals looked petrified: they'd thought they were threatening three poncey city boys and instead all kinds of hell had been unleashed on them. (The bouncers were like a team of velociraptors.) And yet, at the same time, one or other of them would make a snatch at gallows bravery and yell something over the shoulder of The Nat or Rachel before retreating back into their pasty-white shells.

When the attack came, finally, it was horrific. It was also horribly fast. What I witnessed was not quite chaos; no, the (velociraptor) violence the bouncers meted out was brutally controlled and well-orchestrated (choreographed, even), as though they all knew their assigned roles in the hellish scene. All the same, it was *so close* to being out of control that I kept thinking: *This, this will be the second they finally kill those lads.*

The final carriages of the Manchester-Leeds train were still shuddering the brickwork of the archway. In a shipwrecked moment, I thought the train might bring the whole archway down. Brick dust sprinkled in my hair. I blinked some out of my eyes. And once they were clear again I saw Captain Bouncer grabbing The Nat about the waist and then lifting her out the way in a fireman's lift; her legs kicking, kicking away at him but barely registering. And then he came back for Rachel. But he didn't have to manhandle her away. She simply melted at his stare. Fell away from the lads and slipped down onto the floor, where she dropped her head in her hands.

Then the bouncers descended on Rhys and Dan like raptors on carrion. Neither Neanderthal managed to get in a single punch or kick in response to the battering they took from all sides. Rhys went down first. Dan, who'd apparently been trained in mixed martial arts, stayed up longer, perhaps sensing that playing dead wouldn't work, not with men like these. For even as Rhys hit the deck, the assault continued. Savage kicks to the ribs, to the stomach, to the face. Oh God, the face. Rhys had one eye half-open and for some reason that eye happened upon mine and for a beat, we shared a look. Then I looked away and when I looked back, I couldn't even see an eye, not amongst all that blood. And then I tried to convince myself he'd never looked at me in the first place; that I'd never seen that plaintive gleam in his baby-blues.

Then Dan was down. He went down growling, like some kind of animal. But soon he was keening. And the sound of it was like nothing I'd ever heard before. It was the sound of a lad who'd once thought he was ten men becoming a little scared boy all over again; his masculinity seeping away with the blood which soaked into the cobbles.

The worst was yet to come though. The stamp.

Someone – Captain Bouncer – shouted: 'Someone shut that fucker up already.'

And someone else – I only saw the black blur of a bomber jacket, the bending of a knee and the flash of a shitkicker boot plummeting back down to earth – obliged.

After that, it was silent as the grave.

Carl broke it. He stalked over to Captain Bouncer and high-fived him, and the slap of it echoed around my head as though Carl had slapped me round the face.

The noise of it woke me up, and then I heard all kinds of other noises. Maybe there'd been sound all along. Maybe that moment had only played out silent movie style in my own head. But that didn't matter: now I heard it all. The scrape of the wheels of the bouncers' Zippo lighters as they sparked up post-fight (post-coital?) cigarettes. Ads and Carl laughing their heads off. The girls screaming. The Nat had broken free from Captain Bouncer now and she raced over to the prone Rhys. She stood over him for a while, as though afraid to touch him, as though she was scared he'd already be cold. But then she dropped to her knees. With a trembling hand she reached for his wrist. Felt for a pulse. Evidently she didn't find one, for soon she was scrambling for his neck. She knelt and closed her eyes, closed all of herself off to the chaos of the scene, and then, finally, just when it must have seemed like all hope was lost, she must have found a faint pulse. And then her eyes snapped open and she glared at Captain Bouncer with such ferocity I thought she might turn him to stone.

She pulled out her Nokia. Weighed it in her palm. Then, calmly as you like (though her voice was *dripping* with rage), she snarled: 'I'm going to call the police now.'

Captain Bouncer shook his head. 'No you're not, love.'

From somewhere – I couldn't take my eyes off The Nat – Rachel howled: 'Call an *ambulance*!'

The Nat held the phone up. Thin blue light shone out from the screen of it. 'I'm going to dial.'

Rachel: 'Is Dan all right? Natalie, did you check on Dan?'

But neither of them acknowledged her. Right now their eyes were locked on each other like this was some kind of showdown outside a Wild West saloon bar. The Nat had already drawn, and now Captain Bouncer did too. From out the top pocket of his bomber jacket, he produced a small baggie. White powder. About a teenth. Then he produced what he probably thought was a winning smile. 'Put down the phone, love. We found this on one of the kids. Soon as the police arrive, that's exactly what we're going to tell them. We're on a real drive to cut down on dealing at the moment. Police and the bouncing community working together to eradicate—'

The Nat set her jaw. 'You planted that on him. Rhys and Dan... they don't...'

'Yeah, you sure about that, love? The police won't be. And besides' – he nodded down at the prone Rhys, whose trouser leg had rolled up slightly now; the prone Rhys who was sockless and had clearly sacrificed his sock to hold the pool balls they'd half-inched from the Elbow Room – 'I can see your man's got form. That ankle-bracelet. He's *tagged,* for fuck's sake.'

'I don't care. You guys. You beat the hell out of them. The police will see that, too. Tag or not, you can't just go round—'

Another sinister smile from Captain Bouncer. 'We *can* just go round. Especially when lads like that' – a jerk of a fat thumb down to Dan this time – 'come into *my* club, dealing *their* drugs, and then when we chuck them out they play hell with us.'

There was a round of gruff laughter from his fellow bouncers.

The Nat sniffed. 'It's not *your* club. You're just a... a doorman.'

Captain Bouncer narrowed his eyes. 'And you're just a slag. And *they're* just fucking no-marks, one of 'em fresh out of Armley nick, I'd think. Look, I can see you're angry – '

'*Angry?*'

'But you're not helping your boyfriend here kicking up a scene right in the middle of town. You're making things worse. All you need to do is fucking *back off* and we'll call an ambulance for you and we can all forget all about this.'

The Nat bit her lip.

A bloody snot bubble blew itself out of Rhys's nostril.

Rachel sobbed. 'Just leave it, Nat. Just get an ambulance here. Stop fucking… fucking making things worse. He's right. You and your temper. It's no wonder you and Rhys – '

Natalie looked forlornly over at her friend. Then made one last stand. 'I'm going to call the police. Right now. This isn't right.'

It wasn't right. And right then I was so sick of the whole thing I just wanted it over. I wanted out of here. I could taste bile in my mouth. I needed to slope off back to The Townhouse for a strong drink to wash the taste of it away. But still, I surprised even myself by speaking up, and I regretted it ever since.

'She can't call,' I said. 'She's got no credit on her phone.'

Captain Bouncer swung round to me, making a *what the fuck* gesture.

I gulped.

The Nat hailed curses down on my head, calling me the worst kind of scum. And I wished I could take the words back. Somehow, although the two lads had been *threatening me with assault by pool-ball,* calling me a *MUPPIT* and all, and although Ads, Carl and I had been a team, so close we were sometimes accused of being *cliquey,* and although the beating the bouncers had doled out to them had – in a way – saved Team Ad-Carl-and-I's skins, I felt as though I'd betrayed this stubbornly brave girl who I'd only known five minutes.

Then Ads said: 'I think you can still call, like, emergency services on your moby even if it's out of credit. I think it works like that.'

Fucking just like him to be pedantic. I wondered, absently, if all people of Polish descent were as pedantic as him, or whether it was just a trait of his family.

But pedantry has a point in this world, and our pointless delay drew the sting from the situation. And all the energy had been leeched out of The Nat, too. She slumped down next to Rhys and she laid her head on his chest. I watched her head going – slightly – up and down (he was alive, *ALIVE!*). And then Rachel slipped over to Dan, too, and *mushed* over him. And one of the bouncers pulled out a moby and called an ambulance. And Carl, Ads and I kind of shrugged in appreciation to the bouncers before all of us slipped off into the night.

We tucked into another round down in Norman on Call Lane but by then our hearts weren't in it, not after we'd heard the sirens. Still, we persevered, tried to drink ourselves into a livelier mood. And I tried to convince myself they – meaning Dan and Rhys – were Neanderthals who'd gotten what they deserved. But I kept coming back to the fact it had been too much.

At one, Niall, on the door, came over to give us an update. He had a connection worked security at Leeds General Infirmary Thursday, Friday and Saturday nights, when the worst drunks were shipped in.

The headline news: both lads were alive.

At two he came over with another scoop: one of the lads – Rhys he thought – had woken up 'screaming the fucking place down'. But he was okay. Battered and bruised but okay. Apparently the pigs had been hanging around at A and E and had already been in to see him, but he wouldn't be pressing any charges. He said he'd fallen down the stairs at The Townhouse. Said he'd been mixing his drinks too much that night. Niall said the pigs were more concerned about Rhys being out and about with his tag. He'd broken curfew.

Carl made us celebrate with a round of shampoo. The good stuff. You could tell by the size of the bubbles. But every time I looked at the glass all I could see was that bloody snot bubble in Rhys's nostril after he'd been taken down.

While Carl was off talking to the DJ, Adam nudged me. 'It's all good, mate. The news. Those fucking no-marks will know better next time. We're in the clear.'

But that wasn't the news. This was the news: I was a shit. So were my mates. So were the men we were connected to. We were no better than Woody and Bow and everyone who'd fired into that student on Mill Hill that night a year ago.

It was just how The Nat had said: the big boys had threatened us, so we'd gone running to the even bigger boys to sort out our problems for us. Fucking *spoiled brats* is what we were.

II

Norman laid on a lock-in for us. Cleared the common-or-garden out the place and left it for the rare breeds such as us: the princes. We were taken into a back room with a couple other dirty stop-outs and Carl held court, telling the story of the assault over and over again until Niall had to go over to him and tell him to chill. We might have been in a room full of rare breeds but still, there were ears everywhere. Carl took this with typical good grace and told Niall to go fuck himself. Stop being a party-pooper already. And Niall had the good grace just to smirk, shrug, and tell him 'Whatever, Trevor.'

So in the end we went back to Carl's place. He had some powerful skunk which would see us through 'til morning. We cabbed it over to his. He had a penthouse south of the river in one of the new blocks at Clarence Dock. It was set over two storeys, but he reckoned he could have knocked through to the flat below and taken that too, because the developers had barely managed to sell a single pad other than his penthouse which he'd bought off-plan and at a price he now reckoned was daylight robbery. Ten years' time, he told us, they'll be fucking giving these flats away as social housing. Mark my words.

We did mark his words, we always did. Privately Adam and I had been keeping a tally of all the places which appeared to be in the deck of Carl's property portfolio. He never actually let slip how many places he owned, but we knew about two houses in Hyde Park which he rented to students, an end-terrace in Meanwood which he rented to a couple of our colleagues and a fixer-upper in Adel at which he was constantly having problems with his builders.

Made it quite hard to take when he persistently mislaid his wallet when it came to time to pay the cab fare. But anyway, that was Carl and we both knew Carl was a one-off. He wasn't close with his family. His mum and dad had moved out to Marbella when he was eleven. They established a successful bar-stroke-club which was populated by the princes of the Costa del Sol (in other words, ageing East End crooks and ex-soap stars) and Carl was shipped off to private boarding school. To be fair, it appeared they'd washed their hands of him much earlier than eleven. Like, when he was first born. Carl was named for his dad, Carl Senior. Only, confusingly, Carl Senior preferred to go by his middle name, Allen. Carl Junior hated his name too, and wondered why, if his dad so clearly hated it, he'd lumbered on the hand-me-down to his only son.

So Carl treated us like his surrogate family. He bickered with us like we were his little brothers; he took liberties we wouldn't have let anyone else get away with. He just assumed we loved him as much as he loved us. And most of the time we did.

Carl had a big, blown-up print of the three of us right inside his front door in the otherwise spartanly decorated hallway of his penthouse. It was like his way of announcing who he was and where he came from. Whereas in my pad, the hallway was a gallery of snaps of my family, a few collages of mates from school (which embarrassed me now, but not enough to pull them down: that would have felt too much like a betrayal of who I was) and then a few recent ones of the three amigos, and Adam's hallway was littered with pics of him and a litany of different girls, Carl had made a point of *only* displaying us.

The picture, Carl said, captured his favourite ever night. Us princely brothers had dressed up as the Lost Boys (the Lost Boys from the vampire flick, not *Peter Pan)* for a party. Carl loved the gear so much he wanted to stay as Kiefer Sutherland the rest of his life until Ads told him all that leather made him look like one of the crowy-type moshers who roosted on the steps to the Corn Exchange all day and all of the night. In the picture we looked like we shared the same blood. We were wrapped so tightly around each other that at certain points of the print you couldn't tell where one of us ended and the other began.

There was very much a sense of the Lost Boy about Carl. It was as though boarding school had arrested his development. In the open-plan front room/lounge/balcony area there were huge numbers of film posters: *The Godfather, Goodfellas, Scarface, A Clockwork Orange, Breakfast at Tiffany's* (because, as he said, *if I ever stumble across a chick as hot as Hepburn then I'm hanging up my pulling boots*). But though his taste in films erred towards the gangster, the main living space of his flat reminded me mostly of Tom Hanks' flat in *Big* (when the Hankster played a kid in a man's body). There was a table-football table (which Carl insisted on calling *babyfoot,* like they did in France). A Scalextric set, set up in a figure-of-eight on the breakfast bar. Remote-controlled cars skew whiff under the dining room chairs. Comic books strewn over the coffee table.

We kicked some of the junk off the sofas and flopped down. Carl instinctively reached for the remote and clicked on a DVD. *2001: A Space Odyssey.* He kept the sound down and for once didn't provide a soundtrack of his own; remarking on how it was 2001 now and fuck, we were nowhere near where Kubrick imagined we'd be. He tossed me an old dominos case which contained his weed and works. Said he was still too wired to roll, and Ads – he nudged him in the ribs – was too antsy.

They were forever trying to get me to skin up. Practice made perfect, they said. But I never seemed to get any better at it. Maybe it was because I only practised at the end of nights like this (well, not quite like this; we didn't make a habit of getting bigger boys to beat up the big boys for us). No matter how many times I tried it, I wasn't in the same league as them when it came to Rizla origami. As Carl had so often remarked, if I'd have tried to roll the famous Camberwell Carrot from *Withnail,* we'd have ended up with a Potternewton Potato.

I managed to get a flimsy, single-skin joint going and slumped back into the sofa. On Carl's ultra-widescreen TV, I watched Kubrick's famous jump-cut in which the bone thrown by the caveman spun out to become a spaceship, and I thought

– in the rather maudlin mood which had overtaken me ever since I'd seen Carl high-five Captain Bouncer – about how the three of us had surely reached the highest point in our trajectory. Hadn't recognised it when it had arrived. And from now on it was a spin; down all the way. We were going to crash. Things were going to catch up with us. Ten years from now, we'd be as decrepit and regretful as Carl's fucking flat-block.

I passed the dutchie to the left hand side, to Ads, who took a long toke then coughed. He looked at the cherry of the joint like there was something wrong with it. Like I'd fucked up somehow, but then said nothing. Passed it on to Carl.

Carl tasted it like some kind of connoisseur. 'This is lousy,' he declared. He stubbed it out in the ashtray and began rolling one of his own. This seemed to demand every ounce of his concentration and, for the longest time, he sat there like some kind of guru, with his tongue sticking out the corner of his mouth.

I wondered whether either of them was going to show any form of remorse for what we'd had done to the lads Dan and Rhys. So far all I'd seen was self-congratulation (Carl) and relief we'd gotten away with it (Adam). But I couldn't think of how to broach the subject without being accused of being some kind of party-pooper, like Niall.

Eventually Ads went off to fetch some beers from the American-style fridge and I decided I'd follow him over because it was always easier talking to Adam about feeling-stuff when Carl wasn't around.

Ads cracked a Bud ('Fucking shit-arse Bud! What is Carl playing at?') and handed it over to me and then cracked his own.

'*Na zdrowie*,' he said. 'Cheers, ears.' Adam was, as I've said, of Polish descent. His full-name was Adam Warshawski. Most people called him Adamski because they couldn't pronounce his surname (and also because of Adamski, whose record 'Killer' was fucking boss back in the day). We called him Ads because he looked like he should be in them.

I slugged back some of the brew. Then: 'What are we cheersing to?'

Adam didn't answer at first. First, he drank. He drank like he was a snake swallowing a whole goat. Opened up that great gullet of his and poured oceans of it down into the chemical hell of his stomach. Didn't matter what the drink was. Could've been protein shake. Could've been my dad's lethal home-brewed 'wine' – you had to put the inverted commas around the wine just as you had to line your stomach and throat with milk before drinking it: to avoid puking at the sheer *wrongness* of it – from when the three of us had been back to my parental home last summer (Dad had warned me about Adam and Carl, later: told me he thought they were bad news, didn't matter how high-flying their jobs were. 'Those two'll come back down to earth with a crash, mark me. Just don't be there when it happens.').

He drank like the kid who'd been raised in an orphanage, or amongst wolves, ate. Snaffling it all down him in case that was all he was going to get before the bigger wolves took it off him.

He drank like he was in an ad. Like he had to bend his arm in a particular way in order to best display his arms; his arms which resembled thickly knotted ship's ropes, no doubt made from hemp. When we'd first met him Adam had been a stoner's stoner and he'd been as skinny as your common-or-garden pot-smoker. Past two years he'd thrown himself into gym work with the sheer abandon he showed for smoking, once, and drinking, *always*. Course, the 'roids helped. Ads didn't care *what shit* he pumped into his body; never had. And none of it seemed to do him much of any damage.

Lucky son of a Polish bitch.

'We're cheersing to life, man. Life!'

I rolled my eyes.

'The fuck, Neal. What's the *problem* with you? You been like a fucking woman all night.'

'They could have killed those lads. Rhys, Dan,' I hissed. 'You know it.'

Adam shook his head. 'Coulda, woulda, shoulda. They didn't. End of story. Fucking hell, Neal, sometimes I think you must have been swapped at birth. You were raised in a goddamn pub. You know shit happens. This type of shit. And you know it – most of it – gets brushed under the carpet. Always, usually.'

'Always, usually?'

He flapped a paw. 'Whatever. You're in one of your moods. Just don't bring us down with you, eh? Drink your drink. Enjoy a smoke. Or just go to bed. Get your head down.'

I shrugged. 'What if I can't? What if I keep seeing that big bad bastard stomping on that lad's head?'

Adam offered me an encouraging wink. 'For that, my friend, we have coke.'

Then he sloped off to the sofas again and stuck his size elevens on the coffee table. Carl passed him the spliff. And I stood for a moment, shuffling my thoughts. Trying to let them find their places in the narrative of my life. But failing. How in fuck had I ended up friends with these two... two psychopaths?

Adam held up his arm over the top of the sofa. The joint spilled out smoke through his fingers. 'C'mon, Neal, don't leave me hanging here.'

I sighed, shuffled over to them. Took the joint and carried it over to the single-seater chair over by Carl's voluminous CD rack rather than sitting on the long sofa with them as I usually did. This, of course, elicited wolf whistles and the usual banter from Carl and Ads, but I ignored them. Got my lungs into the first toke and felt my head disappear way out west. I kept thinking *I'm okay now, have mellowed the horror right out of my system,* and then the next I'd see that horrific stamp or that even worse high-five.

Carl and Adam started up one of their usual stoner chats. Who was the real killer in *Twin Peaks*? Who would you rather fuck – Princess Leia or the chick out of *Blue Velvet*? How exactly, given carte blanche, would you *torture* Dale Lightwood at work if you knew you could get away with it free as Scot? Who was the greatest – de Niro or Pacino? If you could live in any decade of the last century, which would it be? Will you ever give up smoking blow? Have you seen the new secretary in that office on the third floor – the law firm? Fancy a bet who can steam into her first?

I tuned them out, stared at the CD rack as though it would give me the inspiration to stand up and walk out of here. Go home, for Christ's sake, and get some shuteye before I had to go back into work (as if: all I'd see was a stamp and a high-five and Carl doing his best Rusty Crowe impression, talking about unleashing hell). The only CDs in Carl's collection were film soundtracks. *The Beach*, *American Psycho*, *Requiem for a Dream*, *True Romance*, *Human Traffic*, *Reservoir Dogs*, *Jackie Brown*. (We'd slipped a CD single of Zombie Nation's 'Kernkraft 400' into the rack also, for fun.) And I got to thinking, in some tangential way, about how Carl didn't really seem to have any concept of what was cool, what he liked (or should like) other than those things suggested to him by celluloid. Perhaps that was how he managed to process the assault on Rhys and Dan so quickly and easily. Perhaps he saw them as little more than extras in the great film of his life.

I was pondering this for the longest time as the skunk worked its magic. After a while I must have slipped into some kind of waking trance in which all the CD covers kind of rippled and snapped together like cards being shuffled and dealt, and then the covers morphed into a rat run, and I saw tiny miniature versions of Carl, Adam and me scrabbling along it. Yes, we were rats. Clever rats who'd figured out our way around the rat run. But rats nonetheless. Rats who'd bite and claw at other (bigger, but not as big as the biggest) rats who got in our way. And the very thought of that disgusted me and I tried to think of a way I could skitter out of the rat run, but at every turn great big floating CD cases which were actually doors got in the way (and I do believe at one point a bouncer with a big Cheshire-cat smile greeted me at one particular door with the phrase: *If your name's not Dan you're not coming in.*

It was hella-wicked skunk…

And then some more time had passed too – hell, maybe I'd even slept (shock horror!) – but I kind of came to and I was rocking back and forth on the singleton chair and light was spearing into the room from the not-quite closed blinds – blinds which were always closed, so that you could never look out through the vast panoramic window which made up an entire wall of the flat, and see the mighty works of Leeds and despair – and it was somehow dawn. The crack of. And a minute earlier – it seemed like – it had been the wee smalls of the night.

Carl and Ads were over by the breakfast bar, sniggering away at something, but it wasn't them had woken me, I realised. It was the insistent buzz, the *get-me-get-me* message tone of my moby in my pocket which had yanked me out my reverie. With my fingers feeling like thumbs I fished the Nokia out my pocket. Sniffed it for some reason. Then checked the screen. I had 2 NEW MESSAGES. I clicked the 'read' button not really thinking about who might be texting me in the middle of the night (or now the crack of dawn).

For a while I stared at the message, not quite comprehending it. I screwed up my eyes and read it again. It didn't seem to make sense. None of my friends sent messages like this. I wouldn't have *been* friends with anyone who could mangle language so. But there it was.

It said: *LIKE I SED. SPOILT BRATTS. BUT U R WORSE. U R A COWERD.*

The message was followed, almost ironically, by what I first mistook for a triple-x, but then realised was three kisses.

Still fuggy in the head, I checked the number of the sender. I hadn't got it stored in my phone. So there was no name attached. But already, the cogs and wheels of my mind were grinding back into gear. *SPOILT BRATTS.* Someone had said that to me very recently.

And then it all came crashing back: the girls, the drinks, the lads, the bouncers, the stomp, the high-five.

I presumed the message was from The Nat, but how in fuck-a-doodle had she gotten hold of my number? I mean, it wasn't like I went out giving it to people willy-nilly. Why, only last night I'd fobbed off that lad at The Townhouse and he'd walked off muttering 'what a dick' and –

Oh shit. What a goddamned idiot I was: I'd texted one of the Neanderthals – Rhys, or was it Dan? – from my phone and told him to clear off or some such. Because The Nat's phone had run out of credit.

The Neanderthals. Currently in hospital. Had my phone number. The Nat had my phone number. The police could have my phone number. Or – surely – they'd have means of tracking me down from it. Fucking Ads. Fucking Carl. All about saying we'd gotten away with it last night. But they didn't know what I'd done.

How could I have been so stupid?

I felt panicked. Paranoid. Watched; like maybe there could be a police chopper hanging right outside Carl's penthouse, spying on me through that crack in the blinds. I gulped. Knuckled my eyes with the heels of my hands. My hands were sweaty. Stunk of something strange. *Almost* like gunpowder. But how could that be possible? It wasn't. It was the skunk. Surely it was the skunk.

I put my phone back in my pocket, hoping by putting it out of sight I'd stop worrying about it. But then I thought: *I'd better check. Just in case I imagined the whole thing about the message. After all, I was pretty out of it last night, staring at the CD rack and all.*

And then I thought: *2 messages.* The screen had told me I had two messages. I'd only read one. I pulled the phone back out again and checked my texts. Sure enough, there was another message from the same number lying right below the one I'd already read. The timestamp for this second message was earlier than the first message I'd read.

I opened it up.

DAN N RHYS AWAKE N HV NT SPOKE TO POLICE LUCKIE U. XXX

And as I was reading the message, the Nokia vibrated again and, in my state, I dropped it.

Carl and Adam saw I was awake. 'Fucking hell, Neal. Thought you'd gone in a coma then,' said Adam. And Carl

42

said, at exactly the same time: 'Who's texting you this time on a morning? You got a missus you've not told us about?'

Then the two of them were running across the room and dive-bombing me, trying to grab my phone and – frankly – I couldn't be bothered with it. And – frankly – I *really* couldn't be bothered with the pair of them finding out that the 'missus' texting me was one of the girls from last night, using the phone of one of the lads we'd caused to get busted up. So I threw them off me, Hulk-style. They'd been only playing (of course they had: had Ads really wanted to pin me down he could have, no trouble).

They got off me, looking like I was the worst kind of walking, talking black hole. Carl said: 'Oh for Christ's sake, we were only messing about.' But Adam said nothing. He rubbed at the birthmark on his face. He always did that when he felt nervous or conflicted. I wanted to tell him he didn't have to feel conflicted about me – never me – but he might want to have a think about last night... But of course I didn't because I was a rat and rats had to be very shifty in what they did and what they said. It was in their nature.

I pocketed the Nokia once again, and for a while it was very awkward, but then we heard Carl's alarm clock bursting into life in his bedroom, on the mezzanine level. At some point in the night Ads must have changed the wake-up song from the usual, ridiculous Dolly Parton ('9 to 5') to Zombie Nation's 'Kernkraft 400' and he cracked up laughing when he heard it and stopped with the rubbing at his birthmark, and suddenly, the mood was leavened again.

Adam brought out the coke. Chopped out three massive lines on the breakfast bar with his platinum credit card. 'Just to get us through Friday, boys.' Carl bounded over, and Ads produced two rolled-up twenties. '*Na zdrowie,*' he said, and then the two of them bobbed and sniffed.

Adam squeezed his nose and his eyes watered, then he held out a fresh twenty to me. 'You not partaking?'

I shook my head. 'Believe it or not I thought I'd go for a swim. Clear my head.'

Carl narrowed his eyes. 'You still in a mood with us, Neal?'

I lied. 'Course not.'

'So we cool?'

'We cool.'

I shambled over and kicked on my shoes.

Carl called over to me: 'We should go in together. Like we always do. The three amigos.'

Truth was, it had never felt *less* like we were three amigos. I'd seen something dark in my two friends last night, and now I'd seen it I couldn't *unsee* it. I flapped a paw, Adam-style. 'I'm fine, boys. Just need... Feel like I need to get a little bit sober, that's all. I mean, I was seeing some very strange things in your CD rack last night.'

Adam guffawed again. 'Zombie Nation, wherever you look!'

And I nodded. 'Yeah, good one.' Then I picked up my new coat from Ace (wincing at what might have been a red wine stain or might have been blood on the lapel) and I left.

At the door, I bumped into Carl's cleaner, Liz. He paid her to come in three days a week and she played Mum for him: ironed his shirts, cleared up his toys, the like. She was carrying a boatload of shopping bags from Morrison's; evidently it took a hell of a lot of cleaning product to get Carl's penthouse shipshape. Or else he also paid her to pick up his beers (Bud!) and whatever grub he kept in his American-style fridge. Trying to extricate her keys from her handbag without dropping the shopping. I held the door for me and she seemed grateful and embarrassed at the same time. Kind of limbo-ed under my arm and over the threshold. As she passed me, she caught my eyes. Picked out the red fissures in them. She pursed her lips, then rapidly unpursed them. Asked: 'His lordship out of bed yet?'

I saw no point in lying to her. She'd soon see the truth for herself. 'Don't think he's even *been* to bed yet. You've got your work cut out for you, I'm afraid.'

She set her jaw and, for a beat, two, she reminded me very much of The Nat last night when Captain Bouncer was trying to talk her down from calling the police. And I wondered whether she too thought of us, the three amigos, as a set of spoiled brats. And I wondered whether she spat in Carl's coffee just to attain a measure of revenge for the way he treated her, or rather the way he made her feel.

But then she struggled off down the hallway, resolutely not looking at the print of us as the Lost Boys, and I let the door swing shut.

In the lobby I could smell the fresh paint on the walls; could feel the recycled chill of the aircon; could hear the squeak of my shoes on the virgin wood flooring. The place felt so *temporary*. I kept thinking that if I reached out and touched the exposed brickwork of the walls, I'd find them to be made out of cardboard. And behind the set would be the developers, sniggering into their hands about the fact that they'd managed to pull the wool over so many people's eyes. Right then, it felt like Leeds, this place, my pals, and most of all me were all part of one gigantic con trick.

I called a lift, and while I was waiting, I picked out my Nokia once more to check on that last message. Wondering what The Nat was setting her jaw about now.

COWERD. R & D MIGHT OF FORGOT WOT U DID BUT I NO. FUCKIN PLEEZ SIR SHEZ GOT 0 CREDIT ON HER PHONE. PLEEZ SIR. XXX

Ah, not everyone was fooled by outward appearances. The Nat, it seemed, had seen right through to the very core of me. Understood instinctively that I was an impostor. A fraud.

In the lift I realised I was sweating. I hadn't felt the guilt, running in rivulets out of my (slightly bed-head) hair and onto my furrowed brow, but, under the harsh lift-lights, I saw it. And I saw those red cracks, like streams of lava or blood, running through my eyes too. It looked as though I'd cried the night away. I'd have to call in at Boots on the way to work, after the pool. Or at least go in stinking of chlorine so I could blame it on something else (though the excuses offered up by the three amigos for our increasingly worse-for-wear states were, I understood now, becoming more and more transparent: surely someone soon would *see through us*. See us for the frauds we were*).*

Clarence Dock was like a ghost town. Eerie. My footsteps echoed off the concrete of the apartment blocks. Wasn't this place supposed to be, like, some kind of bustling arena for the young and beautiful of the city, like a modern version of a royal court? Weren't there supposed to be mime artists lining the walkways of the courtyard, trapeze artists swinging through the sapling trees and groups of people on benches discussing existentialism?

Wasn't there supposed to be the constant buzz of things going on, things being created; life?

The courtyard was dead. The waterfront was dead. The Royal Armouries was dead.

Again, I got that feeling that the whole place was just too *temporary* for my liking; I knew what would happen if I looked too closely behind the scenes and I could almost hear my old dad – who, though hardly a builder was at least a know-it-all, as all good pub landlords should be – cackling about the poor workmanship and about things in this day and age not being built to last.

My route into town *should* have taken me across the river and onto The Calls, but I wanted to avoid that area – the railway arches, Assembly Street, the Corn Exchange – for obvious reasons. I also avoided the route which would have taken me up into town via Mill Hill (that other scene of violence). So what that left me was a longer hike; along the riverbank and then through City Square. I turned the collar of my new (and stained) Ace coat up in case any early bird from work – and there were many such suckers – should happen to see me.

I needn't have worried. I found safety in the crowds. Though it had been quiet as the grave down in Clarence Dock, here commuters were spilling out the various egress routes from Leeds train station, all of them looking suitably miserable at the prospect of another day's work about to commence. Most of them hung their heads over their mobile phones, checking their messages. *HAVE A NICE DAY LOVE.*

DON'T LET THE BASTARDS GRIND YOU DOWN. REMEMBER IT'S POETS DAY. That kind of thing.

By the time I reached the International Pool I was exhausted and I thought about knocking the whole, stupid idea of going for a swim right on the head. But then I remembered: the swimming was my cover story. I'd go in and I'd be all like: *I forgot my goggles and they must have just replaced the chlorine and, honestly, Dale, it feels like someone's been at my eyes with a potato-peeler. Yeah, yeah, Mr Lightwood, sir, I know you're a keen swimmer yourself. After all, you can't learn to sail a catamaran without first learning to swim. I know, I know! That's the first lesson they teach you. Well, best be off now. You know what they say: I must have done something really bad in a previous life to have been landed with so much work in this one! Or is it: the devil makes work for idle hands?*

So I forced myself through the double-doors and into the rat-run corridors (everything about the place save that chlorine stink reminding me of a hospital, and not just any hospital: the LGI, just five minutes' walk away, where two lads were lying broken, thanks to me and mine). And dragged myself into the changing rooms, those silent, silent changing rooms – a ton of silence from the male changing room at the International Pool in Leeds would surely be heavier than a ton of lead – where thankfully everyone avoided everyone else's gaze (it was like a twisted version of the Emperor's New Clothes in which we *all* pretended we weren't naked) and where, thankfully, I rented my own locker by the year and in which I kept a spare (slightly crinkled) suit, shoes, the works, as well as a wash-bag, spare towel and swim shorts. And cringed into the freezing pool. Couldn't seem to get myself properly warmed up. Whenever I felt like I was getting close to finding the rhythm of my stroke someone – an old juffer keen to lose that timber he'd piled on as he climbed up the ladder: all those corporate lunches and hotel suppers; a slowcoach newbie who was desperate to impress the ladies with the new six-pack he thought swimming would help him get – would get in my way. I thought about changing to a faster lane, but the fast lane was always serious stuff. There, the swimmers almost breached gifted amateur status and strayed into the professional territory. There, the swimmers ploughed through the water like they wanted to kick (stamp) the shit out of it. High-fiving it over and over; practically swimming over the top of anyone got in their way. And I didn't want to get in their way. I wasn't in their league: not today. Not when even the chorine was having a tough job scouring away the ripe reek of last night.

When I got out, I felt worse than when I'd cringed in. My joints were aching. So was my chest. I should really have knocked skunk on the head by now. Or at least stopped mixing it with tobacco. It was playing hell with my lungs and throat. At the end, before my dad took the final plunge off the high-dive board, he'd had to cart around an oxygen tank with him because of the fags. Should have been a cautionary tale. Wasn't.

So I stayed in the shower far longer than I should have, letting the hard rain of it beat down on my shoulders like I was in for a particularly enthusiastically administered bout of acupuncture in one of those small and very dodgy Chinese medicine places above the Chinese supermarket round back of Eastgate. Pressing my forehead against the dank wetness of the tiles. And slowly I started to come round. Started to fill my body again. My last thought before I twisted the shower head to face the wall, like some dunce student, was how incredibly nice it was to have five minutes in which I couldn't hear that motherfucking Nokia message tone drilling into my skull.

I climbed into my work scrubs. The suit smelled slightly musty. But that was all right. Better than it smelling boozy. The very act of pulling on the suit reminded me of the person I was now, and it was only when I was tightening my tie in the mirror that I felt myself grow whole again. Once upon a time, I could have never imagined going to work in a suit. But now it was as though the suit completed me. Otherwise I was just a Lost Boy all over; ripe for boyish temptation (that all familiar top three: drink, drugs, girls, and now with a new entry in the chart: violence). Sad, but true.

I wasn't like a lot of people I met during my first years in Leeds, when I moved in the admittedly small, admittedly uniform circles of university life (there wasn't much diversity; there certainly weren't many Natalies). I didn't have any idea what I wanted to do when I graduated. My degree – history – wasn't exactly vocational – it wouldn't push me straight into law or whatever, like some of the lads I knocked about with in halls. And in truth, I really didn't want to feel funnelled in that way. Nor could I imagine being miserable and feeble enough to be tied down to a common-or-garden nine-to-five office job. I'd seen how that had broken some of the guys who stumbled, blearily into my dad's pub, wanting, needing a drink to blur away their days. But at the same time I couldn't imagine jacking it all in and becoming someone like my dad, in the pub game or something like that. The hours were terrible. They robbed him of his best moments, so that when he was with us – Mum and me – he turned into a veritable mute.

I told myself I was keeping my options open, but in truth I was just shying away from having *to become*. And perhaps it was because I knew I was fooling myself (and nobody else: Dad for once took off his mute-mask and kept telling me *For fuck's sake, Neal, just get your arse in gear will you?*) that I forced myself to schlep on down to the graduate recruitment fair at the Parkinson Building. Just to see how miserable and lost everyone was.

I almost turned back, right at the last. For it seemed my fellow students – some of them at least – had been utterly shocked by what they'd encountered inside that famous white building (the real world: the world of work). As I climbed the famous Parkinson Steps I had to fight against a tide of students running the other way, screaming in fright at what they'd been told the rest of their lives would really comprise (compromise, duty, responsibility, boredom, hatred of yourself and everyone else). They tossed the flyers they'd been given up into the air and fled for the safety of the Old Bar in the Student Union. I really thought about joining them. But I didn't. I took a nip of whisky from my hip-flask and then stepped inside.

Mostly I just mooched. Sometimes I'd pick up a flyer from this or that company and try to work out exactly what these companies – and there were many of them – did. At the Arthur Andersen stall I picked up a flyer and it had pictures of fellas looking like Next models in their suits, poring over what might have been architectural plans or else an interior map of the human body or else the Magna Carta. The point was you couldn't see what they were looking at. The next picture had the same models in Next cazh gear, riding fucking horses of all things. And the final picture had the Next guys, like, high-fiving (a premonition of Carl's high-five with the Captain Bouncer after the assault outside The Townhouse?) in a lift, for some reason (I suppose the picture was saying: these guys, these princes, are going all the way to the top. Ding. The lift stops and you're on the top floor with a corner office; a place where you've really, truly arrived, and – hot God! – you're so *inner sanctum* you can even use the gilded top floor loos in order to lay your morning cable.)

I was sneering down at the flyer trying to work out whether the ads could be any *more* American. I mean, people were more cynical over here. Couldn't they have, like, changed the brief for the UK market? Hadn't they got the fucking memo? Had they done, they could have had the same guys, only with crappier teeth and in crappier rooms, and instead of riding horses they could have been playing killer-pool and drinking, and instead of riding the lift – or should that have been elevator? – they could have been walking dank, piss-stinking stairs.

One of the reps on the stall came over to me. Tall guy. Enough oily-greasy product on his hair to clag up the wings of a whole flock of seabirds. Crappy side-parting. Slick suit, though, I had to give him that. And I liked his tie-pin too. You had to look real close, but when you did you saw it was a light-saber. And I was a sucker for *Star Wars,* just like any kid born in the late '70s.

Slick Suit came over; proffered me a paw to shake. Began to introduce himself and his company, Arthur Andersen, then paused. 'Say, aren't you Justin Cunliffe's baby brother?'

For a beat, I thought about pretending I was. That was the level of high jinx I used to get up to as a student. I thought about spinning him all kinds of yarns, telling him yeah, I was, and wasn't it great our Just had come out as gay now... But, ah, what was the point? For all I knew, Slick Suit might be Arthur Andersen himself and maybe that was what Arthur Andersen did: maybe they made, like, lie-detectors or something.

I shook my head.

People were always confusing me for other people at uni. I used to find it very funny but just recently I'd decided it annoyed me. I wanted to be me, the unique and one and only me... I didn't want to be so bland, so uniform, I could have been anyone else.

'Sure?' he pressed. Like I didn't know my own siblings or family history. Like I maybe had had too many nips from my hip-flask and had temporarily taken leave of my senses. 'Cos I could've sworn you... Maybe not, no. But I do recognise you. Did you go to Gateways?'

I didn't know what Gateways was, but it sounded kind of like a rehab centre for fucked up kids. Turns out it wasn't. Turns out it was a prestigious private school in Leeds.

He shook his head. Wincing. Pulling this face like, *I'm really trying to place you here. Toss me a bone, why dontcha?* 'Are you an oarsman, then?' he asked, at last.

I shook my head. All that shaking was making me feel sort of dizzy.

Slick Suit flapped a paw. 'Ah, well, never mind. Let's start again, shall we?' He proffered that paw again. 'Nick Byers. Pleased to meet you.'

That handshake changed my life. In many ways, it was a golden one. But in a lot of others it was like we were shaking on a deal: I'd just sold my soul to he of the cloven hoofs.

Byers was devilish, I'll give him that. He had the patter. Exactly the right sales technique. He knew exactly what buttons to press with arrogant and yet impressionable (half-drunk) big fish in the small pond of uni. Even before he told me what Arthur Andersen did (and it wasn't making fucking lie-detectors; in fact, in hindsight, that would have been all kinds of ironic given what they did get up to) he set up working for the company as some kind of challenge. He made it seem like some kind of new and exciting extreme sport. He told me if I picked Andersen and if Andersen picked me, there was still an even chance I wouldn't be at the company in ten years. 'A lot of people don't have what it takes,' he told me. 'They fail.' He talked about the high rates of burn-out. He told me that in all likelihood in five, six years' time, I'd find myself doing something else entirely. Like, he told me, there was a girl in his graduate intake group had run off to Africa to set up a women-only safari company. 'She learned how to shoot guns and fix engines and everything,' he explained.

And I liked the sound of that. Either I'd succeed or fail. Cut-and-dried. No fucking fannying about. No shying away from myself. And even if I did fail, it wasn't proper failure. It wasn't running-a-shitty-pub-into-the-ground failure. No, it was an exciting new brand of failure (I rather liked the idea of going on safari *with a gun,* protecting an all-women group, and then huddling up with them all at night to keep them warm).

Then Byers started talking about what life at Andersen was like if you were a success. If you had what it took (balls, I presumed). He told me to pick a number, any number, like he was a game show host (and in truth, he did look like one).

Wilful ole me plucked a million out the air, because of course I knew he was talking salaries.

And Byers surprised me by not pulling a surprised face. Instead he nodded sagely. 'Sounds about right. If you make it as a partner.'

Then he told me what I could expect to earn in my first month and it was nearly as much as my dad made in two years at the pub. We were talking telephone numbers. Byers wrote the number down for me on my flyer, alongside his actual telephone number. 'That's your takeaway,' he told me.

And I took it away. Didn't scatter it to the Leodian breeze as so many others had. Instead I studied it intently. His telephone number was a mobile number and that also impressed me, as there weren't many of them about then. But the monthly salary, underlined five times, was what made me eventually call him back. (Well, that and the dream of an all-woman safari.)

He said he knew I'd call. He remembered me. I supposed he said that to everyone, but I still felt a Ready Brek glow in my belly: *he'd remembered me, above all those others. Me. Little ole me. I was unique after all, even though he'd at first confused me with someone else.*

Then he asked me to guess where he was right now.

I couldn't think of anything witty or amusing to say. I'd been so nervous when I'd called (working out the astronomical rates it would cost to call a moby and telling myself the call was an investment). So I said, blandly: 'The office?'

Byers made a noise which roughly approximated the *eee-uuuuhhh* noise which accompanied a wrong answer on a Les Dennis-hosted game show. 'Guess again, chief.'

So I guessed the pub. Then the cinema. Then Elland Road. And my every answer was met with that same *eee-uuuuhhh* noise, and all the while I was calculating just how much the call was costing me on the BT bill which my flatmate Henry went through with a fine-toothed comb every quarter. In my mind's eye I saw an odometer, moving fast, going into triple-digits. And I thought, again, of game shows and how the sweet-talking devil of a host always encourages the contestant to take a gamble, even though they've already got a good amount stashed, and they wind up losing and he smarms *Better luck next time.* And the contestant is left with a lifetime of regret. If only they'd been strong enough to turn away from temptation.

There was a guy like that used to come into Dad's pub back in the day. Proper alcie. Worked for the council in the refuse department (though not actually on the bins; in some kind of back office, allocating routes or whatever). He used to moan into his pint about how he could have left his shitty job ten years ago if only Bruce Forsyth had not persuaded him to take a spin on the 'All or Nothing' wheel. That guy had hooked a big fat zero in the end, and in the intervening years his wife and daughter had left him – hell, even his once-faithful dog had left him – because he couldn't bloody shut up about being *this close* to winning 'a life-changing' amount of moolah.

'Give up?' said Byers, finally.

And I told him no way. I told him I never gave up. Which wasn't exactly the truth, but as near as damn it.

And Byers said: 'Good. *Great.* That's the type of person we like at Andersen. A tenacious person.'

I closed my eyes and felt myself floating out of my crappy little bedroom (actually half a bedroom; the unscrupulous landlord had split what was already a tiny room in two, using a wall which was as cardboardy-feeling as the walls at Carl's apartment block, and through those walls I could hear every bottom-burp the eternal bean-eater Henry ever emitted) and out over the red roofs of Hyde Park and over the litter-strewn fields of the park proper and down, down into the city itself. And I saw Nick Byers, the great Nick Byers, standing on top of a very high building – so high he could spit on pigeons – smoking.

I saw this so clearly I'd given my final 'All or Nothing' answer before I'd even realised I'd spoken. 'You're up tall,' I said (childishly). 'Looking down on creation, like in that song.'

There was a momentary pause, then the sound of Byers' latest exhalation. (I pictured a smoke ring, floating fragile as a butterfly, but gradually growing larger and more solid. So that eventually it came to resemble a roulette wheel.)

'Very good, Neal,' he said finally. 'I won't presume to know how you did that, but... spooky. I knew there was something about you the first time I clapped eyes.'

Then he invited me to come down for an interview, at One City Square, which turned out to be the very tall building he'd been standing atop of, fire door propped open, in the shadow of the lightning rod, as he talked to me that day. He warned me not everyone would be as easy-going as he was but I should stick to my guns. Let my natural charm win me through. And by the time I put down the phone, my hands shaking some, I'd signed up for the gamble round of the Nick Byers show.

The night before the interview I got woefully, ridiculously troll-eyed at Vod-Soc. Henry had finished his exams that day and he demanded I come along to help him celebrate. Of course, I should have ignored his banter – 'You're not the lad I thought you were, Neal. I thought you were supposed to have grown up in a pub?' – said no and tucked myself up bright and early. But then again, I've always been great at self-sabotage. The first time Dad trusted me to run the pub by myself I was sixteen, green and incredibly happy. I was also incredibly stupid, and invited most every girl in my new sixth-form centre to come down and enjoy a few underage drinks. Of course they told their friends and they told theirs and in the end we crammed *hundreds* into the place. To soak up my worry, I ploughed into Dad's whiskies and by the time Mum and Dad arrived back from wherever it was they'd been (it couldn't have been a night at the theatre: they weren't that type of parents; perhaps he'd taken her to the snooker at the Crucible) I was so drunk I'd passed out in the cellar, little knowing folk were running off into the night with whatever booze they could take and even, at last, some of the brass from the walls.

The morning after Vod-Soc I woke up feeling as bad as I had the morning after the great ransacking of the Golden Goose. I felt as though a goose had laid an egg in my throat and also taken a shit on my tongue. My brain felt full of feathers. I reached out to check my alarm clock, my whole body screaming in complaint, and then I *actually* screamed when I saw the livid red numbers flashing *00:00*. There must have been a power cut overnight; our shoddy rented house was prone to them. I'd planned to borrow another alarm clock – Henry's analogue one – when I got home, as a just-in-case, but clearly the booze had made me forget that good intention.

Henry, having been woken by my scream, which of course was just as loud in his room as mine thanks to the thin walls, stumbled into my room rubbing his eyes and reeking of vomit. 'Keep it down, why dontcha?' he growled. Then: 'Oh, I thought you had a girl in here. Did you not have a bird on your arm last night?'

I couldn't remember. It didn't matter. 'What time is it?' I demanded.

Henry checked his watch. 'Two.'

That didn't help. I'd been known to sleep off a drunk for twenty-four hours. Longer if I'd mixed the booze with some weed. '*AM* or *PM*?'

'Uh.' Henry scratched his stubble. For a guy who'd most likely ace his applied chemistry exams and end up building nuclear warheads or something, he was all kinds of slow at doing everyday things, like telling the bloody time. '*PM,*' he said, finally.

'But what *day?*' I felt like someone who'd awakened from a coma. Or maybe *he'd* woken up from a coma. At any rate, my next question might be what year and the one after that would be something about the prime minister, or the FA Cup.

After the longest time, Henry confirmed it was Wednesday. Which meant I had an hour to get scrubbed clean, dressed, on the bus, into town and sober. It was some ask. I jumped out of bed like I'd pissed in it. I hadn't: it was Henry was prone to bouts of incontinence after a night on the tiles. I did piss in the shower though, thinking it would save me time. I also shaved in the shower. That didn't save me time. I used up pretty much the last roll of bog-roll sticking square after square of it on the various Edward Scissorhand cuts on my face.

Then it was back to my room and, *oh fuck,* where in cock had I put my *suit*? I knew I'd put it somewhere for safe-keeping, somewhere it would hang properly and hopefully lose its wrinkles. But it didn't appear to be in the wardrobe, the place any normal or sane person would have put it. Nor was it under the mattress on the bed, which is where me, insanely drunk me, might have put it, thinking, *that'll flatten out those creases.* So where was it?

I spun around the suddenly spacious-seeming room, desperately seeking it in all the usual hiding places, until I felt sick and had to sit down on the end of the bed. Nick Byers' voice echoed around my head. I imagined him saying: *I'm very disappointed in you, Neal. I had such high hopes for you. Unfortunately, however, there is no vacancy at Arthur Andersen for a boy who cannot dress himself.*

This gave me a new lease of life. I pulled all the drawers out my chest of drawers and looked behind them and under them, and then I lifted my crappy Ikea rug which covered that red wine stain on the floor which would doubtless see me lose my whole security deposit from our unscrupulous landlord, and then I tried – with a strength I didn't know I possessed, especially when hungover; the *kind* of strength which mothers can sometimes summon to lift whole cars off their babies – to lift the bed. I did some, too. But still no suit.

Sheer desperation forced me back out my bedroom door. Downstairs, into the basement kitchenette; with my every step thinking *Please, God, don't let me have burned it in the oven,* or else *Please, don't say I've been stupid enough to have tried to wash it in the machine.*

I didn't even notice the smell. Not then. My every sense was concerned only with searching out the suit, wherever it might be. That suit had served me well over the years. Funerals, weddings, a few nights out at the posh casino down on Clarence Dock. But now it was refusing to play ball.

Henry was in the kitchen, sweating over the hob. I knew better than to ask him what he was doing. 'Have you seen my suit?' I shrieked.

He swung round. There was a mischievous grin on his face.

'What have you done with it?'

He nodded to the front room. I imagined what he might have done with it: cut off the arms and legs like some vengeful stay-home wife of the businessman who'd been having it away with his secretary for years. Used it to mop up one of his spills (or incontinence stains). Hell, Henry might have done anything with it.

But he hadn't. Henry, God bless him, had – at some point during our drunken night – taken an iron to it. And, remarkably, he hadn't wrecked it. Damned thing looked good as new. Fuck me, I almost cried. It was practically the nicest thing anyone had ever done for me. Still is, actually, and when I thought about pulling the pic of Henners down off my hallway wall, thinking of that moment was the thing that stopped me in my tracks.

I pulled on the suit. It was still warm from the iron, so maybe he hadn't done it last night. Maybe he'd been in my room and got it when I was in the shower. As my reflection was tying his tie in the turned-off TV screen, Henry clomped into the front room carrying that smell with him and, fuck me, I was so antsy and so hungover that instead of saying thank you for the suit what I actually said was: 'Don't get your fucking bacon smell all over me, thank you very much.'

Henry was used to my moodiness by then, and well-versed in stepping around it. He handed me a plate containing a bacon butty. Then he handed me a vodka. The bacon made me feel sick and I couldn't even look at the vodka.

'Chin-chin, Neal. Down the hatch with both and then you'll be fighting fit all over again.'

'I can't eat. I certainly can't drink that.'

'Nonsense. Hair of the dog that bit you? You'll be right as rain in five minutes. You'll be knocking down the door at Vod-Soc wanting seconds.'

'I'm not going to Vod-Soc. I'm going to a job interview at a big five accountancy firm.'

'And once you've knocked that back, you'll be buzzed all over again. These guys – they love enthusiasm. And right now you look about as enthusiastic as a... a... cardboard box. And besides, you can't smell vodka on someone's breath.'

'That's a myth,' I countered. 'One of our history profs used to wolf it down in lectures. Pretended it was cough mixture or water or whatever. Always you could smell it on his breath though.'

Henry winked. 'Ah, but your history prof won't have been drinking Stoli.' He went to the kitchen and brought back a bottle. 'This is my all-time favourite. I'd been saving it for when I finished my exams. I was going to bring it out when we got in last night, but by then it was pointless. We'd already ruined our taste buds by then. All that low quality stuff they serve at Vod-Soc. Honestly... But the Stoli. Tastes smooth as water.'

I was doubtful.

'Here, sniff it.' Henry unscrewed the cap and held the bottle under my nose. I gipped. But it wasn't because of the smell of the Stoli – that didn't even seem to have a smell – rather it was because of the close proximity of Henners, who took great pride in only showering once a week, incontinence or no.

I took up the glass Henry had poured. Stared at it as though in challenge.

Then, without giving myself any more time to think about it, I sunk it in one.

And all at once I felt fine. *Better* than fine. This hairy dog didn't bite me, it nosed my knee, looked up at me with lovely hazel eyes and begged me to take it for a walk. Hell, I could walk it all the way down to One City Square if I wanted. Honestly, the Stoli hit me that day better than coke ever did in the following years.

I still couldn't face bacon though. And I didn't have time to wait to see if it would seem more appealing in five minutes. So I left. Picked up some gum on the corner shop just in case Henry and I were wrong and had totally fucked up our sense of smell last night, and then waited for what seemed like an interminable ten minutes for the number 57 into town. On the way, I chewed my way through the whole pack of Airwaves.

Suddenly it seemed everything was working in my favour. After the terrible start to the day I'd been sure I'd never make the interview but now every light clicked on to green as the bus approached and, wonder of wonders, the driver chose to sail past a number of stops which were thronged with students, the type of students who took their own sweet time to get on the bus and then copper up to pay the driver. *Here's ten, twenty. No wait a minute I have a few five pence pieces I want to get rid of.*

I made it into City Square with five minutes to spare before my interview and only then did I think I maybe should have considered exactly what I was going to say to these people; these people who Nick Byers, the sharp-as-a-tack Nick Byers, had claimed were maybe not as easy-going as he was. Oh sure, I'd genned up on a few standard interview questions. But I barely knew what Andersen did. I hardly knew more about them than I had when I'd reckoned they might have manufactured lie-detectors.

What's more, as the bus spat me out, I heard an ominous grumble and at first thought it had to be something to do with the bus's pneumatic braking system, but soon realised it was *my empty stomach.* I couldn't very well talk over the sound of that for an hour, or however long this damned thing was supposed to last. And now, rather than accountancy – *what is accountancy?* – all I could think of was bacon butties dripping with Tommy K.

It was this basic, primal instinct – hunger: I needed to eat, tear my teeth through the flesh of something – which finally talked me out of my extreme nervousness (and maybe it was the still-settling vodka, too). I thought back to my first meeting with Nick Byers and how I'd thought Andersen seemed like a win-win because I could fail or I could succeed and either way come out on top, and I thought about whether I really wanted to be an accountant at all. I mean, wasn't

60

accountancy plain boring? And I'd never been *that* great with numbers.

So I told myself I didn't care. This – the whole thing – was something I could chalk up to experience, and, who knew, maybe in twenty years when Henners and I met up for family holidays, the both of us with our 2.4s and buxom wives, we'd maybe stay up late one night drinking too much wine and we'd get to reminiscing and I'd say something like, 'Remember that time I nearly became an accountant?'

And Henry would still have that hyena laugh and he'd bark it out and splutter wine all over himself. Finally he'd get composed, and he'd say, 'Remember you necked a voddy before you even went? I mean, who necks a voddy before a job interview apart from someone who doesn't want the job?'

And then we'd both be off and laughing and maybe one of our wives would slipper on down to us and tell us to keep it down because the kids were sleeping, and we would, for a bit, but then one of us would say, 'And you couldn't even find your suit! I mean, what big five accountancy firm would employ a guy couldn't even dress himself?' And we'd be banging the tables, such was our jollity.

Basically, we'd be laughing because it was such a close call. You can always laugh at your near misses given the benefit of hindsight. You're laughing because you're half mad with the thought that had your life but taken that whisker of an offshoot turn, you'd have been a completely different person.

So, I went into the interview with that kind of take it or leave it attitude. And aced it, grumbling stomach or no. The panel contained four Andersen-ers. There was Nick Byers, of course, who tipped me a helpful wink as I entered, and there was a short-arse named Dale Lightwood, who I was soon to discover would be my new boss, and then there were a couple of bods from HR.

Lightwood chaired. He began by asking me to introduce myself, but before I'd gotten much further than providing my name, he'd interrupted. He began to tell me a long and winding story about Arthur Andersen and how they were founded. I got the impression that it wasn't just me bored. Hell, the two bods from HR looked as though they wanted to smash the jug of water into their own faces, *anything* to get out of hearing this crap another time. Then Lightwood moved on to more general subjects.

'What,' he asked, 'do you think accountancy is all about?'

I wondered whether it was a trick question. 'Numbers,' I said. Then I said it louder to cover up my stomach, because when I'd said *numbers* for some reason I'd thought of the three bottles of tomato sauce in our fridge and the two rashers of bacon and the couple slices of bread.

Lightwood nodded. 'Okay. Yes, well that's certainly something to do with it. But what I'm really trying to get at is the *principle* of the thing. The essence of it. You see' – he steepled his fingers; the choir he was preaching to tried hard to stifle yawns – 'an accountant is a person who audits and inspects the finances of individuals or businesses and prepares financial reports. But primarily an accountant is *accountable.* Reliable. Trustworthy. Authoritative. Are you this type of person, Mr, uh, Grace? Do your friends at university think of you as the honest one? The one with all the integrity?'

I gave a non-committal answer. It didn't matter. Lightwood had gone off on one. I could have walked out the room and he wouldn't have noticed. The other members of the panel looked as though they'd have given their eye teeth to have done exactly that. Lightwood stood up and began pacing the room. 'Arthur Andersen,' he said, 'is a rare beast. We are one of the big five, sure, but we're not *lumberers,* Grace. Not like PWC. Basically what I'm saying is this: have you ever been on safari, Neal?'

The question caught me by surprise. I muttered something about Knowsley Safari Park.

'I'm talking Africa. The great plains and savannahs. The Masai Mara. Serengeti. The wondrous beasts. At migration time. Simply nothing better! Up there in a hot air balloon looking down on all those animals, and you've got your spotter's jotter and you're ticking off your big five.' He reeled off the list, counting them on his fingers. 'The rhinoceros, the lion, the elephant, the Cape buffalo. And the leopard. Oh, everyone sees the rhino and the elephant. They're too big to miss. And the buffalo roam in herds. Scores of them. The lion is rarer. But most everyone sees a lion on safari. The leopard though? He's stealthy. No lumberer, he.' Lightwood V'd his fingers between two slats of the blind and clicked them open, looking out over City Square. 'We – the royal we: Arthur Andersen – are the leopards of this particular Leodian savannah,' he pronounced. 'We're vicious hard workers. We're not *obvious,* like lions, like elephants, like rhino. We're individual. Unique. A rare breed in the accountancy world. We march to the beat of our own drum.'

Snap, the blinds closed.

'Great,' I said.

He nodded. 'Great. So, will you tell us a little about Neal Grace? Are you a rare breed?'

I gulped. Suddenly the only stuff I truly knew about myself was the fact I'd downed a record twenty vodka-Red Bulls at Vod-Soc last night and that I had once been quite good at Subbuteo but I'd given it up when I stopped liking football. I could have told him I'd once been in a rock and roll band – I'd been the singer; I wasn't patient enough to learn guitar – but I'd knocked that on the head too when the regular routine of Saturday morning practice interfered with my free time too much. I could have told him the only time I'd ever been in love was with a French girl on a school exchange and when she kissed me I cut my tongue on her brace. I could have told him our rented house had been burgled four times that year; twice after Henry had forgotten to lock the front door. But apart from that, I had nothing.

Nick Byers mouthed *Come on,* and I realised I was starting to resemble a grounded fish; my mouth bobbing open and closed but nothing coming out. And, for some reason, I found myself thinking about that first time Nick and I had met, at the graduate recruitment fair at the Parkinson Building, and how Nick had had me confused with someone else: Justin Cunliffe's brother, wasn't it? And my first instinct then had been to pretend to *be* Justin's li'l bro, only I'd bitten it back then. But why couldn't I play *let's pretend* now?

'Well,' I said, 'the number one thing about me is I was once described as the most talented young British lacrosse player for thirty years. I mean, nobody had ever seen anything *like* me before. I had it all and everyone wanted me to play for them. The school. The county. England. I sacrificed everything for the game. Even my two front teeth. But then, in my final year at sixth form, disaster struck. I'd been called up for the national team yet again and we had a night game in, um, London. But my school still needed me to play for them because for the first time in their history they were close to reaching the national finals and we were putting that old place on the map. And my head teacher practically pleaded with me to play for the school in the afternoon, and in return he'd drive me down to London in time for my date with the England side. So in the afternoon, I booked us a place in the final and then we set off down the M1. The head teacher was going much quicker than he probably should have, but the accident wasn't his fault. I would still tell him that now, were he alive. And I know he'd barely be able to forgive himself, but I'd tell him I was willing to let it go.'

I croaked.

One of the HR bods gave me a sympathetic look and the other one poured me a glass of water. Nick Byers positively glowed. I knew he'd love the lacrosse bit. Hell, even Lightwood looked like he was on board with my lies: as I was later to discover he was a keen amateur yachtsman and looked all kinds of sorry for a fellow sportsman who couldn't pursue his dream any longer due to injury. Actually, maybe I'd laid it on a bit thick with the injury... Probably I had with the national team stuff too: those kinds of things could be checked up on. But would they *really* check?

Shit, maybe they would. Accountants lived and died by auditing and checking. Still, I couldn't worry about that now.

I gulped the water.

'What happened?' said Lightwood.

'A lorry happened. It crashed through the central reservation. Later they did tests on the driver and he'd had some kind of seizure. And my head teacher could have avoided the lorry but... but he was fiddling with the radio dials, trying to find a station with traffic reports because he was worried we weren't going to make it to London in time. They had to cut me out of the wreckage later, and my knee was busted so badly I'd never play lacrosse again. But I was the lucky one. My head teacher died instantly.'

One of the HR bods silently wiped his eyes. Shit, I'd gone far too far with this now. I needed to stop talking.

'Poor, poor man,' said Lightwood, and I didn't know whether he meant my made-up head teacher or me.

And then it was as though a cloak of silence had been thrown over the room for the longest time. Nick Byers finally broke it. 'Sorry to hear all that, Neal. Maybe we should move on to something else.' And I felt all kinds of grateful to him for throwing me that bone; later I wondered whether he'd known I was bullshitting, but I never quite plucked up the nerve to ask. 'Why don't you tell us about your university career?'

I played with a straight bat now. Other than adding in some pointless anecdote about being a member of the theatre club, I didn't make anything up. I told them I was the first member of my family to have attended uni and that this had made me work harder than I otherwise might have done. I told them about how I had a passion for history, especially European history, and that I thought the research skills I'd learned at Leeds would surely only help me in a role at Andersen. Lightwood almost wrong-footed me by asking what my dad did and I almost answered as the Cunliffe sibling, but I forced myself to say 'landlord'.

'Property?' asked Lightwood.

'Pub,' I answered.

'Ah,' said Lightwood. He stood up again and wandered to the window, cracked the blinds once more. It was, I thought, as though he was embarrassed by my answer. But perhaps that was a good thing. At uni I was always getting away with stuff – missed coursework deadlines, my frequent absenteeism from 9am seminars – because, as I liked to remind my tutors, here I was, this working-class boy made good, but I'd never had any real mentors, so why couldn't they cut me some slack this one time?

'Why don't we throw some proper light on the situation?' mused Lightwood, and when nobody answered – what was there to say? – he opened the blinds fully. He looked down onto City Square and said: 'Anyway, there's respectable pubs.' And it was as though he hadn't realised he'd spoken out loud.

'Ahem,' said one of the HR bods. 'Neal, moving on, we have a few procedural questions we need to ask you, if that's all right.'

I nodded, and got on with it.

I thought, my flights of fancy notwithstanding, I was getting on pretty well. I'd gotten into the swing of things and when I spoke about history, I'd talked with real authority. But what really sealed the deal, Byers later told me, was my answer to one of the last questions. Prior to that they'd been undecided about me. As I said, I'd genned up on answers to standard interview questions. I knew that in answer to the question *What do you consider to be your weaknesses?* you were supposed to say something smarmy which still showed you in a good light. Something like *I'm a perfectionist.* But just before I answered I had a change of heart. I'd seen Lightwood drifting, his concentration lapsing. He was looking out over City Square, watching pigeons roosting on the statue of the Black Prince. I decided to shake him up a bit. So I said: 'I'm afraid I've a real weakness for a good glass of port and a few slivers of Stilton. I'm also a sucker for a good Burgundy.'

Lightwood looked round, sharply. Then muttered something which sounded very much like *Bravo!* He loved it, my comment. It pinned me down as someone memorable, and also it rescued me from the ignominy of being the boy who was brought up in a pub (which to Lightwood was probably akin to being raised by wolves).

Byers laid on another wink. Hell, even the HR bod, the one who was forever scribbling notes on his pad, for once put down his pen and for a beat, two, I thought he was going to give me a round of applause.

They told me they'd get back to me by the end of a week and let me know about the success, or otherwise, of my application to be on the grad scheme. Byers accompanied me down to the lobby in the lift and told me he already knew I was in. 'Nailed on, chief,' he said. And so it was.

Byers took me under his wing as the graduate scheme commenced. It seemed to be one of his unofficial duties to 'acclimatise' the new blood to working at a place like Andersen (to working, full-stop, after three years of partying). He took us all out for dinner every night that first week and we got to know his wit and charm as well as his familiar rallying call. He told us, repeatedly, that we were knights working for King Arthur. He told us this – the dining table at Piccolino or at Casa Mia or at Aagrah – was our round table. Most of the green grads took these speeches as Gospel. They'd nod along and say *Yes, sir* to him. But Carl, Adam and me, we just knew Byers was choking our chains. You could see this, like, glimmer of mischief in his eyes whenever he said stuff like that. It was kind of an in-joke   maybe he'd had someone like Lightwood acclimatising him when he started at the company and maybe this had been one of Lightwood's lines – but at least we recognised it *was* a joke.

There were other in-jokes too. Least that's what I thought they were. At the end of the night, Byers made it his habit to call a toast. 'Three cheers to you all,' he'd say, 'and, lest we forget, three cheers for Neal Grace's former head teacher, who's sadly no longer with us.' And he was forever saying to Adam 'Most of my friends consider me good-looking' because, apparently (and inexplicably) that's what Adam had written on his application form (turned out he'd forgotten to erase it when he'd copied and pasted the 'personal interests' section right over from his application form to be on *Big Brother)*.

Later, it was Nick Byers came up with the 'Zombie Nation' nickname for Carl and that was the biggest in-joke of the lot. You see, Carl had failed the ATT (Association of Taxation Tacticians) exam three times, which was unheard of at one of the big five, but he kept coming back from the dead. Rather than be annoyed, as me and Ads were by some of the jibes, Carl revelled in the nickname.

But then again, we all of us found it easy to forgive Byers practically everything. Mainly this was because he was such engaging company. When I was little, my parents insisted on family dinners, sat around the (decidedly square) table in the dining room. It was a real squeeze to get in and around the table, what with that huge Welsh dresser taking up the whole back wall. Inside it were Mum and Dad's wedding presents, the dinner service for 'best', which as far as I knew they only used once and that was later, much later, when they cooked me a dinner to celebrate my getting on the grad scheme at Andersen (not, I noted, to celebrate my degree). That day Dad chinked my glass of fizzy wine and told me he was all kinds of happy I was about to become a man and pay my own way in the world; making out like he'd shelled out hand over fist for my (extended) education, when in fact it had been an unholy trinity of hardship grants, credit cards and a weekend job flyering for a night club which had seen me through three years at uni.

Anyway, I used to think it was the tightness of the fit of the table which constricted us, made us suffer those awful dinners in silence (save the scraped plates and the gulps as Dad knocked back *another* glass of the good stuff and the occasional barked laugh or chinked glass from through in the pub section of the house). I used to think that were we in a bigger room, we could have acted bigger, *talked* bigger. Had conversations.

I decided later, after having met Nick Byers, that actually the silences were because nobody was prepared to act as 'host', guide the conversation, suggest topics and the like. We were too woefully working class to have training in that kind of thing, especially Dad, whose role it would traditionally have been (and hell, he *could* do it; I'd seen him in the pub sometimes and he could have blokes in stitches, even that maudlin fella who'd lost out on the 'All or Nothing' wheel on the Bruce Forsyth gameshow). But Nick had been bred differently and he knew how to work a table just as he knew how to work a room.

He was very particular, even down to the place settings: always boy-girl-boy-girl. Always keeping guys like us – Carl, Ads and me – apart, so we'd get a chance to speak to people other than ourselves (though we orbited back to each other afterwards).

Nick had the gift.

During those dinners, Byers used to say: 'Despite the fact accountancy is boring as old rope and dried paint, *we* don't have to be boring. In fact, the very opposite. We have to be interesting and engaging. We have to be approachable. We have to have interesting conversation. *That's* how we hobnob with our clients. Not by sitting there letting them listen to us crunching the numbers and then picking them out our teeth to show them.'

Sorry to say it though, but most of our graduate intake were decidedly *not* interesting and engaging. There were twelve of us; six girls, six boys (HR must have run the numbers through an equality calculator to have come out with such a perfectly balanced equation). Most of the girls looked as though they'd spent their three years at uni chained to the radiators in the library and I couldn't imagine a one of them quitting and going off to run her own all-female safari company in deepest, darkest Africa. The only one of them had *anything* about her was Sarah Nicol, and she soon became so besotted with Adam that she suddenly lost all ability to talk, and spent most of the time during our dinners mooning over him and then running off to the toilets to cry over her lost love. Ads' big mistake had been to have what he thought was a one-night-stand with her. Apparently the next morning, she was already talking about bringing her toothbrush over and which drawers she could use for her stuff. Most of the boys were worse. Tom Green *should* by all rights have been my friend. He had a similar background. Came from Sheffield just like me. Had attended a common-or-garden secondary school just like me. Hell, I even discovered he'd once been Yorkshire Subbuteo champion when he was fifteen. But Christ, talking to him made you feel like peeling off your own face with a spoon. He was the dullest man alive. He talked *soooo slowwwwwwwwwllllllllyyyyyy* and so utterly uninspiringly about subjects which would put a fucking computer to sleep. He was so boring you shut off even as he was introducing himself: Carl spent the entire three months of his probationary period at Andersen labouring under the misapprehension that Tom was actually called Ben, until Ads set him straight on the subject. But by then the name Ben had stuck and Tom simply accepted it. Hell, even some of our clients called him Ben, and, dullard as he was, he'd probably change his name by deed poll just to avoid any embarrassment.

So it was no wonder Carl, Ads and me became fast friends. And really, we shouldn't have been friends. During my three years at Leeds I'd come to hate public school boys with a passion. I couldn't stand the way PSBs carried themselves, like they owned the place. I couldn't stand the way they talked. Couldn't stand their confidence. And sure, I knew some of it was jealousy on my part – why couldn't I be like them? – and sure I knew I was acting just like my prejudiced old dad, that working-class hero to end all working-class heroes, but at the same time they were just *so annoying.*

And Carl was like the ultimate PSB. I mean he had no idea how to do anything for himself. He'd always had someone – a housemaster, a matron – to do it for him. When we started up an after-work five-a-side kick-around, Carl bought himself a book – a fucking book, for three-year-olds – called *Teach yourself Football in Ten Easy Steps.* And when he bought his first flat he was forever calling up, begging Ads or me to come round on account of he didn't know how to use his new washing machine or his cooker or his toaster. Once he caught a bus to come meet us in Headingley for a few jars and after an hour, when he still hadn't shown, Ads belled him on his new moby. Turned out Carl had never gotten a bus before and he didn't know you had to ring a bell to get off, and, seeing as nobody else had gotten off in Headingley, he'd been stuck. Had wound up in Horsforth. Where in Horsforth? 'I dunno. I can see sheep, though.'

Ads wasn't a PSB but he was a pretty boy. Even in the very early days, before he'd bulked himself up, when he was still a bit waif-like and still carried that stoner's air to him, he was... well, he was just effortlessly beautiful. His suits all looked like they'd been tailored for him. His shirts looked as though he'd had some top designer chasing him down the street screaming 'Please, sir, let me make a shirt for you'. His ties didn't resemble nooses, as Carl's and mine did, but comfortable masterpieces of fashion textile technology. His shoes looked as though they were very happy to be clothing his feet.

And he was just so effortlessly *nice* with it. He was like, 'What, this piece of junk, this shirt? Nah, it was just from Primark,' or, 'What, she likes me? I'm not so sure. Maybe she's just staring at my birthmark.' And even when he did do the dirty – Sarah Nicol, for example – he did it in such a way that *she* came off thinking she'd been the one in the wrong. If it had been Carl – sleazy Carl – who'd said 'There's no way I want your toothbrush in my mug' he'd have ended up de-balled.

Still, Carl, Ads and I became thick as thieves right from the very first dinner. We were at Bibi's. Bibi's was *the* Italian restaurant for the footballers' wives generation in Leeds; the ostentatious, almost tongue-in-cheek décor reflected the opulence of this people-watching paradise. It was a place where appearances counted, and despite the fact that Bibi's was incongruously found on the ground floor of a new-build multi-storey car park, it oozed panache. Notwithstanding the seeming revolving-door style of filling and emptying tables, the food at Bibi's proved that there was some substance behind the style.

As a student I could never have imagined going to a place like that. I mean, it was kind of a symbol of the glitz, glamour and *confidence* of new-millennium Leeds. Of course, Carl and Ads took the whole experience in their stride, but for different reasons: Carl because he was from money, and Ads because, from the very moment he walked through the door, you could see the heads of all those same footballers' wives turning, giving him the once over, liking what they saw.

They fitted in. I didn't feel like I did.

But then, just before we were shown to our table, Carl tapped me on the shoulder. He asked whether I wanted to go to the Gents with him. Then he burst out laughing. 'Honestly, your face! I may be a public school boy but I don't want to play soggy biscuits with you, Neal. I'm talking' – he lowered his voice – '*this.*' He opened up his suit jacket like some kind of dodgy watch salesman and showed me the baggie in his inside pocket.

It was speed. It was always speed in the old days, before we changed our game up and caned it on the coke. I'd never had it before. I watched how they took it, then rubbed a fingerful into my gums. It was very chalky, *so* chalky in fact that I asked him whether he'd not been duped. But Adam, who'd also eloped to the Gents with us, said it was definitely legit. He said it was good shit and where did Carl get it from?

Speed, I discovered, wasn't great to have just before a meal. It dampens the appetite. Once upon a time, Ads said, it was an over-the-counter diet drug. Apparently the equivalent of the footballer's wives lot outside would have been all misty-eyed with it in the '50s or whatever. But one thing speed was really, really good for was helping you drink. That night, as Carl, Ads and I kept the party going right into the wee smalls, I drank more than I ever had, even in the Vod-Soc days, and yet, it seemed to me at any rate, I stayed sober as a judge. Probably that's what kept me out so long, when on any other night I'd have staggered home to bed, already dreading the raging hangover of the next morning.

The next morning, I felt right as rain, and the sixteen-hour working day which followed it barely put me off my stride. Speed, as much as my suit, helped me to become a new person. A more confident person. A workaholic person.

It enabled me to live the kind of fast-forwarded life Andersen dictated we lived. I mean they sucked up so many of your good hours you had practically nothing left when you said good night to Paul at the security desk and exited the revolving doors. Sometimes I felt like lying down right there on the pavement, or else I thought I might as well follow the revolving door right round and go back in the building, bid a hasty 'morning' to Paul and then call the lift back up to our floor.

There was an expectation we work ridiculous hours and a kind of unspoken rule you couldn't leave before your boss – Lightwood or Byers – left. And those guys stayed until *late*. Nine, ten on some bad nights; even later if they were working on one of their big accounts. The good nights we left at seven.

The hours got to all of us. Tom Green got so drawn and pale he looked like he'd never seen sunlight. Sarah Nicol lost a stone in weight in a week. Carl, Adam and I just about got by, thanks to the chemicals we pumped into ourselves, and when it got really bad, I promised myself it would get better, or at least easier, once we'd gotten that tough first year, in which we had to make a good impression, under our belts. But all it took was a quick look at Nick Byers, or Dale Lightwood, to show that was a fallacy. For though they were a few more rungs up the ladder than us, there was always *someone* they had to impress. Nobody swanned about this place looking like they were on holiday. *Everyone* was busy.

Nobody had free time. I mean, in those early days I didn't have the time for a lot of things: sleep, films, a girlfriend, books. (I used to read a lot, and not just for my uni course: I read widely. A Latvian flatmate – a guy into wrestling and heavy metal and, I'd thought, not much else – randomly (and fittingly) introduced me to the works of John Irving (a writer who also liked a good grapple). And I lapped up everything he'd written. I rediscovered Stephen King, a writer I'd mistakenly believed was only for early-teenaged boys who wanted a good scare. Henry lent me his Iain Banks (and his Iain *M* Banks) collections. But now, zip. Nada. I read only numbers on spreadsheets.

Nobody at Andersen seemed to have families to go home to. Either they were divorced (Lightwood) or separated (one of the HR guys) or they'd never had time to make a family in the first place. Look around most places of work and you see framed photos of kids on desks. Not here. If you wanted those things you had to go get a less demanding job and if you did that, you didn't have the right stuff and you were a failure, spoken about as a cautionary tale from thereon in.

But we were raking in money. All of us. It came in so fast, so thick, it was like a snow drift in my bank account. I couldn't spend anything near what I was pulling in. Didn't have the time for it. And most of the time when we did go out – to dinners, to networking events – it was on the company. Ads bought a fancy new Audi TT. Never drove it. Carl collected houses and flats. I frittered *some* cash away on clothes, and the amount I spent in Ace I might as well have bought the place, but still my account was growing exponentially. Once, I called up Henry. As soon as he answered I asked myself why. He told me he was working for five quid an hour doing some ridiculous call centre work, calling up folk and asking them if they'd ever considered changing their gas and electric supplier. He was trying to pay back his student loan, but the meagre amounts he put away barely touched the sides. I didn't have the heart to tell him I'd covered every debt I'd incurred at uni *already*. And that included the credit cards. I used to have six, one of which I only signed up for because you got a free cyber-pet (mine died within a day). Now I had only one, and it was platinum. My credit limit was *immense*. I could have bought a jumbo jet if I wanted, had I got the time to actually research where one could buy such a thing.

And sometimes I took a masochistic pleasure in the work. Sure it was dull and repetitive. Almost as dull and repetitive as calling up folk and asking them to change their utilities supplier (and then getting effed and jeffed at for having the temerity to call in the first place). But if you broke the whole exercise down to its constituent parts and then ticked each done thing – opening a fresh blue cardboard file; photocopying the contents of last year's file; gradually filling *this* year's file – then you felt like you were getting somewhere.

Most of the accounts which crossed our desks were either the small fry discarded by our superiors like Nick Byers or Dale Lightwood, both of whom had a select handful of big-fish accounts which they'd work on all year round, or else the slightly bigger fry generated by the telesales arm of the company, a couple floors down from us.

But we took what we were given. It was the way things worked here.

That's what made it so remarkable that Carl managed to turn up a customer – and not just a small-fry one – all on his own and in his first year on the grad scheme: SAS. This *go out and get it even if it's not the done thing* attitude impressed everyone and got Carl's name known within the upper echelons of the business (which kind of pissed me off because, actually, I'd thought *I* was supposed to be the remarkable one, after everything Nick Byers had said). And it was probably why they allowed him to get away with failing his ATT exams so many times. For Carl, after bringing in SAS, it wasn't a matter of 'Two strikes and you're outta here' as it was for any other Tom or Dick in Andersen. It was a friendly arm over the shoulder from one of the partners and an encouraging 'You'll do better next time, Sport'. And Nick Byers laughingly doing the Zombie Nation dance all over again.

Close as I was to Carl, I had to find out how he'd swung it. I mean, I knew he had the gift of the gab. Most public schoolboys did. But SAS were *bouncers* for Christ's sake. This was no old boys' network thing. Talking them into employing Andersen must have been a whole other ballgame. So I talked my way into the meet-and-greet session Carl set up at One City Square just to try and work it all out.

It was me, Carl and Ads. Ads was effectively there to minute the meeting. Dale Lightwood was there too, 'Just here to tend the tiller, kids, not to steal your glory', as he claimed. The bouncers took an instant dislike to Lightwood. Most likely this was because of his use of phrases such as 'Just here to tend the tiller, kids', which he actually said out loud and in front of them. When he asked them what exactly they did (*sniff*) I thought the main guy, a chap named Nathan Long, was going to toss him straight through the window and into City Square.

Nathan Long was a very wide man. He had huge, broad shoulders and the largest chest I'd ever seen. His belly was something else entirely. It looked like he was pregnant. As I was later to discover, that hour-long meeting was probably the longest he'd spent *without* eating since he was about ten. He was forever waffling down chips or crisps or chocolate bars and then joking 'But my body's a temple'. Carl, who often pushed his luck right to the edge with people, even Long, said: 'Yeah, with a great big bay window, you fat bastard.'

My first impression of Long was that he was quite possibly the scariest man alive. When a man like that, with his sheer *width* and that goatee beard and shaven head combo, clamped your hand in his, you felt like your knuckles had been smashed with a bowling ball. Yet, though he *looked* like a Hells Angel, Long was as nice as pie. Hell, Carl told me that these days Long preferred cheesy pop music (ridiculous boy bands and the like) to heavy metal on account of his daughter Phoebe.

Long had come along with 'back-up' as he called it; another brick shithouse of a man named Chris. Chris didn't offer up his surname and none of us dared ask for it, having suffered his surly gaze for what felt like two weeks. Chris *stared*. It was what he did. *All* he did. I'd not seen someone stare like that other than a young kid who didn't yet realise it was rude.

But that was okay. We'd – Carl, Ads and I – seen enough *your name's not down you're not coming in* types before, so we let him be. And besides, Long did the talking for the both of them. In response to Lightwood's sniffy question about what, exactly, they did, he offered up a long and detailed explanation of the nature and history of SAS and where he thought they were headed in the coming years. Basically what they were was a collective of bouncers (I wondered what the collective noun for bouncers would be: a rumble? A herd?) Each 'member' of SAS had the same rights and privileges as everyone else and each year they elected one of their number to be 'head'. At the moment, that was Nathan Long, but (a shrug) 'if the guys don't like the direction we're headed, they're totally within their rights to vote me out and give someone else a shot.'

It didn't sound like they would. From the numbers Long gave up, SAS were doing remarkably well. They'd pretty much sewn up the Leeds market – they had practically every pub, bar and club in the city centre – and were thinking of expanding into Bradford and maybe Sheffield. They'd recently won contracts with the universities, with LGI, and even provided some stewarding at Leeds United matches.

Long had always done the company's books himself, along with his wife Debbie, but, as he said, SAS were expanding too fast now and the accounting was taking up more and more of what he called his 'Phoebe time'. Hell, he said, 'I don't hardly do any bouncing no more either, and that's what I love. Haven't seen the outside of a door for *months* now. Not with all the new clients and the books and everything.'

'And what's more,' he said, 'I'm not like you guys. I'm not trained in all this stuff. So when they say we owe this much tax I pay it, but, you know, they could be totally fucking us over – 'scuse French – and there's ways and means of… well, avoiding paying some of it. So when Carl here comes to me and he says he can help, then I think: how can it hurt?'

Lightwood nodded at Carl, pleased, and I felt like saying, 'Carl's as qualified as an accountant as you are, Nathan. He's still not passed his ATT.' But of course I didn't. Instead I busied myself trying to work out just how Carl had first 'got in' with Long. From my perspective they had nothing in common other than the fact they were both wearing a suit (Long looking obviously uncomfortable in his, as though he'd had to be shoehorned into it; his pal Chris hadn't even bothered with that nicety. He was still got up in his SAS bomber jacket, zipped right up to the neck). In the end I got to thinking Long probably liked Carl, or at least found him refreshing, because the other company he kept was so wordlessly sullen. While Chris sat with his arms crossed resolutely across his big chest like some kind of muscular cordon, Carl was talking, talking, rattling off nonsense anecdotes and telling Long just how much he reckoned he could save SAS and, sure, one of these days he'd *love* to meet little Phoebe. Was it Boyzone she liked? It was, wasn't it?

By the time the meeting concluded, Long and Carl shook hands on the deal. SAS's business would be coming Andersen's way. And that handshake, just like mine with Nick Byers, was, in hindsight the sealing of a wholly different type of deal. And though my first impression of Long had been wrong, my second, that he was some kind of cuddly teddy bear, was *also* wrong. In the aftermath of the night Carl got the bouncers to kick seven shades of shit out of the Neanderthal lads, Rhys and Dan, we'd come to discover exactly how wrong we'd been.

And, by then, there was no turning back.

III

I *almost* turned back at the revolving doors. Saw my reflection in the glass and realised the eye-drops I'd picked up at Boots hadn't quite done the trick. But then someone *reeking* of aftershave pressed in right behind me and I was caught up in his tide. While we were spinning round, my moby blatted out another text message alert signal and whoever it was behind me – I didn't want to turn and face him; we'd practically be *kissing* in here – said: 'That's yours, not mine, I believe.' His breath tickled the back of my neck and made me feel all kinds of uncomfortable and I felt like I *had* to check the text right then and there.

What I saw made my blood freeze.

U SHLD CUM 2 LGI N SAY SORRY IN PERSON. OR R U 2 COWERD? CHIKEN? XXX PS. BRING UR WALLIT.

Shit. Shit, shit, shit.

A hand pressed on the small of my back. A hissed: '*Come on,* we haven't got all day.' And then the revolving door spat me out on the other side, onto the polished floor of One City Square – so polished you fair glided across it – and the guy was elbowing past me and hurrying for the lift.

I took a moment to get my breath back. Fucking hell. Bring my *wallit.* Was The Nat trying to blackmail me? She couldn't, could she? She had nothing on me. And I hadn't actually *done* anything. It had been Carl called the 'hit' and his mates at SAS who'd carried it out. Well actually, maybe that was the point. I hadn't *done* anything. I hadn't intervened. I hadn't shouted *STOP!* All I'd said was that ridiculous thing about The Nat's phone being out of credit.

She was right. I was a *cowerd.*

But that didn't mean she could extort money from me, did it?

My head was spinning. I'd never been in this kind of situation before. Of course I hadn't. Although I'd grown up in a pub, you could hardly say I'd grown up on the wrong side of the tracks. Mum and Dad were respectable people. My friends at school were respectable (save that day the Golden Goose got cooked and loads of them ran off with the booze and brass when I was dead drunk). And uni was, well, uni. The worst I'd ever done was take (too many) drugs. That was it. And even though I took drugs, I never actually encountered any dealers. That was always Carl's domain. Or Ads' at a push. Never me... I never did anything. And maybe that was the point too. Maybe The Nat had seen through me. Seen the naivety at my very core. And now she'd seen her opportunity to punish me for it. She must have known she'd never have gotten a penny out of Carl. He was too... connected. And Ads. Nope. Too brawny. But me; I was the right mix of unworldly and weedy-looking, and I was ripe for the picking. Whereas I'd thought people looked at me and saw a prince, she'd looked at me and seen a mug.

Shit I should never have turned my phone on again after the pool. Shit I should never have sent that message on my phone – so she had my number – in the first place.

Maybe I should just dump my phone. Buy a new one. Christ, it wasn't like I didn't have the money. And it wasn't like I'd be losing a load of numbers off of my old Nokia. It wasn't like *I* had Rio Ferdinand on speed dial like Carl.

I felt another hand on me; this one gentler than the one which had pushed me in the back in the revolving doors. I spun round. Saw the guy from the security desk in his crisp uniform. The name *PAUL* on his nametag. Guy worked even longer hours than we did, or so it seemed. He was always here in the morning, to call over to us 'Don't work too hard, boys', or at the end of the day, when he released us back into the wild, usually with a friendly 'You been working your hands to the bone today, Mr Grace. Make sure you go grab some me-time... All work and no play, sir. All work and no play.'

Paul was a little Irishman with salt-and-pepper hair. Didn't look like he could harm a fly. But right then, I cringed away from him. Had to be his uniform, and that uncomfortable reminder of what I'd seen last night which it brought with it.

'Y'okay, Mr Grace?' he said, softly. 'You look like you've seen a ghost.'

I nodded, then shook my head.

'Maybe you should just come take the weight off a minute. I've a comfy seat at my desk.'

I washed my face with my hands. Then: 'No, I can't. No time. I gotta…' I gestured over to the lift. 'Stuff to do. Thank you though.'

His smile was glorious, like the sun coming out. 'Ah, no worries. You're one of the good ones. That pal of yours, though. Carl. Never remembers my name. Always calls me Paddy. A fella could take offence at that, you know.'

'Carl never remembers anyone's name,' I said, absently. 'You know Tom Green? Well Carl always calls him Ben.'

Paul nodded enthusiastically, as though there was more to my anecdote than that; as though I'd just proved myself a great wit, a real *raconteur.* Then he announced he'd better get back to his desk and his security screens, in case 'brass' came down and caught him 'chin-wagging'.

I might as well have spent the morning chin-wagging for all the work I got done. I was too distracted. I was jumpy. I kept feeling Dale Lightwood's eyes spearing into me and even though I'd not had any coke, not like Carl and Adam, I must have looked like I had, and I got to thinking a meeting with HR was surely in the post and I could just imagine them saying: 'Do you have a problem, Mr Grace? Arthur Andersen is a caring employer, but if this problem of yours continues to escalate, then we will have no choice but to sever our ties with you.' And I got to thinking that might not be a bad thing because if they *did* fire me then I could escape from here. Run away; dump my phone. It wasn't like I had any real ties here, other than Carl and Ads and my flat. Hell, I could start again somewhere new. Maybe not Africa, not yet. But London. Yeah, maybe. Henry was in London now and he'd finally stumbled into a job which suited his immense talents and intellect. I forgot where. But that didn't matter. I could bed penny up to his door and, after berating me for never getting in touch, he'd welcome me with open arms. Let me couch-surf for as long as it took before I got myself settled.

My Nokia blatted in my pocket. I read the new message which was almost the same as the last one. The Nat, *ordering* me down to the LGI today. Do not pass go, do not collect two hundred pounds. Now. But I couldn't go now. It was only half-ten in the morning (and that first hour and a half had dripped by at around about the same pace as a stalactite grows). Nobody left their desk here. We never took dentist's or doctor's appointments on work time. Sometimes I thought that if there was a real fire, and not just a weekly test, it would kind of be expected we'd stick around at our PCs while our flesh melted off our bones.

The only legitimate reason to leave your desk was to do lunch, and that wasn't for another 90 minutes. And boy would that be a distance run. I checked the time again. Fucking hell. It wasn't even a minute since I'd last checked. Work days went faster on coke. Fact. All that slipping off to the second floor toilets where you didn't know anybody and having a little sniff just to get you through. All that ducking away from Dale Lightwood whenever he happened by your desk and having to ride out the paranoia whenever your email inbox pinged or your phone trilled. And I envied Carl and Adam their morning buzz, I really did. And then I got to thinking if I just went over to them and asked for a snifter, everything would be hunky dory all over again and I'd stop with all this *feeling.*

But then I imagined the come-down and having to deal with these texts which kept winging their way onto my Nokia when the shakes were on me, and it felt like the whole world wanted to hurt me and it was too much to contemplate. So I stayed sober.

Finally midday slouched into view, and those rough beasts Carl and Ads were soon at my desk. They neither of them *looked* particularly rough. Indeed Adam looked as well-pressed and smelled as beautiful as he usually did; and Carl looked *money,* right down to his ubiquitous Aviators tucked in the top pocket of his suit jacket. But you could just tell they were hanging; pranged out; lost somewhere way out west. How the fuck had nobody else noticed?

Carl fidgeted with my stationery. 'What do you say the three of us get the hell out of Dodge?'

Adam twitched from foot to foot. He was kind of hanging on to the divider on the desk which separated me from Tom Green (and Tom Green didn't look too happy about the close proximity of Ads; he spirited his Montblanc pen out of view as though Adamski was some kind of common thief: this was actually a pretty wise move; when we worked late sometimes Carl and Ads conducted night raids on the desks of our colleagues and pilfered all sorts).

I stalled them. 'I don't know... I got a helluva lot of work on.' I gestured to the pile of files in my in-tray. There was stone cold nothing in my out-tray.

'Aw, c'mon,' said Adam, 'La Scala calls.'

La Scala was a little Italian café on Albion Place which we habitually haunted because of the quality of its coffee – the cappuccinos were to die for – and because, famously in local Leeds circles, it had opera pumping out of it at all times of the day, like some form of high-culture *club,* and thus we could talk about some of the dark things we talked, like a bunch of Leodian Machiavelli, about without fear of being overheard. We'd become such a fixture at La Scala that Carl now called its owner, Camilla, *Mama,* and, eventually, he'd gone on to make it his second account won for Andersen. And, sure, it was only small fry but think of the benefits... Free coffee, free pasta, free *bruschetta.*

Before the pair of them had come over to my desk I'd been undecided as to what to do. But now, suddenly, I knew. I knew what I *couldn't* do, which was to go round as though nothing had happened last night. I couldn't go to La Scala and receive a customary hug from *Mama* and when she asked 'Are you three being good boys?' answer in the positive. I couldn't sit there in the back of the café, opera screaming into my ears, and *not* be reminded of how The Nat and Rachel had screamed last night. And I couldn't stand to sit there and receive threatening text after threatening text and not know what the hell I was going to do about all of it.

'I'll give it a miss today, boys,' I said.

Carl sneered. 'Got a better offer? What the fuck's wrong with you at the moment, Neal? Honestly.' Then he flounced off.

Ads flashed me his Colgate-whites and then a shrug, and then he followed.

I gave it five excruciating minutes longer, then locked my screen and took the lift back down to earth, my wings well and truly clipped.

LGI was over the north-west side of the city centre. If you imagined Leeds as a skull, it would be the left eye-socket. During the morning, whilst I'd been locked up in the cell of work, it had hammered down with rain and it was still coming down at a fair clip now. Paul, on the security desk, offered me a brolly from his collection and I crawled up the closed face of Leeds under the mushroom shadow of it. Everyone else was in their own little pod too, dry under their shields, and the pavements resembled a Roman siege formation. The wet hustle and bustle of it as I was frequently forced to step *off* the pavement – and *around* fellas whose larger umbrellas and *more important* places to get to meant they occupied the higher ground – soon inspired a roiling feeling of misanthropy in my gut. I hated these people hard. Felt my knuckles whitening on the handle of the umbrella as I navigated my zigzag path. But then, in the back of mind, there was the stinking reminder of what misanthropy really was: the face of the Neanderthal lad ground into the concrete under that railway archway last night. And I tried to let the hatred drip off me like rain. I was going to make amends. I wasn't being a *COWERD*.

Pedestrian traffic thinned out past the Town Hall and the art gallery, but the rain remained so thick it felt like smog, so cloying it was as though you could wear it. If I'd have closed my eyes I could have imagined myself in an older, wiser, *dirtier* Leeds. A *Dickensian* Leeds. But you couldn't close your eyes. Taxis slunk by and sent up huge waves as they hit the puddles which had accumulated by the kerbs. Occasionally I'd hear the blare of an ambulance siren.

Meant I was closing in on the infirmary.

A sprawling accumulation of buildings showcasing almost the full range of architectural styles, from the art deco Brotherton Wing to the imposing Victorian edifice of the main entrance on Portland Street, the LGI was a town in its own right. In principle, I knew my way around it: Ads had suffered a broken leg in some kind of snow-boarding accident a year or so back and Carl and I had spent a good few hours labyrinthing our way around it, trying to find his ward.

In *principle* I knew my way around it. In fair conditions, I did. But not with the Chicken Licken sky of Leeds hanging so low it felt I could scrape the top of my head against it. Not while the grey-gloom of the day was such that *everything* seemed to be conspiring to muddy the waters of my thoughts. Not while every section of open land turned into sixty seconds' worth of distance run, just to keep dry. Not while I was wrestling with an umbrella which threatened to turn itself inside out at every imposing gust of wind.

After ten minutes' dashing around and much cursing, I tucked myself into a doorway and fired off a text to The Nat. I'd suddenly realised I had no idea where I was supposed to meet her; what ward they were keeping her boy on. And I didn't want to spend my whole lunch hour wandering aimlessly. I asked her to get right back to me with the details.

Right back took all kinds of too long, and the rain began to change its angle of precipitation in order that it could target me better in my little cubby-hole. It sneaked its way under the lip of the building, zigzagged underneath the umbrella and slicked my face wet all over again. The spray of it – like that of a shaken-up can of Dandelion and Burdock – wet the trousers of my suit and made me thankful it was charcoal grey and wouldn't show up.

Finally The Nat got back to me. Told me she'd meet me at reception in the Jubilee Wing. I thought I knew where that was so I set out again but soon found myself hopelessly lost. Closer to Millennium Square than the Jubilee Wing. I backtracked. Stumbled across a small, extortionately priced car park. Scurried over to the toll-booth where a man in a yellow coat – not, thankfully an SAS bomber jacket - was sitting, blowing into his hands.

The parking attendant was Eastern European. Polish, at a guess. He asked me: 'Where your car?' I told him I had none, but I was on the hunt for the Jubilee Wing. He tried manfully to explain my way through the labyrinth and I nodded along despite having lost him somewhere two turns back. Eventually he drew me a map on the back of a betting slip. When I asked him did he not need the slip anymore, he just shrugged, mournfully. It was a gesture my dad would have known all too well.

Following his instructions, I made the Jubilee Wing without further ado. There was little celebratory about this institutionally depressing place. They hadn't exactly put up the fucking bunting (though there was a great deal of litter accumulated along the walkways which might, through narrow eyes, have been confetti). I shook out the brolly and tucked it back, wet, inside its sheath. Looked around for The Nat.

The Jubilee Wing was a hive of labyrinthine corridors, access-controlled doors, and large, airport-style waiting areas in which the seating appeared to have been nailed down to avoid it being thrown. Harsh lighting buzzed out from scores of blinking strip-lights hung from the ceiling. A smell of canteen cooking and common-or-garden desperation in the air. This was perhaps what the staff was attempting to flee from: I saw a hundred and one worker bees scurrying from place to place clutching files or pushing empty trolleys, none of them meeting my eyes or offering to assist me in case I might be ill. Well, it was either the smell or the patients which struck matches under their asses: the patients – most of them from the ranks of the Dickensian poor – wandered around like zombies, shuffling around in their dressing gowns, wheeling their drips in front of them as they ghosted by, *en route* to the smoking shelters.

I squelched through the reception area and a cleaner followed me with a mop, tutting because I'd spoiled her perfect floor.

The Nat wasn't anywhere to be seen and I felt a muffled kind of relief at that. And I'd almost decided to go back out into the rain when I realised the reason I'd come was to put an end to all this and if I did go, then it *wouldn't* end, would it? So I wandered, looking for A & E, because surely I could ask there about Rhys and Dan's admission and find out where they'd been taken to now. After a couple wrong turns brought about by the hospital's altogether mystifying signage system – I'd found myself at one stage wandering through the desperately brightly decorated corridors of the Children's A & E department on the first floor – I found A & E proper. But the nurse there – she was so big she was surely a relative of Nathan Long's – sent me packing. She said she couldn't give out the kind of information I wanted. Not unless I was a relative. Carl would have pretended to be a relative. The old me would have pretended to be a relative. But this new Lost Boy me didn't have the stones.

I headed back to reception and finally saw The Nat. She was standing very close to the entrance, tapping her feet impatiently, still dressed in last night's clubbing gear. Probably she'd been there all along and I'd walked straight past her, busying myself with the brolly. But probably the main reason I hadn't seen her, or had looked straight past her, was the fact she wasn't on her own. She was with a kid. Three, four maybe. Maybe younger. I'm not very good with the ages of small children. Never been around them much.

We spotted each other at the exact same moment and she grabbed the kid's hand and marched him over to me. 'Well,' she snapped, clamping a hand to her hip and wagging a finger as though she was on *Jerry Springer,* 'look what the cat's dragged in. Thought you weren't going to show. Thought you'd, like, wimped out or whatever.'

The kid looked up at me with wide, wide eyes. He smirked. Probably on account of his Mum calling me a wimp. She'd said worse to me. The kid was dressed in a Leeds

United shirt with *BATTY* on the back, but his shock of blond hair made him a dead ringer for the Elland Road club's young tyro Alan Smith. He also looked a lot like Rhys, and the idea that Rhys had once been a little, innocent kid like this, with perfect skin and a cute little button nose, made me feel sick all over again at what we'd done.

'This must be...' I'd forgotten what she'd called her boy. Was it Jack, or Jamie, or James?

'Jake,' seethed The Nat. 'Jake's nan had to drop him off this morning. She had work and, as you can see, I've not been home.'

I felt the colour rising in my cheeks. 'Hello, Jake,' I said.

Jake didn't respond.

'I've told him not to speak to you. I've told him you're a bad man.'

I sniffed. 'And I wanted to tell *you* that I'm sorry. For all of it. I didn't mean any of that to happen. How are they both?'

The Nat pulled a face. 'You can see for yourself, if you've got the guts. This little guy's dad's face looks like... like pummelled meat. And his arm's so badly broken he couldn't even hold Jakey's hand when he came to visit with him. Dan's worse. They're... They didn't deserve what happened to them. They've both of them done... stupid stuff in the past, but nobody deserves *this* as a comeback.'

'I'm – ' Before I could finish another apology, little Jake surprised me by slipping his tiny hand in mine.

'Can you buy me a biscuit?' he asked.

His mother shot him a sharp look which I'd last seen as she tried to stare down a brick-shithouse bouncer. *I* wouldn't have messed. But Jakey obviously had his mum's number. Mine too. Clearly he'd seen right through me just as The Nat had, and saw me as his best chance of getting a snack around here.

'A biscuit,' he said. '*Peeeeeaaaas.*'

The Nat cracked a teenth of a smile. 'We're – his nan and I – trying to get him to say his pleases and thank yous. So far the only way we can get him to say it is if he says *peas* and, for thank you, *fangoo.* And by the way, when he says biscuit, he means a Mars bar or something like that. His dad. Spoils him rotten when he has him.'

I wished she hadn't told me that. The more she told me about herself and her life, the more whole a person she became for me, and that made it less and less likely I could think of her as an extra in the film of my life, in the way Carl thought of people who brushed past him during his scrabble to the top. Still, I didn't know whether I should be saying yes to this kid who was still tugging at my hand and muttering over and over 'biscuit-biscuit-biscuit'.

'Maybe we should... you know... go somewhere we could talk properly.' The Nat frowned. 'You know, instead of malingering around here like a couple of lemons.'

I said okay and she led us back across the reception area and into a sad-looking café which was called, simply, *EAT.* We picked up some wood-effect trays and queued for the counter, where the oldest woman in the world slowly, feebly, poured us a cup of lukewarm, dishwater tea each and cut Jakey a huge slice of chocolate cake. I paid, and when I made to return my wallet to my pocket The Nat said: 'You might as well keep that where we can all see it, eh?' And I winced, remembering her text.

We sat around a table which bore the Olympian ring-stain marks of a thousand other cups of terrible tea and, for a beat, I thought about Ads and Carl enjoying the finest cappuccinos known to humanity at La Scala; Mama fussing around them, bringing them out bowls of olives and other healthy and delicious snacks. Everything here gave off a sickly vibe. The chair I'd picked had a wonky leg which needed to be amputated. Jake's high-chair looked as though it carried all manner of diseases; you could still see an old fish finger mashed into one of the straps and peas rolled around in the seat-section. The Nat picked up the sugar bowl and looked inside it at the tumours of stuck-together grains and promptly pushed it back into the middle of the table.

All around us, folk hacked rattling breaths into face-masks or struggled to wheel their chairs into too-small gaps. It was like death's waiting room. And I was in purgatory until The Nat would tell me exactly what she wanted from me.

First though she had to cope with Jakey. The boy seemed to want to wash his face with the chocolate cake rather than stuff it into his mouth; so then it was out with the wet-wipes, which she kept along with everything else including the kitchen sink in her Tardis-like handbag. And then it was the negotiations: 'Are you going to eat this properly now, Jakey?' And the distraction techniques as she took up the fork herself and fed him by her own hand. And, honestly, the whole thing was so tiring, so time-consuming, and I couldn't see how in hell anyone could do both; work at a place like Andersen *and* have a kid.

Finally, he finished and she set him up with a few crayons and a napkin which looked as though it had been here since the last Jubilee. Then, at last, she turned to me.

'Sorry about that,' she said. 'I really didn't want to drag this out any longer than it has to be. But once you mix Jake with chocolate cake, it's all hands on deck.'

I nodded, pretending I understood. Pretending I could compute *this* Natalie with the Natalie from the previous night, at The Townhouse.

'Okay, so, brass-tacks. I have your names. All three of you. I have *your* telephone number. I could describe all three of you pretty well. Especially Adam. Mind, when the police ask you about distinguishing marks or features?' She patted her cheek. 'He has a birthmark right here. And Carl. Smarmy as hell. The Aviator shades. The slick hair. You I'd have been less confident about describing. Last night, after, when we were here and I was trying to remember you?' She shook her head.

The sinful, prideful part of me took great offence at that. I *was* remarkable. A prince. I was… Okay, I had one of those faces. As I've said, people were forever getting me confused with someone else. Still.

'But now you're here, I think I know exactly how I'd describe you.'

I longed to ask but, at the same time, didn't think I had the onions to take whatever insult she'd fire back in response.

'So what we have is a conundrum.' I raised an eyebrow. She ignored it. 'We have Rhys and Danny and they're all, like, not pressing charges. They're scared, you know? And Rachel, too. But me? I've been through enough in my life. I'm not scared. And do you know why?'

'Search me.'

She narrowed her eyes. 'I will do, later. And I hope you've had the presence of mind to visit a cashpoint on the way here.'

Christ, who was this woman? Here she was talking like some kind of experienced hustler, some kind of wordy, experienced hustler. Last night, she hadn't been able to stop the Yorkshire burping out of her, but today? Today she was something else. And I was something else too: that sheen, that bubble which usually surrounded people like me. It wasn't there today. Not after the night I'd had. Not after the rain had washed it away. Shit.

Shit.

Jake asked whether he could have a biscuit and The Nat told him not now. He slumped back in his seat, his bottom lip jutting out. And I reckoned I probably looked the exact same way. Sulky. Unsure. Like a Lost Boy.

'Okay, so what I think is this. I could make life very difficult for you. I got enough to at least tell the police something, so they might come to your place of work and embarrass the hell out of you, asking all sorts of questions. Or, I could make your life easier. I can see you're worried about all this. You looked like a drowned rat when you walked into reception and you've got, like, bin bags under your eyes.'

'You're talking,' I lowered my voice, 'about blackmail.'

She rolled her eyes. 'No need to make it sound so dramatic. Christ. No, what I'm talking about is people like you, who've had it cushty their whole lives, who get away with everything because the bigger boys can always sort out the big boys for you... Well sometimes, you have to pay something back.'

I gulped. This was it.

'Last night I was so shook up, so scared, so *vulnerable* about it all, but this morning I'm thinking differently. You see, what I reckon I got here is an opportunity. I can spin the wheel, like, and take a gamble. I can ask you for some money.' She lowered her eyes. Then forced herself to lift them again. 'See, I know Jakey's not had the best start in life. Not with what happened with his dad and Armley nick and everything and now he has to live with his nan and me... And you see the boys around our estate and they're lost. Don't know what to do with themselves so they do wrong because it's all they can think of. And I don't want Jake to end up like that. I don't want him to be like Rhys. I couldn't come visit *him* in a place like this.'

My throat was suddenly very dry. I tasted the tea and almost vomited it back up again. 'How much?' I growled. 'What are we talking about?'

The Nat set her jaw. 'Oh, I don't want to be greedy. I'm not talking telephone numbers here. Just something to get us started somewhere else. Away from Leeds. Away from *all this*.'

'Just give me a figure,' I said. 'Ballpark.'

'The park!' called Jake. 'Are we all going to the park?'

Natalie hushed him. 'Two grand. That suit of yours must have cost more. Heck, that *umbrella* of yours was probably nearly that.'

'It's not mine,' I said, pointlessly.

'Whatever,' said Natalie. 'Now, I don't expect you to have that kind of money on you now. I mean, no matter how much you guys flash yourselves around at The Townhouse, it's not like I reckon you've got a money-clip or whatever. But you can give me a down payment now. The rest I'll expect by Monday. That's when they reckon they'll be letting Rhys out and that's the day I want to *go*.'

92

'Two grand,' I said. Part of me was thinking *Fucking hell, she should have asked for more.* Part of me was thinking *Why should I give her that kind of money?* 'I'd have to... I don't know... Cobble something together. I'm not sure. Maybe I should talk to Carl and Adam.'

She shook her head. 'This is just you and me. The other two don't have to have anything to do with this. Now, are you going to open your wallet or am I going to have to do it for you?'

I did it, and I felt strangely liberated as I handed her the hundred and twenty pounds in tens, fives and twenties which was inside. The Nat's hands, however, were trembling as she reached for it. I kept the money bunched in my fist. Looked deep into her eyes. 'And this... this will be the end of it?'

She nodded. 'Once you give me the rest, yes. You'll never hear from me again.'

I gave her the money. She deposited it quickly in her handbag, as though she feared I'd snatch it back. She wouldn't have done so had she known the relief I felt that the end was in sight.

'When and where on Monday?' I asked, thinking if I asked now it would at least stop another text from winging its way over to me.

She wrinkled her nose, like a rabbit. 'I was thinking somewhere a bit nicer than this. Do you have any suggestions? You must know all the nice places.'

I shrugged. 'This is your deal.'

'Okay, let me think about it. I need to take this little guy off for a nappy change. Stay here. I'll think about it and let you know when I get back.'

'Right,' I said, and I watched them slinky their way out the caff. The Nat and her little Alan Smith. And I felt something like admiration for her, though my feelings for her were so complicated I couldn't put my finger on exactly what it was I admired.

Someone tapped my shoulder. Christ, what was it today with people touching me? I swung round. An old dear on the next table, wizened as a crone, said: 'You lot make a lovely family. Your boy's really bonny.'

And it made me feel all kinds of terrible. Because maybe that was what I'd admired in Natalie. The mother in her. The way she was going to all this trouble for her kid.

She came back eventually, looking flushed. She suggested we meet at The Townhouse in two days' time and, despite my misgivings – I didn't really want to go back to that place, not yet – I relented, if only to be out of there. Still, I felt much better about the whole thing, and when I was walking back to work it had even let off raining. And by the time I reached City Square and saw the height and majesty of the building I worked in – One City Square, a place which looked like an ad for a building rather than a building proper – I had something of a spring in my step because now I had a deadline. I knew when this would all be over and I could get back to being me again.

I swung round the corner and made for the revolving doors but before I got there I was waylaid by Carl and Adam. They'd been waiting for me, they said. We needed to talk. And my heart sank like a stone. Straight away I knew this wasn't over. Not by a long chalk.

Ads and Carl kind of hustled me down the street away from Andersen. We wound up sitting at one of the bus stops on Vicar Lane. Carl sparked up a ciggie and Ads worried at his birthmark with his pinkie finger.

'Okay,' I sighed, 'what's going on, guys?'

Carl heaved out a factory chimney's worth of smoke. 'He's asked us to return the favour.'

'Who has?' But I already knew. 'Nathan Long? What do you mean? How's he even know what happened last night?'

Carl winced as he sucked in another drag. 'Long *is* SAS. He knows everything that happens with every one of his employees. I mean, he calls them "members" of the firm but really they're just guys who work for him. He knew about last night before even *we* did.'

A thought struck me. 'Hell, there wasn't CCTV or something, was there? In the archway?'

Carl made a face. 'Course there wasn't. Why do you think they herded those Neanderthals down to the archway in the first place, genius?'

A bus drew up at the stop. An ad for *Ocean's 11* plastered all over the side of it. Right now it was starting to feel like we were living in some kind of low-rent crime caper. The bus doors hissed open. The driver gave us a dead-eyed stare when we didn't climb aboard. Then the doors hissed closed again and the bus pulled out, the driver shaking his head at us as he passed.

'Okay, I'm officially worried,' I said. 'We're talking about favours and returning them. We're talking about CCTV footage. What the fuck have you gotten us into here, Carl?' We were also talking blackmail, of course, but I wouldn't mention that. Not yet. 'Last night you were all like *watch me unleash hell.* Showing off that the bouncers were all at your beck and call, at the click of your fingers. Now you're saying you cut some kind of deal?'

Carl shook his head. 'I didn't make a deal. But it looks like they *do* want something in return for what they did for us.'

I was angry now. 'And what did they do for us exactly?'

'They took care of some people for us. Some people who wanted to kill us or whatever.'

'Listen to yourself. *They wanted to kill us or whatever?* They were no-marks from some estate somewhere.' I was standing up now, prodding my finger into Carl's chest. 'Those bouncers, they didn't do it for us. They did it for themselves. They enjoyed it. And now they're asking for something in return? Already?'

Adam stepped between us, acting the peacemaker. 'Look, *chill,* the pair of you. I was there too. It's really nothing to worry about. Nothing at all. Nothing serious in the grand scheme.'

But my head was still buzzing and my heart was racing and I felt a million miles from calm. 'The grand scheme? There is no scheme, not where we're concerned. We're just blundering along like we always do. But we've blundered into something we shouldn't have now. Those guys, SAS. They're dangerous.'

Carl spat. 'Dangerous? Nathan Long's a pussycat. A big, fat fucking pussycat. He listens to Boyzone, for fuck's sake.'

'Exactly. So he's a psychopath,' laughed Adam. 'No, seriously, Nathan Long is fine. A good guy. He just needs us to scratch his back is all. All that flab he can't reach around.'

'You seen him? Today?'

A round of nods from Ads and Carl.

'He came to La Scala. Surprised us.' Adam fingered his birthmark.

'Surprised you? That doesn't sound good.'

Carl flapped a paw. 'Not *that* type of surprise. He just showed up, that's all. I mean, you know how tight a squeeze it is in Scala? Between the counter and the wall? He, like, blocked out the light when he was walking down. Almost got caught between the tables. Mama had to bring him out a reinforced seat. She was all, like, *Don't you break-a my chair, signor.* And Nathan, pussycat that he is, was all, like, *yes ma'am*-ing her. She kind of mellowed on him then and brung him out the biggest plate of meatballs I've ever seen. You know how she fusses over fellas? And I mean, she must have looked at Long and thought Pavarotti himself had just walked in her place. Give her a minute and she'd have taken his photo. Stuck it on the wall, like with the Vialli print and the picture of that guy from the Housemartins.'

I didn't want to know all that. I wanted to know the other stuff. 'Did he follow you there? Or have one of his SAS guys tail you?'

Carl sighed. 'Now it's you talking like you're in a gangster movie. Neal, I hate to break it to you but we're creatures of habit. Anyone wants to find us between the hours of twelve and one, they know to look in Scala. Nothing sinister about it at all.'

'Fine, fine.' I felt suddenly tired. 'Nobody followed anybody. But still he asked you a favour. What is it?'

Carl and Ads shared a look I didn't like. Then Carl said: 'Well, he wants... Well, what it is is basically SAS have accumulated some funds and they need a way of putting it through the books, to make it *accountable*. You know, so there's a history to it.'

'You mean he wants you to clean his money for him? You're talking about laundering money. You know that, right?'

Adam told me that wasn't strictly true and Carl began talking himself in financial knots, but neither of them actually issued a full-on denial.

'Seriously, you're considering this?'

I'd considered giving in to blackmail. Hell, I'd made a first payment. But this was on a different level. I couldn't help but think of the baggie Captain Bouncer had produced to plant on Rhys and Dan if he had to, and I thought about how much money was coming through SAS on a weekly basis and I thought about how easy Carl found it to get ahold of drugs when he needed them. And then I put the pieces together, and they seemed to fit.

'What's the alternative?' said Adam.

I smiled, bitterly. 'You tell him no. He'll take no for an answer. He's a pussycat, like you say.'

Carl mirrored my smile. 'I said *he's* a pussycat. Not some of the other SAS guys.'

'But what you're talking about *isn't legal*.'

Carl sniffed. 'Neither's coke. Neither's speed. And yet you don't get on your high horse about them, do you?'

I rolled my eyes. 'Okay then; let's play what if. What if you *do* go ahead with this? How do you actually plan to set about cleaning his money? I mean guys like Nick Byers are lax but they do *check* occasionally. And Lightwood? He'd be on you faster than – '

Carl held up a single finger. 'Not if we work the money through some of the small-fry companies.'

Suddenly I knew exactly where this was going. 'You're talking La Scala, aren't you? Places like that.' *The accounts he'd brought in.*

Carl nodded. 'Zactly. Byers and Lightwood never trouble themselves to look into that stuff. We put it through their books. Make like they're paying for security services or something and, hey presto, you got clean money.'

'But La Scala doesn't exactly *need* security, does it? I mean, it's a mom and pop restaurant. Why'd they need a brick-shithouse bouncer on the door?'

Carl grinned. 'Maybe some of the other shops on Albion Place got pissed off at the constant death by opera at full volume. Or maybe who gives a shit. It's a story. Nobody will check. And once we're done, we're done. Favour settled. Slate wiped clean. Free like Scot.'

I wanted to tell him it didn't work like that, but then I realised I'd fallen into exactly the same trap with The Nat. What if she took her two grand and then kept coming back for more? Shit, I felt trapped in on all sides. Where the fuck was I going to go next?

'So are you in?' said Adam.

And all I could do was launder myself some time. I told them I needed the afternoon to think about it. And, reluctantly, they let me take it.

We headed back to the office. Lightwood was hovering near my desk when we got back. He shook his head but chose not to make any more of an issue out of it. Which I was all kinds of grateful about because right then I felt like if one more person started in on me, I'd just snap.

Over the past twenty-four hours my life had proved to have as strong moral foundations as a house of cards. Once one card was pulled away – incitement to assault – they were all coming tumbling down. And now, *money laundering.* When I thought of money laundering I thought of men wearing green golf visors plugging notes into counting machines in the shady back rooms of casinos. When I thought of money laundering I thought of the kind of oath which Andersen forced us to swear as a part of our induction process back in the day. That had been one of the Ten Commandments we were to swear never to break. *Thou shalt not launder money.* And though Carl, Ads and I had kind of giggled our way through the saying of those oaths – it seemed all kinds of stupid they made us stand up there, in front of the whole company, and reel them off – I'd never imagined I'd *break* one of them.

Once again, I thought about running away. And then I thought about black-bomber-jacketed, SAS-logoed, brick-shithouse sniffer dogs on my trail and I thought about being hunted down. They'd find me, whimpering and begging, and unleash the same kind of hell they unleashed onto Rhys and Dan.

And besides, running away was what kids who specialised in self-sabotage did. I wasn't that kid anymore. I had to admit that. Because then it might come true.

At six, when most sane people in most sane organisations were packing up and going home or, hell, already *were* home, I got sick of staring at the same beige cover of the same file and I picked up my desk phone and decided I had to call someone. But as I listened to the dial tone and as my fingers twitched over the number buttons, I couldn't think who I should call.

So I dialled Henry's number. He answered, but only after the longest time. From the sounds of it, he was already in some boozer somewhere in the Smoke. I could hear chinked glasses, the odd cheer, the common-or-garden hum of conversation that was not about work (or money laundering).

'Neal!' he cried. 'Wait a minute, mate. Just let me try and push through the crowd. Get somewhere I can hear you speak.'

I took the receiver away from my ear and was *this close* to putting the phone down. But the thought I might go mad if I didn't speak to someone sane kept me on the line and soon Henry had negotiated his way out of the pub and was, he said, set up outside.

'How did you know it was me?' I asked. 'I'm calling from a work phone.'

'You're the only person I know who'd be calling me from an 0113 number, Neal.' He whistled. 'Boy, it's been a long time. *Beards* since we last spoke.'

Verbally, I flapped a paw. 'Aw, it hasn't been *that* long.'

'Nearly two years, mate,' he said flatly.

I thought back to all those times I'd turned my phone on silent or switched it straight to voicemail when my old uni buddy had called. I thought about all those weekends which had started with me having the good intention of returning his call before getting dragged down into another weekend-long bender. But two years?

'How are you, Henners?'

Deadpan: 'You called me up after all this time just to see how I was diddling?'

'I've been busy,' I said, pathetically. 'You know the kind of hours I was working even when you were up in Leeds with me.'

'Right,' said Henry. 'Busy-busy-busy, greasing those financial wheels, eh?'

'That's right.' I should have put the phone down when I could. Too much time had passed. We couldn't get the teeth of our cogs and wheels to match up anymore. I just felt all kinds of awkward speaking to him. And to think, I'd been – what? – about to ask for his help working my way out of the moral conundrum I found myself in? Ridiculous. Henry didn't even know me now.

'Don't get me wrong. I know you've been in your work bubble up there. Those first few times I spoke to you, it was like I was talking to a different person: Mr Corporate.'

Mr Drone, more like. I'd hit the ground running at Andersen and had barely had a moment to pause and think since. Maybe it had been that – the constant forward momentum without ever being able to consider exactly which direction I was heading in – which had caused me to end up where I was. 'Stop riding me about it,' I said. 'You've always been so superior about me working for Andersen. Like I'm not helping humanity or whatever.'

'I'm not trying to ride you about it,' continued Henry, 'but *fuck,* man, you missed my *engagement party.* Didn't even have the bottle to reply to my email. Things must be going really well for you up there, eh?'

'Wait a minute: you got *engaged*?'

A spluttered laugh. 'Fuck, Neal. Course I didn't, but I just wanted you to think – if only for a minute – that maybe I had, and you'd missed it. I wanted you to feel that pang of guilt. Regret for a good friendship flushed down the pan. I wanted you to think: *Why hasn't he asked me to be his best man?'*

'I haven't flushed us down the pan, Henners.' I was twisting a pen round and round in my fingers. Cat's-cradling it. It was a fancy pen with a silver clip. Every time I turned it *this* way I caught my own reflection in it, and I saw a liar.

'Neal?'

'Sorry, miles away there. Henry, listen to me, we'll always be friends. We'll meet up for family holidays, the both of us with our 2.4s and our easy-on-the-eye wives, and we'll stay up late, drinking too much wine or port, and we'll get to reminiscing and I'll say something like "Remember that time I nearly became an accountant?". And you'll still have that hyena laugh and you'll bark it out and splutter wine all over yourself. And then we'll both be off and laughing and maybe one of our wives will slipper on down to us and tell us to keep it down because the kids are sleeping, and we will, for a bit, but then one of us will say…'

'*Neal,*' said Henry. 'Neal, I don't know what you're talking about. Are you drunk, mate, or have you made yourself kite-like?'

I closed my eyes. Of course he didn't know what I was talking about; that was just a story I'd told myself once upon a time, before my interview at Andersen, when I'd needed to cure my nerves. I'd rehearsed and rehashed it a few times over the intervening years, trying to remind myself of the *endgame* of all of this work, work, work-work, play, but I hadn't realised just how far away I was getting. Every day I put a few more miles between me and the me that could be.

I tried a laugh which came out sounding laundered. 'Sorry, mate. Just working too hard is all. Don't worry about it.'

He sniffed. 'But I am worried now. You sound... off-kilter.'

I twisted the pen. 'Don't worry about it.'

'Hey. We should get some dates. I could come up there or you could come down here and see me. Reminisce some more.'

I nearly said, 'Yeah, fine, I'll have my secretary call you, set it up.' And then I nearly said, 'Well, make sure your couch is free because I'm going to be training it down by Monday.' But actually I said: 'Fire me up an email. I'll see what I can swing.' Henry sighed. 'Look, I gotta go now, mate. Still got work to do before close of play.'

'It's supposed to be poet's day. Piss Off Early Tomorrow's—'

'I know what poet's day means, Henners. Look, see you, mate. Don't go off getting engaged. Not before I can vet your potential missus. Christ knows, I saw some of the mingers you brung back from Vod-Soc back in the day.'

I rang off with Henry's hyena laugh still echoing in my ears. Then I dropped my head into my hands for the longest time. Near the end of that time I began to be aware there was someone standing over my desk. Snorty breathing. A looming presence. Yet even though I knew it would be advisable for me to do so, I still couldn't bring myself to take my head out of my hands.

'Neal?'

Oh shit, it was Dale Lightwood's lightly-woody-with-a-nutty-aftertaste voice.

'Mr Grace?'

At last I looked up.

Dale Lightwood frowned. 'Is there something wrong, Neal?'

I forced myself to smile breezily. But from the expression which spread across Lightwood's face, my own face must have looked like a hurricane had hit it. 'I'm, uh, fine. Just got a lot of work on. Nothing to worry about. Plain sailing.'

Lightwood, a fanatic for all things nautical, seemed even more displeased by my use of a shipping metaphor.

'Look,' I stammered, 'I've just been burning the candle at both ends is all. Once I get this little lot' – I patted the pile of files in my in-tray – 'sorted, the doctor orders a quiet weekend then I'll be up and at 'em come Monday.'

Lightwood narrowed his eyes. At first I thought he was staring with disapproval at the files. There were a lot there. There'd been a lot there that morning. The pile had not changed, not one bit. But then I realised he was looking at something at my desk. I followed his eyes.

Lightwood picked up the Montblanc before I could. He twisted it around in his fingers just as I'd been doing. He paid particularly close attention to one side of it, like he was some kind of pen evaluator and he'd just found a defect which might push the potential sale price down at least a couple points. '*Tom Green*,' he read. '*Huzzah on the new job, love Mum and Dad.* This pen yours, Neal?'

My tonsils bungeed up and down in my throat. 'No... But I don't know how it came to be on my desk... It just... One minute it wasn't here, the next it was. Someone must have left it there, or perhaps I picked it up by mistake. Hold on: what are you accusing me of here?'

Lightwood patted the air with the heels of his hands. 'Look, I'm not accusing you of anything, Neal. But calm down, will you? Remember where you are: in the lair of the rarest beast amongst the big five.'

'I am calm.'

'Good.'

'I am calm and I am not a thief.'

I suddenly became aware that all extraneous noise on our floor had stopped; the whirr of the photocopier, the buzz of the phones, the shuffling of paper, the stomping of staplers, the clattering of keys, the ripple of conversation. Everyone, it seemed, was watching this exchange.

Lightwood offered me a reassuring smile. 'Not a thief, no,' he said, utterly *un*-reassuringly. He leaned in close: 'Now, Neal. We don't want a scene here, do we? But what I'd like you to do is stand up, walk with me over to Pomegranate' – Pomegranate was one of the ridiculous names they'd come up with for the small meeting-rooms which were dotted about the place; my initial interview had been conducted in a room which I later discovered was named Kumquat, of all things – 'and we'll have a little sit down and a little chat.'

'But I don't want to chat,' I said pathetically, like the schoolkid who's just been asked to step into the headmaster's office a while.

'I think you do,' hissed Lightwood. 'And I think you should come quietly.'

Come quietly? What, like some fugitive who's been rounded up by the sheriff and his volunteers?

I climbed up onto legs which hardly felt seaworthy. Lightwood patted me on the back – *there's a good boy* – but held his hand there in case it was needed to push me on. In case I made a run for it. Then we performed the walk of shame, me shuffling like there were shackles attached to my ankles, Lightwood trying to hurry me along. My head drooped, and I couldn't meet the eyes of a single one of my colleagues. No, not even Ads, who as I passed, hissed 'Neal, what's going on, mate?' Probably he was worried I was about to grass them up for their money-laundering plan.

The worst day of my life was just about to get all kinds of worse.

Lightwood sat me down in Pomegranate then he told me he needed to leave me there a minute – 'Just a minute, Neal; no longer than a shake of a lamb's tail' – while he popped down to see whether there were any of 'those work shies' in HR still in the building.

'What do you need HR for?'

Lightwood shrugged. 'Ah, nothing. Protocol. Just have to do everything by the book, don't we? Remember: accountancy's about being accountable.'

My lip trembled. 'Is this about the pen? I didn't even know what the deal was with the pen. It just landed on my desk and I happened to be playing with it.'

Lightwood shook his head, solemnly. 'It isn't about the pen, Neal. Tom Green did complain someone had taken his pen. Kicked up all kinds of a stink about it. And I will ensure it is returned to him properly. But this isn't about the pen.'

'What is it about then?'

Lightwood winced. 'Let's just wait 'til HR gets here, shall we?'

Then he went out the door and locked it behind him. The key he left on the outside. Effectively, I was now in gaol.

Shit. Shit-shit-shit.

I told myself I wasn't the real one they wanted. Hell, I'd not even been party to the meeting with Nathan Long. No, they wanted me to point out the ringleaders: Carl and Adam. They wanted me as a witness. A grass. Perhaps they too saw the same weakness The Nat had spotted in me. That yellow streak.

I stared at my hands, at my lifeline. I'd never noticed before but it appeared to end prematurely, little more than halfway across my palm. I'd never set much store by fate before but, suddenly, in that small, chrome and teak room, I understood everything that had happened today was a comeback, a punishment, for my presumption. I'd sealed my fate, my doom. I made a fist so I wouldn't have to consider such weighty subjects.

Then another terrible thought struck me: what if Lightwood *wasn't* going to fetch one of the *work shies* from HR in order to dot the i's and cross the t's of this meeting? What if he had a cop lurking somewhere in the building? What if things had escalated that far already?

When I heard the key turn in the lock again I almost jumped straight out my seat. Lightwood strolled into the room first, his hands clasped behind his back like fucking Poirot or something. Thank Christ though; he wasn't followed by a cop. He *had* fetched someone from HR. Poor guy looked like he'd been just ready for the door – he was already wearing his coat – and he looked none too pleased to have been waylaid. He slumped into a chair like a deflated balloon; let his briefcase drop to the floor like a sunk stone. I didn't recognise him. Us 'princes', us knights of the round table of King Arthur, didn't tend to hobnob with stiffs like him. Stiffs like him who thought he could go home at half-six on a Friday night.

Lightwood made himself chair of the meeting, as usual. He introduced the HR guy but I forgot his name almost immediately. Lightwood announced this was just an informal meeting for now – 'just a chat' – but he'd requested the presence of the HR guy because of certain allegations which had been made about me. I wanted to know exactly *what* allegations he was talking about but of course Lightwood wouldn't let me off that easily. First he had to waffle on about the moral integrity of Arthur Andersen and to throw off a lot more crap about us being the rarest beast amongst the big five. Finally though, he asked whether I recalled the oath I'd taken in front of the whole company.

'Sure,' I said. But inside, I was squirming. I decidedly did not like the direction this meeting was taking: that oath, of course, made reference to money laundering.

Lightwood offered an eighth of a smile. 'Of course, our oath isn't as binding as the Hippocratic oath which doctors have to take. But' – he rapped his knuckles on the table – 'by the same regard, we don't expect that it will make hypocrites of our staff.' He was clearly pleased with that line. Waited longer than he should have before continuing, as though he wanted one of us to interject with applause. Then: 'So of course, we have to take all allegations of drug-taking on the premises extremely seriously. You remember the line, don't you, Neal?'

I gulped. Of course I remembered the line: some junk about not muddying our brains with junk. But what I couldn't wrap my head around was this: *this was all about drugs?*

'Mr Grace?'

'You want me to, uh, say it right now?'

The HR guy interrupted. 'I don't think we need to make him do that.' And Lightwood looked as though he wanted to throttle him.

'I'm not... I don't understand,' I said.

The HR guy opened his briefcase, rooted about inside then plonked a file down on the desk. Lightwood took it up and flicked through it. 'These,' he said, 'are all reports filed stating they have seen you – Neal Grace – looking worse for wear on company premises, repeatedly slipping off to the toilets on work time. Sniffing.'

'Sniffing?' I said, incredulous. 'I'm in here for sniffing?'

The HR guy was quick to step in. 'These reports are all uncorroborated. You are not on trial for anything here. All we want to do is get to the bottom of this. We want to find out whether you have a problem, Neal, and we want to help you if you have. Remember, the first step to recovery is admitting you have a problem.'

'Yeah, but *sniffing*? That's one giant leap to take. Someone sees me sniffing and you jump to the conclusion I'm some kind of addict?'

Lightwood sighed. 'There's more. Today, after I received another statement regarding your, ahem, general shape – '

'Wait a minute. A statement. You're putting together some kind of case on me. Who's your witness? Let me guess: Tom Green. Tom Green doesn't have a life of his own and he's jealous I might have one, so he makes up... Hell, I bet he put his fancy pen on my desk just to seal the deal.'

Lightwood frowned. 'How many times do I have to say this? This isn't about the damned pen.'

I seethed. 'Okay. So what's this *more* you're talking about.'

Lightwood made like a Cheshire Cat. 'This morning, at oh-nine-hundred hours, I was granted permission to monitor and record any or all telephone conversations made on your desk phone – '

'You don't have the right,' I yelled.

'We do have the right, I'm afraid, Mr Grace,' said the HR guy. He produced another file from his box-of-tricks briefcase. Pulled out a sheaf of paper held together by a clip. Passed it over to me. 'This is a copy of the company policy and procedures on the use of company equipment.' I didn't bother to read it. Didn't have time. He also passed me a second clipped document. 'And this paperwork outlines the company's attitude towards drink and drugs in the workplace. You accepted both policies and signed to that effect when you passed your three-month probationary period.' He passed me a third paper, where an arrow-shaped Post-It note pointed directly at my signature.

Lightwood took up the reins of the conversation. 'And so, I was waiting a long time for you to pick up the phone today, Mr Grace. An awful long time. What were you doing all day? That stack of files in your in-tray never seemed to move. And you sure didn't do anything on your computer.' A tight smile. 'Yes, we're monitoring that, too. Your keystrokes, websites visited. All that jazz. And then at eighteen-hundred hours, you made a call didn't you, Neal? Do you remember what was said on that call, Neal?'

I scratched my head. That was the Henry call. Neither one of us had said anything *Not Safe For Work,* had we? Sure, it had been a little *bantery.* We'd sworn. But nothing worse than that.

The HR guy handed Lightwood another batch of paperwork. 'This is a transcript of the conversation,' he explained. 'You can request the actual recording if you'd like.'

'I thought you said this was just a chat. Informal.'

'Just making sure we cover ourselves, Mr Grace.'

'Indeed,' said Lightwood. He licked his thumb and, like a well-practised librarian (or else a green-golf-visor-capped money launderer in some seedy back room of a dodgy casino) flicked through the pages. He found what he was looking for: a highlighted passage right near the end. He cleared his throat. 'This is a Henry Something speaking. We don't have his surname yet, but we can find it out, if required. *Are you drunk, mate, or have you made yourself kite-like?* Mr Grace, does this or does this not make reference to drug-taking?'

'That's it? That's all you have? It's a figure of speech: like, say someone says something stupid and the other person says "What, are you high?" I could ask you if you were high because *you've* said something stupid.'

'Okay, Mr Grace, that's quite enough of that.'

I stood up. 'But it's ridiculous. I'm not on drugs. Never have been. This is just... well, it's trumped-up, is what it is.'

'Sit down, Mr Grace,' said the HR guy. 'Please?'

'Fine'. I sat. 'But it doesn't change anything. This is... this is a slur on my character. I should... You should... This isn't fair.'

'Life isn't fair,' grinned Lightwood. 'Not unless you go out there and grasp it by the throat like a big-five animal. But I take your point. If you're innocent of this, then you certainly don't want any *insinuations* cast upon your character. And there's an easy way of sorting all of this out. Would you like to know what it is?'

'Hit me,' I said.

'We test you. We take some of your hair and have it tested – that's how it works, isn't it?' – he glanced over at the HR guy, who nodded in agreement – 'and when you're all clear we say sorry, Neal, and none of this ever makes your permanent record. Course, if there *is* truth to any of this – and, Neal, you have been looking *wan* recently – then, we sever our employment with you forthwith and report you to West Yorkshire Police.'

Shit. Shit-shit-shit.

'Do we have your consent to perform the test?' The HR guy's pen was hovering over his notes.

I gulped. I literally had no wriggle room left.

'Neal?' said Lightwood.

'Okay. Do it,' I said. Because things couldn't get any worse, could they?

I think Lightwood was hoping I'd just admit to the drugs then and there, and I might have done had their evidence not been so cobbled together. I think he was trying to call my bluff. I *know* he was. But right then, sticking or twisting, they neither of them seemed like a good option for me.

But the HR guy saved me. 'Well,' he said, 'we don't have the staff on site to conduct the test right now. So what do we say first thing Monday morning instead, Mr Grace?'

'And we'll take it on point of honour that you don't shave your head in the meantime,' said Lightwood sulkily.

'That's settled then,' said the HR guy, rising from his seat. 'So if you don't mind, I've a home to go to.'

Lightwood fluttered his fingers. *Just go.*

As soon as the HR guy had left, Lightwood snarled across the table. 'You're out of here, Grace. You know it as well as I. You might have a stay of execution for now, but come Monday, that's it.'

I stood up once more, resolved I couldn't listen to another word.

At the door, Lightwood stopped me in my tracks, Columbo-style. 'One more thing,' he said. 'I'm placing you on immediate suspension while this investigation plays out. Do not go back to your desk; do not collect your things. I will call security to escort you out the building.'

Security was, of course, our old pal Paul, and Paul came up looking all kinds of apologetic he had to make me suffer the indignity of being escorted from the building. In the lift on the way down, a Friday night trip in which I used to feel the day sloughing off me all the way, I now felt like I was riding a snake on a Snakes and Ladders board.

Paul, his Irish eyes kind of *gleamy,* told me everything was going to be all right.

But I told him there was *too much* everything right now, and even if one thing miraculously turned itself around, there were other crises ready to rear up in its place. I told him I'd had enough.

He told me he felt like that sometimes.
I asked him what he did about it.
He told me: *Bushmills.*

IV

I went to a bar nobody would know my name. Bar Cenessa on Boar Lane. Sure, it was packed with the usual after-work Friday-night revellers, but they weren't the Andersen crowd; despite it being one of the closest bars to City Square it wasn't *quite* the right calibre – it tried a bit too hard; it was too big, too spread out to have any intimate VIP-type areas; and it looked too *chainy*: those loops and swirls of paint on the walls which were supposed to make it look individual instead made it look as though it had been decorated by a guy who moonlighted as the artist who churned out those identikit modern art prints you got in crappy hotel rooms – and besides, Andersen hadn't booted out yet and, really, you weren't too cool for school if you were out and about this early. The people we knew went out fashionably late and looked their best just when everyone else was starting to look just that little bit dishevelled. We sailed past bouncers – even the ones who weren't SAS – without them needing to take a look in our eyes or hear our slurred speech.

Cenessa was an in-between, passing-through kind of place. Folk could hop off of the train and straight into it, before heading off to Yates' Wine Lodge and Square on the Lane (both of which were also characterless and, on Saturdays, stag and hen central). You could never be a regular at a place like Cenessa. You'd never have your own glass behind the bar. And, sure, your feet didn't stick to the floor like they did in some of the spit-and-sawdust dives I'd enjoyed during my time as a student in Leeds (Big Lil's Saloon Bar springs to mind) but it wasn't that much of a step up from the Golden Goose.

While I was queuing at the bar, I overheard two try-hard lads talking. They were discussing 'the professions', law and accountancy. One of them had a friend of a friend who.... 'But you know, mate, when you reckon it all out, the hours those fucking desk-jockeys work, when you equal it all out, their hourly take-home ain't much bigger than ours.' Once upon a time, I'd have whopped my wanger out on the bar. My wallet I mean. Showed them a recent bank statement. Told them, divide that by whatever and you still get a bigger girth than you fucking no-marks. Carl, Adam and I were always doing stuff like that. Carl especially. But no more. No more. Cenessa didn't even boast SAS bouncers on the door who could bail me out when these two lads took offence. Hell, that was the very main reason I'd come here.

There weren't many other reasons to stay. They didn't have Bushmills, for one, just common-or-garden variety whiskeys. The bargirl I asked didn't even know whether they were Scottish or Irish. So I plumped for a G and T instead. The girl said they definitely had that, and wasn't it my lucky day, it was happy hour so that meant I got two.

I told her it most definitely wasn't my lucky day, but seeing as though it *was* happy hour, I'd take two gins. So she poured me two, and I had to painstakingly explain that I actually wanted four. And honestly, it got a little embarrassing trying to sort it all out and in the end I just took my two and sloped off into the crowd, looking for a safe and lonely place to lay my hat.

Turned out there were plenty spare tables once you got past the crush at the bar, so I helped myself to one by the window which looked out over Mill Hill. From here, I'd have had a ring seat as the static between the Leeds players and the students finally came to a head.

I thought of my own crimes, slowly but surely stacking up; crimes I'd already committed as well as those which were in planning stage. I felt guilty for all of them, but perhaps the one I truly couldn't get past was one which I could only punish myself for. Though it didn't exactly make it onto my rap-sheet the worst thing I'd done was pretend to be someone I wasn't. I'd pretended to be a prince, a knight, when I was but a rat and a coward. What Henry had said about me being Mr Corporate, stuck in my bubble, was like a poisoned spear slowly working its way into my flesh and my blood.

Because I knew it was true. I knew I'd become someone else over the past three years, someone even my own dad wouldn't have recognised should he have blundered up and out of his grave in north Sheffield and then lumbered into here like some zombie.

I thought: I have until Monday to save my own life, otherwise I'll just plunge headlong into more of this. I thought: But how does one escape in just a weekend?

My Nokia's insistent trill intruded on my thoughts, but even had it not, I'm not sure I would have found an answer. Not then. I put the phone on the table in front of me, watched it drill itself into the varnish, having a fucking hissy fit that I wouldn't answer it.

When it had finished, spun itself out, I checked the screen. *3 MISSED CALLS,* it informed me. The caller was *CARL.* Ads tried next, but I ignored him, too. They wanted an answer from me: I'd asked them for the afternoon to decide whether to help them clean the money and return it to the SAS books. But I still didn't know what to say. Maybe if I'd gone to a bar which stocked Bushmills everything would have sorted itself out and *BINGO!* it all would have come to me. But I hadn't. And now I was writing another instalment in my adventurous life story in which I sabotaged myself at every turn.

Another call from Carl came in. I stared at the phone, willed it away. And, miraculously, it did stop, after only four rings.

I let out a sigh of relief, then the ringing started again.

A voice: 'You not going to answer that?'

I looked up.

Carl was here. 'Of all the bars in all the world,' he said, smiling. He took the phone away from his ear and sat down, blocking my egress route from the table. Sat so close that were it not for the fact he was my friend, I would have thought he was threatening me.

'How did you find me?' I asked, miserably.

He tapped the side of his head. 'Intuition, baby, intuition. I thought about it and I reckoned there was only one

114

place you'd want to go after a grilling from Lightwood and that would be a bar. And then I thought some more... You're a *sensitive* soul. You wouldn't wanna go in a bar had SAS bouncers on the door. But you'd want somewhere close, nonetheless. Hey presto, Cenessa.'

He'd read me like a pulp fiction book.

'Where's Ads?' Carl reached out for one of my G and Ts. Slugged some back, and I was like: 'Help yourself...'

Carl looked like he'd just eaten a whole lemon. 'Fuck, that's not exactly Bombay Sapphire, is it? More like' – he spat on the floor – 'Mill Hill Grit or something. And this place – Neal, how could you? – it's not exactly The Townhouse. Hell, it's not even *Norman.* It looks like the kind of place Han Solo would set up a meet with his old pal Greedo. You know, the cantina bar at Mos Eisley? A hive crawling with scum and villainy? I'm surprised they don't have a live band: Sy Snootles and his Mob.'

I sighed. 'Where's Ads?'

Carl poured some more of the gin down his throat, gargled, then spat again. 'Adam... Adam?' Pretending like he knew the name, just couldn't remember where he'd heard it. He held up a finger. 'Ah, right, *that* Adam. The guy you blanked at lunchtime – along with me, I hasten to add. *That* Adam. Right, well, our Adamski's not handling things too well at the moment. He's a bit like you in that respect. Only, his, like, unease manifests itself in different ways. Ads has gone off to score some more shit. I told him, "Look mate, you're already wired and Lightwood's getting watchful," but he was like, "I can handle it."'

'So you know what Lightwood had me in for?'

Carl sucked his teeth. 'Seems like you've been a very naughty boy, Grace. The rarest of the big five animals does not go round stealing – what's his name? Ben? Dick? Harry? – Tom Green's fucking Montblanc, does he?' He wagged a finger. 'Least that's what's swinging around the office grapevine. That's it, isn't it? There's no more to it, Neal? I mean, you'd tell me if there was, wouldn't you?'

His eyes were like icebergs and I was the *Titanic*, crashing right into them. I'd tell him everything. I would. 'They had me in because there'd been allegations I was *on the sniff.*'

Carl snorted a laugh. 'Is that all?'

I hated him for his breezy contempt. '*All?* They've suspended me. I was *escorted* out the office. I can only come back Monday and only then when I've passed a drug test.'

'Like I said, is that all?'

'Carl, they talked about getting the police involved.'

'They won't. Too embarrassing for the company.'

'Yeah, but even if they don't, something like this goes on your record. If I'm given the bullet and I apply for another job and they need a reference, they'll call up Lightwood and he'll say, "Yeah, yeah, officially he was diligent, a good time-keeper, proficient in accounting. But off the record, he was trouble. Drugs, you know." And my CV will be straight in the bin.'

'Won't come to that,' said Carl. 'We're knights. We get away with things like this.'

'I won't. I'm not like you. I'm not... I don't have the old boys' network backing me up. I'm not, like, a Mason or something.'

Carl laughed. Eighteen months back, the three of us had finished work on a Friday night like this one (but different, because then I was a prince, and gung-ho) and we'd been debating whether we should chip on down to The Townhouse straight away or maybe call in somewhere for a nip on the way (not Cenessa; not Square on the Lane either). And just like that, Carl had said: '*Monte motherfucking Carlo.*'

We took an EasyJet from Leeds-Bradford to Lyon that night, then upgraded quite considerably, taking a train First Class over to Monaco. Saturday morning, we were princes amongst a whole population of princes. We headed for the casino, and all of us came out well up. Adam had done so well the three of us got invited to some kind of private party on a yacht belonging to a famous oligarch who'd later go on to buy a Premier League football club. The oligarch wasn't in attendance then, he was over in LA, but everyone else who was anyone was there, living it up.

The three of us found ourselves at the prow of the yacht, looking out onto the azure-blue sea in which three topless supermodels frolicked in a dinghy. Cool Croc – the actual Cool Croc: two DJs wearing huge crocodile masks – pumping out beats and spinning the tunes. Carl raised a toast – to us – and said we should do this more often. I laughed and said yeah, course we should, but it was easy to sing when you were winning. But Adam remained silent. When we asked him what was wrong, he pulled one of his incredibly Polish faces at the same time as giving this hugely Gallic shrug.

At last, he explained. Adam said he felt like his dad might be in the Masons, and had maybe signed him up too without telling him. We told him that was ridiculous; the Masons were a traditional English organisation, they wouldn't go round accepting Polish people as members. But Adam was wearing his indignant Adam Ant hat. 'No, honest to,' he said, 'that's the God's honest. I feel like my way's been smoothed. Like someone has come along before me on the beach and swept away all the wrinkles and the broken bottles and the used condoms and I can just flip-flop through. People come up and shake my hand and carry me up to the next rung of the ladder. All these smiling blokes, all these lovely ladies. I just feel like I've sometimes been too lucky, yes? Maybe I just didn't recognise those handshakes for what they were. They must have been Masonic.'

I laughed and shook my head. Told him it sounded like there were too many bubbles bouncing around in his head.

But Carl said: 'That, what you're describing; that's what it's like if you went to public school.'

In Cenessa, which was about as far away from an oligarch's yacht as it was possible to be, Carl gave off similar confidence. 'But *I* know people. You might not be a…a Mason, but… Okay, put it this way. Do you think you're the first person at Andersen who's had your particular problem?'

I sighed. 'I don't have a drug problem, Carl. Who was it went swimming this morning instead of firing down another line off your breakfast bar?'

'I don't mean that kind of problem. I mean, an HR interfering kind of problem. Can you keep a secret, Neal?'

'Oh, for fuck's sake, Carl. You really have to ask?'

'No, I mean a proper one. You can't let this one out the bag. Not even to Ads.'

'Okay.'

'Nick Byers.'

'What about him?'

'His first year at Andersen he fails his ATT, just like me. Yeah, I know, he's the one goes round making up all that Zombie Nation business, but back in the day, he must have been just like us. And I mean *just like us.* Anyway, after he got the ATT test scores – you know they issue them at midnight, online – he went out and got blasted, and I mean blasted, and the next day he turned up still in his party clothes. Lightwood collared him. Threatened him with all sorts. Trying to get him to admit it. But you know how Nick is. Course he wouldn't back down to *Lightwood* of all people. The test, it's a bluff. They want to back you into a corner so you come out sobbing, admitting to everything. Nick never took the test.'

'Why not?'

'He had words with the right people.'

'But I don't know the right people. And anyway, how do you know all this?'

'Nick is the right people and Nick told me.'

'You think Nick would be able to help me?' I felt a surge of hope.

Carl patted my knee. 'I think he'll know what to do. Let's put it like that. In fact, let's put it another way. I think Nick Byers has something on Dale Lightwood; something big, something juicy. And of course I don't know what it is because Nick closely protects this thing. It is valuable. A get out of jail free card, maybe.'

'And he'd use a get out of jail card for me?'

Carl shrugged. 'He likes you. Hates Lightwood too, of course. So that'll work in your favour. I'll call him, later.'

'Why not now? Please? Can't you call him now?'

Carl looked as though he'd have loved to have, if only damned red tape hadn't gotten in the way. 'I can't call him now because you haven't given us your answer yet.'

'What answer...? Oh right. The money laundering.' That spark of hope which had kindled in my chest fizzled out.

'Well?'

'Well, it doesn't look like I have any choice, does it?'

Carl nodded. 'That's right. And that's how you sell it to yourself if ever you start to have doubts. I'm not trying to force you into anything here, Neal. But the situation you're in now, well, you need a favour, and I've one to give. But I also need a favour. We all scratch each other's backs and this all goes away, I promise. And that, *that* is what the old boys' network is all about. People on the outside think it's all kinds of sinister, but really it ain't. We're just kids trying to get into someone else's garden, offering each other leg-ups on the way.'

It didn't sound like that at all. But I was in no position to argue. I was in a bind; Carl was right, and I hated to say that more than almost anything. Basically, what it amounted to was I was out of choices.

'Good,' said Carl. 'That's settled. Now drink up, Neal, we got places to go; people to see. I'm still on the clock here, mate. You don't think I'd have just got let out before eight so easy if we didn't have a client meeting to go to, do you?'

'A client...? Oh, right.' I drained the gin and tonic; Carl poured the rest of his on the floor. He offered me a ciggie; a Benson and Hedges; he smoked them sometimes instead of Camel Lights because he thought the name sounded more elegant. I declined.

At the door, Carl stopped to talk to the bouncer; offered him a card and suggested if he ever fancied stopping 'playing at' being a doorman and wanted to step up to the A-League, all he needed to do was call him and he'd be able to get him through the door at SAS. Remarkably, the bouncer – a guy built like the concrete reinforcements holding up a bridge – did not punch Carl in the face but instead took the proffered business card and placed it in his pocket, with a gravelly 'Thank you, Mr Carl.'

We set off down Mill Hill, past greasy kebab houses and run-down pubs and betting shops, and once we'd gotten a safe distance away from Cenessa I asked Carl whether he was starting up a fucking recruitment agency now.

'Nah,' he said, 'just keeping my fingers in all the pies is all. Eventually, I don't want to work for Arthur Andersen.'

'What?' This was the first I'd heard of it. As far as I could tell Carl *loved* the place, really bought into that knights of the round table of King Arthur bullshit.

'Yeah,' he shrugged, kicking an empty chip-tray out of his path. 'I mean, it's all very well working for some massive corporation, but one day I want to be my own boss. Run my own thing. Client services. Something like that. I can supply a business like SAS with everything they need, from their books done to new blood through the door. I been thinking about it a while now.'

'When were you going to tell me about it?'

We passed under the Dark Arches, which did exactly what it said on the tin. Long dark archways too shadowy to see the rats scurrying at your feet; too loud to hear the man with a knife running up behind you to mug you for your Nokia. The rumble of trains up ahead; the clank and jangle of barrels being loaded at the Scarboro' Taps; the din of the kitchens at the Queens Hotel. The ground squelchy underfoot; the air stinking of piss.

'It's only in the thinking stage at the moment, Neal,' said Carl. 'But if we can stay in with clients like SAS, then at some point I'll make the jump. And of course, I'd want you and Ads to be my wing men.'

I wasn't sure whether this was Carl's way of using a carrot as well as a stick in making me do what he wanted with regard to cleaning the money. I wasn't even sure if I liked the idea; I mean, without the set structure, the back-up, the organisation of Andersen, Carl would most likely spend all day in front of his massive TV, watching film after film, doing line after line. But then again, there was something shrewd about him: witness his property empire; witness his bringing the accounts on board in the first place, something which was virtually unheard of in a first year on a grad scheme. And when he really set his mind to something, Carl was like a dog with a bone.

Soon after he won SAS as a client, he started work on their books. What he found was an unholy mess. There seemed to be all kinds of inexplicable and unaccountable monies entering the accounts. There were black holes; wormholes; time warps; asteroid fields. He said he couldn't *move* for obstacles, or digressions, or anomalies. It was like their books were a fucking sci-fi computer game, for Christ's sake.

He said it was all kinds of easy to tell the books had been glued together by the husband and wife team which was the Longs. He said he *could* have gone to Byers, or to Lightwood, told them he'd been wrong – the SAS account wouldn't be a workable one after all.

But how pleased would Lightwood have been then?

And so, on the sly, Carl got permission to bring Adam and I in on the deal. I always wondered how he'd swung that, but, given the benefit of hindsight, I reckoned he'd asked Byers to scratch that itch for him. And so, the three of us spent a couple weeks ensconced in the SAS offices on David Street every night as soon as we shipped out of the Andersen offices; we weekended there too. Carl promised us it would be worth it; he'd negotiated a fat commission. And not only would he give us our share of it, he'd also take us away with him for a weekend when he visited his folks in Marbella. That was just the incentive we needed.

And Carl was as good as his word. Soon as we filed the audited accounts at Company House, we filed our holiday forms with HR and the three of us went over to the Costas for ten days of absolute debauchery, all of it on Carl's family. (The all-time best night was the Saturday of the last weekend, when Carl Senior and Carl's mum left us to babysit the bar while they went off for a 'dirty weekend stop-over' somewhere up the coast. Just like when I'd been handed the keys to the Golden Goose, we invited everybody. I mean, we literally rounded up girls off of the beach and helped them down the gangplanks of the yachts their fat old husbands had bought for them. We partied like there was no tomorrow, but when mañana eventually did show her ugly face, Carl hired a whole clean-up crew from a nearby building site and we put our feet up; enjoyed our last day at the private pool.)

I'd not been back to the offices on David Street since those two, red-eye weeks (which we'd survived by wolfing down takeaway pizza after takeaway burger; copious amounts of Red Bull, and Pro Plus – Carl wouldn't allow us to be high on *his* job – and, on our occasional breaks, watching nervous punters cruising the streets, waiting to pluck up the courage to wind down their windows and negotiate a price with the been-round-the-block prostitutes which populated that district: we always used to sing 'Roxanne' whenever we saw a customer one of us thought we recognised.) But as we headed over the canal, I saw the area had been given something of a facelift. Sure, there was enough of the old hag left to recognise: derelict buildings stuck out from its nearly sunny smile like rotten teeth and there were still a number of tramps gathering down by the locks, launching their empties like barges into the polluted water, but in the most part it looked *almost* acceptable, like the madam who used to work the punters but who now ran the whole show. A couple old mills had been done out into new media centres and now, in an area which was once upon a time famous for its streetwalkers, the only pedestrian traffic other than us were those suited and booted men and women scurrying to their cars from places like the Round Foundry.

According to Carl, Nathan Long had had quite a lot to do with the gentrification of the area over the past year or two. Apparently he'd gotten sick of having his wife and daughter visit him at work and have to look at the whores on the street and he'd petitioned the council, wrapped it all up in a more general concern: shouldn't they *house* these ladies of the night? It didn't matter if those homes were shitholes as long as they were homes. If they were left to just rot on the street, they'd hardly make a bean. And local businesses would suffer too.

Other than the odd derelict building, the only thing of the old David Street to survive the regeneration had been, against all the odds, a greasy-spoon of local renown. Apparently Nathan Long had quite a lot to do with that, too. He *lived* for their chip butties, their bacon barms, their jacket spuds in a way I'd, until just a few minutes ago, thought Carl lived for Andersen. The Gubbins Café was hardly a loveable place, hardly a place of historical significance, despite the fact it was an ever-present in an otherwise changeable line-up of industries and building types in Holbeck. From the outside it looked ugly; a relic. On the inside, the Gubbins was gloomy and the tables were all set back against the walls, separated into booths: it looked the kind of place where grizzled detectives would take their slippery snouts. Which wasn't entirely an unfounded observation: the café *had* once been *that* kind of place and it had a history as a hang-out for many of the streetwalkers. The great and good of West Yorkshire Police vice squad, all decked out in their tight, crotch-hugging trousers and decidedly *un* casual after-hours scrubs, could often be found inside, comparing notes with their short-skirted informants. Once upon a time. Now the ladies of the night had been moved on to different nights in different dimly-lit streets *away* from the city centre, I wondered who the hell the café's clientele could be. I could barely imagine any of the young professional/media types who came suited and booted to work at the new offices around here would choose to while away their lunch hours here. The Gubbins Café didn't exactly boast hummus wraps.

Long must have been keeping this place going all on his own, and according to Carl his ever-expanding bay-window proved it.

At the door, Carl stopped me with a warning. 'Don't, whatever you do, even if Long twists your arm, even if he threatens your dear old mum, eat anything in here. You hear me, Neal? The only things that should pass your lips should come from sealed containers. Cans of pop. The like.'

I grinned.

'I'm not fucking joking, Neal. Environmental Health would have shut this place down *beards* ago if it wasn't for Nathan.'

I nodded, then bit the bullet; stepped inside first while Carl held the door. A tiny bell announced our arrival.

The little girl perched on a tall stool behind the counter didn't even look up from her mobile phone. She sat there, biting her lip in concentration, every so often tapping the buttons. Snake, I guessed. She was playing Snake. Other than her, there was nobody in the café.

The girl looked to be about six, give or take. But I was no expert. She could have been twelve. She could have been three. She had incredibly dark hair and a half-moon face. Lit up from below, her face was all chin and nose. She might have been a goddamned witch's daughter. Most likely she was the daughter of one of the streetwalkers. Even at six (or three) she looked life-hardened and world-weary. The way her shoulders slumped inside her over-sized bomber jacket made her seem disappointed somehow. She kicked her trainer-clad feet against the bottom rung of the stool as though she wanted to hurt herself.

Carl closed the door with a bang and the girl didn't even look up. The pair of us stalked over to the counter – a display cabinet which showed off some decidedly limp-looking pies and pasties lit by a blinking strip-light – and drummed our fingers on top of the glass. The drumming echoed the chattering of my teeth. It was fucking freezing in the Gubbins, and somehow *damp* too, as though the rainstorm of this lunchtime was still going, but only in this one very specific location. There were two electric heaters behind the counter, one of which looked as though it would be condemned if ever a qualified leccy took a peek at it; the other looked as though it already had been, on numerous occasions. Judging by the wear and tear on it, it had probably arrived with the latest batch of flotsam and jetsam washed in on the polluted canal water.

I tried not to think of the adverts for carbon monoxide poisoning, of all of those poisonous fumes being belched out into the atmosphere and into that little girl's tiny lungs. Carl cleared his throat and I couldn't tell whether he'd done so in order to attract the girl's attention or because the fumes were getting to him too.

The girl puffed out her cheeks, let out a long, bored breath. She looked like she was performing a well-observed impression of a streetwalker confronted with the same vice cop for the fourth time in the space of a quarter-hour. Slowly, she fingered the phone, perhaps pausing her game so she could come back to it later. Then, finally, she turned her half-moon face on us full beam.

'All right, love; your mam or dad in?' said Carl.

The little girl placed the Nokia carefully on the side, next to the cash register, and then she simply sat there and stared at us. Her eyes looked as though they were coal-powered. They burned with her disgust at us; that we'd walked into *her* café and disturbed *her* game. She stared at us so hard I felt like stepping back away from the counter. And it was so *odd,* the way her eyes seemed so young and so old at the same time.

I whispered in Carl's shell-like: 'Maybe she's deaf or dumb or – '

The little girl sneered. 'Not deaf. Not dumb.' She spoke in a strange, halting voice. It was as though she was a computer reading out a message sent in text-speak.

Carl squeezed my arm and I realised he was trying to tell me something, and all at once I *got it.*

He made his voice go all mystical. 'You look like a Philippa. Doesn't she look like a Philippa, Neal?' I kept schtum. 'Or maybe a Pauline… Something beginning with "P", at any rate. You know there's some around here think I'm a little psychic, and the spirits are telling me you're definitely a "P".'

She gave him a look as though to say *I'm not stupid enough to fall for that one*. Then she said: 'You're not psychic.'

Carl pressed his fingers against his temples, closed his eyes. Made an odd humming sound in the back of his throat. Then opened his eyes again. 'I am too,' he said, 'and right now the spirits are telling me you should go and shout your dad and tell him his guests are here. I'm touched, I promise you.'

The little girl rolled her eyes. 'Touched in the head,' she said, like she was seventy-three years old.

Carl carried on manfully. Foolishly. 'Okay, okay. I got it now. But it was a real tough one on account of you've *grown* so much. You can't be *Phoebe*, can you, love?' Even I was embarrassed by the tone Carl took with the girl. Even I could tell she didn't want to be condescended to like that. 'The Phoebe I saw in photos was only very little, but you look like a big girl. Aren't you a big girl, love?'

She studiously ignored him.

'We're not *strangers*, Phoebe,' said Carl. 'You *can* talk to us. It's okay. It's not against the rules... We're here to see your dad, Nathan. Here, I'm Carl... You remember me, don't you? Your dad must have told you... I'm the one bought you all the Boyzone CDs for Christmas. You remember?'

She tutted. 'Already had all them CDs. Should have known that, if you was psychic or whatever. Anyway, don't even like Boyzone no more. They're, like, yuck.'

'Okay love, that's great,' said Carl, 'I'll remember that for next time. I'll get you something else. But will you be a good little girl now and tell us: where's your mam and dad? Actually, it's your dad we're really after. He asked us to meet him here. We're going to have a very important meeting. Do you understand?'

The little girl ignored him. Now she was staring directly at me, her eyes white-hot and... and cruel somehow. 'Who are you?' she said.

It was a question I'd been asked many times, in many different ways. My old dad used to ask me in such a way, he'd

126

really bring out the *are*. My dad was all about what a person did for a living (he'd respect you if he liked what you did; if not, well, he'd behave *otherwise)*. When I showed a certain academic bent he couldn't understand where it had come from. I think he thought I was going to follow him into the family business, no questions asked. I think he wanted me on the board over the door of the Golden Goose: 'Grace & Son: licensed premises'. My decision to go to uni made him question my bloody parentage.

Then there was Nick Byers, who was, for a spell, before he took Carl under his wing, my old mentor at Andersen. He told me the best way to get a handle on clients and clients' needs was to put yourself in their shoes and ask who you were. Emphasising the *who*.

And every goddamned time I looked in the mirror these past couple days I'd ask myself that same question. Stressing the *you*. Staring into my eyes like I didn't recognise myself. Like I couldn't understand what purpose I'd been placed on this earth for. Asking myself how I was going to make up for the series of failures which were fast becoming the central premise of my life.

This little girl asked me the same way I asked myself, with the same bitterness in her voice. Summoning all of my strength, I slapped my prince-mask on my face and told her I was Neal Grace. *The* Neal Grace.

And the little girl said: 'Oooooh. Fancy.'

And then I could think of absolutely nothing to justify my existence to her. I was out. Out and, at last, saved by the toilet flush. Then the very heavy tread of catering-sized feet on creaky floorboards above our heads. Then those same feet clumping down a set of stairs. There were two doors close to the counter. One contained a luminous orange sign with a hand-drawn arrow pointing downwards and the legend *TOIL-LETS*. At the bottom of the door a pair of large, black, wellington boots stood on a wad of newspaper. The other wasn't strictly a door at all; rather it was the same kind of hanging beads which my mum and dad used to have separating the bar from the living room at the Golden Goose. I used to love running through the caul of those beads, imagining that one day I'd somehow magically arrive at somewhere *other* than boring old Sheffield. Imagining I could somehow conjure myself into another life with other parents if I wished it hard enough.

The man who stepped through the beads and into the main room of the Gubbins looked as though he'd long since stopped dreaming that such a transformation could occur. And while some adults might have still stepped through those beads once in a while as though they were stepping through the curtains onto life's grand stage, this man stepped through like he'd *never* stood on ceremony. He was still yanking up his trousers at the back with one hand.

Nathan Long.

If his daughter Phoebe's face was half-moon, his was most definitely the full-moon version. He was much fatter, much rounder than when I'd seen him last. His cheeks were chubbier and ruddier. His chins seen in quadruple. He was fair bulging out of a white apron which was covered in a litany of stains which I hoped to Christ were red and brown sauce and not something more sinister.

'Welcome to my humble abode,' he said. 'You've met *Feebs*, I take it?'

Phoebe chimed in: 'Dad! I've told you. Don't *call* me that.'

He mussed her hair then shuffled over to us, offering his great ham-hands for us to shake. Carl first, who asked, 'What, you *living* here now?' and Long erupting into a volcano of a laugh which fair shook the Gubbins to the rafters. 'Course I bloody don't. Owner took the compulsory purchase money and did one, lock, stock. Left all his, well, gubbins here. So I says to the council, I'll keep the place going, least until you need to knock it over to make room for another media centre or something.' Then me: 'Good to see you again, Mr Long.' A wince as I was released from the vice-like grip of his fist (but not from that of his eyes), and him saying: 'Sorry we missed you at lunch today, Mr Grace.'

And then, for a beat, two, it was complete and utter silence.

Long broke it. 'Fucking hell, you two so high and mighty you can't come in a greasy-spoon these days? Honestly, the pair of you look shell-shocked. If I'd have known I'd have called the meeting in the offices. But I thought I'd make it a bit more relaxing for you… Or has Phoebe said something to you? She's got some mouth on her, that one, I tell you.'

'Phoebe's been lovely,' said Carl. 'We've been comparing notes on Boyzone.'

Long frowned. 'Yeah, well. Says she doesn't care for them anymore. *That's* what passes for loyalty nowadays.' I saw a flash of *something* cross his dull, cowish eyes, as though he might turn bull. But he didn't. Instead he became something else entirely. He became Nathan Long, *café owner.* He clapped his hands together. 'Anyway, what are we doing standing around shooting the breeze? *Drinks!* Phoebe, haven't you asked these two fine upstanding gentlemen what they'd like to drink?'

She shook her head.

He shook his. 'Ah, well, bred for better things than fixing drinks, I'll warrant. But right now, you're seven years old and you have to do what I say, girl. So I want you to ask these guys what they're having and then I want you to fix the drinks. Okay?'

Phoebe slid off her stool, slouchy as a teenager. 'What do you want?' she asked in dull monotone.

We gave our orders.

Phoebe made for the kettle.

Her dad stopped her dead. 'Wait, Phoebe. Wash your hands first, please. We don't know where those hands have been.'

Wherever those hands had been, it wouldn't have been filthier than the sink. The taps were rusty. The soap fossilised. Just above the sink, right next to the sign which read *NOW WASH YOUR HANDS,* there was a smear of snot wiped on the wall and left to dry.

Phoebe looked up at her father, moon-face to moon-face. Something passed between them. Then he clicked his fingers (Carl-style), and she *schlumped* over to the sink. When she turned on the taps, there was a great clunking and rending-metal sound as though the plumbing system were about to give up the ghost. We all listened to it shaking, rattling, rolling and then Carl made some joke about the water supply, which none of us laughed at at all.

'So,' said Long, once his daughter's back was turned, 'I believe you guys had some kind of trouble last night?'

'We talked about all that before,' said Carl. 'At La Scala.'

Long sniffed. 'Yeah, well, don't go expecting no skinny cappuccinos in here, boys. Not like in *that* place. No opera neither. But Carl, I wasn't talking to you. I was talking to Mr Grace here.'

'Uh,' I said. 'Yeah, there was a bit of... static. Over at The Townhouse. Your guys – SAS – they sorted it.'

'And what did you think of that?'

'Pardon?'

'What did you think? Were you relieved? High on the smell of blood? Or did it make you feel sick? What?'

I didn't know what to say. I couldn't look at Long. Instead my eyes strayed behind the counter. Phoebe turned off the tap, dried her hands on a tea-towel so dirty it *should* have necessitated her washing her hands again. And in that moment it was so quiet I could hear the crunch of the towel as she rubbed it against her skin. The crispiness of it. The dried crappiness of it. But then, another sound which was more piercing in the near-silence: Nathan Long cracking his knuckles as he bunched his ham-hands into fists. In a low voice, he said: 'I asked you a question, Mr Grace.'

'I was... Look it all happened a bit fast. I haven't really processed it yet.' Nathan Long rolled his eyes. 'Okay. Maybe I was pleased we... well, we didn't get battered ourselves. So that was good. But, I dunno, maybe it all went too far.'

'*Maybe it all went too far,*' mimicked Long.

I tried to placate him. I didn't know how Long had turned like this. Back in our initial client meetings with him he'd been... well, quite meek, like the location intimidated him somehow. Like wearing a suit constricted him. But now he was on his own turf. In a small voice I said: 'Look, maybe we got off on the wrong foot here – '

Long gave a bitter laugh. 'Aye, and you'll be saying *my guys* did that too. Only they was wearing shit-kicker boots and – ' He stopped. Phoebe was shaking his arm. 'Ah, the drinks are ready,' he said, in an altogether different tone.

Long picked up the tray and we followed his wobbling progress over to one of the tables. Above the table was a calendar which was three years out of date. 'Shall I be mother?' he said, and, had I been anywhere else in the world, at any other time, and in different company, I would have cracked up laughing. As it was, I nodded, sheepishly.

He sat – and so did we, taking his cue – and poured three mugs of builder's tea from the pot; the tea was the colour of tanned leather and looked as though it had the same consistency. Phoebe also sat down. She'd helped herself to a can of Dandelion and Burdock – Christ, I'd not drunk that since my Golden Goose days, but the distinctive smell of it took me right back – and a straw. She sat by her father, kicking her legs out under the table. I felt the displaced air from her every swing against my shins. The slurp as she sucked the fizz up the straw sounded like clogged drains.

I glanced at Carl: *Is she really going to be a part of this meeting?* But Carl made this really weird gesture, like I should keep my eyes front.

Long placed his hands, palms flat, on the table and examined his fingernails. I did too: they were clean. He let out a long, raggedy breath. Then: 'I called this meeting because I wanted to look each and every one of you boys in the eyes. And not just me. I wanted my Feebs' – '*Dad! I told you!*' – 'to have a look-see too. See, 'cos she's a very good judge of people. Very good indeed. Now, *Phoebe*, can you tell me what you think of Carl here?'

Unconsciously (I thought) Carl adjusted his position in his seat. Sat up straighter.

She shrugged. 'He's all right. A bit funny, mind, when he pretends to be psychic or whatever.'

'But you reckon he's okay, yeah?'

She nodded.

'So do I.' Long picked up a teaspoon, levelled it at me. 'But what about this one?'

Instead of straightening in my seat, I felt myself slipping down it.

'I don't know.'

Long thunked the teaspoon back down on the table. 'Neither do I, Feebs, neither do I. And, you see, that's the problem. I don't allow anyone to work for me unless I've looked into their soul. Every guy working the doors for SAS, they've been for interviews like this. And they've passed. Your friend Adam I saw this lunchtime so he gets a pass also. Carl, I know I'm okay with because he's about as slippery as they come, and the slippery ones don't tend to go running off to the police at the merest hint of trouble.' Carl made some meek noise as though to object but was over-ruled. 'But you, Mr Grace, I've never been sure of. I can't make my mind up. I don't think you can either. Sometimes I think you think you're bang-on the same as Carl and Adam, but sometimes I think you get to thinking you're different.'

I squirmed. It was true. A lot of the time I didn't know who I was. The essential Neal Grace was a changeable thing. 'I'm sorry,' I said, 'I'm just a little bit under the weather today.'

Carl kicked me under the table. *Let me handle this.* 'You can trust him,' he said. 'I'll vouch. He's like family to me.'

Long frowned. Even his forehead was flabby; like a stack of flat tyres. 'But he *isn't* family, is he? Not really. Not like me and Feebs.'

'No, I suppose not,' admitted Carl. 'But in some ways he's better than family. *My* family, at least. I mean, they fucked off – 'scuse French – to Marbella when I wasn't much older than Phoebe here. Left me to fend for myself at—'

Long roared with laughter. 'Fend for himself, he says! You went to one of the poshest private schools in the country.'

'Boarding school, though. Being away from home isn't for everybody... But what I'm saying is, I couldn't choose my family but I can choose my friends, and I chose Neal. I chose him because in a lot of ways he was like me. You know, no real roots. A bit lost. Don't get me wrong, he has – had – a family, but they weren't anything like him, you know. He was like... like that Mowgli, raised amongst wolves.' Long raised an eyebrow. Carl ploughed on. 'I suppose what I mean is, he found himself at Andersen, just like me. We found our calling.'

Long snorted. '*Calling?*'

Carl shifted in his seat. 'Yeah, I suppose that's it. We found what we were good at and what would make us whole people and... And we found ourselves together. Adam too. His parents can't even speak English properly so he had to make his own way, in a new language, and – '

'Enough with the life stories, Carl. I'm not here to hear about Peter Pan and the Lost Boys. I'm here to decide whether I can trust' – he jerked his thumb at me   '*him.*'

'Neal is Mr Trustworthy. He's incredibly loyal, too.'

Long drummed his fingers on the table. Then: 'I've made my decision. Have you, Feebs?'

It was ridiculous, I wanted to protest. How was my fate being decided by a fucking seven year old?

Phoebe nodded, clinked her can of pop down on the table. 'I don't think he is trustable,' she said.

'Now wait a minute!' Carl yelped. 'I need him. *We* need him. He has skills... I mean, when I first met you, Nathan, I hadn't even passed my ATT tax exams. Neal did, first time.'

'You don't understand,' said Long. 'There's different types of trust. On the one hand, you have *this* kind of trust: is he an honest man full of integrity? And on that score do we trust him? No, we don't. Not as far as I could throw him. Mind you, I'm a strongman. I could throw him into the canal. From here. Hell, he's an accountant, you're *both* accountants, and to me that makes you only one step farther out the swamp than a bloodsucking lawyer.' He paused, supped his tea. 'But there's another type of trust too, and that's what's important here. Can I trust you to do what I want, whatever the circumstances? I know you'll do it for me, Carl, and I know you'll do it right. And I reckon your Neal here will be exactly the same. I can see changes in him from last time we met. I mean, back then he could barely look at me. Now... Well, he's seen the dark side, let's just leave it at that.'

'So, you trust us in that way?' said Carl, in a reedy voice.

Long sighed. 'Yup. Hell, if I thought you'd be trouble, don't you think I'd have had back-up here? Don't you think it would have been a whole SAS squad rather than just me and Feebs on the interview panel?' Then he leaned in close. Hissed: 'But if he fucks up, Carl, I *will* throw him in the canal. Mind you, that'll be after. After my boys have been to work on him. You got that?'

I'd got it.

Long turned to Phoebe. 'Go get that bag from behind the counter, will you?'

She nodded, slipped out her seat and headed for the counter. She ducked behind it and came up holding a sports hold-all. *SLAZENGER* written down the side. The logo looked like a leopard, that rarest of the big five beasts. And here we were, about to change our spots and work for the other side.

The bag looked heavy. Phoebe carried it with both hands and still had to drag it the last part of the way. Long took it from her and lugged it onto the table, where it thunked down so hard it spilled my undrunk tea. 'Care to take a look inside?'

Carl obliged. Worked the zip. Then whistled. Then kind of fell back in his seat. 'How much is there?'

'Three hundred grand. The rest of the bag's packed with weights, just in case someone takes it off of you and makes a run for it.'

Carl gulped.

'But don't worry. Nobody'll do that. They know you work for me now. And if they don't, it's the canal or the railway arches for them. Ain't that right, Feebs?'

She nodded. 'That's right. But, *Dad*, stop calling me that.'

Suddenly Long snapped back into pussycat mode. He stroked his daughter's hair. 'She's tired, boys. Do you see that? It makes her snappy. Not her fault. I've kept her up too long. She should be curled up on the sofa right now with a nice glass of milk and a Disney vid, just about ready for bed. She's only seven, you know?'

'We know,' said Carl.

'Good,' said Long. 'Now get the fuck out of here so I can lock up and drive her home so we can enjoy some family time together.'

We jumped to our feet. Mumbled our goodbyes. Then hurried for the door. At it, Long called after us: 'So I'll expect to see that little lot in the SAS account very soon, eh?' And we both pretty much bowed, and then we were out of there.

Soon as the door closed behind us, announced by that little tinkling bell, Carl kind of dropped to his haunches. Spat into the gutter. '*Fuck,*' he moaned. '*That was intense.*'

I grabbed his arm. 'Come on, mate, this is Holbeck. We don't want to linger around here with that kind of money on us.'

It had grown gloaming dark since we'd been in the Gubbins. Carl looked up at me, bright-eyed and still kind of fierce. 'Right, *right*. What's your suggestion, genius? We schlep up through the Dark Arches, where you can't even see your own face or even your hands? Then, like, dump it in your locker at the International Pool for safe-keeping?' He pulled out his Nokia. 'No. We call our driver.'

'Our driver?'

'*Ads,* you numpty.' He plugged a number into his Nokia. Gave it three rings, then pressed the *END CALL* button. Within seconds, the half-beam headlights of Adam's blood-red Audi TT flashed around the corner from Globe

Road and pulled up – rather haphazardly – at the kerb. He buzzed down the electric window.

'You two lovelies looking for business tonight?' He grinned rather maniacally. Was clearly wired.

Carl, who'd made a miraculous recovery from his spitting-into-the-gutter moment as we emerged from the Gubbins, performed an excellent if alarming impression of a hooker's roll-walk; then he ducked down into the window, wagged a finger. 'You couldn't afford my ass, Warshawski. It's outta your league. Even if you do drive a TT.'

'This TT's been in cold storage. I haven't drug it out for the longest time. But for you, my sweet, I bring out the big guns. Climb in; have a feel of my gear stick.'

Carl snapped out of it at last and caught me unawares by calling shotgun. Meant I had to ride in back like some kind of seven year old. There wasn't much of a back seat in a TT, more of a package shelf, and even then I shared it with the *SLAZENGER* bag.

We took off. Almost literally. Ads revved the engine and then screeched away from the kerb, smoke pouring off the tyres. It was as though Ads was a getaway driver, racing through the streets with our booty – the *SLAZENGER* bag – safely ensconced in back. He tonned it down David Street, hand-brake turned it back into Globe, then *flew*. It was as though the cops were already on our trail, an APB out on the TT.

Ads threw the car into the bend at Bridgewater, laughing shrilly, like Murray Walker morphing into the Joker. I had to hold on to the back of Carl's headrest. Carl had to tell him to calm the fuck down unless we really did want the police on our (sweet) asses. The lights of Asda House flashing by; other cars snailing out of our way. We swung out to pass a bus, and into oncoming traffic. A chorus of beeps sounded, but by that time Ads was back on the right side of the road and flooring it, and then braking, almost too late, as we thundered around another bend and into the tighter streets south of the river.

We stopped at lights on Bridge End. At first I didn't think Ads was going to stop. I thought he was going to floor it, sail right through onto Swinegate. But at least he jammed on the brakes and we screamed to a halt outside the Malmaison hotel. *The bed house. And we were bad men.*

The car thrummed below us and I at last let loose with the breath which, until that moment, I wasn't aware I'd been holding.

Adam said: 'I can't help it. I've had this thing a year and it's still yet to get past four digits on the clock. It's like a horse got to be rode fast. It's itching for it.'

And Carl said: 'Nope. What's making you drive like a lunatic is all the coke. Here, give me some.'

Ads handed him a baggie and then the two of them set about snorting lines off of the steer-wheel. A taxi pulled up next to us, turning right, and the kid driving it looked over. Saw this going on. Then resolutely looked the other way. Christ, I thought, it was as though I was driving with the guys from *Scarface*. And when I caught Carl's eye in the rear-view I saw he thought this too and it made him the happiest man alive.

After the lights, Ads took it a little calmer. We followed the loop up past the station (and City Square; the lights still on at Andersen) and then up past the Town Hall and then back down again, past the Merrion Centre, past Europa nightclub (drunken students being made to queue by bored-looking SAS bouncers despite the fact it was generally empty inside at this time of night) and out of the city centre.

'Where we even going, anyway?' I asked. I'd gotten over the motion sickness now, but was beginning to be overtaken by a different type of queasiness. Basically, I hardly ever left a one-mile radius surrounding the beacon of One City Square. Everything I needed was on my doorstep. Outside of that, I was abandoning my comfort zone; I was becoming positively agoraphobic about it. Besides, Ads had whacked the hot-air blowers on full and it was hot as hell in the back of the TT. I'd already removed my jacket and loosened my tie, but I could feel the guilt-sweats creeping up on me regardless.

'We're going to see Mama,' said Carl. 'Day like we've had, I could kill for some of her home cooking.'

'Mama? But isn't La Scala...?'

'She doesn't *live* in the café, Neal,' snapped Carl. 'Just like we don't live at One City Square. Even though it sometimes feels like it.'

We continued in an irritable silence. I pressed my face against the glass and looked out on a wider Leeds which I didn't recognise. Harehills; Chapeltown. I tried to find something, anything, I recognised but couldn't. All I saw was dark looming shapes. Frazzled lights. Boarded-up buildings. Dilapidated warehouses. Endless rat runs of rain-slicked terraced houses. None of it snagged in my brain.

We threaded through Chapel Allerton, which I kind of knew; the bars at any rate. Hardly surprising: Chapel A was the stop-off point for many young professionals between Headingley and Hyde Park, where they'd lived as students, and some of the more familified suburbs where they'd finally admit they were no longer young. It was a Peter Pan kind of place, where nobody admitted they weren't twenty any more. I kind of thought Ads might end up there.

And then, finally, Moortown. Carl seemed to know it well. He sat-navved Ads down a couple side streets, past St Gemma's Hospice, which for many was the end of the well-travelled road which led from Headingley through Chapel A, through somewhere like Shadwell or Adel, and then onto a quiet little cul-de-sac which miraculously *remained* quiet despite its close proximity to Scott Hall Road.

At first, in the fizzing light of the streetlamps, you might have confused Mama's house for a common-or-garden unassuming semi, but when Ads pulled into the driveway and the TT's lights caught the place full-beam, we saw it was anything but unassuming. The house was *pink*. Maybe she liked her places as loud visually as they were noise-wise. Must have *delighted* her neighbours, just as La Scala's constant high-decibel opera did in town. Every windowsill was dripping with flowers and where there weren't flowers there were window boxes containing a veritable supermarket aisle's worth of herbs. The front garden was a ramshackle affair which contained not-quite-life-size replicas of the Statue of David and models of the Leaning Tower and the like. It looked like a miniature golf course gone to seed.

Even before we clambered out the TT, we could smell garlic, heavy on the night air. Despite my misgivings (and the car ride) my stomach grumbled. By the time we had crunched onto the loose gravel of the driveway, we could hear opera, too. Not quite so loud as it was in town, but still, loud enough that when he knocked on the door Carl had to practically perform a policeman's knock in order to be heard. And even then, he had to try it a few times; I noted a few curtains twitching on the street but no movement from within Mama's house until, at last, the music shut off.

Then we waited a few moments more before we caught sight of her through the mottled glass of the front door. She kept the door on the chain as she answered. And in that moment, when she poked her head between jamb and door, I saw Mama as nothing but a scared old woman. During the day, she wore make-up as loud and operatic as her musical tastes but now she was bare-faced and the wrinkles which she hid so well were painfully apparent. Same with her hair. As the Leeds Institution café owner she wore her hair scraped back and decorated it with (pink) flowers, but now it was down, and scraggly, and decidedly grey.

'Mama, it's us,' said Carl.

And still she peered out through the crack and didn't seem to *see* us. Perhaps we'd roused her out of her bed. Perhaps she kept up the operatic white noise just to soothe her into the land of nod. Certainly she'd taken her own sweet time in answering the door, and certainly she was now wearing a dressing gown. Maybe she'd taken those moments to pull it on, to cover up the sins which lay beneath.

Then, suddenly, it dawned on her who we were, and suddenly she was all birdsong and hugs, and in those moments as she wrapped her arms around each of us on her doorstep – me more than most; she pulled me to her, and then, still holding me, looked at me as though she'd not seen me in a decade and was trying to work out just what aspects of me had changed; I'd only missed one lunchtime – her wrinkles disappeared and her face changed and she became Mama again.

'What am I thinking? You must come inside! We must eat!' She bustled her way around us, harrying us over the doorstep, sweeping us into her front room – she called it her 'reception' – and whipping us up drinks. Birra Morettis all round. And then she was bringing us out trays laden with little plates of *antipasti* left over from the day. Olives, cooked meats, bread. The like. 'Children, children,' she kept saying. 'Make yourselves at home!' She practically tugged Carl's shoes off his feet. Barrelled a footstool his way and forced him to 'take a load off'.

Her other children were cats. I saw three of them dotted around her reception room and another two skittered hurriedly away when we entered. The remaining trio looked at us green-eyed, licking their lips at the cooked meats. But judging by the size of them they didn't exactly go short in that regard. The cats, I felt, told the story of Mama. She rounded them up, little lost things, from all corners of Leeds. Fed and watered them. Pampered the hell out of them. Took them to bed with her, most likely. She must have been making up for what was missing; *actual* children. She'd told Carl once, after a few glasses of wine, that her husband (now dead) had never wanted kids. And she so obviously had. But, as she told Carl, 'those were different times; then, your husband spoke for both of you, and it was final. Not like some of these couples you see in La Scala now.'

It made me all kinds of sad when I thought of how she thought she was trying to care for us Lost Boys, trying to mother us, little knowing that we had bad-pennied in that night to take advantage of her. And it made me feel even worse to think that maybe she didn't *care* if she was taken advantage of; if all she wanted was a little company to see her through the dark hours.

She cuckoo-clocked between kitchen and reception, kitchen and reception, emptying her larder and her fridge of

140

everything she could lay her hands on and then bringing them to us as offerings. *Please stay.*

On the way through, she'd squeeze Ads' cheek. 'Oh Adam, Adam! How happy you make me! To think, everyone on the street will be looking out their windows and seeing that lovely little sports car of yours in *my* driveway! They'll think I have a footballer over for dinner. Or a prince. You look like a prince!'

Or she'd fawn over me: 'Isn't that a nice new watch, dear,' and, 'What a lovely tie; you do dress well. Like an Italian!'

But she'd always return to Carl, patting him on the knee as though to say, *Don't worry, I still love you the best.*

Carl told her to come sit down, but she said she didn't have the time. 'I'm cooking up a storm in the kitchen, children. Just you wait and see!'

So we waited, played stare-out competitions with the cats, whose seats we'd clearly taken. We waited; I checked my phone. It was the first time I'd done so since Cenessa, and I was gratified to see there were no new messages from The Nat. We waited; Ads pulled out a baggie and Carl wagged a finger. *No, not here!*

We waited until a bell tolled; Mama calling us through to dinner, to a Last Supper, if things went badly. Her dining table fair buckled under the weight of a steel-drum-sized bowl of spaghetti and meatballs; there was a granary wharf full of very garlicky bread; a salami salad which looked like a rockery. Once again I felt guilty as hell. We were here to con this woman, that was the long and short of it. And we'd come round mob-handed to do so. While we'd been sitting in the reception room, I'd wondered why Carl had brought Ads and I along in the first place. After all, he already had Mama wrapped round his little finger; our presence was only incidental to her. But now I decided it was because even Carl had a conscience. And, sure, it was smaller than the average bear's, but it was there nonetheless: he wanted *all* of us to get our hands dirty in this business.

Mama played mother a whole lot better than Nathan Long had. She scooped out great platefuls of food for us all; enough to feed an army of accountants who'd been on the razz all week and had only had time for the occasional Pret a Manger sandwich. Conscience or no, Carl dug into his meal with an abandon I'd only seen him previously exhibit when caning it on the drugs. Ads was a little more restrained; he didn't slurp up his spaghetti like a kid, splashing tomato sauce all over the napkin tucked into the collar of his shirt, but still it seemed he had an appetite. I sort of stabbed at meatballs with my fork; avoided Mama's concerned gaze.

The whole thing struck me as remarkably filmic. Carl must have wanted it that way. It felt like that scene in *GoodFellas* where De Niro and Pesci go to Pesci's mother's house (Pesci's mother played by director Martin Scorcese's mum) and discuss, over a slap-up meal, their problems in disposing of a body. They make like they've run over a deer on the road – it got its hoof stuck in the front grille – but actually the body they have belongs to a fellow wise guy.

Carl wasn't discussing whether a hoof was the correct name for a deer's foot, but he was chatting some of his usual shit. In between mouthfuls, he'd share his thoughts on everything from global warming ('a crock of shit') to new business ideas (he'd had a eureka moment, apparently, and decided he could make a mint hiring PCs to students by the hour). And Mama simply gazed at him affectionately and agreed with everything he said.

Then Carl started talking about his family. He didn't do this often, and I noted   how Mama's lips pursed in disapproval to hear 'her' Carl talk about his real mum. The tale was long and convoluted, but the gist of it was, Carl's Mum had been scouted by a modelling agency when she was just seventeen (well, you know what I mean) in Glasgow. They'd paid her train fare down to London and given her a couple jobs on the spot (a campaign for some new sheer tights and a poster for a jeweller's which was running a deal on engagement rings). And she'd thought she'd made it. She rented a swanky flat in Soho and hobnobbed with the stars in

Covent Garden. But gradually the work dried up. Some weeks the agency would act as though she didn't exist anymore when she called them up; they had a conveyor belt of newer, fresher models all the time. Some weeks they'd tell her they'd had a last-minute cancellation and could she high-tail it across London? At twenty minutes' notice. For an ad for a new shade of nail polish.

For some reason – maybe she'd just been pigeon-holed after one of her earliest jobs – Carl's mum began to be used exclusively as a hand model. And that wasn't where she'd seen herself a few months down the line. She'd seen herself on billboards in Leicester Square. She'd seen herself being spotted by some movie mogul and tried out for the films. Nobody was going to put her in a film because she had good hands.

The money began to dry up too, and some weeks she really struggled to make the rent. In fact, her flat-mate got so sick and tired of subbing her she suggested Carl's mum take a 'proper paying job'. Which of course made Carl's mum fly off the handle because she was a *model*. She wasn't cut out for the common-or-garden nine-to-five. But eventually she came round to the idea and, ironically, the new job was working with her hands too, in a typing pool. Even more ironically it was through this and not through modelling that she'd enjoyed her own, minuscule, taste of Hollywood.

Carl's Mum and the rest of her typing pool cronies had, in the late seventies, been hired by someone from the Elstree studios in Borehamwood to type up eight hundred pages of 'ALL WORK AND NO PLAY MAKES JACK A DULL BOY' for the scene in *The Shining* where Jack Nicholson starts his descent into madness at the Overlook. Apparently Kubrick was such a stickler he wouldn't allow anything which would ruin the emotional realism of the scene and so, instead of simply getting one page of 'ALL WORK AND NO PLAY MAKES JACK A DULL BOY' and photocopying it, or installing a load of blank pages underneath the top page, he'd had some underling hire the typing pool to do the entire eight hundred pages. And Carl's ma, as the quickest typist, was the one who'd completed nearly all of them. Her handiwork, on celluloid forevermore.

A year after *The Shining* was released Carl's mum met Carl's dad and her life changed dramatically all over again. She'd kept her looks and still hung around Covent Garden enough to brush shoulders with many of the young princes of the time. Carl's dad wasn't exactly a *young* prince but he was certainly wealthy enough. He worked, rather amorphously, 'in business'; he always had all kinds of deals on the go: property; import/export; he had a stake in a couple nightclubs, one of which went on to be sold to Peter Stringfellow. Carl's dad had been looking for someone pretty to hang off his arm at club nights and Carl's mum was only too happy to oblige. But then she became pregnant and then Carl's dad ran a mile; *many* miles, in fact. He fled to Marbella, where he bought a stake in another club along with a decidedly dodgy character he knew from the East End. Two months later, he returned, unable to live without Carl's mum. Their wedding was so shotgun you could smell the gunpowder.

Carl was born three weeks later and for a while the family was content with life in the Smoke. But Carl's dad had been bitten by the Marbella bug and he was desperate to move the family out there, lock, stock, and live the proper high life. Carl's mum wouldn't countenance that. She wanted Carl raised in the UK. She didn't want him to be one of those peripatetic kids had no roots; didn't know where they were from, let alone where they were at. The arguments went back and forth.

They divorced when Carl was eight and then got back together when he was nine. Separated when he was ten and then remarried when he was ten-and-a-half. As a wedding present, Carl's dad gave Carl's mum keys to a new bar he'd bought out in Marbella, and at last she relented. Carl wound up in boarding school and Carl's mum wound up meeting Stan Kubrick at last, one hot late summer night at their club. When she told him she'd typed all those pages for the film, Kubrick didn't believe her. He claimed he wasn't *such* a pedant that he'd have wanted eight hundred pages all identical.

I wasn't sure whether I believed Carl. The tale sounded tall. But it also sounded like a distraction technique. He was luring the table into a false sense of security before he pounced. I watched him mop up the rest of the tomato sauce with a slab of garlic bread, then he placed his knife and fork down carefully.

'How's business?'

Mama, who was still eating, took a fork and squashed a meatball with it. 'Pah. They try everything they can to stop La Scala. They hike up the business rates every year; the chain stores, they complain about me; now they are trying to tell me I cannot play opera! What kind of a nanny state is this?'

'No opera?'

'They say: *noise pollution.*'

'Leeds Cathedral bangs out the bells every Sunday from about nine in the morning and nobody calls that noise pollution. Wakes me up every time.'

'Poor thing,' said Mama. 'And you work so hard in the week. You deserve some shut-eye in your down-time.'

'Bravo,' said Ads, raising his bottle. 'Well said.'

Carl looked at him sharply. Then: 'Know the guy came in with us today?'

Mama puffed out her cheeks. 'The fat man? Man like that he must be careful. A heart attack waiting to happen. Has he a family? Children?'

'Yes. A girl, seven. Phoebe.'

Phoebe wasn't like any other seven year old I'd ever met though: I mean, what other little girls interviewed prospective partners for her father's criminal enterprises?

'Sad. She will end up without a father.'

Carl nodded. 'I think that's why he's now beginning to make a number of shrewd investments. He is taking money and he is trying to make it grow in places... He wants to be able to leave something for her. A nest egg.'

'Phoebe must be very pleased she has a wise father, then.'

'I want to show you something,' said Carl. 'Neal, nip out to the car will you? Pick up Mama's surprise.'

Ads tossed me the keys and I did as I was told. As I walked out the room, I heard Mama cooing. 'A present? You should not have. You boys. *Too much!*'

We were too much, I thought, and as I bipped the central-locking button the temptation to climb in the front of the TT and get away into the night was very difficult to resist. What forced me to bend over the seat and retrieve the *SLAZENGER* bag from in back was the thought of Nathan Long's face and how he'd set the hounds on me as soon as Carl clicked his fingers and made the call.

I lugged the bag back into the house. In the dining room Mama was still busy telling Carl and Ads how they should not have, how they needed to save their pounds for when they became fathers themselves. Ads met my eye and cleared a space on the table and I thunked the money down right where the vat of spaghetti meatballs had been.

Carl said, '*Ta-daaaah.*'

Mama remained seated. 'What is this?'

Carl drew back the zip, revealing the packets of money. One wad rolled out onto the table, coming to a rest between Mama's gigantic salt and pepper shakers. 'The fat guy,' he said. 'Nathan Long. He wants to invest in your business.'

Mama narrowed her eyes. 'This does not look like typical way of making investment,' she said, carefully. 'This looks... like *problem* money. Drug money, even.'

Carl made himself all sweetness and light. 'Mama, the three of us work for one of the largest accountancy firms in the world. Everything we do must be above board. We are held accountable for everything we advise our clients.' He flapped a paw. 'You, of course, are not just a client. You're... well, you're like family. And when Mr Long approached us with his proposal, we of course considered all of the ramifications of the offer. This might not be – yes, you chose the right word – typical, but believe me this is a good deal. With the business rates and all, you need it. '

Mama was transfixed by the wad of notes which had rolled out the bag. She looked as though she wanted to take it, but at the same time she looked scared, too.

'Pick it up,' said Carl. 'Smell the green. You'll feel better about it, I promise.'

She reached out; laid a single digit on top of the wad gingerly, as though it might burn her. Then, when it didn't, she gathered it up. 'It feels... All the notes are brand new.' She licked her lips.

'Pristine,' said Carl, laying it on thick. 'You see, the reason Mr Long felt he had to provide the money in note form was because he was worried about the tax implications of simply sending the cash via a bank transfer. He doesn't want Phoebe to lose out on any of her due because of inheritance tax issues.'

Mama looked doubtful, but not doubtful enough.

Carl reached over and laid his hand over hers. 'This is the answer to your prayers.'

Mama sighed. 'Okay. I'll take your word. I love you like a son, Carl.'

Carl beamed. 'All we need you to do is bank this. Not all at once but in small increments. With the weekly take would be good.'

Mama looked doubtful all over again. 'I... it's a lot of money, Carl. Won't he – this Mr Long - have a controlling interest in La Scala? Am I saying it right: controlling interest?'

Carl nodded, proudly. 'You are. You are saying it very well. And don't worry; Mr Long has no interest in taking over your café. He has, shall we say, other fish to fry. He wants you to remain at the helm, running the place just as you always have done. You're a Leeds Institution, Mama. He'd be loath to change that.' He squeezed her hand. 'And I wouldn't let him.'

Mama gushed. 'You're a good boy. Just promise me one more time. The money is not from the drugs?'

Carl became all kinds of solemn. 'Cross my heart and hope to die. It's clean.'

Suddenly I couldn't breathe, I felt so guilty. Here we were duping everyone we knew, shitting on our own doorstep.

And it *stank*. I had to go outside, now. Breathe some clean air. Get my head right. I blundered to my feet. 'I need... I'm just popping out for a cigarette.'

Mama looked up, a flash of anger bolting across her deep brown eyes. 'You shouldn't smoke, Neal. Bad for the lungs. You know how my husband – God rest his soul – passed, don't you?'

Thankfully Ads took the sting out of the situation. 'You know what, Mama? It's been a long day for everyone. We'll leave you now to get some rest.'

Carl patted her hand one last time. 'We'd offer to wash up for you but I know you'll just tell us no.'

She sniffed. 'That would be rude. You are guests.'

Carl shrugged. 'Well, I tried... And don't worry, Mama. We won't let naughty Neal here smoke on the way home. What he chooses to do in his own flat we can't do anything about, but in Ads' car? No way.'

We made our long goodbyes. There was plenty of hugging; plenty of gratitude. Then the cats saw us off the property. As Adam pulled out the driveway the beams of his headlights struck on at least five sets of cat's eyes, watching us go.

We stopped off in Chapel A at the Mustard Pot for a last drink and a chat about whether everything was sorted now. Carl patted his distended belly. 'I think I got some kind of wheat allergy or something,' he said.

'You got a truth allergy,' I said.

Carl growled. 'Hey, we're all on board with this. Snap out of it, Neal. All I'm saying is, I'm FTB: fit to bursting. You, Neal, barely touched a meatball. Hell, mate, I know it's a bit harsh pulling the wool over Mama's eyes like that, but believe me, she *wants* the wool pulled. She doesn't want to have to see the truth; that her café is going down the pan. We've done what we had to do.'

That, it seemed, was that.

But things weren't over, not by a long garlic baguette.

V

The next day was Saturday and for the first time in a week, I woke up in my own bed in my own flat reasonably *compos mentis*. Well, when I say *compos mentis*, I mean not weirded out by drugs. As it happened, I'd had something of a disturbed night; Parmesan dreams had had me being chased up and down Mill Hill by a Captain Hook-alike Nathan Long. Even as I emerged from the land of nod, batting away the cobwebs of sleep, I could still feel the sweep and zing of his hook as he thrust it towards me, attempting to skewer my neck.

Long as Hook had made for a nightmarish vision; he'd looked clumsy, walrus-like, and yet at the same time he'd been razor-quick. Every time I thought I'd put distance between me and him, I'd hear the thrust and stab of his hook again and his guttural cry: 'I'll have your guts for garters, Grace!'

Guts for garters. Who even said that anymore? Mind, with a shudder I recalled thinking nobody shook their fist anymore either, and then I saw one of the Neanderthals – Dan or Rhys – doing exactly that, before the SAS bouncers beat seven shades of shit out of them.

And just like that, the remembrance of my crimes crept up on me. Goosed me. Tap-danced on my grave. And just like that, I decided I was too sick and too tired of being a fucking *culture* for all this guilt and I had to try to forget. Make a new start. I'd taken a wrong turn, pushed through the beads in the doorway and come out somewhere dark, but I could shuffle out of that place just the same. Let the beads close. Pretend I'd seen nuffink, guv.

I lurched into the bathroom, pissed for England; thought about heading down to the International Pool for a dip, then thought better of it. I hacked at my stubble, brushed and then rebrushed my teeth and tongue (I could still taste

149

Mama's garlic), then finally showered away the rust of yesterday, and took my time about it.

Fresh and clean, the clag of the past couple days washed away down various plug-holes, I felt almost like a new man. Or at least, a little like the old one again. I reminded myself all I needed to do now was meet The Nat and give her the rest of the blackmail cash, and then have Nick Byers sort my Lightwood problem out, and I'd be in the clear. To use a Carl analogy, it was as though I'd had to crawl through a mile of shit (à la Shawshank) but soon I'd emerge out the other end and I'd be free.

For a heady moment as I brewed up, I wondered what the hell I wanted to do with the rest of my life. Maybe it was time I started making plans.

I took the coffee up to the rooftop garden, a stinking euphemism of a place. Because it was a communal area for every resident of the block, everyone decided it was someone else's business to look after the upkeep of it. Someone had partied up here last night: the place was stacked with empty beer cans and discarded homemade filters made from old Rizla packets and I thought I might have seen a used condom too before I stopped looking so closely. Nobody had thought to take their crap home with them.

To be fair to my neighbours they *had* left behind a deckchair, and I pulled this over to the balcony section and looked out over my portion of Leeds City Centre. My place was at the bottom of Eastgate. The Bookends. Close to the Playhouse and the City Markets (and Millgarth Police Station, that great hulking depression of a building which reminded me of all the crimes I'd been involved in). Akbar's Curry House was just up the way and there were pubs aplenty on my doorstep.

It was an okay morning. The sky was almost a bare blue; there were only a few speckled clouds over to the west and I had a pretty much perfect view of the giraffe necks of so many cranes building up the new Leeds. Work appeared to be going on everywhere and I wondered how the hell we'd find enough people to fill all the new apartment complexes which were going up. Or were they just going to be empty shells, like Carl predicted for his place in ten years' time?

I thought I was much happier living here. Noisy though it was – and it *was* noisy; you could already hear the cacophony of buses wheezing up and down Eastgate – and shabby though it was (the lift was never working and the rooftop garden wasn't the worst of the communal areas; no, that was reserved for the basement storage area, which I had a strong suspicion homed various tramps as well as rats, mice and probably fucking crocodiles) it was at least *real*.

The morning air had cooled my coffee enough to drink and I slugged back a mouthful. It tasted, vaguely, of dishwashers, though mine was broken (I'd tried to wash my trainers in it). But what was good about it was it wasn't boozy and it wasn't served by Mama. Nor did I happen to be in a café at Leeds General Infirmary or down on David Street.

No, I was on home territory. Home and dry? I didn't think so. But again, at least up here I got some perspective. Up here, I was still small fry. There were people out there had done a lot worse than me.

A good night's sleep: works wonders for the system.

As if to prove my good mood wasn't for nought, a text message winged its way onto my Nokia. The sender wasn't The Nat. Nor was it Mama already having doubts. It was Carl, and he was promising a 'meet' with Nick Byers that afternoon. It was all set up.

I drained the rest of my coffee, stretched, then decided, seeing as though I had some time to strangle, I might just attempt a little retail therapy. See if Ace had any new lines in. Maybe I could even wander over to the Corn Exchange and pick up some new gear in there (if I could stand being so close to The Townhouse and those arches on Assembly Street).

Some mornings you get up and everything's a red light: you're hung over to buggery and you can't work the kettle, let alone the *cafetière*, and there's no Henry anymore to fix you a bacon butty; you Hannibal Lecter up your face when you attempt to shave; a bus splashing maliciously through a puddle ruins your suit; you get to work and realise the clocks went forward an hour last night and you're late. And, fuck, if you had to *commute*... Today, everything was coming up green. I called the lift, fully expecting to receive a game-show wrong-answer *eee-uuuuhhh* in response. But fuck me, didn't the little 'call lift' button light up like a candle and then the display above the door showed the count-up as it climbed up from ground.

As I lifted it down to the ground floor, I even found the courage to look myself in the eye in the mirror. I winked. *Looking princely, Grace.* Then came over all embarrassed and looked away.

But still, I was *improved*. Even as I stepped right out of the flats and straight into the sludge of the city, even as it got right up over my shoes, into the turn-ups on my jeans (which I wasn't sure I liked; they seemed too Teddy Boy), I felt somehow above it all. My place wasn't far down from Primark, and even now, in dull mid-morning nothing time, the place was rammed. Primark was like some ancient Roman forum: billions of people were milling about, waiting for friends or simply whiling away the time, talking. Mostly, when I was hung over, I had some trouble cutting through their massed ranks, but they seemed to clear a path for me today, as though they saw the green shoots of the new old me starting to sprout.

I crossed the street and headed down Briggate, Leeds' main shopping street, and I was just passing through the deepest, knottiest part of the throng outside Harvey Nicks when I felt a hand grasping my arm. I spun round, immediately on the defensive. Immediately the scared-rabbit me of the past two days slipping out. Saw an incredibly tall Jack's Beanstalk of a fella dressed in a grey rain mac, grey trousers and grey shirt. The only thing which stood out from this ocean of grey was his brown tie, whose knot was pretty much level with the top of my head. I trained my eyes upwards, took in the grey man's face, which looked as though it had been moulded out of clay. He'd got one of those imploring faces; he wanted something.

'Can you hear Jesus knocking on the door to your heart?' said the grey man.

'Uh… Pardon?'

'Can you hear Jesus knocking on the door to your heart?' The grey man had raised his voice now; was practically shouting at me. 'He's knocking. With all his might, he's knocking. Are you going to let him in?'

I bit my lip. Tried to think of a witty comeback which would shoot him right down.

Jack's Beanstalk in grey glared at me and then repeated his question, as though to a dullard. 'Can you hear Jesus knocking on the door to your heart?' he said, intoning every sy-lla-ble.

And I got to thinking about this documentary I watched once. It was about madness. It ended with this neat little definition, kind of a cut out and keep takeaway, and I'd cut it out and kept it. According to the documentary, the definition of madness was trying the same thing over and over again, expecting different outcomes. I imagined I wasn't the first person this grey man had confronted like this, and he expected I wouldn't be the last, and yet the grey man still seemed surprised at the fact I was seemingly rendered speechless by his question; that I didn't simply drop to my knees, beg for forgiveness and pray tell Jesus my heart was open now (I'd lost the key before).

Could I hear Jesus knock-knock-knockin' on the door to my heart? No, but I could hear *something*. I could hear the penny, dropping in my brain. All of a sudden I realised *I* was the one slowly going mad. Definition had it down pat. I'd been trying the same thing over and over again; going out getting snarled up on booze and drugs so that during the long, long working days I was so tired I was phoning it in, barely even realising what I was doing half the time. Any time I made a mistake – and there'd been a few, business and personal – I was taking it on the chin, stewing over it for a couple days, then going back out into the world with an empty heart I could only fill with more drink, more drugs, and a little retail therapy, *still* expecting good things to come to me. Like big accounts. Like a corner office. Like a girlfriend. Like a future.

Christ, and just like that I was depressed all over again.

After weighing me up for a few more seconds, the grey man shook his head and walked away, back into the crowd. I watched him go, cursedly. The man walked in the same kind of jerky way that the little man in the old cuckoo clock in my childhood bedroom back at the Golden Goose used to emerge, on the hour every hour before popping straight back into his hole again, ready to try the same mad scheme again in another hour. I watched him as he woodenly wobbled back to what was apparently *his spot* outside the department store. He'd got a small 10 watt amp set up there and a mic, and soon I heard his voice crackling out, echoing back from the concrete, glass and chrome. And because he was now officially the loudest looney, the mouthiest madman on the street, an even larger crowd started to congregate around him, for no other reason than to laugh at him, it seemed.

The grey man started in on what was now becoming a pretty familiar refrain. 'Can you hear Jesus knocking on the door to your heart?'

The crowd pressed in closer around him. They were, I saw, mainly baseball-capped young lads. They'd been meeting up, *plotting up,* outside Primark earlier and were now shouting their own responses, egged on by their sparklingly-white-trainer-clad mates.

'There's a hole in your lives, a Jesus-shaped hole,' continued the grey man, his face a stern mask of concentration. Whatever these boys were shouting at him, he wasn't going to give in to the temptation of shouting back at them. But he played uncomfortably with the knot of his brown tie and shuffled his feet.

'You are lost! And alone! Let Jesus in,' he continued, and for the first time, I heard the quiver in the man's voice.

A group of older lads, uni students perhaps, had now elbowed their way to the front of the crowd, all bravado and bounce. They'd clearly chosen to dress like 'individuals', like some of the new breed of lads who populated the bars on Call Lane, but all looked uniformly as though they were auditioning to be in the latest indie band; they were all skin-tight black jeans and deck shoes, striped T-shirts, and mop-style hair. They'd tried very hard to look so scruffy.

'...for He said, "I am the Resurrection, and I am the Light"...' said the grey man, voice rising to a high-pitched crescendo.

'... I couldn't ever bring myself to hate you,' sang a voice from the crowd, reprising the Stone Roses number. It would have made me laugh, usually, ten minutes ago, but now I wasn't really in a laughing mood. I *was* lost. A lost boy. An orphan after my dad had popped his clogs. Not that I bought any of the Jesus shit but, still, part of me felt the same existential angst as the grey man must have done before he was born again; the same emptiness...

'Most of the people walking around today are the walking dead, because their hearts are empty,' continued the grey man. His eyes were now fixed directly on me, lasering into my very soul, it felt like; identifying my faults and my crimes. And the next passage was surely meant only for me: 'You are walking around with something missing. And Jesus is that something. He's got the key to your heart, but he's polite, so he knocks. Can't you hear him knocking?' The grey man thudded his fist against the mic now, replicating a policeman's knock. And suddenly the spell was broken and I remembered this was a madman and I was a prince and fuck him; if Ace had a new line in, then that'd be worth a *Hallelujah, praise be to God.* But I wasn't going to stand around getting fucking *shamed* into feeling something.

Most of the crowd evidently felt the same. Started to move on. They moved on to the guy in the army-style trench coat just further down the walkway; a man who was becoming more and more animated, windmilling his arms as he railed about the outsourcing of call centres to India. Or if not him, the shrill woman in the man's coat who was blurting out a litany of complaints about animal testing; or the shaven-headed brute of a man who was apparently dead set against the butchery of the English language on the internet.

And I found that I was whistling that old Louis Armstrong number, 'What a Wonderful World'. What a world it was where crazies like this were allowed to push themselves to the front of the queue just because they were shouting. What a world it was when everyone thought they had a right to be heard, even when they were speaking nonsense. What a world it was, and I blamed the internet. And I blamed reality TV. Both seemed to make people think they were far more important than they were. Everyone seemed to think they had the right to their fifteen minutes of fame every day, and so, on streets like this, on days like this, I could barely hear myself think over and above the inane chatter, the meaningless fucking bullshit.

Everyone was talking, shouting their stories, but nobody was listening.

I wondered whether, if I screwed up my eyes and tried, really tried, I could make them all disappear. Make them vanish just like that; clearing my path so I could head through their massed ranks and go wherever it was my Rick Rogers Nikes led me. I wasn't loopy though, not like every bloody other person in town today, so I didn't actually try screwing up my eyes. Instead, with a new steely determination, I walked into the midst of the madding crowd.

A couple of people muttered as I elbowed past them. I paid them no mind. Someone tried to stop me – possibly the grey man again – but I ignored the hand which brushed against my arm. I *thought* I might have trodden on someone's foot – my admittedly air-cushioned Rick Rogers left trainer made a decidedly different, fleshier sound as it connected with something which was not concrete – but I didn't care.

Soon I was round the corner, past McDonald's, and onto Boar Lane and I could breathe more easily because Ace was in sight. Soon as I pushed the door I felt bright and airy all over again. Cool Croc was laying down some mellow beats on the sound system and a couple of very sexy girls were perusing the womenswear section. Marco gave me a *Top Gun-*

style salute from behind the counter, but gave me some space to go explore the racks.

I found a couple of tees I liked straight away. One Parker number which had a print of a triple-X shop's neon sign which arrowed down to your crotch and said 'Adult Material Downstairs'. It was just the right kind of ironic to be funky. Another, a V-neck Criminal design, which showed a cityscape skyline. I'd think about them.

Eventually Marco ambled over, all piercings and jagged hair and muscle. He greeted me as he always did: 'How's my favourite style-conscious number cruncher?'

And I answered as *I* always did by asking whether he had anything new in. Sometimes they held the good stock back from the hoi polloi – at least at first – to set a buzz going about this or that tee or denim or belt.

Marco gave me a conspiratorial wink then disappeared out back for a while. He came back clutching – my heart skipped a beat! – a very full-looking *SLAZENGER* sports bag. 'Ready for this?' he asked as he unzipped it. He pulled out a slinky-looking black tee with a very gruesome picture of Jesus on the front, all bloody from his crown of thorns. Above it, in cursive text, was written the legend: *FORGIVE YOURSELF.* Marco held it up to my chest and it felt like fate. 'Thought it was your size,' he said. 'These are new in and they're going to be big. So obviously only our most discerning customers get a look-see right now. They're' – he lowered his voice – '*French.* Designer straight out of Paris. Its rumoured she has something going with those Cool Croc guys.'

He dug deeper in the *SLAZENGER* bag. Produced a couple more tees and then a long-sleeve shirt and a pair of new combat pants, but my heart was already set on Jesus. He'd knocked, and I'd let him in. Marco rang up the till. Children would have cried when they saw the price, but I simply slipped him my platinum card and made off with what might as well have been the wing of a jumbo jet.

I headed home to change. Helped myself to a Corona from the fridge and sat, surfing the TV channels until Byers swung by to pick me up. He was late. I was standing by the window looking through the blinds when he arrived, parking up his midnight-blue Porsche Cayenne – a car so beautiful it would have turned even the grey man from town into a sinner – round back of the flats. When he bleeped the central-locking and walked away all the bods from the Chinese supermarket came out to take a look at it; one of them even posed for a photo with it.

I buzzed Byers into the flat. He blustered inside. For the first time I noticed strands of grey in his usually sleek black hair. He seemed distracted. He flitted; one minute he was examining some of the pictures in my hallway, the next he was picking up something from my telephone table, and the one after that he was giving me the eye. He seemed unconvinced by my new Jesus tee, but chose to say nothing about it.

I offered him a Corona. He said yes, then, once I'd popped the top, said no. He was driving. He'd forgotten. I slugged mine back then poured his down the sink. He drummed his fingers on my breakfast bar.

'You all right, Nick? You seem...' I couldn't finish my sentence.

He washed his face with his hands. 'I need to hit something real hard,' he said, finally.

'Look,' I said, 'sorry you had to – you know – come here and bail me out or whatever. I can see you've got a lot on your plate.'

He looked at me, miserably. 'You don't know the half of it.'

'Anything I can help with?'

He shook his head. 'Nope. And you need to be as far away from this as possible.'

'I don't understand.' But I thought I did. Maybe Nick Byers had gotten wind of the stunts Carl, Ads and I were pulling with SAS and Nathan Long and La Scala. Shit, maybe he'd even caught up with the bouncers and what they'd done to the Neanderthal lads on Assembly Street.

He sighed. 'You know, maybe I will take that beer now. After all, I can have one and still drive, can't I?'

I popped the top on another bottle of Corona and handed it to him. He socked it back like Ads, like a snake swallowing a goat, then wiped his mouth with the back of his hand. And then, for the longest time, he was silent. He simply stood there, staring into space. He looked like he was in shock. Like he'd just received some very grave news.

'Nick,' I tried. 'Mate. If you're not up for this, we can do it another time.' Thinking, *When?* I had a day and a half to sort this.

Nothing. No reaction at all. It was as though he hadn't heard me at all. I could have clicked my fingers in front of his face and he wouldn't have blinked. I thought back to him at the graduate recruitment fair when I'd first encountered him. How *impressive* he'd seemed. How sharp. He'd seemed like a higher breed of human than everybody else in the Parkinson Building. A true prince amongst men. I wouldn't have dreamed of clicking my fingers in front of his face then.

Finally, he sighed. Then: 'We need to go somewhere we can talk.'

I kind of shrugged. 'We can talk here. It's fine. I mean, it's not as though the walls have ears or anything.'

Byers looked startled. Practically jumped out of his skin.

I tried to calm him. 'Just a turn of phrase, Nick. Look, we're fine here, aren't we? If you like we can chip on up to the roof garden, get a nip of fresh air. There's some good views from up there and – '

He shook his head. 'No, like I say, we need to get out of here. This city. I feel like...' He trailed off. Picked up his beer and studied it as though he'd forgotten he was even supposed to be drinking it. I wondered whether he was drunk, then. Or stoned maybe. Certainly he seemed *slower* than usual. Discombobulated by something. And generally *nothing rocked his boat.* I'd seen him blasted on enough shampoo to sink a fucking Leeds-Liverpool Canal barge and yet he was still always *on it* enough to play the grand host. Not today.

'Fine,' I said. 'Lead the way.'

He did. We went out to his Cayenne and I shooed off the loitering Chinese supermarket workers like they were pigeons. Nick didn't even seem to *see* them. He went round back of the car and popped the trunk. Then scratched his head as though he couldn't remember what he was looking for. The trunk was packed full with his golf clubs.

'We going for a round, Nick? That what you were talking about when you said you wanted to hit something real hard?'

He pinched the bridge of his nose as though trying to *pain* himself into remembering. Grimaced. 'Um... I've already played a round with the pro at Alwoodley today,' he said slowly, and then, picking up the pace, as though growing back into his own well-moisturised skin: 'Completely mullered me of course but there were a couple times I caught him dickering with his score so at least for a while I had him worried.'

'Nearly beat the pro, eh?'

He grinned. It came out looking a bit lopsided. Wasn't anything like the usual Colgate beam he gave off. And I thought back to last night, to Ads smashing his TT around the streets of Leeds; me like a pinball in back. And I wondered whether I should be getting in the Cayenne with Byers.

I needn't have worried. Nick drove slow as an oldster out for a weekend drive to the garden centre. He drove as though doped up. Even when we got out onto the open roads as north Leeds gave way to green belt. Ads might have lost his driving licence in ten minutes on roads such as these but Byers seemed reluctant to really put his foot down. He seemed reluctant to speak too, and after a while the heavy silence in the Cayenne got to be oppressive. I tried to make small talk – 'What about that rain yesterday?'; 'See that new bar which opened on Call Lane?' – but it only served to spice up the tension. All I wanted to say was *What the fuck is wrong with you?* But I didn't dare ask.

We made it up to the driving range at Leeds Golf Centre on Wike Ridge Lane. The car park wasn't full, not by a long stretch, but there was at least ten mill worth of car parked up. Only when we'd climbed out the car did Byers think to ask me whether I'd played golf before. 'I just kind of assumed you would have,' he said.

He assumed right, but that was only half the story. I had started lessons a while back. Andersen got us whopping discounts on account of golf was very important when it came to entertaining clients. I'd gone along for the first couple of Saturday mornings and initially I thought I'd gotten the hang of it straight off the bat. My teacher – an old pro who spent all morning eating oranges; he knocked back so many I thought he might overdose on vitamin C – told me I was a natural. And I could certainly whack the ball quite far (especially when I got to thinking the ball was Dale Lightwood's face). But it turned out my drive was the only part of my game was any good at all and even *that* was kind of inconsistent. Soon as I got my Lightwood angst out of me I could barely hit at all. After three more weeks the old pro told me he thought I was maybe wasting my time as well as his. I wouldn't listen to anything he told me about my stance. He told me I was too hunched. Why couldn't I get loose? I said I didn't know. He told me to go on home and have a good think about it and if I was still interested next week he'd be more than happy to welcome me back. *As long as I listened.* Then he sent me packing with a quarter of an orange and the tail well and truly between my legs.

I hadn't bothered going back. I decided the old pro probably called everyone a natural.

Byers was reluctant to let me use his clubs – if I didn't have any of my own that was a sure-fire bad sign I was a hacker – so we hired some from the Pro Shop. At the counter, the old man serving – he was a dead ringer for my old pro teacher, and if he'd have been wolfing down an orange I would have been convinced they were one and the same – looked at my Jesus tee like I'd just come in wearing a shirt with *FUCK THE POPE* emblazoned across it. Probably this was exactly the effect the newbie Parisian designer was looking for. He gave us some clubs in the end, but the deposit he asked for was far more than the advertised rates. Maybe he thought I'd go all Happy Gilmore on his range.

As we walked out onto the range Nick sucked in the fresh air. It seemed to rejuvenate him some. He limbered up. Performed some stretches, his driver behind his back. I watched and copied. He dumped a basket of balls on the tee and kicked one into place, slightly ahead of the rest. Then, with the explosive force of a raptor bird attacking its prey, he struck: I lost sight of the ball almost immediately and only found it again when I heard it *ching* against the back fence, three hundred yards away.

'That was great, Nick,' I kiss-assed.

Byers pulled a face. 'Ya think? I thought it pulled left too much. C'mon, Grace, you're up.'

I knew I was going to fuck it up. I knew that after the majesty of Byers' drive mine was going to look all kinds of puny. But even I couldn't have imagined just how bad it would be. I connected. But only just. I clipped the top of my ball and it skewed off right, so close to another driver a few booths up that he ducked. Called out 'Watch it!'

'Shit on it,' I said, raising a paw in apology.

'I thought your hand-eye'd be better than this, Grace,' observed Nick, raising a typically Byersian eyebrow. 'What with you being a lacrosse champ in your heyday.'

I felt the blood rushing to my cheeks. 'It's been... well, a long time. I'm rusty.'

'Rusty? Christ, if you were a car, they'd send you down the wrecker's yard. Why don't you have another go?' He came up behind me and tried to arrange my body so I could follow through with my swing better. It was all kinds of embarrassing, like slow-dancing with a guy in the changing rooms at the International Pool would have been. 'Now,' he said, his breath tickling my ear, 'give it some air.'

This time I completely missed the ball, almost staggered off the edge of the tee section and down into the no man's land of the range. Nick grabbed me. Righted me, then raised another eyebrow, like he had hundreds of them, like throwing an eyebrow in now wouldn't diminish his stock at all. 'You need to give up the poltergeist, Grace,' he said. 'You're fooling nobody.'

And for at least three beats I didn't know whether he was talking about golf or life in general, though for some – my orangey old pro – that amounted to the same thing.

'Why don't you just stand back and watch?'

I did as I was told, and for a while the only sounds were the sweep and zing of his driver racing down on the ball (it sounded like the sweep and zing in my Parmesan dreams, when I'd been chased by Nathan-Long-as-Captain-Hook) and then the *ching* as the ball struck unerringly off the back fence. Hell, even the golfer a couple booths down stopped to watch the precision of Byers' hitting.

At last he spoke. 'Your friend, Carl, Mr Zombie Nation, as he's better known to me, called me about you. Calling in a favour. I told him course I would help, and in any way I could.'

'Thanks,' I gushed. 'I can't tell you how much I appreciate it. I mean basically you're saving my life. Calling Lightwood off, letting me come back to work, it's – '

'You're not coming back to work, Grace,' he said, flatly. *Sweep-zing-ching.*

'Pardon me? I thought you said you could help. In any way you could.'

'I am helping you. I'm telling you what you need to hear.'

'But you're not. Carl said—'

Sweep-zing-ching. 'I thought you'd have learned by now to take what Zombie Nation says with a pinch of salt.'

'But Carl... I mean, he was talking old boys' network, that kind of thing. He said you could pull strings...'

'I have pulled strings.'

'And yet I'm out. Not coming back to work.'

'Don't' - *sweep-zing-ching* – 'sulk, Grace. It doesn't become you.'

I kicked a ball off the edge of the tee. It landed with a plop in a puddle. 'You've been acting weird ever since you came round. Is this something to do with that?'

Sweep-zing-ching. 'You could say that. Look, I'm not going to tell you what you want to hear. Not now. But one day you'll understand. You'll see what I've done for you today is *more* than a kindness. It's more than pulling strings. It's – '

A flare of rage went off in me then. 'It's because I was brought up in a pub, isn't it? It's because I never went to private school. The first time we met, you thought I was someone else. If I'd have pretended I was Justin Cunliffe's baby brother and that I went to fucking *Gateways,* I'd still be in a job by now. You'd have scratched my back, no questions asked.'

Byers swung round. For a moment I thought he was going to hit me with his driver. Instead he leaned on it, louche as a motherfucker. And I hated him then more than I'd hated anyone in my life. 'You're wrong. But you're also right. You're not like your friends Zombie Nation and Adamski, and the sooner you accept that and move on, the better. You're different.'

'Move on? Move on where, exactly? You've seen my flat. It's not much. Not when you compare it with Carl's pad. But the mortgage payments are crippling. I can't... If I don't work, how am I supposed to pay for that?'

'You'll be fine.'

'Fine? How is any of this fine? How is any of this a kindness?'

He winced. 'I like you, Neal. Always have. I saw a spark in you right from the off. Not many people have it. Not your friends, certainly. Maybe that was why I thought I knew you, but I couldn't place you. Turns out why I thought I knew you is you reminded me a lot of me at that age.'

'*You?*' I spluttered.

'Me. All that lacrosse jazz you gave it in the interview. That *sucker for a good Burgundy* crap you gave as an answer to the *what do you consider to be your weakness* bullshit. Still cracks me up now. You could do whatever you wanted in your life, but you let yourself get dragged down by them two. You let them dull your brain with all that sniff and all the *nonsense.*'

'But Carl said you – '

'Got dragged over the coals for my own problems with the sniff?' He flapped a paw. 'Yeah, a lot of people think that. But it never happened.'

'*Because* the old boys' network got you out of it.'

'Nope. Because it never happened. I just let the story stay out there because, well, it never hurts for people to believe you're protected. Bullet-proof.'

I shook my head. 'I don't get this. I don't get any of it.'

'And praise be for that. Because if you *did* know then you would be bricking it, just the same as I am. Look, you wanted my advice and I'm giving it to you. Get out now, while the going's still good. Say you've burnt out, need a new challenge. Say whatever you like. Just get out. Because a whole shit-storm is coming and you need to be well clear when it comes.'

'This shit-storm,' I said, in a low voice, 'has it got anything to do with Nathan Long?'

Byers evaluated me for a long time. Then: 'Maybe. That's all I'm saying. Maybe.'

'But,' I gulped, 'I'm… as guilty as the other two are, as far as that's concerned.'

Byers jabbed his fingers in his ears. 'I didn't hear that. I didn't hear any of that.'

'Nick, this is serious. I'm—'

He grabbed me by the shoulders. Squeezed. 'No. *This* is serious. Shut the fuck up now, and I'll tell you what your next move is. Then I will drive you home. Then you will open your laptop, boot up your emails, and you'll fire off an email to Lightwood tendering your resignation. Okay?'

'Course it's not okay, it's… I don't understand.'

Byers sighed. 'Here's what will happen. When I said I was playing a pro this morning, I wasn't telling you the whole truth. I *was* playing a guy dickered with his scorecard though. He's notorious for it in accounting circles. I'm talking Robert Henderson. You heard of him?'

I was puzzled. 'He's kind of a big deal at PWC.'

'Bingo,' said Byers. 'He practically *is* Price Waterhouse Cooper in Leeds. Genius, is what they say about him. What they don't say about him is, he's a comedian. But, honest to goodness, Grace, he is. Funny as a fruit loop. And when he heard what you said at your interview about your weakness for port and good Burgundy wine… man, he said he was going to steal that line for his own repertoire.'

'Great,' I said, deadpan. 'So if I don't make it as an accountant I can at least write people's jokes for them so everyone thinks they're all kinds of a funny fucker at dinners and the like.'

'Grace, you need to drop the attitude. Henderson's already seen your file. Likes what he sees. He wants to meet you. You'd be going in at a higher level than the one you're at with Andersen. You'd have more responsibility. You wouldn't be answering to no Lightwood there. You'd be, well, *me.*'

'I still don't get it. Surely it doesn't matter how much he likes what he sees on my file and surely it doesn't matter if he likes my stupid jokes. As soon as he asks for a reference from Andersen he sees I was slated for a drugs test and he sees I'm up for leaving before the test can take place. It doesn't take a top accountant to work out that two and two makes four.'

'Dale Lightwood'll see to it the drugs stuff is expunged from your records. You have my word.'

'*Why?* Why would he do that? Come to think of it, why would *you* do this?'

Byers winked. 'I told you. I like you, Grace. Always have. We can swing this. I promise.'

'I don't know what to say.'

'Say yes. Then meet Henderson. Sign on the dotted line. *Then* take your gardening leave. Go on holiday. Get away from Leeds. Get away from Adamski and Zombie Nation. Then come back refreshed and start your new career. It'll be the best thing you've ever done.'

'What if I say no?'

An old-style Byersian grin. 'Then, my friend, you're fucked, and also you're out of help. But you won't say no, will you?'

I flapped. 'I can't just – '

Byers' eyes were steely. 'Remember what you told me on that first call? When I invited you in for an interview? You said you never gave up. I told you I liked that in you. Your tenacity. Here, there is no such word as *can't.'*

'What are you? Yoda?'

Byers ignored me. 'And your leaving Andersen? It's not giving up. Think of it as a tactical retreat. And then, at PWC? After a break? You'll come out fighting. All guns blazing.'

'Right,' I said. 'Like, *okay.*' Thinking Byers sounded more than a little mad.

''Zactly okay.' He fished in his pocket and pulled out a business card. Handed it over. It felt heavy. The text was embossed. *Fancy.* The name on the card was Robert Henderson. Partner. 'Call him. He's expecting you.'

'What? Now?'

Byers sniffed. 'No time like the present.' And then, in a prophetic echo of another leader of men backed into a corner (though I didn't know what *kind* of corner Byers was in; not then), he said: 'Now, watch this drive.' And he struck the ball so cleanly it *squeaked,* like washed windows.

I pulled out my Nokia and plugged in Henderson's number from the card as though on auto-pilot. The guy took his time answering and I was on the verge of ending the call when he finally picked up, sounding somewhat flustered like he'd been on the loo and had had to make the mad wipe and dash in order to get the phone. He also sounded *old* and gruff. Instead of answering with his name, he answered by rattling off his entire telephone number, which was exactly how my old mum used to answer the landline in back of the Golden Goose. Once he'd finished, I quickly gave my name before I lost my nerve.

'Grace, you say?'

'Yes. Neal. Nick Byers spoke to you about me. He said you were expecting my call.'

'Neal Grace? Never heard of you. Is this some kind of prank? Are you trying to sell me something?'

I opened and closed my mouth like some grounded fish.

'Because, young man, if you *are* trying to sell me something you've got two hopes, Bob and No, and Bob's made like Elvis and left the building.'

'This is, uh, Neal Grace from Arthur Andersen. I'm not trying to sell you—'

'Arthur *who?*'

'Andersen. The accountancy firm... Look, I'm sorry. Is this Robert Henderson? Maybe I dialled the wrong number or something.'

Henderson answered with a snort and then a great rumble of laughter. 'I'm pulling your leg, boy! I know who you are. Of course I do.' *Ah, that famous Henderson comedy Byers was telling me about: Christ what a weirdo.*

'Right,' I said, and forged a laugh. 'You really got me there.'

'Should have heard yourself, Grace. Stammering and stuttering! Wait 'til I tell Byers about this.'

'Nick's with me now. We're at the—'

'Don't bloody tell me. The driving range. He'll be getting some practice in after I whupped his arse this morning.'

'That's right.'

'In that case, I need to get out into my garden and play some practice shots of my own. Grace, why don't you come see me Monday? You know where we are, right?'

In that instant, I completely forgot, even though I must have walked past the PWC building on Wellington Street thousands of times. 'Um,' I said.

'Um, he says.' Henderson rumbled with laughter once again. 'How does 2 pm suit you?'

I felt railroaded. 'Suits me fine,' I said.

And with that, Henderson rang off. It had been one of the strangest telephone conversations I'd had in my life.

'Told you he was a card,' said Byers. But he didn't sound jovial. He sounded distracted again. He checked his watch, a great station clock of a thing which glittered in the weak sunlight. 'Anyway, look, we'd better make tracks. I've got to see some people.'

I knew better than to ask *what* people. In fact, all the way back into town, Byers and I adopted a silent partner named Schtum. Our business, it seemed, was all settled. Didn't feel that way to me though. To me it felt like everything was up in the air and I didn't have a handle on any of it. Byers was acting as strangely as a concussed clown; one minute depressed as hell, the next coming on strong, telling me he really liked me, was *saving* me. Henderson seemed like a joker. The whole PWC set-up seemed hinky. There was some aspect of this I just didn't get; couldn't grasp. Maybe I should talk to Carl again. But I didn't really want to do that. For some reason, even *thinking* about leaving for PWC felt like the worst kind of betrayal, even though Carl was the one set up the meet with Byers in the first place.

Nick kept the motor running back at Eastgate. I exited, stuttering and stammering all over again, half thanking him, half trying to wheedle out of him any more info regarding what was going on. He drummed his fingers on the steer wheel and told me he'd already said more than he should have, and what he *had* said I should keep under my hat for now. Then he told me I should make sure Robert Henderson never saw me wearing a shirt like the Jesus one and then he wound his window back up and pressed pedal to metal and sailed away from the kerb.

I spent the rest of Saturday afternoon trying to piece it all together but was about as successful at that as I had been at the driving range. By seven I had the mother of all headaches and I decided that the only way to cure that was to crack open another Corona and think about something else. For some reason, I found myself thinking of Natalie. I wondered what she was doing right now. Was she visiting with Rhys at the hospital or was she down the spray-tan place, getting a top-up? Or was she watching out for her kid, Jakey? Or was she *packing*?

I tried to imagine what *she* might want for a new life. Safety and security for her kid. Perhaps a new fella for her. But, beyond that, what hopes and dreams did she have? I couldn't imagine. Mind you, I couldn't even think what *I* wanted from life these days. An end to the madness of the past few days, sure. A little safety and security for myself. But beyond that? Could I picture myself at Wellington Street, slaving for PWC? Did I want that? Did I want to sacrifice my next decade working every fucking hour God sent just to save face and ensure the fat pay cheques kept rolling in? Wasn't there anything more?

I couldn't answer my own question, and that worried me because in a way I was still as clueless about my life as I had been when I'd wandered into that graduate recruitment fair at the Parkinson Building. Maybe I was still waiting for a different kind of life to simply present itself to me and I'd think *Yeah, that.* Maybe I was just procrastinating.

Carl called me at nine and said he and Ads were going down to The Townhouse and when should they pick me up, and even though they were the last people on earth I wanted to speak to and even though I should have stayed in and kept my head straight, the weird aimlessness of my life made me think it couldn't really hurt to take my mind off things for a while, and, besides, Carl wasn't taking no for an answer so what was the point in fighting?

He loved my new tee. Of course he did. I'd masked the kind of desperate stench of the day with a barrel-load of John Paul Gaultier and felt almost better about myself when they rocked up at ten. We laughed and drank and bantered like there was no tomorrow, but despite it all I felt empty. If Jesus *had* happened upon me and started braying on my heart it would have come off sounding hollow. And, of course, that was what we all were, amongst the dirty lights and polished surfaces of The Townhouse. A bunch of fucking puppets. I found myself wishing The Nat would come along, try and talk her way into the VIP section all over again, because at least she was real. But of course she didn't and of course Carl wanted to talk to *this* girl and Ads wanted *that one.* And couldn't their mate sit down with me, too?

I found myself talking about hopes and dreams with the girl. I never once looked at her face so I had no idea whether she was a sort or not, and in the end I must have bored the pants off her because she slipped off to the toilets and never came back. So Ads and Carl *ripped* into me because I was a fucking loser and she'd been begging for it, mate, and I'd just let her walk away. What was wrong with me?

A while later, when it had all become blurry, I banged shoulders with a guy who looked as though he was in *Hollyoaks.* I believe I asked him whether he was, and I believe he asked me whether I wanted to step outside. And then Carl and Ads were bundling me out of the place and back to Carl's because none of us wanted a fight then, and then we were wedged into Carl's sofa with a bong on the go and Ads was the maudlin one, not me. He kept muttering that people were looking at us different since the night we got the bouncers to beat seven shades of shit out of the Neanderthal lads and maybe he now wished we hadn't done it. In the end he bored himself to sleep and then it was just me and Carl, Carl and me.

I wasn't going to, but I told Carl about the PWC thing. About Byers not being able to smooth things over properly with Lightwood. Carl told me not to worry. He'd soon be out of Andersen too, and together we'd start up that new company he'd spoken about on the way down to the Gubbins café to see Nathan Long. I told him I liked the sound of that, and part of me did: the two of us, out there alone, against the world, answering to no-one. But a large part of me didn't, too. And I realised, with no real surprise, that I didn't trust Carl. Couldn't imagine me and him out there alone. Could only think it would all end in tears.

We cracked open some shampoo to celebrate our brilliant plans and before I'd even reached the bottom of my first glass, Carl was asleep.

I walked home as the city was just coming round after a heavy night. I walked so fast my feet could barely keep up with my legs; stumbling some, staggering some, but getting there all the same. Nobody paid me any mind. Not even the rats, the first of which were starting to emerge from the cracks in the pavement and the ginnels between buildings. Those nocturnal scouts burrowed and worked at their dark early morning goings-on and they didn't even twitch as I scuttled past them, thinking of how much like them I was; a rat in a run. Blinkered. Only a CCTV camera responded to my movements, sweeping in an arc as I passed a slumbering hotel.

I drank in the dawn. It tasted bitter, like shampoo left out too long from the night before. I felt outside of time and small, like whatever I chose to do with the rest of my life didn't matter a fucking jot.

At the bus station, the dregs of last night were waiting for the first buses home. I had to walk in the gutter so as to avoid a few of them who'd set up camp right in the middle of the pavement. One of them asked me for a cigarette when I passed, and I ignored him, eliciting a volley of complaints which followed me right round the corner and onto Eastgate. Maybe I wasn't nothing, then. Maybe I wasn't small and unremarkable. Maybe what I did, or didn't do, mattered.

Maybe I was still drunk.

I got home and threw myself into bed fully clothed. Slipped into a thankfully dreamless sleep almost immediately. No Nathan-Longs-as-Captain-Hook chasing me *this* night.

I woke late, and I'd managed to kill most of Sunday, which was great. Still, a kind of dread had descended on me by four and all I could think of was tomorrow and what it would bring: my final meeting with The Nat and my first meeting with Henderson. It felt strange that the dread *wasn't* in relation to having to wrench myself back into Andersen all over again.

I imagined Tom Green slipping quietly into his seat behind his desk next door to mine; incessantly checking his watch when I didn't roll in at eight-thirty or nine. And then, by ten, he'd maybe have the nerve to pluck his posh bloody pen out of his briefcase and put it on his desk without fear of the demon Neal Grace pilfering it. Hell, Tom Green would probably go against his rigid 'no drinking during the working week' code and go out for a few that night in order to celebrate my leaving.

A couple of the girls might miss me. Might. They might circulate an email regarding a collection; they'd want to buy me something nice. But not enough people would contribute and they'd end up handing whatever money was raised right back, because it would be downright embarrassing to buy me something obviously crap, obviously cheap and all that.

There'd be whisperings about what had happened to me. Dale Lightwood would convene some kind of emergency meeting in which he'd distribute my workload. He'd say he couldn't say anything about Neal Grace, but then, on the hush-hush, he'd tell everyone anyway. He'd say he'd known right from the off I was a bad sort. *I mean, do you remember what he said about good Burgundy in his interview? Too cocky for his own good, that one.*

Carl called at seven to see whether I was up for a Sunday evening session. Just a few games of pool, a beer and a bite down at the Elbow Room, but much as I'd grown sick of staring at the four walls, I knew it would make me even sicker to be out and about and on display, so I cried off. It was never easy crying off with Carl. He had no qualms about *begging.* Had no compunction about playing the *my mum and dad never loved me and you're my real family* card. You felt like you were shattering his fragile dreams, you really did, but I knew exactly what excuse would stop him in his tracks.

'I've an appointment at the bank tomorrow,' I told him. 'I need to be fresh as a daisy for it.'

Carl already knew about my jumping ship to PWC and must have – as I knew he would – accounted two and two and made the four of *I was broke,* or at least having money troubles. And, though he thought of me as family, Carl was tighter than a *real* Leeds man when it came to money. He was all, like, an embarrassed cough, a 'Right, say no more' and a quick ring-off.

I should have used the same excuse in the past.

Still, it left me in a kind of no man's land for the rest of the evening, and because I'd only gotten up late, there was no way I was sleeping, even if I did have an early night. I forced myself to watch a couple DVDs: no gangster stuff. Nicole Kidman in *The Others,* which even distracted me enough to jump at one point, and then the execrable *Peal Harbour,* which almost defeated the point of watching a DVD in the first place by making me think even a nightcap at the Elbow Room would be better. But I was stoic as a motherfucker and held off. The effort this took, however, *the strain* of it, meant I was sleepless in Leeds-attle until *way* past four *am.* And by that time I was already worrying about how I'd explain to the bank I wanted two grand cash, pronto.

I needn't have worried. As the cashier told me, I was 'a very valued customer' of the bank and if I wanted to take a seat in one of their plush booths and wait, somebody would be along 'quicker than a shake of a lamb's tail' to give me my cash. How did I want the money? What denominations? I said I quite fancied seeing a lot of Charles Dickens' face in the pile. A smile: 'Of course, sir'.

A Tale of Two Cities. As I looked out from the booth I could see a couple of bedraggled looking students arguing the toss about overdraft charges with a wall-faced teller who wouldn't even listen to their cock-and-bull excuses. 'A break-in at your place, you say? Well, shouldn't you be talking to your insurance company, not us?'

A guy in an off-the-peg suit came into the booth. On his name tag it said *MANAGER,* and I reckoned he was on probably a fifth of what I was on as a fifth-tier at Andersen. The ratio got even worse when you compared it to what I hoped to be on at Price Waterhouse. The manager seemed flustered. He must have seen the girth of my bank balance and had been made to feel small by it. He might have been supposed to, but he asked me no questions about what the

174

moulah was for, simply licked his fingers and counted it out –
twice – and then handed it over.

'And will that be all, sir?'

I stood up.

He looked all kinds of uncomfortable. 'Um, you still
need to sign the paperwork.'

I must have looked put out because he offered me a
cup of coffee while I signed. In the bank, at least, I was still a
prince amongst men.

I asked him to leave me in the booth a while as I
signed and stashed the money away. 'After all,' I noted, 'one
can't just wander through Leeds clutching a wad of notes, can
one?'

*I wondered why I still did that? Pretended to be
someone else.*

He left me and I separated one hundred and twenty
notes from the rest and put them back in my wallet. That
covered the down payment I'd given The Nat in the café at
LGI. The rest I tucked into the inside pocket of my suit jacket,
behind my mobile phone. I could have asked for a baggie to
put it all in, but in a way I wanted The Nat, the *grabbing* Nat,
to reach for it and in her haste knock it all onto the floor.
Maybe then she'd see the shame in what she was doing.

There was a café on the ground floor of The
Townhouse, round the side of the building looking out onto
the back of the Corn Exchange. As I rounded the corner of
Assembly Street I saw Natalie right away. She was sitting on a
tall stool by the counter which ran around the room and she
had her back to me. But I knew it was her because of the hair
and the tan and because she kept checking her watch. She
didn't *seem* ashamed. Just anxious to get this over and onto
the next chapter of her life.

I walked round to the entrance. There was a bouncer
on, even at this time of day; even though there wasn't
anything like a lunchtime rush. The moment I saw his black-
bomber-jacket-clad form, my heart bungeed in my throat, for I
was sure it was Captain Bouncer from the fateful night. But
when I drew up close I saw that, though they shared the same

shape, build and demeanour, nothing else about them was similar. This guy was a younger model, learning the ropes before they let him loose on the night shift.

Still, he seemed to know me (or at least, my type). He greeted me with a polite smile and a 'Hope you're having a good day' and then a 'Let me know if there's anything I can do for you'. And, for a beat, two, I couldn't think of what to say because the last time a bouncer did our bidding all hell was unleashed. But then I found my tongue, thanked him and told him no worries, I was fine. 'I'm meeting someone.'

'Bird in the café bit?' he asked. 'She's been here ages, mate. Don't know if she's been at the Dutch but she's got up for a piss about five times. Maybe she's just nervous.' He took a look at my face. 'Or maybe that's just too much information.'

I walked past him and into The Townhouse. It felt like an age had passed since I'd last been in, but in reality it was less than a week. Time flies when you're having fun, or when you're living a double life as a criminal. Still, this would be the end of it, I told myself. *And remember, she's nervous. You've got the upper hand here.*

Turned out she had the upper hand. The moment I saw her and our eyes locked I felt brain-freeze, like I'd just slammed down a vodka ice lolly far too fast. She looked... *different* somehow. And it wasn't just the fact she wasn't as heavily made-up as I'd seen her previously. Nor was it the fact she was wearing jeans – bone-tight – rather than a very short skirt. She looked – goddammit – like a real person. Not someone I could just dismiss as sink-estate desperate. The fact I ever had made me realise just how much of a princely knob I'd been recently.

She slipped off her stool and stalked over to greet me. She wasn't cold, like I'd been expecting. 'You came,' she said, and she made a move to touch my hand, then thought better of it and smiled instead.

I thought she'd be all about *I want my money* and that was it, she'd be running for the hills. But it wasn't like that at all. I thought it would be all like, this was *my* turf, not hers, but it wasn't like *that* at all either. She'd staked out this place and made it her domain, her territory. She seemed at home in it in a way she hadn't been when she was with her friends the other night.

She seemed composed. 'Should we get some food in?' she asked. Then quickly: 'I'm paying, don't worry.'

So we wandered over to the display and she picked out a slice of quiche (I hadn't thought she'd be able to pronounce the word, so go figure) and I opted for some pizza. She ordered a Coke, so I followed suit, even though I'd have loved a dash of vodka in it and *na zdrowie*, down the hatch, instant composure.

The waitress told us she'd warm the food up and bring it right over. So The Nat led us over to the tall stools and we sat. I patted my jacket pocket and whispered: 'I got the money'. And Natalie looked at me as though I'd made the worst *faux pas.* And that made me angry because, *look, I'm sorry, I've never been blackmailed before. I don't know how to handle this…*

I took a swig of Coke. 'Okay,' I said. 'Got that one wrong. Let's try this instead. How are the lads? Rhys and Dan?'

'Do you know what? They're both on the mend. Still in the hospital, mind. But improving. That was what the nurse said: "There are signs of improvement." Both of them are conscious and eating and whatever. I had my first proper conversation with Rhys since he came round yesterday. And do you know what? He called me a slag and a whore. In front of our son. He told me this was all my fault. Jakey started crying. I was so angry I couldn't even speak.'

I didn't know what to say, so I said this: 'It isn't your fault.'

She gave me a *yeah, right* look. 'If I hadn't insisted on going checking out *this place* and if Rachel hadn't jumped at the chance to go inside on your friend Adam's arm then none of this would have ever happened.' Then she did something very strange. She started arguing with herself. 'No. That's not right. Rhys and Dan are *hard-wired* to do stuff like that. Going mental at the VIP-cordon things. Getting chucked out. Fuck's sake, the reason Rhys got sent down in the first place was he brayed the barman of the working mens' club at the after-party for Jake's christening.'

'Fucking hell.'

'Fucking hell is right.'

We neither of us had noticed the waitress whispering over to us on her soft shoes, bringing our food. The way the waitress said 'Excuse me' while she dumped the food in front of us made us understand she hadn't exactly appreciated our conversation.

It felt strange eating in front of my blackmailer. I don't know why but I felt all kinds of awkward. I kept trying to be *too* polite; eating my pizza with a knife and fork instead of getting stuck in and eating with my hands like any normal person. We neither of us spoke and I became aware of the noises my mouth made when I ate, and I didn't like them. Once I saw Natalie had taken two small forkfuls of her quiche and pushed the plate to the side, I did the same.

The Nat twisted her glass of Coke in her hand so the ice jangled. Then: 'The minute you walked through the door you had this *why is this happening to me* look on your face.' It wasn't quite true, but I didn't want to tell her what I'd really been thinking (or *not* thinking: my brain-freeze as she materialised into a real and actually quite pretty… not that that should count for anything… person).

'Let me tell you something. I used to be that way. I used to think *Why is this happening to me?* I'm pregnant just before my exams at school. *Why is this happening to me?* My son's father has been sent down to Armley nick. *Why is this happening to me?* We've fallen behind on our rent and need to go live with me mam. You know the story. Most of the folk our way are the same. Never think to think about what they've done to get into the situation in the first place and done nowt to change it in the run of it anyhow.'

I thought about telling her I wasn't like that, but actually she had me down pat. My whole shitty weekend had seen me cycling closer and closer to the plug-hole and I'd felt

178

sorry for myself with every turn, every new thing which dragged me down. Why hadn't I tried harder to think what I could do about it?

'You're talking yourself out of your money,' I said. 'You're having me think about *why is this happening* and maybe I won't let it happen now.'

'You will.' She smiled sweetly, confidently.

'How do you know that? How do you know I'm not... I don't know... In cahoots with that bouncer out there? I mean, it's lunchtime. The place isn't exactly rushed off its feet. What's he there for? Have you asked yourself that?'

She didn't answer my question. She answered a wholly different one instead. I don't hate you, Neal. I'm past that already. In fact, you helped. You just showed me how rotten it is up here. So don't hate yourself, all right? I've had a lot of time to think about this whole thing and none of it is good. Yep, not even what I've done. I can see that. But at least something good can come out, you know? In the wash. This way, you, like, ease your conscience and I get to take Jake away from all this. That's how you justify this to yourself.'

It felt like a corrupted version of Stockholm Syndrome. South City Centre of Leeds Syndrome maybe. I was her hostage, in a way, and yet I was feeling all kinds of positive towards her. She was offering me a way out of my own head, my own masochistic head. And I was jumping at the chance.

I pulled the money out of my jacket pocket and dumped it on the counter. It was a fairly thick wedge on account of I'd asked to see a lot of Charles Dickenses. The Nat stared at it for the longest time, and for a while I had great expectations she would turn it down, have second thoughts. But eventually she gathered it up and stuffed it in her handbag.

She looked up, met my eyes. Said: 'A pleasure doing business with you.'

And I really, really wanted to say something witty, something condescending, in response. Something like 'Don't spend it all at once, not even in Primark'. Or something cutting which would make her regret this moment for the rest of her days. But I couldn't think of anything on the spot. I suppose I was kind of under her (Stockholm) spell and I suppose in a way she'd given me a way out by telling me I was – well, the money was – helping her and her son to get away from all this. She was allowing me to think that, in a dog-legged, arse-about-tit way, I was rescuing her. And what red-blooded male *doesn't* want to think of himself as a prince who rescues a beautiful princess. (Even if she wasn't beautiful or a princess.)

She left first and I followed her out after giving her a couple minutes' head start. I saw her round front of the Corn Exchange, just a girl waiting for a bus. I hoped I'd never see her again. Hoped this sorry chapter of my life was over. Wished it was nine months, a year later so maybe I'd be able to look back upon this moment and laugh, or at least not cringe. At least not cringe.

PART II

I

There was a girl waiting in reception I thought I recognised. As I glided across the dinner-plate-clean floor towards the lifts, our eyes met briefly – and only briefly – but something passed between us. That instantaneous thought: *I know you.*

She didn't look like a client or a friend, or even an ex-conquest. She wasn't dressed right: she'd gone for the double-denim look – short skirt and tight shirt – which didn't exactly suggest *business.* At least not my type of business. She didn't look comfortable here, spiky thin amongst the plump leather sofas. She had a magazine on her lap but wasn't even pretending to read it. A beaker of water on the table in front of her that looked untouched. Instead she kept fiddling with the ends of her shoulder-length rusty-blonde hair – you could see the muddy brunette roots sludging through – and fumbling with her necklace. I decided if she was here for anything at all, rather than just a long sit, it was to start a new job as a cleaner.

In that moment when our eyes met she gulped; adjusted her skirt. Then looked away first.

If she'd have been dressed differently I might have gone over, but I decided not to. The security guy on reception at PWC wasn't a Paul. No, I suspected the little Irish guy with the salt-and-pepper hair from Andersen might have been kindly enough to allow someone like this girl to sit all day. But not the PWC guy. He was younger, more jobsworth-y. I'd had a run-in with him a couple weeks back after I'd forgotten my ID badge for the third time that month. 'Should be three strikes and you're out, Mr Grace,' he'd said, before reluctantly issuing me with a visitor's pass. Ever since then he'd looked at me funny, and I suspected that if I did go over to the awkward girl on the leather sofas, by the *blunk*ing water machine, I'd only provide him with more ammunition. Security had gone crazy since 9/11 and, to be fair to him, he was only doing his job. But for fuck's sake: did it really look as though the awkward girl was carrying high-powered explosives in that tiny little handbag of hers (a Gucci: clearly knock-off)?

So I walked over to the lift, called it, waited, then climbed in without even a single look back, and once I was inside, squeezing in alongside a batch of grey-suits from my floor, I forgot all about her. Leeds is a small city. You see the same faces a lot. No biggie.

In the lift there was muted talk about weekend plans and whether anyone else had signed up for the charity dragon boat race up at Waterloo Lake, Roundhay Park. They'd heard Andersen had a very strong team this year. 'Ringers,' was the whisper. 'They're getting as bad as the Oxbridge boys at the boat race. Not a one of them a bona fide employee.'

As soon as the doors swished open on the fifth floor, we were all business. Robert Henderson's office door was open and though you could see he was practising his putting with the machine we'd all chipped in for for his fiftieth, we were all watchful. He'd not shown much of his 'comedian' side recently. Though Price Waterhouse were still doing well in Leeds, we'd fallen well behind Andersen and he didn't like it. Sometimes I got the impression he held me personally responsible, as though I was some kind of bad-luck charm had been palmed off on him. But my figures were good. *Everyone's* figures were good. Better than they'd ever been. It was just Andersen were doing way better.

I shared an office with a guy named Bill. Great name for an accountant – almost as though he'd been chosen at birth for this line of work. But in fact he'd only come to the game late. He was as old as Henderson and as boring as Tom Green back at Andersen, but I liked him all the same. I'd relished quietness and calm ever since that terrible, terrible long weekend last year. Bill was always in early, but he never rubbed it in, not like some. 'I just like to get up early is all, Grace. I'm a lark, always have been. Means I get all my good work done before owls like you have even wired yourself back into the system with a bucket-load of Starbucks.'

Today he greeted me in the usual way. A glance up from his paperwork, a brief nod and then a quick quip about the weather. He thought they should start the cricket season early this year. When it got as hot as it was now in June then you just knew you were in for a crappy July, August and September.

And I, as usual, yawned a lion's roar of a yawn and told him he sounded like someone's dad. Not *my* dad, of course. He didn't go in for cricket: he couldn't bear to invest so much of his time in something as trivial as that (couldn't even bear investing time in me, his son).

Bill chuckled then went back to his work.

I settled down to mine, and was just about getting lost in the EyeSpy Security account when a call buzzed through on my desk phone. I answered, still navigating my way around a spreadsheet. Crooked the phone receiver between my shoulder and ear and manipulated the mouse. 'Yeah?' I said.

(Bill muttered, 'Is that any way for someone to answer their phone? Youth of today; I don't know,' then grinned.)

It was the security guy from reception. He sounded like he was crowing. 'There's someone to see you, Mr Grace. Want me to send her up?'

And in a flash I remembered the awkward girl at reception. 'Who, uh, what's she want? Who is she?'

'She wouldn't give her name. Says it is *personal* business.' The way he said 'personal' made it sound a lot like 'sexual'. 'Shall I send her up?'

'Um... I should come down.'

'She's been here nearly an hour, Mr Grace. We can't have her clu—' – he was about to say *cluttering up the place* – 'I'm going to need to send her up.'

'But who is she? What does she want?'

An icy pause. 'I don't know what she wants, Mr Grace. But she is very insistent. Frankly, I am concerned she might' – he lowered his voice – 'cause a scene down here. And I am not having that.'

'But doesn't this go against all of your security protocols... or whatever.' *Fuck's sake. It was as though I was conversing with C3PO.*

'Not if I escort her up to the fifth floor, it doesn't. And Mr Grace? Please don't tell me how to do my job. You don't see me coming into your office and fiddling about with the calculators, do you?'

Before I could respond, he rang off. My heart was beating hard and low in my ears. A little wire behind my ears thrummed with anger. I slammed the phone down.

Bill raised an eyebrow. 'Trouble at' mill, Neal?'

I sighed. 'Don't know, Bill. Don't know what the fuck's going on.' But it certainly *felt* like trouble. Nine months had passed since that terrible, terrible long weekend in which Trouble had become my middle name and my life had come to resemble something out of a crime drama. Those nine months had been a pregnant pause. I lay low at Price Waterhouse. Kept my head down. Steered clear of anything which smelled hinky.

Meanwhile, events in America changed the world irrevocably. The towers were brought down. I'd had to take three months' gardening leave after I walked out on Andersen and I'd started at PWC in the first week of September. A week later, I was still on my induction training course, locked into a bare basement room which felt like a bunker along with a couple graduates and Bill. We were snoozing our way through talks on anti-bribery and corruption, stuff we'd all heard before, even the grads, when, weirdly, an old fax machine in the corner spluttered into life. The trainer, a middle-aged man who looked exactly like Peter Pan had in an old picture book back at the Golden Goose, right down to the jug ears, went over to investigate.

He pulled off the sheet of paper which spooled through the fax and then his knees kind of gave way and he wobbled badly, before one of the grads raced over and helped him to his chair. The grad passed the fax around and silently, almost reverentially, we studied it. It was a picture, almost a cartoon. Whoever had sent it had hand-drawn that eternal image of the plane smashing into the second tower of the World Trade Centre. Underneath that was a small message of explanation.

None of us knew what to say and for a while we all sat there staring vacantly into space. We felt kind of outside time because right then we knew everyone else in the world was staring at a TV screen, watching the horror, and here we were, trapped, our only lifeline to the rest of the world that ancient fax machine (we hadn't been allowed to bring our mobile phones down; they'd distract us from the anti-bribery and corruption spiel). Someone up there, in our own tower on Wellington Street, must have felt kind enough not to keep us in the dark any longer. But still, it felt like we were learning of the tragedy via fucking *cave paintings*.

Eventually Bill said 'Fuck this' and climbed to his feet (this decisiveness was one of the reasons I first liked him). And me and him unlocked our bunker door and lifted it back up to reception. There, the whole of PWC were gathered in front of the large flat-screen TVs, watching the disaster continue to unfold. Nobody spoke. It felt like we were in church.

Leeds changed too, to a much lesser degree. Leeds United had been on trial, in the form of Bowyer and Woodgate. After the collapse of a first trial (due to a newspaper publishing what they shouldn't have done) a second trial finally wound up in December 2001. Both players, it was reckoned, got off lightly. Bowyer was cleared of his charges whilst Woodgate was convicted of affray and given community service. But behind the scenes the trial traumatised the club. They'd once been a bright, shining advertisement for Promethean Leeds, living the dream, but the trial brought the house of cards tumbling down. A terrible run of form on the pitch coincided with the trial of the players, and this ultimately meant the club finished fifth in the league, outside the Champions League places.

Cause and effect. The club had over-reached; they'd staked millions on continued involvement in the money-spinner which was the Champions League. They'd gambled. In September they'd unveiled plans for a brand spanking new stadium in the outskirts of the city. They'd invested unheard of amounts in players. They'd hired the most expensive goldfish money could buy for their offices. And yet, without the guaranteed income from European football, they were suddenly on the brink. The manager, David O' Leary, was sacked. But this would not arrest the freefall. Leeds had flown too close to the sun and they'd been burnt.

I couldn't help but think there was a cautionary tale in there for me. The bubble felt like it was bursting, and I kept myself to myself, hoping the fallout would not be too bad. I didn't see much of Carl and Adam at all. It was a conscious-unconscious decision. I don't think it *looked* as though I was deliberately distancing myself from them. Certainly there was never a decisive moment in which I blanked them, or told them to *go away, never darken my door again.* It was just that we moved in different circles now. And the fact Andersen and PWC were such fierce rivals helped in this way. We weren't exactly encouraged to mix with 'the enemy'. Even at Christmas there wasn't much of a truce. Ads invited me along to the Andersen Christmas party at the Queens Hotel, but then had to call back a while later and tell me he'd been wrong, all the tickets had gone. Sorry. I knew Lightwood must have scoured the guest list, seen my name and black-balled me all over again. Carl offered me tickets to the Test Match at Headingley and I took them off his hands, only to pass them on to Bill.

Like I say, I was quiet. In hibernation mode. I barely left the flat at weekends and rarely went out on the razz. And sometimes, when I did, I'd have trouble with the bouncers, who no longer recognised me as 'a face'. Instead of kicking off with them or arguing my case, I'd simply shrug my shoulders and move on. Or go home.

At one point in March I thought I had a girlfriend. Sarah. Turns out we had our wires crossed. She seemed to want me for my flat, for a crash-pad at the weekends so she could enjoy the shopping and the clubbing. Nothing more. She definitely did not want to travel down to Sheffield to meet my mum. I don't know what I'd been thinking. Even I didn't really want to see my mum anymore and it didn't seem to matter if I saw her or not. On the rare occasions she did recognise me, she thought I was my dad. Perish the bloody thought.

As I waited for the lift doors to whoosh open, I was trying to picture Sarah. Trying to work out whether she'd have changed enough in four months for me not to pick her out of a crowd. But there hadn't been a crowd. And Sarah wouldn't have been seen dead in double denim. Not unless she'd seen Naomi Campbell wearing it. So if it wasn't Sarah and if it wasn't –

An awful thought struck me. What if the awkward girl from downstairs was a nurse? From Mum's care home? What if she'd got some awful news, the kind you can only give out face to face?

It wasn't Sarah. Nor was it a nurse from the care home. Not unless the Hollies Residential insisted their nurses show up stinking of booze – *bad* booze, *cheap* booze – at half-past-nine on a weekday morning. My guest exited the lift alongside the security guy. The security guy was half linking her arm, half frogmarching her. She was struggling a little bit.

It was Rachel Stonehouse. For some reason I identified her instantly now whereas I hadn't had a fucking clue downstairs. Hell, I even remembered Ads' terrible chat-up line from the night we all met at The Townhouse: 'You're Stonehouse; well, I'm penthouse'. From the townhouse, through the stone house, via the penthouse; was the final destination the big house? Because just then it felt like my crimes were catching up with me all over again.

I must have looked like I'd seen a ghost, for the security guard, not even bothering to wipe a godawful smirk off his face, said: 'You okay, sir? You look a little... unsteady?'

Rachel Stonehouse. I stared at her, baldly and terrified. And I saw the reason I hadn't recognised her at first was the dye job. She'd been brunette before. Now she had a kind of dip-dyed dog look.

'Sir?'

I improvised. 'Yes, I'm fine. This is my sister. She's here to talk about my mother. Mum's in a care home. Not doing so well. In Sheffield.' *God, I was talking too much.*

'That right?' The security guy weighed up Rachel doubtfully.

She nodded, and when she did so it seemed to waft the booze fumes so the reek of her redoubled.

'Well okay then, if you're sure.' He paused. 'But miss, may I ask that next time you visit us, you call in advance and have your' – snort – 'brother here raise a request for a visitor's badge. We have' – his eyes burned into me – 'protocols, you know.'

He flounced off, for the lift and I was left with the drunk.

'Rachel,' I said, 'hi… This is, um, unexpected.'

She sneered.

'Are you all right?'

She growled. 'All right? All right?' She was talking too loudly. People were turning round to have a look at us, trying to work out what was going on, what exactly the relationship between our odd couple could be. Embarrassed, I ushered her into a meeting room. Should have closed the blinds. I saw Henderson lingering, peering through, trying to work out what in hell the girl was doing. Probably guessing something bad: pregnancy, an unpaid debt at the golf club bar.

She unzipped her handbag and produced a hip-flask. Took a good nip before I could tell her to put it away.

'What's all this about?' I asked, although I already had a sneaking suspicion. Natalie must have talked. Spilled the beans about the blackmail. Now Rachel wanted a piece of the cash-cow.

She sucked her teeth. 'Your fucking *sister*? I don't look nowt like you.'

I blushed. 'That's not true. We're both brunette.'

She looked at me as though I was the kid who couldn't graduate from first-year infants'. Then: 'Where's The Nat?'

I rubbed the back of my neck with my hand. The meeting room felt too hot. My tie was choking me. 'Pardon me?' I coughed.

'Nat-lee. Where is she? Nobody's seen her for – what? – nine months. She left everything. Her phone, her stuff, her mam, me. Took off. Last person she went to see is you. I been trying to track her down ever since. So has her mam.'

'What makes you think I know where she is?'

'Because you give her the money she had.'

I tried to stay calm. 'What money?'

A long sigh. 'Don't play silly beggars with me, sunshine. I know you give her money. *Jake* told me. And then you met her again and you give her more. And then the next day she's gone and nobody knows where.'

'I don't know where.'

'You're lying. People like you. Smarmy fuckers. They *track* their money, like. They don't just give it away.'

'I still don't know what money you're talking about.'

She rolled her eyes.

'How did you find me?' I asked.

'You don't wanna know.'

'Actually, I do.'

'Your phone number. We paid a fella round our way to track the number what had been sending all the texts to Rhys's phone. Actually Rhys paid it on account of he wanted to find you and beat the living shit out of you. But I wanted you found because of Nat-lee. I want to see her again.'

'Hmmm,' I said.

'First we went to that City Square place. Tall, fancy one. They said you'd left. Then you was like, off the radar for ages. Then we got a sniff you was back in the game. I was going to come and see you in September but then all the stuff with Dan started up again – '

'What stuff?'

'Him and Rhys were at it again. Fighting. Rhys managed to get away when the cops came but Dan had a busted knee, see, so he got rounded up. Sent to Armley. Damned near broke my heart, it did. He's still inside on account of he had another fight in there, so God knows when he'll ever get out.'

'Right.'

She hung her head. 'With Nat-lee gone and Dan gone I… I been through a rocky patch. It's taken me best part of six months to come here and see you. Get the courage like.'

'And what is it you expect me to do now you're here?'

'I said: tell me where The Nat is.'

'She never told me where she was going. She just said she was striking out for a new life.'

Soon as I said it I knew I shouldn't have. Rachel looked up sharply, the suggestion of a smile playing at the corners of her red, red lips. 'Ah, so you did see her then.'

I floundered. 'Yeah, but only to, like, apologise for what had happened with the bouncers. I came to the hospital. LGI.'

'Yeah, Jakey said he seen you there. That's where he seen you giving her money.'

'That was it, though. Just a few quid. She just said she needed it to pay for—'

'You're lying. Wanna know how I know that? Your smarmy lips are moving.'

'I swear I don't know where she is. Haven't you tried… I don't know, that same fella tracked *me* down for you?'

Now I'd caught *her*. She pretended like she hadn't thought of that, but really, I could see the whole Natalie thing was just a smokescreen. She was here for the money. Of course she was here for the money. Everyone was here for the money.

For a beat, two, we stared each other out just like The Nat had with Captain Bouncer on the night his crew beat seven shades of shit out of Rhys and Dan. Then: 'I want ten grand.'

'That's ridiculous. I don't have that kind of money.'

'I want ten grand else I'm going to the police about what you boys did, siccing the bouncers on Rhys and Dan like that.'

Suddenly I realised something about Rachel: she was a flake. The Nat had been the strong one, holding her up. Alone, she was a no-hoper chancing her arm. Suddenly I felt calm. I showed her nine fingers. 'That was nine months ago. You've already told me Dan's down for assault or the like. Natalie had a proper plan. She came to me and tapped me for the money, but it was *two days* after what happened happened. You've waited too long. The dust has settled.'

'I want the money.'

'But you're not offering anything in return. Your friend Natalie promised to keep her mouth shut. And she has. You... you're just chancing your arm. Well, I'm calling your bluff. I'm not giving you anything.'

She looked as though she'd been slapped around the chops. Her lips quivered. Tears pooled in her eyes. 'But...' In her head she'd already spent the money. She'd had the imaginary shopping spree to end all shopping sprees. She'd spruced up her house. She'd lived it up in *Eye*-beefa. She'd thought I was the same easy target as The Nat had tapped up. But I wasn't. I'd changed. I wasn't as lairy anymore. I wasn't as showy. But I was harder. I'd at least weekended at the School of Hard Knocks. And it had taken this encounter to show me exactly that.

'You should leave,' I said, calmly. 'I'll show you out.'

She scrubbed fiercely at her face, trying to scratch her tears away. 'But you can't just... It's not fair... You're... You can't get away with this. I'll scream this place down. I'll... I'll say you touched me up.'

I smiled a very Carl-like smile. 'They won't believe you. I can smell the booze off you from here and everyone else will be able to too. Besides, you're my *sister*, don't forget.' I winked.

'This is... You can't... People like you just think they can get away with everything, don't they? Well let me tell you, some people are fragile and they break easy... but... but...' She was talking herself into hysterics now. 'But sometimes when we snap we have sharp edges and you better watch out you don't get scratched or cut.'

'And *you'd* better take another hit from your hip-flask and try and calm down.'

She did exactly that. Finished the whole lot, it looked like. Then she kind of puffed herself up and sat forward in her chair. 'I'm gonna tell Rhys.'

'Tell him what?'

'Where you are. And not just you, your poncey friends too. I seen them. When I went to that City Square building looking for you. They was outside having a crafty fag. Didn't even recognise me, neither of them. But I clocked them all right.'

This worried me, a little. But I didn't show it. 'Great,' I said. 'And you know exactly what'll happen when your friend Rhys shows up again, threatening us? We'll call the bigger boys. Those bouncers will love nothing more than getting to tune up on his Neanderthal arse all over again.' I leaned in. 'Don't do it, Rachel. Let this go. Forget it.'

She sniffed. 'I never will. Because of that night my best friend has gone.'

I sniffed right back. 'She would have gone anyway, eventually. She had her head screwed on. She was intelligent. Brave. She had what it took to get out. You don't.'

I saw a flare of jealousy behind Rachel's eyes and all at once I saw how their friendship had been; her following firebrand Nat through everything in life, picking up the discarded dregs; boys, drinks, the like. Her the boring one, the dumb-ass one. She'd thought Jakey had brought Natalie back down to her level, but she'd been wrong. Natalie had gotten out all the same.

I stood up. So did she. I showed her to the door. When I touched her to shepherd her through it, I felt her flinch and I felt guilt rearing its ugly head in the pit of my stomach because really, she was one of the beaten-down and disposed and I'd just relieved her of her dream. But at the same time I felt relief because *I* needed to keep on keeping on too, and I couldn't let her drag me down.

We didn't speak in the lift on the way down, nor did we share a goodbye. She left, walking with her head hung low, into the hard, hard streets of Leeds, and I trusted I'd never see her again. Robert Henderson, it turned out, shared the same sentiment. When I was back on the fifth floor he popped out: 'Quick word in my office, Grace?'

I went in, closed the door behind me.

Henderson rocked back in his chair and stuck his hands behind his head. There were great, yellow sweat patches at his armpits. 'What was that the cat dragged in?' he asked. 'Noel on security tells me it was your sister, but neither of us believed a word of it.'

It felt like I was being talked at by Lightwood.

'We're not like Andersen, here. We don't accept our staff bringing their personal problems to work with them. Oh, believe you me, I'd heard the whispers regarding your conduct at One City Square, but I chose to ignore them. Nick Byers vouched for you and he's about the only one in that nest of vipers I'd trust as far as I could putt him. Is there anything you'd like to tell me about, Grace?'

I shook my head. 'It's nothing. It's sorted.'

And right then, it felt like it was, but the story of the aftermath of the night the bouncers beat seven shades of shit out of the Neanderthal boys had a long tail. A very long tail. And the end of it rattled.

Two days later consequence came back to bite me on the arse. Again, it was heralded by a phone call which I took in my shared office. Ever since I'd taken the Rachel call, Bill had been shooting me worried looks whenever my desk phone rang. When it was my mobile, he looked like he wanted to flee for the hills. God knew what he thought was going on in my personal life. We didn't exactly cover that base when we had our daily chat about the weather and maybe shared titbits about good new coffee places in the city centre (I'd long ago stopped going to La Scala).

I eyed the screen of the Nokia miserably, thinking *I should have changed my number nine months ago. Took a hit on the contract and simply moved on.* I didn't recognise the number, which was a bad sign. City code 0113, but otherwise... I was clueless.

I let it ring far longer than any patient person on the end of the line could have stood, then finally grew tired of the Nokia tune and pressed the green 'answer call' button.

An 0113 voice spoke: 'Is this Mr, uh, Neal? Neal Grace?'

I frowned. 'Who's calling, please?'

A pause, a *chup* of masticated gum in that 0113 mouth. 'I need to speak to a Neal Grace.'

'And I need to know who's calling.'

'Are you Mr Grace? Or can you fetch him to the phone?'

'I'm not fetching anyone anywhere until I know who you are and what this is about.'

'Uh-huh, well' – another *chup* as her jaws wrapped themselves around her Wrigley's – 'I *have* to speak to Mr Grace and only Mr Grace. This is important.'

So important you make the call with a mouthful of chewing gum.

A tut. Or maybe just another *chup.* 'Are you still there, Mister?'

I sighed. 'I am.'

'And are you Mr Grace?'

Another sigh. 'I am.'

'Like, *finally,*' she said. 'I got something important I need to tell you.'

'Spit it out.' I meant both the gum and whatever it was she wanted to say.

'Well… First I need to make sure you are Mr Grace.'

'Is this some kind of scam?'

This time there was a definite tut. 'Mr Grace. Don't you think I've got better things to do than play telephone tennis with you? All I wanna know is, can you confirm your date of birth for me?'

'You tell me. I'm not giving that kind of information out over the phone.'

She rattled off my birthday. *Christ*, I was getting old. I told her yeah, she had the right Neal Grace.

She took a deep breath. 'Okay. Right, well my name is Jackie Downes. Nurse Jackie Downes. I work at LGI.'

My first thought was *Mum,* but this was quickly followed with a second. *It can't be Mum. If she'd have been admitted to hospital, it'd be in Sheffield.*

'Anyway,' she said, 'the reason I'm calling is because, well, you're listed as next of kin on the forms and – '

Shit. It was Mum. 'Is it my mum?'

'What? No. Not unless she's grown a pair.' There was an awkward off-beat, then: 'Look, I'm sorry. That came out wrong. It's been a long day. A hard shift. No, you are listed as next of kin for' – a rustling of papers – 'a Mr Carl Sharp.' She rattled off Carl's address in Clarence Dock.

'Carl?'

'Yup,' she said.

And suddenly I thought back to two days previous, and Rachel's parting shot: *I clocked them all right... your poncey friends... I'm gonna tell Rhys...Sometimes when we snap we have sharp edges...*

What if Carl this time hadn't had time to call on the bigger boys to get him out of his mess?

'Mr Grace?'

'I'm sorry... Is he all right? I mean, he's not – '

'Dead? No. But he's took something of a pasting. He's got a broken jaw and a couple black eyes for his troubles.'

Relief coursed through me.

'Has he said anything? You know, about what happened?'

A pause, a *chup* of masticated gum. 'He's not really talking at all, yet. We're running tests, and brain activity seems okay. But you should prepare yourself for a shock when you come down here and see him.'

'Come down and...?' I hadn't planned on doing that. The thought of going to see him hadn't even crossed my mind.

'He's got no-one,' said Jackie. 'And we find our patients get set on the road to recovery much faster if they have friends and family around.'

I gulped. Suddenly I felt all kinds of sad that *I* was listed as Carl's next of kin. That *I* was the best he had. And I didn't even want to go see him. I thought back to that Lost Boys picture he had in his hallway; the three of us wrapped so tightly together we could have shared blood. We'd been family, once, before everything went arse-over-tit. Surely I could at least...

'I'll come down,' I said, sadly. 'Just give me a couple of hours to square things with work and I'll be right over.'

'I'm sure your work would understand. You know, you being next of kin and all that.'

'You don't work a place like I do, Jackie,' I said.

She *chupped,* or tutted, then asked me whether I had a paper and pen; told me what ward Carl was on. Then, without further ado, she hung up.

I was left holding the phone hoping an empty line would give me more encouragement. Finally, I pressed 'end call' and returned the phone to my pocket, sighing for England.

Bill knew better than to ask me whether there was any *more* trouble at' mill.

I went to see Henderson and explained the situation, putting Carl closer to the flat-line than he actually was. The idiot sat there, tossing a golf ball up and then catching, tossing and catching, tossing and catching. And I felt like grabbing the ball and launching it into his face. But eventually he let me go, with warnings that he'd noticed a 'worrying trend in my behaviour' ringing in my ears. Noel the security goon smirked at me as I snuck out the building.

I made it to LGI in decent time on shanks's pony. Couldn't remember a single step I'd taken, mind. I was thinking about what I might say to Carl. Whether I would bring up Rachel's surprise visit. But almost as soon as my mind was on the job – finding Carl – I managed to get all kinds of lost. So I went back to the beginning and started again. This time, after a couple wrong turns brought about by the hospital's altogether mystifying signage system – I'd found myself at one stage wandering through the desperately brightly-decorated corridors of the Children's A & E department on the first floor – I found Carl's ward. Level 3. Ward 24A.

A nurses' station had been set up outside the access-controlled double doors which led through to the ward proper. It was womanned by two nurses must have missed the Florence Nightingale 'care classes' at nursing college. One of them – had to be Jackie unless they all went about gummed-up to the nines – slapped her chops around a wad of chewing gum and wouldn't even deign to respond when I asked her whether a Mr Sharp was inside; the other, more senior member of staff – she didn't so much have crow's feet as crow's legs, wings, fucking *beaks* – told me she was none too pleased I'd come for a visit outside proper hours – 'Our patients need routine, you know'. But then I told her *Jackie here* had called me and asked me to come down, and she relented. I'd have hated to have been in Jackie's soft-soled shoes after, when Crow's Feet got a hold of her. Jackie seemed to know this and was pretty sulky as she buzzed me through to the ward. Crow's Feet called after me: 'Third bed on the left!'

I entered a ward which shook with noise from a nearby lift and rattled with the chorus of coughs, splutters and wheezes from those faulty-engined patients accumulated in the beds. Rolled with memories of my parents in places like this. And, as though underlining that thought, I heard the soulless beep of a heart monitor from beside one of the beds.

Not Carl's thankfully.

Carl's bed was, as Crow's Feet had so helpfully informed me, the third on the left. It was surrounded by damp-looking grey curtains. He was sitting up in bed, living the life of Riley, watching the local news on the pay-per-view TV on low volume. Admittedly, he was hooked up to all manner of tubes and wires and his face wasn't a very pretty picture but, still, he didn't look *too* different from a Saturday morning after the Friday night before.

When he saw me, the first thing he did was flick me the Vs. The second was, he shuffled down in his bed, made himself look a little greener around the gills. The third was, he licked his flaky lips with a tongue so parched it looked like a dead fish, dry and scaled. The fourth was, he croaked: 'Water!' He gestured over to his bedside table, which contained a jug and glass.

'What did your last slave die of?'

'Lack of work,' he groaned. He tried to smile but singularly failed. His jaw was an absolute mess.

I poured him a glass from the jug and handed it over. He took a long slug and gasped as though it had contained whisky. Then he nodded at the TV. 'It's not been on the local news yet that the most handsome man in Leeds ain't so pretty anymore. But it will be, mark my words. Harry Gration'll be sobbing when he breaks the news to Yorkshire's ladies.'

I gave him a *yeah, right* look. 'How are you, Carl? You look like you've been in the wars, mate.'

In the bed next to us, an old man groaned. His breath was a rasp. If he was anything like my dad he wasn't fit enough to survive.

Carl took another swig of water. Now I was closer I could see he was a bit worse than my original assessment (a little worse than hung over). And his voice was all over the place from busted teeth, jaw and lips. It looked as though he'd been in the type of fight which is more like a mauling, but all the same you tell everyone *you shoulda seen the other guy.*

'I'm...' For a beat, I thought he was going to cry, and suddenly he looked just like a little boy in the bed got up in his Colgate-striped pyjamas. His next of kin should have been his mum, or his pops. Someone who could give him proper sympathy. Someone who wouldn't have to bury their feelings under the bushel of *laddishness.* 'Boy, I hate this place,' he slurred, finally.

'Not exactly the Ritz, is it?'

'More like Ritzy's,' he said. 'Or fucking Planet Earth.' Both were godawful nightclubs we used to avoid like the plague. When we were Lost Boys together.

An embarrassing silence descended then, and I decided I could only cover it up by *doing something.* I moved a couple things off the chair at the side of his bed and sat down. The chair creaked. 'What happened, pal?' I asked.

His face creased into a frown. It looked very painful. 'Ten of them. Big meat-house fuckers. Came at me from out of nowhere. If Ads was there, we could have put up a fight. Hell, if *you* were there, Neal. Where've you been, man?'

'Working,' I said, truthfully. 'You guys at Andersen are wiping the floor with us at the moment, so it's all hands on deck.'

Carl tssked. 'It hurts me almost as much as my face does to hear you refer to PWC as *us*.'

I showed my teeth. I hoped he read it as a smile.

'You've been flying under the radar, is what you've been doing.' He wagged an admonishing finger. His nails were manicured and, set against the wasteland of his face, they looked kind of *not his.*

'Yeah, well,' I said. 'Tell me the truth about what happened, won't you? Were there really ten of them?' He winced. 'Okay, I'll ask you an easier one. You spoken to the police about it?'

He stared at the TV. 'You know, they got a couple movie channels on that thing. But could I find a film I wanted to watch? Could I buggery. It's all rom-coms and bullshit. What I'd give for a blast of *GoodFellas.*'

I snapped my fingers. 'Could you give a description of any of the guys got you, Carl?'

'Why, you gonna go after them?' he slurred.

'No, I just mean, any detail might help. Had you seen any of them before? Might any of them have held a grudge against you?'

Carl tried to smile. 'I thought you worked for PWC but that was just a front. You're undercover fuzz. You got the dialogue just right.'

'Okay, if you want to play it like that: were there any other witnesses? Besides you, of course.'

Suddenly he couldn't speak properly at all. 'No… Dark alleyway… Mill Hill… All over too fast…'

'*Mill Hill?*'

A groan. 'Yeah... Down by the arches... Dark Arches... Nobody around... Too dark... Too dark to see.'

'Feels like you're knockin' on heaven's door,' I mused. 'But had you seen anyone, you know, following you or stalking you or something?'

'Apart from every good-looking girl with an LS postcode? Nope.'

We were getting nowhere. Maybe I had to ask him flat out: was it Rhys? One of the Neanderthal boys from the night of the SAS bouncers? I thought about how I could frame the question, but before I could, Carl let loose with a coughing fit which I feared would break the wires in his jaw. I was at the point of pressing the *NURSE CALL* button before he contained himself.

I poured him another drink. His eyes were streaming. And in that moment he looked very, very ill indeed. He reached over and grabbed my hand and, though he wouldn't look at me while he said it, I still felt the real feeling, the *raw* feeling in his words. 'You're my next of kin, man. That's almost like being my best man. I've missed you.'

And I felt like I had to say something. Anything. So I said what you're supposed to say in this kind of situation. 'If there's anything I can do, mate. I mean it, anything.' *Thinking, I'd stop by his pad and pick up his 5001 Great Film Quotes book or else go buy some grapes for him.*

Not thinking about what he actually asked me to do. How, to paraphrase another of Carl's favourite flicks, just when I thought I was out of this business, they dragged me back in.

'Thanks, pal,' he said.

'Do your mum and dad even know about what's happened to you?' I asked. 'If I'm your next of kin, has anyone even thought to tell them?'

He shook his head.

'Want me to call? Chuck me your phone and I'll do it.'

He looked away again. 'They don't care what happens to me, Neal. Never have. Call them and you'd only be disturbing a very nice siesta. I can't see what good it would do. They'd never fly out here... And I wouldn't want them to even if they did.'

'Okay. What about Ads, then? Does he know?'

A strange look passed over Carl's admittedly beaten-out-of-shape features then.

'What?'

'Ads is on his way in. But Neal? Before he gets here you need to make like a good Boy Scout and be prepared.'

That sounded exactly like what Nurse Jackie had said to me about Carl. Prepare yourself. He looks shocking...

'Why? What's wrong with *him*?'

But then we heard feet schlepping down Ward 24A, pausing a couple times to open the curtains which surrounded a couple other beds – eliciting groans and grumbles in response – before finally those feet found the right bed and the man himself, the devil himself – speak his name and he shall appear – popped his head through a gap in the curtains. And I knew right away what Carl had been on about. Because Ads wasn't Ads anymore.

Back in the day, even when he was wearing a suit, even when he was got up in his ridiculous no-lens glasses, Ads still looked like a superhero rather than the mild-mannered alter-ego which was what most accountants at Andersen got to looking like. Hell, even when he was caning it on the coke and the 'roids and he'd been sleepless in Leeds-attle for a week, he'd always *looked* like an advert for the good life. Even when he chelped on to Carl and me about heart palpitations and pains in his kidney he'd always looked clean as a whistle; as though he'd live forever.

Ads walked up to the third bed on the left on Ward 24A looking like the walking dead. He was pale as a vampire and his cheek was red and scratched from where he must have been worrying at his birthmark. His eyes looked peeled. His skin blotchy. He'd stopped going on the sunbeds and looked like he had when he'd whited himself up to play a Lost Boy at our famous fancy dress party. Surely he was getting in darkly with the coke again. It couldn't be the 'roids on account of he looked like he'd lost about three stone in weight, most of that muscle.

He seemed surly. Petulant. Clocked me and said: 'Wow! So *Neal* chooses to grace us with his, like, presence... Did you bring anything good, mate? Or just yourself?'

'Nice to see you, too, pal,' I said, raising an imaginary glass. '*Na zdrowie.*'

Adam gave me a look as though to say *I* shouldn't be using *na zdrowie.* That was for Polish people and honorary Poles only.

'Children, *children*,' gurned Carl. 'Stop bickering at the bedside. You're making me feel like I'm in a bad soap opera.'

Ads stifled a yawn. 'Yeah, whatever. Sorry, mate. How are you holding up?'

'Well,' said Carl, 'I'm not dead.'

'There is that,' said Ads. 'Who the fuck did this to you? Got any ideas?'

'You sound like Neal, here. Both of you trainee fuzz, asking your questions. We're going to have to face it. It all happened so quickly I didn't see anything, and when it was over, I was out for the count.'

Ads cracked his knuckles. 'But don't you *want* us to find who did it? I could ask around. Put a word in with Nathan Long. See if there's anything new on the bouncer grapevine.'

'Leave it, Adam, please.'

Carl's tone stopped Ads in his tracks. 'What do you mean, leave it? Is there something here you're not telling us?' He loomed over Carl's bedside. 'Who was it, Carl? And do we have to be worried? I don't need to be worried. Not at the moment. I got all sorts going on in my head and I don't need to be worried.'

'*Chill*,' said Carl. 'I just mean there's nothing to be done. This, *this*, is the end of it.'

Ads sniffed. 'You know who did it, don't you?'

Carl looked shifty.

Ads growled. 'I fucking well knew it. I fucking well did. All the way chipping down here I was thinking people don't just batter people like us for no reason. There has to be more to the story. And I was wondering who you might have pissed off. You've not upset Nathan fucking Long have you, Carl?'

Carl looked relieved. He might have laughed had he not been so pained. 'Long? Nah, that pussycat and me are still fine. Fine!'

'So who?'

I couldn't hold back any longer. 'It was one of those lads, wasn't it? The lads from The Townhouse that night when your pal Captain Bouncer rounded up the rest of them and took them down the arches and – your words – *unleashed hell*.'

Carl gulped.

'It was, wasn't it?'

'H-how did you know?' he gasped.

'Just an educated guess.'

Ads turned Incredible Hulk then. He upended the table which contained the water jug, kicked over the chair. Tried to beat his way through the curtains. I tried, gamely, to hold him back, but even without that extra three stone of muscle he was still packing power and he shrugged me off like I was as small as The Nat's kid, Jakey.

Ads was yelling and bawling and setting off the other patients in the other beds. I heard about ten *NURSE CALL* buttons going off all at once, but *Ads* didn't hear them. He was still frantic with rage.

The nurses came, saw, chewed, tutted. One of them said: 'Hey! You can't...' And then shimmied out the way as Ads pinballed around the room. Another went off to calm the other patients in the ward.

Eventually I managed to calm Adam, too, though this might have been because there was nothing left to kick or throw over, not unless he wanted to toss *Carl* onto the floor off of his gurney. When the SAS security detail turned up, Ads was perched on the seat – which I'd righted – with his head in his hands and I was kind of stroking his head, talking nonsense soothing words like he was a big fucking baby.

We managed to smooth things out with security. Of course we did; our names still held *that* much weight. But, as one of the black-bomber-jacket-clad guys reluctantly admitted: 'We still have to turf you out, lads. We have to be seen to be doing just that.'

So they escorted us out of the ward and down in the lift and sent us on our merry way in reception. Thereupon, we kind of staggered out into the big turning-circle out front of the Jubilee Ward and we fell onto a bench in the smoking area. A couple cops in a *just in case* meat wagon gave us the once-over then returned their gaze to a few kids pissing about outside the entrance to A & E and the couple having a merry old row over a disabled parking space.

'What the fuck,' I said, draping my arm around Ads' shoulder, 'was that all about?'

Adam started to speak, but then his whole body was overtaken by a storm of shivers and sobs and I was like, *shit, what do I do now?* So I kept my arm about his shoulders and gave it the occasional squeeze and waited for whatever it was to work its way out of his system.

At last it did and Ads said we should get out of here. He had some great cola and we should go fucking bust some away from watchful eyes. And I was like, *what the fuck, Ads? Have you forgotten what's just happened.*

He told me he didn't want to talk about it. And I might have been fine with that if it meant I could simply walk away, leave these ghosts behind with my old life. But then he proceeded *to* talk about it and I had to stay.

'That night,' he said. 'I have nightmares about it. What we brought on for those lads. I tried to… like… justify it at the time, but it kept gnawing away at me.'

'Know what that proves?' I said. 'Proves you're a good guy. You've got morals. A code.' I hoped this was true for me as much as for him.

'We've all had benders before, Neal. Benders which last a long weekend… But I've been on a bender for nine months and I just can't seem to get it out of my head. Every day something reminds me of it. What we did. How we were so cowardly. And then Carl goes and gets in deeper with Long and... and I just can't get away from it. I'm not who I want to be, mate. Not in the least. And I hate who I become on the cola, but at least *everyone's* a shit on cola, so there's that.' He looked round at me. 'How the hell do you cope with it all?'

Good question. 'I just try and live a different life, day by day. But sometimes I feel like I've been in assume-crash position for the last year. I suppose being away from Andersen helps.'

'I suppose it does. I might be being paranoid but every day Lightwood and Byers, they watch me like hawks, man. They're just waiting for me to make a mistake so they can can my ass. And maybe I should just make that mistake and let them do what they want. They're forever checking my files... It's not normal. They look into Carl's too. La Scala. SAS. It's not right.'

I felt my palms becoming sweaty. 'You think they're onto something?'

'Yes,' said Ads. 'No. I don't know. I know Nick Byers is *okay.* He's almost one of us. But Lightwood?'

I thought of the day Nick Byers and I had gone out to the driving range. How distracted he'd seemed. How he'd said there was something he couldn't tell me. I wasn't at all sure Byers was okay. I wasn't at all sure he was one of us.

'Ah, it's the cola talking,' said Ads. 'I'm as paranoid as a cat. Just forget about it. Forget about everything I've said. Let's just go for a drink. Enjoy ourselves. Make it like old times.'

'I can't, Ads,' I said, quietly.

'Aw, *come on.* I'll shout you.'

'I can't.' I stood up, proffered my hand.

'We used to hug,' he said. 'Like men. Not like fucking business partners.'

I shrugged. 'Sorry.' Then I walked off out into the turning-circle.

Adam called after me: 'You're a real dick, Grace.'

But I never turned round. Not once.

II

Never ask anyone in hospital – no matter how badly off they are, no matter how much you love them – if there is anything you can do for them. If you have to, ask them if they want you to go fetch some stuff – books, a new set of PJs – from their home or if you can go buy some grapes. Or *tell* them you're going to call their work for them and explain their absence and you'll call round their friends and family to keep them in the loop about visiting times and all that jazz. Don't whatever you do give them the wriggle-room of that *anything.* Don't give them an inch – even if they can't move their fingers an inch, even if they have their mouth wired shut – because then they'll take a mile. And the worst thing is, you won't be able to do anything about it. Because *you asked.*

You stupid bastard.

Carl called me a day later.

I knew there was something *up* almost as soon as I answered, and it wasn't just Carl's strange new voice.

He introduced the subject of the big anything he was asking me to do for him in a roundabout way, but even when we were miles away from our final destination, I knew I was being talked around into something I most definitely would not want to do. Hell, Bill knew it. He looked over at me from over a mound of paperwork and shook his head at me. Mouthed 'Just put the phone down'.

By then, even he knew about my problems with phones.

I asked the questions you were supposed to ask. How was he doing? Was he still in pain? Was he bored?

Carl told me he'd slipped a porter a couple of Elgars to wheel him down to the smoking area whenever he wanted it. He was down there now sucking on a Benson and Hedges.

I imagined he loved the idea of hiring a personal servant. But it did sound a little pointless. 'Forty quid's a bit steep, mate. Porters are supposed to do that kind of thing as part of their job. Money for nothing, mate.'

'Yeah, but after Ads yesterday...' He trailed off. 'The staff are a bit wary of me. Or of the people I knock about with, at any rate.'

Circles circling. Ask your question. You know you want to.

'Anyway, I might have been able to hold off having a crafty ciggie or two' – *As if,* I thought – 'if I knew I was only in here for a couple more hours. But they keep saying they need to keep me in. Under obs. They're not releasing me yet. They say there's still some anomalies with my bloodwork.'

'Right, well. Probably the best place for you.'

I heard Carl taking a long draw from the cigarette. Then the roundabout circling closer, closer to the favour he had to ask me. 'So anyway, I'm banged up in here and Christ knows where Adam is... Have you heard from him since...?'

'Not since I left the hospital last night. Why?'

'Think you could round him up for me?'

'Again, why?'

A sigh. 'I'm worried about him, is all.'

But it was more than that. I knew it.

'Look, I'll swing by later. Bring you some grapes and a few mags. Keep you going for a couple of hours at least. But Carl, I'm at work mate. I gotta—'

'Wait a minute, matey. Hold your horses. There's something else.'

My heart sank like sewage.

'We've been summonsed,' said Carl. 'I got a call not twenty minutes ago. You know, bat-phone shit. Come now, do not pass go, do not collect two hundred nicker.'

'Summonsed by who?' Like I didn't know.

'Nate.'

Nate? 'You mean Nathan Long. Your client. *Andersen's* client.'

'Our client, Neal. All of us. Don't worry about it. It's a similar deal to last time. Easy as pie. Sweet as a nut. Worked like a charm, didn't it, and then he was off our backs.'

'I'm out of all that, Carl,' I said, slowly.

'I know, I know. But I'm desperate. See, he wants us round his house. I can't go, Neal. They won't discharge me.'

'Discharge yourself.'

'I can't. I'm still too… *woozy*.'

'Well that's fine because I can't go either, and who knows where Adam is? So what you need to do is call your boy *Nate* back and tell him you're ever so sorry but we're all indisposed. Can't possibly go round his at the drop of a hat.'

Carl lowered his voice. 'He reckons we owe him another favour though, Neal. It was his guys working security yesterday in here. They're under orders – from the hospital – to report all such incidents to the police. They could have handed Adam right over to them… But they didn't. They let him go. Ergo Nathan reckons we owe him.'

'Ergo, schmergo. I can't go see Long, Carl. I'm not doing it.'

'Please, mate, you said was there anything you can do. You *said.* And you saw the state of Ads. I can't send him on his own. He'd end up OD-ing in Long's toilet or something. Darling *Feebs* would find him and be scarred for life. And therefore so would we.'

'This is a work phone,' I reminded him. 'So chill out with that kind of talk.'

He spluttered. 'I can't chill out. Way Long put it, we have pretty much no choice. We have to go. Show face. *Represent.*'

'No,' I said, coldly. 'We do got a choice. And I choose not to go. I choose to stay here in my comfy office. Yeah, that's right, *my* comfy office.' Bill raised an eyebrow. 'And get on with my job. I'm not in a bind here, Carl. My choice is simple. And it's made.'

As I believe I've noted before, Carl was not above begging. Playing the 'you're my family' card (like we were in fucking *EastEnders).* 'Pleeeease, mate. You don't understand how important this is… This could be massive, for all of us. It could be the thing that allows us to go it alone. *That* big.' I heard him flicking the flint of his lighter, sparking up a fresh

Benson and Hedges. 'And Neal: you could be part of that. I'm talking a life-changing amount of money. I'm talking a corporate takeover, and we'll be handling it. Us. Independently.'

'I don't know what you're talking about. But it doesn't matter because I'm not interested. I don't want anything to do with this.'

'I'm dangling a carrot here, Neal.'

'I don't like carrots and I can see in the dark fine.'

'*Pleeeease*, mate. If you don't do this for me I could... I could lose everything.'

'Your bad.'

'No. *Our* bad. I keep telling you, Neal. You're up to your neck in this just as much as I am.'

I paused. 'Are you threatening me, Carl?'

'No. Well... I don't know.'

'You don't know.'

'I am asking you, as my main man, as my next of kin, as my number one guy, to do this for me after you told me you'd do anything. But yeah, I suppose if your answer's still no, I might as well pull out the big guns. You got no choice, Neal. None of us do.'

Suddenly my hands were shaking. Of all the rotten luck... I was being *blackmailed again.* But then I thought back to what Natalie had said about the whole *why is this happening to me* thing and I decided this wasn't just *happening* to me. I'd brought it on. Something in my character – the one I'd created for myself here – was *blackmailable* and that was because I didn't really have a moral code. And now I'd fallen, and was floundering – still, despite everything, all the changes I'd made I was floundering – I was a Lost Boy who could be manipulated to do whatever anyone else wanted.

'Tell who you want about my involvement, Carl,' I said, decisively. 'I don't really care anymore. Just know, I have a choice in this and my choice is, I'm having nothing to do with it.'

'Fine,' said Carl, and he hung up the phone.

Two minutes later the desk phone rang again, and it rang and rang until I had to pick it up and put it straight back down again. I dropped another call like that and then my moby began to ring. I didn't even bother checking the caller ID. Simply turned it face down on the desk where the vibrations of it caused it to seem all antsy and desperate.

Bill said: 'Want me to answer? Tell whoever it is you're not here?'

I frowned. 'Nah, but promise me one thing, pard? If I'm in this office next week with the same Nokia and the same number, shoot me. Honest to God, you have my permission to put a gun to my head and *bang*.'

'That bad?'

'Worse.'

'Woman trouble?'

'Worse.'

'Say no more.' He returned to his paperwork. But when the phone rang again – the moby – I heard his frustrated sigh.

I picked up. 'My answer's the same, Carl. There's nothing you can say would make me change my mind about this.'

'Maybe there is,' he said, and my thumb twitched away from the red 'end call' button. 'The girl, Natalie. You gave her money, didn't you? Paid her off.'

That stopped me in my tracks all right.

'No point denying it, mate. I know all about it. Two grand, wasn't it?'

'H-how do you…?'

'How do I know? Had it from the horse's mouth. Well, virtually. From the horse's mate's mouth. Rhys. He told me before he busted my face.'

'R-Rhys?'

'Don't pretend you don't know what I'm talking about. I know everything. I wasn't going to bring it up. I don't want to embarrass you. But you left me no choice, did you? The other girl, Rachel, she came to see you, didn't she?'

'Well, uh…'

'No point lying. I *know*, remember? She came to see you. Wanted a score of her own. Only, you've come over all Scrooge these days, so you gave her squat diddley. So she tells you she's going to sic Rhys on us on account of she can't send Dan because he's in nick. And you didn't think a polite phone call to warn us would be in order?'

'I didn't think – '

'That's right. You didn't think. You never do. And because of what you did, I'm here. With a broken jaw. With a pair of black eyes. He detached my retina, Neal. Punched me with a sov' ring, and I could have lost an eye. Could have gone blind. And all because you were too *goo-ey* to walk away from that Natalie and all because you were too... You didn't give a shit about me and Ads, did you? So you thought *What does it matter if Rhys goes after them?* Didn't you? Mate.'

I squirmed. 'It sounded like an empty threat.'

'Doesn't matter. You should report anything and everything suspicious. It's the way of the world now.'

'It wasn't my fault... *I* didn't punch you with a sovereign ring.'

'Yeah? Well you might as well have done. And here was me thinking you were my number one guy, my next of kin.'

'I'm sorry.'

'Yeah, well. A little late for that, don't you think?'

'Probably,' I admitted.

Then, his trap bated, the jaws of it ready to snap shut, he asked me the question one more time. 'So, Neal, you going to try and do one thing to make it up to me? You going to go round up Adam and chip on over to Nate's?'

I closed my eyes. Closing off one sense simply caused the others to become more attuned. I heard the policeman's knock of my heart in my ribcage; the devil inside that heart, ripping it in two. 'I don't know where he lives,' I said, softly.

Carl laughed bitterly. 'No, but he knows where *you* do.'

Then he was all business again. He asked me whether I had a pen, paper, then read off an address in Roundhay. 'And

Neal? Make sure you take a new attitude. Nobody likes a sulker but Nate more than most.' Then he rang off.

'Motherfucker,' I breathed into the dead line.

I sat for a while, staring into space until Bill brought me out of my reverie. He told me he was popping out for coffee – he knew a great new place on Commercial Street – and did I want one? I blinked, said no, I had places to be, people to see, and quick as that my life took another K-turn back into the shit-storm.

I made like I was going for lunch, but I knew I wasn't coming back. I scrawled a brief note to Bill – 'Cover for me!' – but then balled it in my fist and tossed it in the wastepaper basket. I dialled Ads the moment the lift spat me out on the ground floor. He ignored my call as I suspected he would so I shanksed it up to City Square and to the Andersen building. A few people I half recognised were spilling out the revolving doors but they were so consumed by the screens of their own mobiles they never noticed me, and, even if one of them did, they didn't bother saying hello. Not now I'd decamped to the enemy.

Paul, the security guy on reception remembered me though. He came out from behind his desk and clapped me on the back. Told me it was great to see me and how was life on the other side and had I found *any* places served a decent Bushmills in Leeds at all? I fielded his queries then set him to work on calling Adam down from his desk. 'Don't tell him I'm here. I'd like for it to be a surprise.'

Paul tapped the end of his (decidedly red) nose and told me to leave it with him. He had a good ruse. He called Ads' desk and told him he'd found a missing umbrella and was it his? I couldn't hear the other end of the conversation but I imagined Ads saying 'The fuck?' Then Paul told him the umbrella had Adam's name stitched into one of the panels and he really should come down and take a look, for the brolly looked all kinds of expensive. And even I heard the sigh from Adam's end of the line.

Four minutes later, Adam was standing in the Andersen reception area, staring at me like I was the Ghost of

Christmas Past. For a minute it looked like he might cross his fingers, tell me to get gone, Satan. But then he shuffled over. It looked like every step he took made his headache worse. I could tell he had a raging beast of a hangover, and, when he got closer and I picked out the crustiness of his nostrils, I could see how he'd tried to self-medicate it away. Christ, even his shirt was unironed.

'Whaddya want, Grace?' he snarled. 'This isn't about no fucking umbrella.'

'No,' I admitted. 'That was a ruse.'

He shrugged. 'If you've come to apologise for walking away yesterday I don't want to hear it.'

'It's not that.'

He shook his head. It looked like it pained him to do so. 'I'm going back up to my desk now, Neal. You know how it is. Carl's not here so muggins here gets lumbered with all his paperwork.'

I sighed. 'We got lumbered with something else, too.'

He narrowed his eyes. 'Whaddya mean? Is *this* some ruse too?'

'No ruse. But you've gotta come with me. Now. We've been summonsed.'

His eyes became shifty. 'Summonsed. What? Like, to court?'

'Worse,' I said. 'Nathan Long.'

Adam puffed out his cheeks. 'Shit. What – now?'

I nodded. 'He wants us up at his place in Roundhay.'

'Okay, we'll go get my wheels. They're in Long Stay down by the International Pool. Then we'll swing by and pick up Carl from LGI... It's on the way to Roundhay.'

'Carl's not coming. Apparently they're not discharging him today and he won't discharge himself.'

Ads snorted. 'What? Zombie Nation's run out of lives, has he? Can't get up like the walking dead this time? This is *his* deal. What's the point in going if he's not there?'

'We've no choice, mate. Not after your little flap back at the hospital yesterday.'

'Oh, that,' said Adam.

214

'Yeah, that.' And I told him about SAS considering their rather gentle dismissal of him from the premises yesterday being yet another favour which needed to be called in. And that convinced him.

He followed me out the building. At the revolving doors, something very strange happened. I saw Nick Byers in the quarter-compartment directly opposite us and he saw me. Our eyes met and I was about to smile, give him the thumbs up: PWC *had* been a good move for me, even though I was in the process of screwing it up (that old Grace self-sabotage in evidence all over again) but he gave me this awful cold *get away from here NOW* look which frankly chilled me to the bone. I was trying to decipher that look all the way across town to the Long Stay by the International Pool so that by the time Ads *blip-blipped* the central-locking of his TT, I realised we'd not spoken a word the whole way.

Didn't matter. There was nothing to say. The both of us felt like puppets being dragged about the place. What we *thought* about the matter didn't count for anything. Not to anyone.

The TT started great, cold. Ads floored it out of the car park. He came *this close* to clipping a parked Merc around one turn and seemed so keen to escape he practically smashed through the barriered exit. Then we were on the way, the little compartment of the Audi fired like a bullet towards its target; us, the prisoners inside.

Nathan (Nate) Long's house was located on Park View Crescent, one of the most affluent streets in Leeds. Not quite footballer-standard homes – the Robbie Fowlers of this world lived farther out, in Shadwell and Harewood – but not far off. This was mega-rich-folk land and with mega-rich-folk amenities on the doorstep – the local golf club was only a good tee-off away and the delis and bookshops of Roundhay were within Bluetooth range – and the *houses.* The houses were huge. Looming stone-built Victorian hulks which in any other area of Leeds would have been converted into flats or assisted living accommodation. More modern glass-and-chrome constructions which *sprawled* across what seemed to be acres. Mock Tudor residences which would have been suitable for Henry VIII himself.

The road was smooth as a ribbon; a ribbon these mega-rich grandees could cling to which could pull them through the labyrinth of Leeds until they reached home, this place whose air was more refined, healthier than anywhere else in the city. Indeed, it seemed lighter here. Brighter. The sun seemed to have speared through the clouds *right above* Park View Crescent and had deigned to shine here, and only here.

On Park View there were no cars parked up, cluttering up the road. All the houses had their own long driveways and large, access-controlled gateways behind which fleets of Jags and Mercs slumbered safely. And on all the gateways warning signs from security companies like EyeSpy, Leeds Alarms and Huntsman were posted. Although these weren't your common-or-garden security signs. Rather, they'd been done out to look stylish and more in keeping with the respectable nature of the area. Same with the streetlights, which contained small black domes that looked suspiciously like surveillance cameras, only they'd been made to fit in with the wrought ironwork of the traditional-style lamp-posts. Everything seemed to say *this is a safe area*, and yet they didn't want to shout about it, because shouting was something the common people did.

Must have been a lovely, quiet place to live. The archetypal leafy suburb: and there were trees – big oaks, ostentatious monkey puzzles, willows – everywhere. Even on the road itself the tarmac was liberally sprinkled with white blossom from the trees. It looked like confetti. Like the residents of these houses were welcomed home every night by this scattering of flowers. Otherwise, the street contained no rubbish, no graffiti, nothing which shouldn't have been there.

Until the two of us, the eternal bad pennies, showed up, that was.

Long's house was actually a bungalow, though calling it a bungalow by name seemed kind of disrespectful. Call it low-slung then. Low-slung and crouching behind a high fence which appeared to be constructed from spears, tall black things topped with gold points, and three obstructive conifers. The house had been built in the 1980s – there was a date-plate on the wall, though they couldn't *quite* make out exactly what it said: '89, maybe? '88? – and though it had been put together using the simplest materials – red brick, which seemed kind of out of keeping with the dark sandstone of the other houses on the street; the brick seemed not to have weathered *at all* in the intervening thirty years – it had *accessorised* up. The huge porch-stroke-conservatory which formed the left-hand side of the house looked like a shoulder-pad. The hanging baskets which dangled from every drainpipe or ledge – or so it seemed – were mad earrings. The blinded windows could have been wearing eye-liner.

There was no way of knowing how far back the house went, but even judging from the length of the front of the house it had to contain six, seven bedrooms. And then there was the carefully manicured lawn out front, which drenched with water features, rockeries, summer seating areas. There were patios – two of them – littered with pot-plants and benches and barbecues. An antique swing under the shade of one of the conifers.

After considering Long's house for a long moment, Ads gave a low whistle, in the manner of a builder or architect. Then: 'This is the house that drugs built, yeah?'

'Yup,' I said. A pause. Then: 'You probably paid for his extension, mate, what with all the cola you've been changing.'

I saw the corner of Ads' mouth twitching, itching to say something. Then at last: 'I don't think I can do this, mate. I really don't. Maybe I should just wait in the car.'

I squared my jaw. 'I don't want to be here either, but we've no choice.'

Still he made no move to get out the car. We watched a gate whirr open about five houses up. The nose of a sleek, black BMW peeked out. I tried to make out the driver, but the windows were tinted and I could only see shadow. Then, after a long moment, the car growled out the gates and purred away

217

down the crescent. We both took in the personalised number plate and tutted.

Then the silence grew between us until it became something I had to pop. 'Let's just get this over with, eh?'

I unclunked, unclicked, then clambered out the TT. Ads, however, remained pinned to the driver's seat. I let him take a moment. I looked over Long's house. I realised that despite the obvious ostentatious *look* of the house, it also seemed guarded. Every single curtain or blind in every single window at the front of the house had been pulled tightly closed, blocking out the 'park view' in one fell swoop.

I walked round to the driver side of the Audi and rapped on the window. 'Come on, pal. Time's up.'

And finally, sulkily, he got out the car. Sighed over to the front gate in my wake. The front gate seemed to have been designed to resemble a portcullis, if portcullises had huge Beware of the Dog signs on them. There was an intercom button on the side of it. I pressed it and the only response was a volley of rabid barks from the dogs we were supposed to beware of.

At last we heard a crackle, some fumbling, and then a huffy voice moaned through the intercom: 'Yeah? What do you want?'

Phoebe.

'Hi, Phoebe,' I said. 'D'you remember us? We met you at the café on David Street. With your dad.'

'I meet a lot of folks,' she grouched.

'Yeah, well, we remember you. It's not often we get to meet a… well, weren't you the number one fan of some boy band or other?'

I could hear the boredom in her voice. 'Why are you here?'

What, on this planet?

'We're here to see your dad.'

'You got an appointment?' said Phoebe in a monotone so flat we couldn't even make out whether it was a question or a statement.

'Yup,' I confirmed. 'He sent for us.'

There was another buzz and then the intercom went dead. The gate swung open painfully slowly and we passed through onto the long loose-gravel driveway which led up to the house.

We knocked, eliciting another fireworks display of miscellaneous barks, whines and growls from the pack inside. *Christ, how many dogs were there?* Eventually Phoebe answered the door. Seven, maybe eight years old and already she was slouching like a regular teenager. She was wearing a crop-top which had the legend *BABE* scrawled across it in glittery font. Leggings. Platform shoes. Her hair was scraped back so much it looked painful. She mashed her teeth around a wad of gum as she weighed us up.

'Hi, *Feebs,*' I said. 'What's this, you training to be a nurse when you grow up?' Thinking of Nurse Jackie at the LGI.

She sneered. 'No. Why would I wanna do that?'

Exactly. She'd probably never have to work in her life. 'Your dad in?'

She folded her arms across the *BABE* text. 'You brought me a present?'

I wondered whether this was the usual way to get past this petulant gatekeeper. Ads fished around in his pockets and came out with a stick of Juicy Fruit. She curled her lip, but took it anyway. Spat her old gum in the foil and replaced it in her mouth with the new.

'So, are you going to show us in now?'

A huge Rottweiler padded up to Feebs and nosed at her belly. She scratched its ears and it seemed to *purr.* But then it looked up at us, and that purr turned into a growl.

Phoebe looked delighted. 'Don't worry. Hog here wouldn't harm a fly.'

'You called your dog Hog?'

She wrinkled her nose. 'Not after a pig, *dummy.* After a bike. My dad loves bikes. Harleys and the like.'

'How many dogs you got in there?'

She scratched her head. 'Eight, maybe?'

'And they all as big as Hog?'

219

She *beamed.* 'Hog's the smallest. A runt, really.'

I gulped.

She ushered us inside. We had to hopscotch around various piles of dog turd on the floor and dance around Hog, too, who kept muscling into our paths and trying to knock us off our feet. 'He's only playing,' said Phoebe.

We passed three, four doors leading off the hallway until at last she showed us into a formal sitting room. It was a vast expanse of *whiteness* (white sofas, white armchairs, white rugs) apart from one gigantic baby Doberman. It seemed delighted by our presence and rewarded us by jumping up, applying a litany of licks to our faces.

'That's Killer,' said Phoebe. 'We bought him to train up as a guard dog. It's not really working.' She clicked her fingers. '*Killer.* You're not supposed to be in here. Daddy would *kill* you if he saw you in here.'

Killer sulked out of the room and joined Hog at the doorway, looking in.

'Why don't you sit down,' said Phoebe. 'I'll go tell Dad you're here.'

I looked at the sofas suspiciously, couldn't believe they'd stayed so white, what with the dogs. Then sat down. The sofa was so low that I didn't quite know how to sit on it properly.

Phoebe left, and the baby Doberman followed her, but Hog, the Rott, stayed on the threshold, shooting us evils.

We waited, and we waited.

'How long do we wait?' said Ads. He was pacing the floor. Kept going to the window, looking out at the car as though he wanted to get back into it by a process of osmosis. (Hog growled every time he touched the blinds.)

I blew out my cheeks. 'Piece of string. Long'll be trying to make some kind of point. We were late so he'll be late. Just sit down, will you? You're making that dog all antsy.'

Ads collapsed into the sofa and began studying a rogue stain on his tie.

I picked up a magazine off the coffee table and began flicking through the pages.

And then Nathan Long sloped into the room. He was wearing a furry, white dressing gown and flip-flops which showed off terribly gnarled, terrifically hairy toes. He was still drying his bald pate with a towel. He stank of chlorine. There must have been a pool somewhere in the house.

Ads seemed to stiffen in his seat.

Another guy followed Long into the room. The kind of person Carl – with his love of all things Americana, especially films – would have called 'a tall drink of water', and which Ads, in a better mood, maybe would have – no definitely would have – called 'a long streak of piss'. This guy was wearing a penguin suit and my first instinct was: *this guy's the fucking butler.* But he made no move to offer us drinks, nor did he bring out a silver platter piled high with Ferrero Rocher. Instead he kind of lingered by the door like he had about as much status here as one of the dogs.

'Who'd you have to kill to get a pile on this street then?' I said. And then wished I could take it back. I caught the smirk which fizzed and then popped, disappeared, on Long's face. Then the steely look of pure hatred which replaced it.

Long rolled up the sleeve of his dressing gown, all exaggeratedly, like, and took the time to read his sundial of a watch as though it was a long, luxurious narrative that consumed all of him. 'You're late,' he growled.

'Yes. You see, our mate, Carl, the one who you called, he's *in hospital.*' I realised I'd probably snapped this too forcefully. Lightened my tone. 'We only got the call late.'

Long smacked his lips together. 'He couldn't discharge himself? There's nowt wrong with him. My guys said.'

I held up my hands in a surrender gesture. 'I can't speak for Carl.'

Long sniffed. 'Right, so you're just the monkey. I send for the organ grinder and I get *you*.' He shifted his gaze onto Ads, but still addressed me. 'And what's wrong with your pal.

He looks *wired.* I can't have fucking druggies coming in my house.'

All at once I felt a wave of nausea crashing through me. The claustrophobia of Long's front room; the stink of chlorine which was seemingly emanating from Long's every pore. The dogs. The guy in the penguin suit by the door. It was all *too much.*

Ads, thankfully, stepped up to the plate. 'I'm not a druggie, Mr Long. I've just been working hard is all.'

Long tugged at a strand of his goatee beard. 'You forget, boy, that you get your gear from *my* men.' *His men. And here was me thinking they were a collective. A co-op.*

'I'm fine,' said Ads. 'Honestly, I am. Straight as a die.'

Long continued to stroke his beard. 'I could test you, you know. I got the gear for that, don't I, Verity?'

The penguin-suited guy nodded.

I decided I'd better step in again. 'Look, we haven't come here to talk about drugs. We came here because *you* asked.* Carl didn't tell me why. He just said it was something along the lines of the La Scala thing.'

Long flip-flopped over to the armchair and fell into it. The chair creaked in complaint at his bulk. From somewhere in the house, we heard the din of Phoebe's music being turned on, and the accompanying howls from the pack of dogs. 'I don't know which is worse: that new crap she deafens herself with or the dogs complaining about it.'

The new crap was, I realised with a start, Cool Croc. And here was me thinking those guys were bleeding-edge. And here was me thinking their tunes were so new nobody – not even their creators – had heard them before. Those guys were getting all kinds of too commercial.

'Shut the door, will you, Verity?'

Verity did as he was asked, and Hog was not best pleased. We heard him scratching at the other side, whining to be let in. Verity, though, was unmoved. Stood by the jamb with his arms crossed, his face a wall.

'Good,' said Long. 'Right, lads, let's get down to business, then, eh?'

We both nodded.

'Okay, so your pal Carl told you I was after a similar kind of deal to the La Scala thing. And that's correct.' He held up a finger. 'But it's not *everything.* You see, I wanna tell you a story. Once upon a time, when I was a little fucker growing up in Wakefield, I had a dream. It wasn't like the dreams my pals had. I didn't want to grow up to play for Leeds United or Yorkshire Cricket. I didn't want to be in the army or whatever. What I wanted to do more than anything was ride hogs. I saw this film about a man driving across America on this lovely big hog and I just thought, *That's for me.'*

I wasn't quite sure where Long was going with this, but I knew better than to interrupt.

'I liked everything about the hogs. How shiny they were. The noise they made. How riding them looked like freedom. And so, when I was old enough, I got about five jobs so I could save up to get a starter bike. Nothing big. Just a 125cc. One of those jobs, incidentally, was working the bar at the local working men's. I was only sixteen but nobody gave a shit in those days. Besides, I was a big fucker by then. And after a while, they asked me to work on their doors for them, and that was my first taste of the bouncing game. Been in it thirty-odd years now.'

I whistled, like I was very impressed.

'So anyways, I got my 125. A little Honda. Crappy thing really but I loved it. Gave me my freedom, it did, so I never had to stay in Wakefield. I could escape. Explore. Go places. But, see, I still needed money on account of I wanted a bigger bike. Believe you me, lads, there is always a bigger bike. So I got in deeper with the bouncing. Got a couple jobs over in Leeds. Made a few buddies. Mostly, they were biker types, just like me. On Sundays, no matter how late we'd worked on Saturday night, we'd go for a ride. We went all over the place. The coast, mainly. Up by Whitby. That way.'

'Nice,' said Ads, probably to stop himself from falling asleep.

Long looked up, sharply. 'Am I boring you, Adam?'

'No… I was just saying I like it up that way.'

Long tutted. '*Anyway*, so what we had us was a little motorbike crew. Oh, we weren't like Hells Angels or anything like that. But we were tight. And we egged each other on to go faster, faster. Always faster. Then this one guy – Brutus, you know him?' We shook our heads. 'No matter. He's not on the scene no more. But Brutus he got this leather with *WHO DARES WINS* written in the studs on back. You know, like the SAS motto? And after that, we all got the same and we got to be known as the SAS crew. And that, in a roundabout way, is how SAS bouncing collective started. We was all bikers in them days.'

I really, really wanted to move. It felt like I was playing Musical Statues and whenever Long paused to take a breath, I had to stay as still as a corpse. I forced myself to think of something, anything else so as to take my mind off moving. And for some reason, The Nat sprang into my mind.

'When SAS started, we had lots of work, and we just kept on getting more. In the end, we had to knock those Sunday rides on the head on account of we needed a day to catch up on all the admin, the tax returns. The like. It wasn't supposed to be that way. And then Feebs came along and we always needed more money. For nursery stuff, for a swing set, for a new house, for a family car, for *every damned thing.* So I worked even harder. But in here' – he slapped his chest – 'I still dreamt of the open road, of a big hog, and of America.'

He paused and, for a beat, two, I thought he was crying. But it was just a snail-trail of sweat from his bald pate.

'Last week, a company named EyeSpy Security – they do systems: CCTV and the like – tabled an offer for SAS. See they wanted a manned guarding and site security division to add to their, like, portfolio… Seven mill, give or take. I shook hands on the deal yesterday at right about the same time Adam here was kicking up such a fuss in the LGI.'

'Congratulations,' I said. 'That must be – '

'Complicated,' said Long. 'I'm leaving a few people in the lurch. Can't help it. I reckon it's a case of now or never.

See, I still got that dream and this might be my last chance to follow through on it. You're not blind, lads. You can see I'm a big guy. A heart attack waiting to happen. Way I see it is, if I don't do it now, take the whole tribe - wife, Feebs, maybe Verity, even – over to the US now, I'll never get to do Route 66.'

'People'll understand,' I said. 'You've worked hard all your life. Now's when you get your reward.'

'Yeah, but as I say, it's complicated. This reward? The seven mill? I won't get all of it. Every single SAS bouncer is a shareholder. You know that. Also, there are conditions to the deal, before everything gets ratified, you know? Before we sign on the dotted line. They want to look into our books.'

'There shouldn't be a problem with that,' I said. 'Carl made them watertight.'

'They also want to look into cash flow. All that jazz. And you see, there are certain *undeclared incomes* we need cleaned up before their accountants take a look. You hearing me?'

'Loud and clear,' I said. Thinking: *Oh shit.*

'So the reason I called you lads here today is I want you to look after the last few quid from our, ahem, sideline operation.'

'How much is a few quid?'

Long stroked his goatee. 'Get the case, Verity, won't you?'

Verity nodded and opened the door. Hog came bounding into the room like the fucking Hound of the Baskervilles. 'Get out!' barked Long. And the dog retreated, tail between his legs. Verity came back clutching a briefcase and it was this – the fact it wasn't a *SLAZENGER* bag – which convinced me we were talking telephone numbers.

'Open it,' said Long.

Verity obliged.

Inside was more money than I'd ever seen in my life. It took my breath away.

'There's a cool mill in there, lads, give or take. And I expect to see every penny of it *clean and new* in my account before we up sticks to America for six months.'

'When's that?'

'Plane tickets are booked for the end of the month.'

'That gives us two weeks. Less. You can't expect—'

'I *do* expect. That's the thing, Neal, I expect.'

'I don't think – '

'Well *don't* think, then. Just do it. Remember, who dares wins.'

I felt like I might faint then. I felt like I might slip into the sofa and never appear out of it again. I glanced over at Ads and saw he was just as shell-shocked as me. His face had gone a whiter shade of pale. He scratched incessantly at his birthmark.

'Right then,' said Long, standing up and dabbing at the sweat on his brow with the towel. 'Storytime's over. Now it's time to work-work-work.'

Verity showed us out. I barely remember anything about our journey to the door. Might have *coated* my shoes in dog turd for all I knew. I *think* we mumbled a brief 'good luck' and a 'bon voyage' to Long before we left, and I think there might have been handshakes all round. But I couldn't be sure.

When we got to the car, Ads was shaking so hard he couldn't work the central-locking button on his key-fob and in the end I had to wrestle the keys off him and do it myself. 'You okay to drive?' I asked him.

'I need a drink,' he said. 'God, I need a drink.'

I had to walk him round to the passenger side and tuck him in the front seat, like he was some kind of elderly relative on a monthly trip to the shops. I felt creaky and old myself, and absent-minded too. After I'd somehow managed to key the ignition and gun the engine, I mirror-signal-manoeuvred out onto Park View and I discovered – thanks to a loud, indignant beep – that I'd somehow managed to blind-spot out the BMW which was already on the road. I only missed hitting it by the skin of my Colgate-whites.

Ads didn't even seem to have registered the near miss. He sat, rigid in the seat, gripping the case like he'd been handcuffed to it.

I drove back into town and it felt like I'd driven the whole of Route 66. Parked up in the Long Stay and Ads was still rigid, gripping the case like his life depended on it. Probably, it did.

'What do we do now?' I said.

No answer.

I pulled out my Nokia and buzzed Carl. No answer from him either.

I looked over at Ads again, and the case. And I decided there was no way I wanted to walk through Leeds with *that* on me. And I couldn't trust Ads with it either. Not in his condition. So what was I supposed to do? I tried Carl again, and again the phone slipped right onto voicemail.

What to do, what to do, what to do?

'Adam,' I said. 'Hand me the case.'

At first he seemed reluctant, or maybe he'd simply not heard me. I asked again, and this time he passed it over. The minute he let go of it, he seemed to collect himself all over again. It was as though the case, or rather what was inside it, had cast some kind of spell over him.

'My dad spoke hardly a word of English,' he said. 'Did you know that?'

'Um, yeah, mate. You've told me.'

'But he did say some things and what he said was, it doesn't matter what you become as long as you become a good man. We're not good men, are we, Neal? This type of thing does not happen to good men. Good men never even get in this situation.'

I thought back to what The Nat had taught me about cause and effect, and choices. And I thought about what I'd learned about myself: which was, I was willing to *try* to be good, as long as it wasn't too difficult. Then I always made the easy choice, took the low road. 'No,' I admitted. 'We're not good.'

'Well then,' said Ads. 'We must drink. Forget about how bad we are.'

'I can't face a drink now, mate. My head's in bits as it is.'

'I can't face *not*-drink.'

'Well, then, you go to the pub. I'll go home. Tomorrow, we talk. We go to the hospital. See Carl. Try and find a way out of this... Or, or a way forward. Something.'

'Okay,' said Ads, and off he went.

Leaving me with the case. I thought about how stupid, how amateur-hour my plan for its safekeeping actually was and then I thought about how stupid, how amateur-hour it would be to actually have the case in my flat, where anyone might find it. And I decided I was right, because there was no other way. So I walked over to the International Pool. It wasn't far. Just round the corner. And I swung into the liquid silence of the changing rooms. And I found my old locker. And I eased it open. And inside went the case, underneath a pile of shirts. And then I closed the door and I locked it and I walked away, into the future and into the past, all my roads converging at once.

The Nat was waiting outside the main front door to the flats on Eastgate. I knew it was her instantly, despite the fact she'd had her hair cut quite dramatically short and had allowed the natural colour – auburn – to return. She looked all kinds of relaxed. She wasn't the ten-to-the-dozen person I'd met nearly a year ago. She was leaning against the wall, her leg tucked up into a lazy sideways V beneath her. An arm hung limply at her side; a plume of cigarette smoke trailing out from the snout in her hand.

I wasn't even surprised to see her. It was just one of those days, the days in which chickens come home to roost.

She hadn't spotted me yet through the Primark crowds and I took a moment to study her in more detail. She didn't look as though she was dressed by Primark now. Nor did she look like she'd been dressed by the kind of high-end stores Primark copied. No, she'd found her own style. That was the white star of a Converse trainer pressed against the red-brick wall of the Eastgate bookend. Her summery dress looked like something I'd seen my mum wearing in old photos from the 60s, before the Golden Goose robbed both her and Dad of their youth and any glamour they'd possessed.

I approached her like she was a rare breed; the real leopard of the Leodian safari. Carefully. Easy does. Don't want to frighten her off. But she didn't look like *anything* could frighten her. She looked kind of above it all.

I wondered what she wanted from me and I wondered at myself that this hadn't been my first thought upon seeing her (no, that had been that she was beautiful). I should have hated her. I should have been wary of her at the very least. After all, she'd *blackmailed* me. But I didn't and I wasn't. And I reckoned the reason I didn't immediately think she was here for more money – which, admittedly would have been all kinds of a safe bet, especially so soon after Rachel's surprise visit – was because she looked so damned *self-possessed*. So easy in her own skin. She didn't look awkward and out of place, as Rachel had. Nor was there that sense, as there was with Rachel, that she had to talk to herself, talk to herself, talk to herself in order to keep herself stuck in place. With Rachel, now that I looked back on the moment I'd spotted her in reception at PWC, I'd had the sense she was rehearsing every threat she was going to make to me, and she was promising herself it would all be worth it in the end.

Somehow, with Natalie, it almost looked as though the end had already been reached. I wished I could have looked so effortlessly happy. I wondered whether I could ever get that way again.

She saw me and she smiled and her smile was genuine; her genuine first instinct after seeing me was to smile. So go figure, you accountants.

I invited her in. I hadn't known I was going to until I opened my mouth. I didn't ask her why she was here, because that would have spoiled things and I wanted something which *wasn't* ruined beyond all repair.

We drank. I'd told Ads I didn't want to, and back then a drink had been the furthest thing from my mind, but in my flat, with Natalie, it just felt like the natural thing to do. Eventually she told me why she was back. At the time, we'd both been closing in on the bottom of, well, it might have been our second, or fourth, bottle. Certainly we'd tasted our way through the couple *good bottles,* the ones I kept in the fancy wine rack in the front room, and had moved on to the ones I kept at the back of the tin cupboard. The vinegar vintages. The rainy day bottles.

Over the past year or so, I'd had a lot of rainy days.

We had pushed the sofa back against the wall and were sitting cross-legged and swaying around the low coffee table, *communing.* It felt a little like black magic, like a séance. And finally, the drinks unstoppered her tongue enough to tell me she was back because she wanted to return my money. My loan, she called it, and I didn't pick her up on the fact it had actually been blackmail.

After that, I told her I had a million quid so I didn't need her money, and then the whole story came out. All of it. At first, talking about it like trying to pull out a splinter which had worked its way so far below the skin even tweezers couldn't wrench it out. But eventually it poured out of me like vomit.

She didn't seem shocked. Perhaps she was too drunk for that. She told me I should take the money and run. What the fuck was stopping me?

'Nathan Long,' I said.

She shook her head in a very exaggerated way. 'Nuh-uh,' she said. 'What's stopping you is your own, like, attitude.'

And yeah, she was probably right.

And the next day, I remembered that feeling of *rightness* very well. But *after* that moment, my mind was a blank. I couldn't remember a single thing which had passed between us. All I knew was, I woke up as the light speared through a slight gap in the blinds and I appeared to be on my sofa, in my front room, only the sofa wasn't where it usually was in the room (*oh yeah, I'd pushed it back against the wall*) and I appeared to be covered with – yes it was! – a towel from out the bathroom.

My head felt like a wrecking ball had been taken to it and my guts bubbled and broiled like some terrible broth was being concocted in it and my mouth was some workshop of filthy creation and I was busting for a piss, but despite all that I felt remarkably *well.* It was as though pulling the scab off the wound of the last year and actually *talking about it* had made me better.

I tossed off the towel and got up. It was something of a mistake: I wobbled alarmingly, like I hadn't gotten my sea legs yet. The world wobbled. And then righted itself on its axis. I picked my way through an ocean of mostly finished wine bottles and empty fag packets and a couple pizza boxes – had we ordered in last night? I had no recollection of doing so, yet the Milano's boxes said otherwise – and out into the hallway, where the lights were blazing.

My bedroom door was open a crack and I desperately wanted to peek through. For surely The Nat was inside. Surely I'd done the gentlemanly thing and let her have the bed (stale though the sheets were). But for now I didn't have the balls to, and besides, I was dying for the loo. So I went into the bathroom and promptly turned around and walked straight back out again. One of us had been sick during the night – most likely me, judging by the terrible taste in my mouth; though that might have been leftover Milano's and bad wine – and had mostly missed the toilet. But then the urge to pee became unbearable and I went right back in there, closed my eyes to the mess, and pissed for Yorkshire.

After I'd finished, I washed up a little and then I steeled myself; went back out and knocked softly on my bedroom door. 'Natalie,' I whisper-croaked.

There was no answer. '*Natalie!*'

Nothing. Gently I pushed the door. Slowly it swung open. A strange gloaming light filled my bedroom and it took me a while to realise it was coming from my reading-light on my bedside table: I hadn't done any reading since I'd embarked on my career as an accountant. Next to the reading light was a half-full glass of red wine and the sight of it almost sent me racing back across the hallway to the bathroom to throw up again.

The bed was unmade. For some reason, whatever mess the rest of my life was in, I always made my bed. It was a hangover from the Golden Goose days, when my mum would never give me my Coco-Pops until she'd performed a spot check on my little cabin room. So Natalie *had* slept here. She hadn't simply done a bunk in the middle of the night. Made off with my good silver (or at least, the collection of pound coins I kept in a jar in my front room). But where was she now? My flat might have been a penthouse, but it wasn't spacious. There were four rooms in it, and that included the hallway. So far this morning I'd been in every one of them and there'd been no sighting of the lesser-spotted Natalie. Bleary-eyed as I was, I couldn't have missed her.

So where was she?

A thought struck me so suddenly, so sickeningly, I had to sit on the end of the bed until the initial shock of it blew over some. *Christ, I'd told her about the million quid, hadn't I? I'd told her fucking everything.* I couldn't recall doing so, but what if I'd also told her about where I'd stashed it, for safekeeping? What if I'd dangled the key in front of her, like some wine-o gameshow host, and told her how close she was to walking away with the main prize?

What the hell had she done?

What in fuck had I done?

What in buggery would I tell Carl, Ads?

How would we explain it to Nathan Long?

I could picture her now, perched on a bench at Leeds train station, the case on her lap and a sunny smile on her face, waiting while the London train pulled in. At King's Cross she'd make a brief stop-over while she exchanged some of the money. And then she'd hot-foot it over to the airport and she'd be away. The world was her oyster. She could go anywhere. Route fucking 66, if she wanted.

No. That picture wasn't quite right. Over our first bottle last night she'd told me, briefly, about her new life. And it still very much involved her son, Jake. So *he'd* be in the picture. Sweet little Jake with his Alan Smith hair. So maybe she'll have hitched back down to – was it Nottingham she said she'd moved? I thought so – Nottingham and picked him up en route to somewhere else. Somewhere good for kids. Where was good for kids?

Why the hell was I worrying about that?

A thought tolled through me clear as a bell: I needed to check on the locker key. I needed *proof* she'd done what I feared she'd done. I kept the key on a, well, I suppose you'd call it a telephone wire; a tight-spiralled cord fixed into my wallet. I patted myself down, like I was searching for drugs. Though I was fully clothed, there was no wallet.

I strip-searched my room. No cigar. Then the hallway. *Eee-uuuuhhh.* The bathroom. No, siree. Then back into the front room.

The minute I clapped eyes on my wallet, tucked almost sorrowfully between two sofa cushions, I heard the front door go, then swing back on its hinges and slam shut. Then Natalie breezed into the room carrying two Styrofoam cups of coffee. 'Morning, sleepyhead,' she said. 'You had no bleeding milk in the place so I went out for some brews. You look like you need one.'

I was speechless.

She wasn't. Just like the first time we'd met, back at The Townhouse, she talked ten-to-the-dozen, like a goddamned machine gun. She filled in some of my huge gaps from last night: yes, we'd ordered pizza and yes, it was rotten, just like she remembered it; Milano's never changed, no matter how long you were away from Leeds. Yes, we'd talked shit. Yes, I'd passed out 'right in the middle of me telling you about Jakey's new school!' And yes, embarrassingly, she'd put me to bed (well, the sofa) and yes, she'd tucked me in under the towel because she couldn't find a blanket anywhere in the place. She'd have put me in my bed, but she tried carrying me and I was a dead weight.

And yes, there was the money. 'What are you going to spend it all on? If it was me, I'd splash out on a nice house. A car maybe. Put some away for Jake. The rest I'd squander on champagne.'

I winced. 'It isn't my money. I'm just holding it.'

'Yeah, well,' she shrugged. 'That was how I justified taking that money from you. And that's why I want to give it back.'

I didn't really know what to say. I didn't *want* it back.

'Take a walk with me, Neal,' she said. 'I want to see how much has changed in nine months. It seems like everywhere I look there's a new building or something.'

So I did, and afterwards I really wished I hadn't, because outside there was another snake, this one a great, twisting, mouthy thing, and it swallowed me up and sent me back right to the beginning.

III

We walked aimlessly at first. The Nat wanted to look in through this shop window and then that one. The crowds carried us this way then that way. For the first time in my life, I found myself looking up, studying some of the beautiful architecture of the buildings *above* the shops. The ornate domes of the markets. The elegant Georgian stonework of this place or that. The like.

We bought hotdogs from a van round the back of Debenhams and I surprised myself by wolfing it down. Soon we found ourselves on Albion Place, where, amongst the many mobile phone shops and jewellery stores and shoe shops, was La Scala. It wasn't in my mind we were coming to La Scala until very late and I realised that this was because there was no opera blaring out of it today. Usually, all you'd have to do was turn onto Albion Place and *La Traviata* or *Turandot* would guide you home. But today, it was silent. And that was odd.

The closer we got to Mama's place, the odder it seemed. Used to be she'd set up a few tables outside in case the sun poked through the clouds for an hour. No tables today. Nor was there a bevy of people outside, queuing to get in. Indeed, the place seemed deserted.

The place *was* deserted. The front door was boarded up. The windows were whitewashed over. There was a sign posted to the door and it read that the place had been repossessed. My heart skipped a beat. Had something happened to Mama? Had we caused that thing to happen?

An Andersen-type guy (though he wasn't Andersen, I didn't think: maybe DLA Piper) in a smart charcoal-grey rain mac approached and read the sign too.

'I keep coming back, hoping I was wrong. Hoping the place hasn't shut. But I'm fooling myself.' I wasn't sure whether he was talking to me, Natalie or himself. Or even the sign posted to the door.

'When did this happen?' I asked him.

'A couple of days ago.' His voice was a shrug. 'Can't get a decent cup anywhere in town now.'

'Do you know what happened?'

The Andersen-type guy pulled a *well, you're talking to the right fella here, mate* face. 'Dawn raid by the police, believe it or not. Closed the place immediately. Carted old Camilla off in cuffs, is what I heard. Financial irregularities, is what I heard too. Mind you, I shouldn't be surprised. She told me her accountants were Arthur Andersen.'

The Andersen-type guy walked off, his hunt for a good coffee beginning all over again.

Natalie said: 'What's the big deal? It's only a café, like. Things change. *Everything's* changed in this city.'

I bit my lip. 'You don't understand.'

She looked a little hurt. 'Yeah, well, whatever. What do you wanna do now?'

'Now I need to make a phone call.' But I didn't know who to call. I couldn't bring myself to try Carl at the hospital, even though he'd surely have gotten all the gen on La Scala, and I didn't want to call Ads because... well, Adam wasn't Ads anymore. So who? *Who?*

I scrolled through my phone book and maybe it was because his name came under 'B' so was near the top of the list, or maybe because I'd been subconsciously thinking of him anyway, I stopped at Nick Byers' number. I called him before I lost my nerve. I didn't think he'd answer. I thought he'd be home, home on the driving range. But I was wrong. He picked up after just two rings, before I'd even collected myself enough to think of what I was going to say, how I was going to broach the subject.

'Grace,' he said, gravely. 'I've been expecting your call.'

'Wh-what? How?'

'Let's just call it my sixth sense. Remember when you knew I was somewhere up high, when I called you to invite you to interview? Like that.'

'O-kay.'

'So, you want to meet up? Now?'

'I definitely need to talk. I need to know what's going on.'

'Not over the phone. I'll come meet you. Where are you now?'

'Albion Place. By La Scala... or what was La Scala.'

'Right. Meet me at Sartori's, then. Give it half an hour.'

He rang off.

'What's going on?' said The Nat. 'Something's spooked you.'

I ran a cold, sweaty hand over my face. 'Seems like the past year all I've been doing is trying to keep all the plates spinning, but now they're all crashing down. I can't think fast enough. I can't *move* fast enough.'

The Nat shrugged. 'So quit trying. I used to feel that way too and then I just thought stuff it, concentrate on what's important. What's important to you, Neal? Keep that plate spinning and sod the rest of them.'

'I... I don't know.' It was true. Used to be the answer to that question would have been my friends, my job, my lifestyle. But not so much anymore. They were all of them compromised.

'Well, you need to take a long, hard think, then. But Neal? Things can get better. They can get fixed. I mean, look at me, for Christ's sake. I was sinking up here. Drowning. A change of scenery was all it took.'

I hung my head. 'I'm not sure it'll be that easy.'

She gripped my arm. 'It *can* be. I mean, look at this place.' She gestured at the empty café. 'Been here donkey's and one day it's just gone. What if that spod in the grey rain mac had it wrong. What if it wasn't financial irregularities? What if that old woman who owned it just woke up one morning and thought stuff it? What if *she* needed a change of scenery? And if she could do it, she who's a proper Leeds institution, then you could too. You're not even from Leeds, are you?'

I thought I could guess exactly what Mama's new scenery would look like but I didn't want to say. I didn't even want to imagine. What had we done to that poor, poor woman?

I checked my watch. 'I'm sorry, Natalie. I've got to go meet someone.'

'And you don't want me tagging along, is that it?' She mimed an offended face, but spoiled it by grinning. 'Don't worry about it. I've already outstayed my welcome with you.'

'It's not that,' I said. 'It's just... I don't want you getting embroiled in any of this mess. I really don't.'

Her smile faded a little but didn't disappear completely. 'You forget. I'm already involved. And I just wanted to say I was sorry again, just in case this is the last time I see you.'

'You don't need to.'

'I do.' She stood on her tiptoes, then surprised me by pecking me on the cheek. Then, before I could do something stupid like kissing her back, she turned away and walked off into the Albion Place crowds. And I stood there for the longest time trying to work out just what in hell I was feeling. Although I lost sight of her, I could still feel the tingle on my cheek from where she'd had her lips, and the farther she got away from me, the more that tingle tingled, as though there was still something connecting us – though it had pulled taut – and that thing might be like chewing-gum on the sole of a shoe, stretching out as the shoe lifted off the pavement. Weird, I know.

Before I could put my finger on it properly, she returned. 'Sorry,' she said, 'I just wanted to say one more thing because I know what boys can be like, never changing their bedding and all that.'

I was confused: what was she talking about bedding for?

'I put your two K under your pillow. I just wanted to make sure it was safe. But then I got to thinking: what if you didn't go back to bed today? You've got that *flight* look in your eyes. I know it well. I used to see it every time I looked in the mirror when I lived in Leeds. So all I wanted to say was, you've got your money back, if you need it. If you need quick cash to make your getaway.'

I tried to tell her I didn't need it, but the truth was, I was no longer sure. Maybe I *could* make a run for it before any of this got any worse. Two grand would see me through at least a couple of weeks while I got settled somewhere; I could charge an estate agency with getting shot of the flat. Somehow, anonymously, send the locker key up to Carl so he could clear up the Nathan Long mess. Write a grovelling letter of apology to Mama... Cut my losses. Escape.

Natalie ignored my pleas for her to take the money back. She walked away again and this time it felt like forever. And I set out for Sartori's.

Sartori's was a new Italian place down on Granary Wharf. Despite its newness, it wasn't a patch on La Scala. I hadn't been but I knew it was the current restaurant of choice amongst the kind of *it* crowd of which I used to be a member, mainly, it appeared, because it was very expensive and, in a kind of Emperor's New Clothes type way, that convinced everyone it was good. At least for now. At least until the next new restaurant opened up and over-cut them with its over-priced menu.

I stood for a while outside Sartori's and wondered whether I'd been mistaken. Maybe the place was the *next* next big thing for it looked as though it hadn't properly opened yet. It seemed as though if I pushed through the glass double doors I'd be jumping the gun, stepping over the threshold *just before* the proprietors could seal it off with a red ribbon some local dignitary was supposed to cut with oversized scissors. But then I saw a couple early diners on a couple tables over by the window which looked out over the river and I decided it was open for business after all. Still, as I walked in, I thought I could discern the smell of fresh paint in the air and when I looked at the arrangement of the tables... well, it looked as though management were in the middle of *feng-shui*ing up the place but had been distracted at the last.

I couldn't see hide nor hair of Nick Byers and I thought about going back outside to wait for him, but before I could turn tail a white-shirted, black-waistcoated, walking, talking stereotype of a waiter meerkatted up from behind the bar and shouted for me to *wait please!* He scurried out from his bar and came out to greet me. He seemed disappointed when I told him I only wanted a drink, not food.

I sat at the bar, just far enough away from a couple Ladies Who Lunched. Their tall stools rose up from seas of Harvey Nicks shopping bags on the floor and they hoovered up their luminous cocktails through straws, barely pausing to draw breath.

The waiter who was also a barman asked me what I was having. They had an excellent house red, if I'd like to give it a try. I couldn't think of anything worse, so I opted for a bottle of Peroni, which, though it might take some of the edge off, wouldn't completely smooth me over into a state of memory loss like last night. The bottle came out the fridge cold and wet and begging for me to down it in one, but I paced myself.

As I nursed it, I thought of the last two occasions I'd seen Nick Byers. On both of them, he'd seemed odd. *Off.* I considered how he'd been at my flat before we'd gone to the driving range up at Wike Ridge. Some of the glamour had been rubbed off him, it seemed. Grey was starting to show around the edges. He'd looked somewhat dishevelled, not at all like the kind of man you'd always imagine standing atop a tall building, looking down on everyone else. I'd always known him as an open, engaging man, the kind of guy who was always the host. But, for the first time, I'd seen a secretive side to him. Frankly, he'd seemed anxious, not at all the man of steely nerve and conviction I'd once known. Same with that final time I'd seen him, in the revolving doors at One City Square. That strange look which had passed between us. That feeling he was trying to warn me off something.

He knew, I decided. I wasn't sure how and I wasn't sure why, but he knew something was going down and he wanted me away from it.

I was so deep in my thoughts I didn't notice him arrive. The Ladies Who Lunched did and it was their slightly over-the-top giggling which alerted me to his presence. I saw them give him the once-over and I saw their appreciation of his get-up; he was wearing the right clothes. Sober but expensive – obviously expensive – tailored gear. Shoes so well polished when he hung his head he could grin at himself, tip himself the wink. But when he got closer, I decided he hadn't grinned or winked in a while. He carried a sad air with him, like he'd been struck down by grief, and the Ladies Who Lunched hadn't sunk enough of their cocktails not to sniff this out. They turned away from him and went back to their drinks.

I climbed off my stool to greet him. There was a rather awkward shoulder-tapping moment which *should* have translated itself into a man-hug but didn't. Byers scratched his head like he was trying to remember his lines for the role of host, then, feigning enthusiasm, rubbed his hands together and said: 'Right, drinks. Whaddle it be?'

I held up my only quarter-drunk Peroni and said I was okay.

Byers ordered a Bushmills. Rocks. Maybe he'd been sharing his troubles with Paul, the security guy in the Andersen building. While we were waiting for this to be served up, a third Lady Who Lunched turned up to meet the pair who were already ensconced at the bar. And then it was all shrieks of excitement and ubiquitous air-kisses and hugs and *oh, don't you look nices* and rummaging around through bags, and I thought, fake as it all was, it was at least more real than the awkward meeting Byers and I had just shared.

At last the waiter brought over the whisky and Byers said we should go find a table somewhere a bit quieter so we could talk. I followed, and we found a pew tucked under the archway and, *ah, didn't that take me back to happier times, to the night when Carl got the bouncers to beat seven shades out of the Neanderthals...? The night which started all this.*

We both took a moment to collect our thoughts. I spun my bottle of Peroni around on the beermat; Byers sniffed his whisky but didn't drink it, simply placed it back on the table. Then, half-heartedly: 'So, Grace, how's it hanging?'

I pulled a face. Then lied: 'Okay.'

'From where I'm standing, that's a lie. You look a little bit – '

'Hung over. Yeah. Plus I feel exhausted from running around trying to keep all the plates spinning.'

Nick hmmmphed. 'I'm not sure how good the old spinning-plates analogy is anymore. Doesn't really make the grade, does it? Not after Al Qaeda made the towers disappear.'

It was surely too soon to be saying stuff like that. But then again, maybe Byers was showing me a sign. Telling me nothing was off the table. We could talk about anything. If so, I should tell him he looked every bit as rough as me, nice clothes or not. 'Whatever,' I said. 'It just feels... Things are getting on top of me, that's all, and I called you because you might be able to shed some light on what's gone on.'

Now Byers drank. He thrust his head back and poured the whisky down his throat so that it barely would have touched the sides, then he made a helicopter signal with his finger. *Another round.* While we were waiting, he fiddled with his tie. Turned it wrong-side up as though his script was written there. At last the waiter came over with a drink each and Byers palmed him off with a twenty and a 'Keep the change'. Then at last he talked. Only, as soon as he did I wished I could stop him somehow. I wished I could take those words and push them back down his throat; replace them with new ones. I didn't like what I heard. Not one bit.

He started with a biggie: 'You need to skip town, Grace. You can't be here. The jaws of the bear-trap are closing in.'

And I, of course, asked him what he was talking about. Bear-trap, indeed.

I should have never asked.

The headline news was this: Nick Byers was working as a snitch for the financial crimes squad. Had been working as such for just over a year, ever since a couple shadowy figures named Blake and Deane had come to see him on the hush-hush one day while he'd been out at the driving range. They'd shown him their badges and their papers and they'd asked him to come have a word with them in the back of their car; a big Land Rover with tinted windows. Byers said if it wasn't for the fact he'd seen their badges he'd have been bricking it he was going to take a shot to the head.

Sub-headline was this: Byers'd been caught with his fingers in the till and creaming off the top and practically breaking every financial services code he – along with every Andersen employee – had sworn to uphold. He could proceed directly to jail. He could *not* collect two hundred pounds. He could suffer his name being dragged through the dirt and the courts. Or he could help them out. See, Blake and Deane had peered into the murky pool of Andersen and they'd seen a lot more in the deeps of it than just Byers' 'misdemeanours'. With Byers they were only just dipping at the surface. Apparently the FBI was looking into Andersen dealings across the pond in America. Eventually they might build a multiple-country case which would be bigger – much bigger – than anything Byers could even comprehend.

They presented him with a take-it-or-leave-it, one-time offer. They would cut a deal with him today, but not tomorrow, nor next year or the year after, when all the murk was brought under the spotlight. They wouldn't press charges now, not while there were bigger fish to fry. But he had to help them in this wider investigation into deeper, more systemic fraud at the company.

Byers knocked back his second Bushmills. 'I took what they offered because really there was no choice.'

And I said: 'Fuck.' Because, really, there were no other words. It sounded like the plot of one of Carl's gangster movies rehashed, reheated and translated into Leodian. And, frankly, upon first telling, I couldn't get the whole of it through my thick skull and at first I refused to believe him. This was all a joke. Byers was the bar-room bore who told the one about there not being the word 'gullible' in the dictionary.

But the more I thought about it, the more it made a sickening kind of sense.

The timelines matched. Just over a year ago, Nick had started to look frazzled around the edges for the first time. Nine months or so ago I'd gone to him to see about trying to get around Lightwood and being able to stay on at Andersen. And Nick had flatly refused. Told me it was better for me if I got out. He'd set me up with Price Waterhouse instead. And, ever since I'd come on board at PWC, Andersen had somehow, miraculously, blown us out of the water. Had to be on account of these systemic fraud and dodgy reporting strategies he was talking about.

And yet – no matter how much sense it made if I talked it through with myself, put it into a coherent narrative structure – this was still *Nick Byers,* and we had history. He showed us how we could be princes amongst men. He showed us how to find ourselves as men – how to live, how to act, how to dress – and how to hide the Lost Boy in all of us well away.

'But *you?* You're a' – I'd been about to say 'rat', like this was *GoodFellas,* but I changed my mind at the last minute – 'an informant? For the police?'

He tore at a beermat. 'I am,' he said. He raised his eyes to meet mine and I saw a flash of pride there, before he dropped them again back to the beermat. 'For my sins.'

'I can't believe I'm having this conversation,' I said.

Byers smiled, sadly. The light of it did not reach his eyes. 'I know, right? That whole Blake and Deane crap when they took me out to their Landie. It was like something in one of the pulp fiction comics I used to read when I was a little lad.'

For some reason, I couldn't picture Byers as a little lad. He had to have come out whole and grown right from the off. And I definitely couldn't imagine him as the kind of geek read comics. But then again, maybe he wore a mask to work. Everyone else did, didn't they? Byers was well-practised at hiding his motives from others, but even he'd let his mask slip when he'd had to try and hide being an informant.

Still, I couldn't get my head around it, though. 'How often do you, like, meet them? What sort of stuff have you told them?'

He'd now torn the entire cover off one side of the mat, so he flipped it over and started again on the other side. 'I've told them a lot. Mostly in the past nine months, since you've been off the scene. When they want a meet, they call me up and they say "Time for little Tommy Tittler to come tittle" and I have to drive out to the Little Chef on the A64 to York. The fucking Little Chef, of all places. I swear they do it on purpose to make me feel like crap.'

'You feel guilty?'

'Yeah. No. I don't know. Do you?'

I gulped, then nodded. 'Guilty but also coerced, you know? It feels like my arm's been twisted behind my back this past year.'

We shared a look of if not understanding then at least complicity. 'Well,' said Byers. 'At least nobody's calling *you* Tommy Tittler.'

I lowered my voice as a waiter passed. 'Who else knows about this? Lightwood?'

Byers sneered. 'Lightwood wouldn't know an investigation was going on even if they turned his office over and demanded the passwords to his computer system.'

'What about Carl? Adam?'

'Well, they've been as much in the dark as Lightwood. But they maybe won't be for much longer.'

'What do you mean?'

'I mean the financial crimes guys, Blake and Deane, that's just white-collar shit to the rest of the police. But now other departments have started to get very interested in how this all ties in with some local businessmen who may or not be disreputable. Blake and Deane've tugged at a few threads and the whole thing is starting to unravel now. Hence La Scala going down. But they're not really interested in La Scala. They're more interested in your man Nathan Long. They've been trying to swat that fat fly for so long now, and finally they think they got something they can hang on him.'

I gulped. 'First up, he's not *my man*. Second up, he's planning to sell up. Liquidate his assets. Go to America.'

Byers nodded, solemnly. 'We know. *They* know.' He held up a paw; narrowed his finger and thumb so a feather could have barely passed between them. 'They're this close to having enough on him to make an arrest. Him *and* his associates.'

'The rest of the SAS mob?'

Byers sighed. 'No, Grace. His *accountants.* Know how they finally got Al Capone? Tax evasion.'

'Everyone knows that, and Long ain't Al Capone.'

'Doesn't matter. As far as I can see, they've been after him for a while now. And this is how they'll get him. Tell me, you spoken with your crony Carl Sharp recently?'

I told him I had; I told him *some of* what had gone on yesterday, our being called-up to Long's place in Roundhay. *Summonsed,* that was the word. I didn't tell him about the money and I *certainly* didn't tell him about the International Pool.

'Yeah, but have you spoken to him *since* yesterday?'

I scratched my head. I remembered trying to call him from the Long Stay by the International Pool. He hadn't picked up. But then again, he was in hospital. He wasn't supposed to be mucking around on his phone in there in the first place. Maybe he hadn't answered because the doctor had called in on his rounds and checked him over. 'No,' I said, 'I haven't.'

'And you'll be lucky to get hold of him at all, now. Blake and Deane told me they were going to pay him a visit. Your friend Adam's next. I'm not sure how much they know about your part in all this yet, and I've certainly not spilled the Heinz, but... but in this past year I've come to learn quite a bit about people and I've come to understand that a person will do mostly anything to wriggle out of a mess. Including shopping his friends.'

'Carl wouldn't.' I stopped, because maybe Carl *would.*

Byers nodded slowly as he saw the realisation dawning new in me. ''Zactly. And who's to say *you* wouldn't, either? You never know what you're going to do until all the chips are down, and by then you're desperate. And desperate men do desperate things.'

'Okay,' I said, 'I see that. So why are *you* helping me? You didn't have to push me towards PWC when I came to you. You didn't have to agree to meet me today.'

Byers looked out into the white water of the river as it ran below us. He looked like, had the glass not been there, he might have jumped in. 'Honestly? I don't know. Maybe it's like I say and I see something of myself in you. You've not quite hidden yourself as well as I used to, even if you think you have, but there it is.'

'I don't understand.'

He shot me a hangdog look before returning his gaze to the water. 'Maybe I was brought up in a pub just like you. Maybe I lucked out and went to university just like you. Maybe I re-invented myself there. Gave myself airs. Graces. Geddit? Graces, Grace.'

I kind of nodded.

'Maybe I wanted to forget all about my past and make a new story up for myself and maybe I liked that new story so much I lost the old me. Or who knows, maybe I'm lying. Maybe I never lived in a pub at all. Truth is, I don't think you're a bad sort, Grace. And I don't think you deserve to get sucked into this. You got morals left. Some, at least. And that's more than can be said for most at our place. They get blinded by the green. *I* got blinded by the green. I can see now, though, and what I see, I don't like.'

'I still don't get it.'

'Yeah? Well maybe that's my point. You got a girlfriend, Grace?'

Why was it, as soon as he asked that, I pictured Natalie?

'Not really.'

'Okay, you got friends somewhere you can go stay with? Old uni pals; something like that?'

'Well, there is Henry.'

'Where's Henry?'

'London. He works doing something engineering-y. Maybe with the Thames tidal barrier. I don't know. I've barely spoken with him in years.'

'Go see him. Not tomorrow, not next week. This afternoon. We're a ten-minute walk from the train station here. Hell, the occasional local train rattles over our heads. So go up there, book yourself on the next rattler to King's Cross. And hole up. Because shit is going to hit the fan any minute now. Like I said, the jaws of the bear-trap are closing. They'll have Carl now, and he can't Zombie Nation out of this one. Then Ads. Then Nathan Long. They won't be able to do much more than question Long for now, so after twenty-four hours he'll be on the loose and like a bear with a sore one. And guess who he's going to look for first?'

I sucked half a bottle of Peroni in one and the world wobbled once again, like someone, some unseen force, had just bumped into the projector. I had to grip onto the edge of the table to keep myself stable and upright. In the distance – sounded like they were down a bottom of a well, or maybe I was – I could hear the trio of Ladies Who Lunched cackling away like well-dressed witches and I could smell too much garlic, which made me think of Mama. From the kitchens, there came the clatter and smash of someone, some poor potboy, dropping a pile of plates. A few of the diners applauded, sarcastically.

I reached for the second bottle of beer and Byers reached out and stayed my hand. 'Wait,' he said. 'Don't fuck this up and get drunk. I'm offering you a way out here.'

And suddenly I felt like screeching with laughter because this was all just ridiculous. 'I can't go on the bloody *run*,' I shrieked. 'And even if I did, how far would I get? I've got a flat here and a job here and… they can track you on your moby, can't they?'

'Lower your voice,' growled Byers.

But I couldn't. I was incredulous. 'What do you expect me to do? Go incognito? Change my name? Live another life? In hiding?'

He sighed. 'No. Just *lay low.* Stay out of the limelight a while. Go somewhere other than Leeds.' Then he pulled out his wallet. It looked fat. 'How much money you got on you?'

I was still having trouble believing this was actually happening and, when I didn't immediately answer, Byers opened his wallet and counted out a few twenties into a pile. That sobered me some. 'I've got dough,' I said. 'Or access to some at least.'

I thought of the money The Nat had left for me under my pillow at the flat. And then I thought of the cool million which I'd stashed in the locker at the International Pool and *that* thought set me off laughing all over again. Because there was no way I was going to take it, was there? There was no way I was going to top all my crimes so far by running off with *Nathan Long's* million, was there?

I got light-headed and it was surprise at myself which made me feel that way. Because I realised I didn't feel entirely averse to taking Long's million. The idea didn't repel me, nor did it scare me. And that was unexpected. And suddenly my mind was running away with itself, making calculations: what if the police *did* round up Long and keep him in for questioning for a day or so? That gave me enough time to take the money and get as far away from here as possible, didn't it? So what if Long had *people* in Leeds? They'd look for Carl first, wouldn't they?

What would I do with a million quid? I'd quit work, for one. Travel, maybe. Catch up with old pals. Make my mum more comfortable. Make myself more comfortable. Read books again. Catch up on a few box sets. Do something good with my life. Last night, The Nat had asked me what I'd spend a million on, and I'd struggled to come up with an answer (though admittedly I was very, very drunk). Today, I was coming up with answer after answer.

So maybe taking the money was the right thing to do. After all, I literally had nothing to lose now, so why not take it? Or maybe I was just making busy convincing myself it was right. Maybe it was my greed talking...

Byers snapped his fingers in front of my face. 'You going to do what I say, Grace? Because for a minute there, I thought you were away with the fairies.'

'You know what?' I said. 'I think I might.'

'Good,' he said. '*Great*. Now I got one less thing to worry about. But now I gotta go.' He stood, proffered a paw. I took it, and shook warmly. 'Good luck, Grace,' he whispered.

'And to you,' I said.

And then he was gone. I sat for a while watching the river, becoming hypnotised by it just as Byers had. Then the rumble of a train above brought me out of my reverie. I walked back out under the arches of Granary Wharf, my head still spinning some. I stopped halfway along in order to catch my breath and it was then I became aware – or *thought* I was aware – of a figure a few arches back, following me.

I couldn't make out anything about the figure beyond shadow, but my mind was already filling in the details. Dressing it in an SAS-branded bomber jacket and shit-kicker boots, perfect for jumping on someone's head.

I faced front. Walked ten rapid-fire paces then spun round, playing 'What time is it, Mister Wolf?'. But when I swung round, I couldn't see anybody trailing in my wake. Not a one. So I tried to tell myself I'd been imagining the whole thing. I was *het up*. Paranoid. I was imagining up a stalker in order to subtly self-sabotage myself, so I wouldn't wind up with the loot. Or else there *was* someone there and it was just a shopper or a tramp or some kid playing silly beggars.

I had to get a grip.

I started walking quickly again, looking back over my shoulder every few paces. Now I couldn't see my stalker, but I was sure he was there. I could *feel* him. Feel his eyes on me. *Christ. How was I going to go fetch the loot from the International Pool if one of Long's goons was watching me?*

I'd have to throw him off the scent, that was how. As soon as I rounded the corner I started to run. I dashed up to Mill Hill and then dived into the off-licence on the corner and stood at the window, watching out and breathing heavily. The shopkeeper asked me what the hell I thought I was doing and if I didn't want anything, could I get out of his shop? He didn't want any trouble. I told him I'd take a packet of Benson and Hedges, but could I rest here a while. He rolled an elaborate tut around his mouth like gum, but didn't push me further to leave.

I watched the corner where the Dark Arches spilled out for five minutes. Many people came. They were rushing for the station, or else for the pubs. They were running for buses, or else looking for somewhere to go eat. But none of them was wearing an SAS-branded bomber jacket, so I eventually decided I'd either imagined the whole thing or I'd lost him. Either way, I needed to get up to the International Pool, take my money and run. Before I lost my mind or my life or both.

And yeah, I realised what I'd done there. I was already thinking of it as my money.

I braved it. Stepped out onto Mill Hill and then followed it around onto Boar Lane and then City Square. I felt like I was making a farewell tour, but one in which I couldn't pause to take stock. Here was Cenessa, the bar I'd sunk into immediately after being called in by Lightwood and told about the drug test. There, looming, was One City Square, the great glass elevator running up the side of it. I'd spent so much of my recent life there and I wondered if I would ever see it again. Here was the statue of Edward, the Black Prince. Carl used to joke that he was the patron saint of guys like us, princes amongst men, because Edward was the first Knight of the Garter. That's why they installed the statue of him where we could look down on him always and remember out nightly conquests. There was Wellington Street, and I had to keep my head down as I walked past the PWC offices.

I didn't notice anyone hot in pursuit, but I might have been cold in my thinking. That beefy guy studying the bus timetable. He wasn't dressed like an SAS bouncer, but what if his off-white Leeds United shirt was only a disguise? And how about him, peering into the window of an estate agency which specialised in city-centre lets and sales? He didn't look the type to want to live in an apartment. Hell, he wouldn't have even fit through the door of some of the places I'd seen, such was the immense breadth of his shoulders. So what if he was simply *pretending* to be interested. What if he was simply waiting for me to shamble past so he could get on the bouncer hotline and alert the rest of the roaches to my progress? And him, lingering on a bench outside a sandwich shop, nose buried in a tabloid newspaper: was he peering through it, at me?

I had to cut out the paranoia. It wasn't helping me. It was slowing me down, like I was carrying a *SLAZENGER* backpack full of rubble on my shoulders. I cut right onto Queen Street, where pedestrian traffic thinned and it might be easier for me to pick out a tail. But I saw nothing other than sharp-suited lawyers. This was the law district of Leeds and there were many firms based around here. Maybe I should have simply gone into one of them, told them the whole story and then thrown myself upon their mercy. But now I had a plan, now I was *acting,* I didn't want to stop.

Still, my heart was thrumming with tension as I pushed through the double doors and into the rat-run corridors of the International Pool. My kneecaps felt like inflatables; they wobbled, weren't firm enough. Goosebumps rippled up and down my arms. With every step I thought I was going to feel a firm hand landing on my shoulder, tugging me back.

Somehow I made it into the changing rooms, with their oppressive silence. The changing rooms were divided into smaller alcoves to provide a little more privacy. In the first section, a couple spindly old men of the type often hogged the middle lane during lane-swim sessions quietly cracked their limbs into tiny trunks. A young lad studied the notice board for details of the next life-saving session. None of them looked like they were out to get me. None of them paid me any mind at all. In the next section, a permatanned grandad preened himself naked in front of the mirror and I hurried past him. And the section after that was empty. My locker, my safe place, was in the final quarter, and I was so close now I could feel my fingers tingling with excitement. Soon, they'd touch the stressed leather of the case.

But when I rounded the corner my heart triple-jumped. Despite the fact he wasn't wearing his penguin suit I recognised Verity immediately. Here was that 'tall drink of water' who'd acted almost like Nathan Long's *manservant* yesterday when I'd been *summonsed.* Yesterday, he'd seemed like he had about as much status as one of the dogs as he lingered by the door, out the way. But in here, away from his boss, he seemed much more *present.*

He was half-turned away from me, drying off with a towel. There was a huge SAS tattoo on his shoulder blade and the motto *WHO DARES WINS* ran down his arm like a sleeve.

Behind him was the biggest guy I'd ever seen in my life. He had to be six-six and three hundred pounds. Maybe more. His bowling-ball head alone had to be fifty pounds. And hanging off it was a single, braided ponytail which swayed like a baseball bat readying itself for a strike. This guy had his back turned to me and his own tatts were legion. Angel-wings covered both shoulder blades and there was a dotted line which appeared to run all the way round his huge neck; underneath it was the legend: *CUT HERE.*

Behind him was my locker. Number 375. Might as well have been 666. Might as well have been in *Tibet* for all the chance I had of getting to it.

Neither of the SAS goons had seen me yet. Everyone only *half* looks in male changing rooms. Them's the rules. But I sensed if I continued to stand there like a goose then Verity would soon pick me out in his peripheral vision and immediately tag me a perv. And then he'd swing round, and then he'd see who it *really* was. And, as Rusty Crowe almost said, all hell would be unleashed.

And yet, I couldn't move. I stood rigid and stared at them and I wondered how much Verity and his pal already knew. I wondered whether the jaws of that bear-trap had clamped fully shut yet.

Verity reached into his own locker and pulled out a tee. For a beat, when he pulled it over his head, I thought about making a dash for it, because at that time his six-six, three-hundred-pound pal was head bowed, rooting around in his wash-bag for a brush or a comb or a fucking tub of moisturiser. So I could maybe smuggle myself past unseen. Throw back the locker door so they couldn't see my face. But then, when I thought about how I'd get *back past* them, my knees turned to water.

My Nokia got sick of waiting. The number of times I should have tossed the damned thing over the past year, and yet there it was, in my pocket. I drew. Instinct made me do it. Instinct made me want to either see who it was or at least shut it off. I saw *CARL* on the display and I pressed *REJECT CALL,* and at the very moment I did so, Verity looked over. And performed the most telegraphed double-take I'd ever seen in my life.

'You,' he said.

And we stood like a pair of Wild Westerners in a shoot-out, staring each other down. Verity's tee was baggy and red and had *TRUTH* scrawled across the front of it like a sponsor's logo on a football shirt, and I had time enough to think that *yeah, Verity means truth, doesn't it?* And to think *yeah, truth bites.* And *also* to think: he's only wearing a tee and his boxers. No pants. No shoes. I could make a run for it.

I made a kind of testing-the-water dart right, and Verity echoed my move. I stopped. He stopped. Then, out the corner of his mouth, he hissed: '*Brutus, Brutus!*' And his six-six, three-hundred-pound pal turned round with the grace and smoothness of a fucking transatlantic cruise ship. 'That's *him,* for fuck's sake. Neal Grace.'

And Brutus growled like a bear.

I made my move. Darted right once more and this time kept going. Past the empty section, past the section which contained the preening, permatanned grandad and past the two spindly old fellas, who looked at me as though I was mad. I almost slipped on a puddle of shower water just before I reached the door but somehow kept on my feet. Yanked the thing open and allowed myself one swift look back over my shoulder before I charged through it.

Long's two goons were hot on my tail: Verity so fast he was almost scalding; Brutus a little more lukewarm. To be fair to the six-six, three-hundred-pound bear, he was clad only in a fluffy white towel which he'd wrapped around his waist. Verity was running like he really meant it.

I pushed the door closed and threw myself into the rat-run corridors. Hadn't gotten far before I heard the door opening again and the slap of Verity's bare feet on the tiles. Then, louder and heavier, the rumbling tread of Brutus too. I tried to waylay them. Pushed over a litter bin so the contents spilled out; hopefully there'd be something sharp inside. Something jagged-edged. I ran through the café and pushed over tables, eliciting angry cries from the staff and some customers. And still they were close. Too close.

I ran past reception, through a knot of kids here for a school swimming lesson; backpacks scattered all over the place; some teacher in their midst trying to read out the register in case he'd lost a kid en route. Dodged and weaved my way through more pedestrian traffic then finally reached the double doors which would spit me back to the outside world. From behind me, shouts and commotion as the clad-only-in-a-towel Brutus and the half-dressed Verity skittled through after me. But I did not look back. Shouldered through; out onto the pavement, half of me thinking *where now?*, the other half begging that half to stop with the thinking already: just go. Then both halves conspiring together to ask: *the fuck?*

There was a laser-blue Ford Fiesta illegally parked on the double-yellows directly outside the International Pool. The driver bipped the horn, but from where I was I couldn't make him out. Could only make out the sticker on the back bumper which read *LITTLE MONSTER ON BOARD* and the vast collection of cuddly toys which were piled on the parcel shelf, practically filling the entire rear window.

Not him. *Her.* The window wound down and The Nat – The Nat! – poked her head out. 'Get in!' she bellowed.

I didn't even consider how weird it was that my blackmailer was now my getaway driver. And I only half felt it when Verity and his fellow goon Brutus crashed out the doors behind me; Verity thrusting out a desperate hand, attempting to grasp my collar. Missing, but the draft of it forcing the hairs on the back of my neck to stand to attention. I simply *acted.* Threw myself at the passenger-side door. For a beat I thought *Oh shit, she's left the child-lock on* as I tried the handle and it wouldn't give, but then I heard a satisfying clunk and I was in.

Natalie panicked, revved the engine, cranked the Fiesta into first and then stalled. 'Shit,' she moaned. 'Shit, shit, shit.'

I looked in the rear-view. The goons were getting closer.

'Calm down,' I told her. 'It's just like riding a bike.'

Natalie cursed, stamped her foot on the accelerator and cranked down the handbrake. This time she didn't stall. She screeched away from the double-yellows, but not quick enough. A goon connected with the side of the car. There was a loud *thunk.* Natalie yelped. I believe I did too. But it was okay. *Okay!* If it had been Brutus who'd smashed his elbow against the glass, the glass would have given up the poltergeist, but it wasn't, it was Verity. The Nat fumbled with the gearstick, tried to shunt it into second. Verity tore at the side of the car; found purchase on the wing-mirror and then clung on. And as Natalie picked up speed he hurried along on our flank, staring in at me, never once taking his ice-cold eyes off of me.

But then Natalie stamped on the gas again and finally managed to throw him off. He slipped out of view for a moment and I felt a surge of relief, but then he was on his feet once more, running; and Brutus was closing in too, barrelling into the road in pursuit, his white towel flapping in the breeze.

Natalie went again. The Fiesta was petulant, reluctant to do as it was told, but gradually, sulkily, it was coming round to the fact it had no choice in the matter. She'd keep plugging away at it until it did her bidding. And right now her bidding was to put as much distance between us and the goons as possible.

On the pavement, a traffic warden waved his arms at us, urging us to slow down. The Nat growled: 'If I could take my white-knuckle hands off this wheel I'd flick that fucker the Vs.'

And I gave a shrill laugh.

I think we both felt mad in that moment. Kind of Thelma and Louise-y. Kind of like we were existing in a different type of reality to mundane traffic wardens, meters, road traffic laws and the like. *Where we were going there were no roads...* I became vaguely aware of the *whap-whap nee-naw* of sirens, many sirens, echoing, cascading back off the buildings and I wondered, absently, whether the traffic warden had sicced cops and ambulances on us. And wouldn't it be funny if the crime which finally brought me down was driving the wrong way down a one-way. And I laughed again.

But something brought me back into reality with a bump. In my peripheral vision I saw a sign telling me we were headed down a one-way street. Natalie hadn't seen it, and dragged the Fiesta up to thirty – felt faster than it was between the closely stacked parked cars on either side of the road. Verity had maybe done us a favour by pulling the wing-mirror off. Still, we were going the wrong way, and if we met a car coming at us head-on we'd smash into it, no question. And if it was an oncoming cop car or an ambulance, no doubt about it, we'd come off worse. And by the time we pulled our crumpled noses off the dash and steer, Verity and Brutus would be on us, red in tooth and claw.

The road wasn't just a one-way. It was a dead end. Even Natalie couldn't miss the white minus inside a red circle sign which blocked our way. We'd reached the end of the road. We could climb out, try and make a run for it across the loose-gravel car park and then over the pedestrian bridge which squatted over the inner ring road. Try and lose ourselves in the entanglement of streets in the northeast of the city centre. But The Nat wasn't in a mind to do that. She let out a long, low sigh of frustration then wrestled the car into reverse. And at first I thought she was going to try and reverse all the way back up the road, but then she swung it round and began a complicated three-point turn which turned into a five-pointer. And, Christ, my palms were getting sweaty.

At last, serenaded by the sounds of sirens, she set the Fiesta back on track. I couldn't immediately see Verity and Brutus running us down – Natalie had driven away too fast – but I knew they wouldn't have let us go that easily. Probably they were getting their breath at the top of the road, just waiting for us to come back.

At the top of the road was a crossroads. Left would take us back up to the International Pool. Right, into town, through the lawyer belt. Straight on was a route to the LGI. Coming from the left, I could see the goons. And they could see us. Verity drew a finger slowly across his neck. And I had to keep telling myself we were at an advantage here. We were in a *car,* for fuck's sake. Neither of them even had bloody *shoes* on...

Straight ahead, the road, the buildings, the pavements, the parking meters, the mailboxes were all of a sudden painted blue. And then we saw the charge of the ambulances, down from LGI. For a moment, time flat-lined. I looked over at Natalie and she looked at me. Then the paddles were applied and time was jump-started all over again. Seconds before the first ambulance in the procession reached the crossroads – Verity had stepped into the road and was virtually thrown back up onto the pavement by it – Natalie made a decision. She kicked the accelerator, wrenched the wheel right, and *threw* us into the turn just before the ambulance could follow.

The ambulance loomed large in the rear-view, and Natalie kicked again. The Fiesta barely responded. 'Shit,' she moaned. 'Shit, shit, shit.'

The ambulance driver let loose with a long, deep honk of the horn and finally Natalie cleared out the way. Found a side street she could tuck down and *just about* made it round the corner without totalling the car. The side street was barely wider than a pavement and numerous large catering-sized bins complicated the route, but somehow she managed to navigate us through. Carl would have said something about the Kessel Run.

Eventually she pulled back out onto a proper road and I stopped gripping the sides of my seat. There was no sign of the goons anywhere.

'Where the hell d'you learn to drive like that?' I asked her once I'd gotten my breath.

She sniffed. 'Rhys. He was good at hot-wiring. Not so good at what came after. You could say that was a, like, sign for what he was like in everything.'

And for a beat I considered just how deeply the lifeline of me, Neal Grace, had changed. Here I was, still knowing exactly what Carl would say about this or that situation, when the chances were I'd never see him again. And here The Nat, and I couldn't second-guess a single thing she'd say. It should have been refreshing, but it was all kinds of sad.

She turned onto Merrion Street and then followed it down past the McDonald's on the corner, and at last I realised I should at least tell her I was grateful.

'Look,' I said, 'thanks. You didn't have to do that.'

'Sure I did,' she said. 'I couldn't leave you hanging. It's not my style.'

I frowned. 'But how did you know I'd be there? At the pool?'

'Let's just call it my female intuition.' She grinned. 'I was following you just in case you got in trouble. And you did. So it's a good job.'

'You were following me?'

'Sure. Went right down to that restaurant place at Granary Wharf. Stood around outside kicking my heels while you talked to that fancy-pants fella.'

'I didn't see you.' But I *had*. I'd seen some shadowy figure behind me in the arches, hadn't I? It had spooked me. That had been *her?*

She tapped the end of her nose. 'That's why I'm such a good spy. So where now, Neal?'

That was the question, wasn't it? We'd escaped. By the skin of our Speedos, we'd escaped. But surely that was only temporary. Verity, Long and the SAS guys had a network, a proper spy network, which pretty much enmeshed the city. By now every bouncer, hard man, dealer and bad egg in Leeds would be on the look-out for a laser-blue Ford Fiesta with 1992 plates and a bumper sticker which read *LITTLE MONSTER ON BOARD*. I groaned. My paranoia was coming back. We passed Europa nightclub and, though it was closed and would be for the next five hours, I was sure I saw SAS bouncers lurking, hissing venom into their walkie-talkies. Same down North Street, where we had to queue to make a right onto Regent Street. Eyes everywhere. Seekers everywhere.

'You've got to have a plan, Neal,' said Natalie. 'You can't just go off half-cocked on this. Otherwise it'll never stick.'

'I don't know,' I said. 'Really, I don't. At least with the money I might've—'

'Sod the money. For now, sod it. You've escaped. That's what counts.' She drummed her fingers on the wheel. 'But if you're *really* concerned about money that bad, I know where you can get some more. So do you.'

My mind was a blank.

'Your *flat*. I left your two K under the pillow.'

'But that's just two K,' I said sulkily.

'*I* managed to make a life on that.'

Touché.

'We're not far away from Eastgate, Neal. Hell, we'll pass right behind the flats on the way down. I can stop by the Chinese supermarkets. Wait a while. You can even pack a bag.'

'What if someone's lying in wait for me?'

'*What if*, Neal? There's always a *what if*. I need to know now. Do you want me to stop?'

I nodded. We sat in silence on Regent Street, waiting for buses to pull in and out. Watching furtive guys slipping out of the sex shop clutching plastic bags to their chests like closely guarded secrets. Watching two drifters on the corner fly-postering for the latest events at Club Mexx and at The Night Garden. Then, when the coast was clear, a left turn onto Lady Lane, finding it hard to comprehend that this might be the last time I happen down this way. As usual, the minute I saw the street sign, an old Bob Dylan number sprang unbidden into my mind. 'Lay Lady Lane'. Song used to be on the jukebox at the Golden Goose. All the old fellas used to put it on when they were feeling particularly maudlin. Which was most nights, the amount they drank.

Natalie pulled into the exact spot Nick Byers had parked his Porsche the day he'd taken me up to the driving range at Wike Ridge and told me he'd get me out of Andersen. None of the workers from the Chinese supermarkets rushed out to pose for photos with her Fiesta. 'I'll wait here. Keep my eyes peeled.' She switched on the radio and that was my cue to get out.

Although I hadn't *any* plans beyond the flat on Eastgate, during the wait on Regent Street I had at least managed to cobble something together in terms of how I'd access the flat without being seen. The basement bin-store could be accessed from the street round back of the apartments proper for those residents who had keys, and I had a key. Inside was like a yard sale in which the browsing customers were rats, but I was able to pick my way through it fine. Then I took the fire-escape stairs right up to the top floor. At the summit I took a moment to catch my breath and to press my face against the mottled glass of the fire door to check whether there were any goons lurking at my door. If there was one, hell, even if there was a *suggestion* of one, then I was going straight back down the stairs. Fuck it. Two grand wasn't worth dying for.

There wasn't anyone there. I steeled myself and pushed through the door. Keyed the lock of my own door, expecting at any moment to feel a thick arm around my throat. A twist. Then nothing. But the arm never came. My front door swung open and I immediately smelled my vomit, stale pizza and crappy red wine from the night before.

I closed the door behind me and tried to find my voice. I couldn't bear the anticipation of being jumped out on. If there was someone here I wanted them out in the open, even if that meant they attacked me. 'Hello?' I croaked. 'Anyone h-here?'

No answer. So I followed a well-trodden path into my bedroom. Turned on the lights. They glared, exposing nobody but little old me. I saw myself in the mirror on my dresser. I looked about ten years older than the last time I'd looked in it.

I rummaged around in the wardrobe and found an old rucksack. Wondered what I should stuff in it. The money, obviously, and I retrieved this from under the pillow first. Placed it at the bottom of the bag and packed some socks, some boxers around it. Then I threw in a few tees, some good jeans, a shirt. But what else? It's a perennial dinner-party conversation starter. *What would you take if...?* Yet beyond a few clothes I couldn't think of anything I wouldn't miss. Pictures: I should take pictures. The *feeling* man always said photo albums. But I had nothing beyond the framed prints on my walls and I decided I didn't want it to be *too* obvious I'd done a runner in case one of Long's goons did come to pay me a visit. Let them sit and stew for a while. Place looked like the *Marie Celeste,* as though someone would return at any minute. Let them think I would.

At the door, I said a quiet goodbye. There was nothing lingering about it. Then I took the fire escape back down to The Nat and the Fiesta.

When I got back in she looked worried. She said she'd seen a clutch of men all got up in SAS-branded black bomber jackets clattering down Lady Lane while I'd been inside. One of them had gone so far as trying the door to the basement bin-store, before eventually giving up. The lot of them had gone round front of the building instead. And I'd been so long, she said, that she was sure they'd gotten to me, but I must have been the luckiest man on earth to miss them.

I still thought I was anything but. I chucked my rucksack in back and told her to step on it. Don't spare the horses.

And Natalie shook her head and said: 'You posh boys. You don't half talk funny.'

PART III

I

There was a guy in my office who reminded me of Bill back at PWC. His name was Martin ('but you can call me Mart'). He was maybe forty years old but he dressed like he was sixty. Mostly, he was easy company because he never asked trying questions. We talked small about the weather and occasionally about sports but he never asked me a single thing about my personal life and I liked it like that. Some people at work thought I was stand-offish because I didn't *share*. They spent all day every day reeling off the minutiae of their home lives as if everyone gave a shit, and seemed somehow offended I didn't give as good as I got back. Then again, I think they thought I was a bit weird anyway on account of I didn't have a single photo of anyone I loved on my desk. They liked that I was always available to come for drinks at the drop of a hat, but not that I kept 'myself' shrouded in mystery.

Weird was okay as far as 'call me Mart' was concerned because he was weird as an accountant. And our office was anything but an accountancy firm. We were Sniper PR and Marketing Consultancy, and we were new-age and we were fresh and we were all about giving people space to think, man, away from the pressures of, like, figures and reports and all that bogus dark stuff, man. Hell, Sniper laid on fucking sleep-pods and table-football machines in case us creatives ever got bored. I sometimes wondered why they hired someone like Mart in the first place. I mean he clearly didn't fit in and he dressed like he didn't even want to try to. But maybe every office needs a Steady Eddie, and Mart was ours.

Though there wasn't a clock in the whole place Mart was the most punctual guy I ever saw. He wouldn't take the Underground because, as a proper northerner, he couldn't trust it. Preferred to walk everywhere, and he had an accountants' spreadsheet on his computer which told him exactly how long it took him to get from here to there to everywhere he needed to be.

Most of the others made fun of him behind his back but I passed the time of day with him, even though I knew that each such exchange between us would mean he'd make himself more limpet-like and attach himself ever more fixedly to me. That didn't matter, I thought. He was harmless.

I felt sorry for him and maybe that was what caused me to let my guard down with him. We were talking one day in the print room (I could see a couple of the younger creatives over the other side of the room listening in and sniggering at Mart's remarks). Mart was saying something about there being a 'piebald sky' (the sniggers almost turned into full-on shouts of laughter then) and I told him, yeah, I knew what he meant: it was the kind of sky you saw over Headingley on a good day at the cricket. I said it off the cuff. I'd been sampling a 'Bill voice' I could use on Mart, so I barely even needed to think of a response when Mart came out with one of his weird weather reports.

I soon realised my mistake. Mart was a proud Leodian – right down to his 'Marching on Together' Leeds United coffee mug – and his eyes lit up at my mention of Headingley. He told me I spoke of Leeds as only a true native of the city would, with love and a little regret (and this elicited more guffaws from the young creatives). And I had to admit I'd lived in Leeds for a spell a few years back.

This admission unleashed hell. Suddenly Mart wanted to talk all things Leeds with me all the time and every time he brought the place up I'd feel this immense *twang* in my belly, like my guts were a guitar string and he played slap bass.

I started avoiding him. If I was at the water-cooler and he ambled along, all amiable-like, some titbit of gossip on his lips – like, 'Did you know J.R.R. Tolkien was once based at the university in Leeds? Oh yeah. It's reckoned he based Mirkwood on the woods in Meanwood' or 'Have you heard? They're talking a new high-speed rail-link between Leeds and London' – then I'd face-palm, make like I'd forgotten something urgent at my desk, and do one. If there was ever a work's night out and I found out Mr Leeds was on the guest list, I'd make my excuses and do something else. Anything but have him make a beeline for me and 'Leeds' me to death. But sometimes it was impossible to give him the slip. Even if The Nat had been my getaway driver, he'd have still found a way to Leeds me into submission. Maybe he wasn't so harmless after all. Maybe he was more like Tom fucking Green at Arthur Andersen than he was Bill at PWC.

I'd managed to wangle my way onto something the company dubbed their Friday Task Force. The task of this force was to hole up somewhere and blue-sky think about the topic of the week: it could be something like *Say a company like Arthur Andersen had existed after 2002 and say it came to you and asked you to alter its image in the public perception, how would you set about doing that?* Or it could be *Say Lee Bowyer and Jonathan Woodgate want a positive spin after all their terrible PR; what would you do, and would you have any moral qualms?* Or: *What do you do with a Prometheus City like Leeds, which reached for the stars but ended up in the gutter?* These weren't actual examples. The city of Leeds was never mentioned (nothing outside London ever was). But you get my drift.

Mostly the topics were just a starting point anyway, and discussions spiralled out every which way but loose from that point. But they always wound up at the same point: they became griping sessions. This or that creative director was stifling this or that guy's creative mojo; they didn't have the *vision* to see exactly how this or that campaign or account should be. Sniper was getting all kinds of too corporate, man. Too *old*. They wouldn't take any risks; they wouldn't push the envelope.

Christ, I wanted to tell them, *this ain't corporate. This is kindergarten. I know corporate and I know what ain't, and that's why I'm here in the first place.* I wouldn't have taken any job working for anyone bigger than an SME. And Sniper was my fourth similar company in five years (I left whenever anyone got too close, started asking questions).

266

The meetings were traditionally held on Friday afternoons at three, which meant we were duty-bound to take it out of the office and across the road to the pub, a place called the Verger's Arms. I liked it because it was a proper old-school boozer. There were a lot of them in London. They seemed to be better protected here from the waves of identikit Cenessas and the like. I also liked it because it reminded me of the Golden Goose, and I'd made my peace with *that* part of my past even if I hadn't come to terms – yet – with Leeds.

Anyway, the task force was a Sniper PR institution (in much the same way Mama's opera which blared out of La Scala used to 'be' Leeds; it was seen in affectionate terms; even if you didn't like the music, it was part of the furniture, the make-up of the place). Creatives *killed* to be on it. They practically took *pay cuts* to be on it; refused promotions and the like (senior management were barred). Most got in in the usual way in the end though; through the helping hand of the old boys' network: some of the other guys reminded me a great deal of Carl and Ads. They were entitled-type people and I had to drink a great deal at the meets just to get through them. Indeed, my drinking skills were what had gotten me onto the force in the first place, and even though I couldn't *share* 'myself', not like the rest of them, I could certainly drink the lot of them under the table. And that still counted.

How Mart wangled his way onto the task force was a mystery. But I knew why, right from the off. Me and the rest of the task force crew rolled in to the Verger's at a quarter-past-three after messing about buying ciggies from the corner shop, making a few calls, grabbing a bite to soak up the alcohol, and of course Mart was already ensconced at the long table in the corner. He'd bought two pints of London Pride and the rest of the guys could go fuck themselves. The other pint was, of course, for me. He patted the seat next to him and said I should sit down. 'Us northerners should stick together.'

The rest of the task force came back with large G and Ts and spritzers and other ridiculous southern drinks and I almost felt glad of having Mart for company, until the man himself nudged me in the ribs with a 'Hey, you'll never guess what I read in last night's *Evening Post*'. The poor bastard still subscribed to the Leeds newspaper: I wondered why the hell he didn't just move back up there if he loved the place so much.

I sighed. 'Dunno, Mart. Has Leeds Town Hall fallen down?'

'Close,' he breathed. 'They're closing down the International Pool. Tomorrow. Wrecking balls are scheduled for early next week.'

One of the guys, a guy who looked so much like Ads he could have cut my one-time friend's face off his dead corpse as it lay there in the morgue and worn it as a mask – *if* it hadn't been so battered, so bruised, so bent out of shape it looked like a wrecking ball had been taken to it – stood up and cleared his throat. He shuffled a few papers and then announced the weekly Task Force Topic, and I didn't hear anything of what he said.

'What do you make of that, then?' hissed Mart. 'Another Leeds landmark bites the dust.' He began singing the bassline to the old Queen number. I didn't ignore him; I could hardly hear him. His voice sounded muffled. Distant.

Meanwhile Ads-mask was still busy introducing the topic at hand, but all I could hear was a *whooshing* sound reverberating through my ears. It felt like the guy was at the end of a long underground tunnel and his voice was only a vibration, a tremulous echo of something which had happened in the past.

Mart was still talking too, and *his* voice was like a lost broadcast from a sunken ship. 'Yeah,' he droned, 'the council wallahs reckon they're going to replace the International with that new place down Beeston way, the John Charles Centre, but it won't be the same. That pool was... Well, October 2007 will go down as another sad month in the history of England's finest city.'

The International Pool had been in a sorry state in 2001, when I'd been a regular. Shabby and poorly maintained, the water was permanently murky even when they blitzed it with enough chlorine to sink a battleship and you had to be careful not to slice your feet open on the sharp edges of the tiles around the pool itself. The less said about the changing rooms, the better. For the first few months of my exile I'd kept a close watch on news about the pool just in case a major refurbishment was slated. Just in case they decided to throw out everything: the bad tiles, the bad water, the *lockers,* and my money with it. But that refurbishment had never come. The pool had kept on doggy-paddling along and, after the recession, there was simply no money to spare *to* do the place up. So I'd stopped checking so much after a while and this had helped me feel a little bit better about having been forced to leave the money where it was, in locker 375.

The money – *my money* – had come to represent many things for me. It was my rainy-day money, my just-in-case fund in case London, my job at Sniper, living with Henry all over again (in a similar kind of squalor to when we were students in Hyde Park) got too much for me. In some ways, I thought of it as a trust fund. Once I thought I was ready, once I'd really learned what I wanted to – and what I should – spend it on I'd take it and do good with it (for me and for others). The money was also an external hard-drive which contained my guilt. By keeping it at arm's length, around 175 miles away, my conscience was reasonably clear and I didn't have to think too hard about what had happened to Ads, to Carl, to Nathan Long, to *Andersen,* even.

The Ads-mask guy rapped his knuckles on the table and our glasses clinked. 'Uh, Rob? *Hell-oh?*' he said. 'You heard a single word I've said?'

And it took me a good while to remember that Rob was my name. Had been for six years, give or take, ever since The Nat introduced me to one of the guys who lived with her, a guy who knew a great deal about computers who'd shown me how I could get myself a new birth certificate and a new identity using an old death certificate from a hospital in Sheffield where some poor mother of a baby she'd only known a couple hours, enough to name him Robert Andrew Deacon but not much else, would have had to watch him wrenched from this earth early, and she'd have had to put out an ad – *FOR SALE, BABY SHOES. NEVER WORN* – never suspecting that someone like me, someone whose real name was Grace, but who should have changed it to *Dis*grace, would have paid more for his name.

The new identity I'd picked out for myself still made me a couple years off the big three oh, which was nice. One day, I thought, I'd pay Mrs Deacon a visit, if she was still alive. Thank her. Throw some dough her way once I got my million. Or maybe that was a pipedream. After all, I never went to see my own mum before she died. Never went to see Mama either.

The Ads-mask guy rolled his eyes. 'Honest, Rob, I know it must be boring as hell sat there next to Mart, but for fuck's sake' – he clapped his hands together – 'you need to get with the programme.'

Mart stood up. 'I'm not standing for that.'

And everyone around the table save the two northerners cracked up laughing. Steady Eddie Mart stormed out and I made a token attempt at following him to check he was okay, but as soon as I'd swung through the saloon-style doors of the Vesper's I stopped. Pulled out my cigarettes and my phone. Called the one person in the world who would understand how much the news about the forthcoming demolition of the International Pool had rocked my world. The Nat picked up after just one ring as I was still watching Mart flouncing down the road, walking at such a clip he'd send his spreadsheet totals way off cock.

'You were expecting my call?' I said.

'Female intuition,' she said. 'Nah, I had my phone in my hand anyway. I was about to take a nice picture of Jakey. You'll never guess where we are.' She didn't give me time to. 'We're at a driving range. We're playing golf. Do you believe it? Anyway, you've spoiled it now. I was going to take a picture of him swinging for the ball but he's already whacked it a mile now. He's going to be a regular Tiger Woods.'

'Great,' I said. 'Look, something's happened.'

'You've not told those idiots at Sniper what you really think of them, have you? Honestly, Gracey-boy, how many jobs are you going to wade through before you settle?'

'It's not that, and nobody calls me Grace any more, don't you remember?'

'Jakey does. He's always asking when *Neal's* coming up to visit again, and he's forever Gracey this, Gracey that after you've been up. And what Jakey says is catching. Sorry, I'll try harder, *Rob.*'

I wasn't playing along with her jovial tone. 'Nat, something's *happened.*'

'Oh,' she said. 'You're using *that* tone.' She lowered her voice: 'Nathan Long's not gotten out, has he?'

'No, not that. It's worse, in a way. Look, I won't keep you guessing. They're knocking the International Pool down, Nat. With my money right inside it.'

'*Fuck*,' she breathed. 'Seriously?'

'I wouldn't joke about something like this. And neither would my source.'

'So whatcha gonna do? Do you think the dust has settled enough for you to go back up there?'

I stood aside as another party of suits cut past me to the saloon doors of the Vesper's. Held my tongue until every single one of them had slipped inside. Then: 'I don't think it'll ever settle that much. Nathan Long may look like an elephant but he also has a memory like one. I expect he has my face on a dart board in his cell. I expect he has chalked off each day of his sentence, and he's not counting down to the day he gets out, or even to the day he can ride a motorbike again, but rather to the day he can come see me, or at least start hunting for me again. Nah, he won't forget. Revenge is like a drug to him. And he makes sure none of his minions on the outside will forget either.'

The Nat whistled. 'Sounds like you can't forget him either. Sounds like you've spent a lot of time imagining him over the past few years.'

'Of *course* I have. The guy practically banished me. He's made it so I can't even set foot in a city I'd come to know as home, for fear someone will take me out. You know there's a bounty on my head, right?'

'I do. And if Jakey doesn't shut up about Gracey this, Gracey that, I might just claim it as mine. Has to be a helluva lot easier than trying to go up there and trying to get your money back from a building they're gonna knock down.'

'It's not a joking thing.'

'I know that, pal, on account of I'm banned from Leeds too. Mind, I should have banned *myself* years ago. Would have saved me loads of trouble.'

I remembered my cigarettes. I flicked open the pack and pulled out a lamp-post-long Benson and Hedges with my teeth. My hands shook a little as I struck the wheel of my disposable lighter. I took a deep draw and spoke around the cigarette. 'How many times do I need to tell you I'm sorry about what happened to your mum, Natalie?' In the wake of our flight six years ago, Natalie's mum's house had burned to the ground. Fire investigators never discovered the cause but arson was suspected. No suspects were ever brought in, however. Nobody on the estate was talking. Nobody had seen anything. But we'd *known*. It was Long's SAS boys, sending us smoke signals which would carry all the way down from Leeds to Nottingham and London respectively.

'Yeah, well,' said Natalie. 'It was only bricks and mortar, pal. *She* didn't burn to the ground, did she? She was out at the time. *Course* she was out. Drinking up a storm at the working men's, if I remember right. And anyway, you should have seen the place. It was like... I never used to have to think about what the house was decorated like when I was little. All I had to do was look out the window. There was the old leather sofa from when I was one, rotting away under the washing-line, and there was Dad's old armchair before he did one, mouldering away by the back fence. Council found her better digs after, so, in a way, Long did her a favour. Burned up the past she found it so hard to get rid of and let her start again with a new slate.'

I sucked at the cigarette. Exhaled. 'I know all that. What I mean is I'm sorry it meant she blamed you. Wouldn't talk to you again.'

'Yeah, well,' she said again. 'That's *her* choice. I can't worry about her any more. Jakey's my priority. Then myself. And we're both better off where we are. And have you ever thought about if she *did* still talk to me? She talks to everyone else, too. And loose lips sink ships. Who's to tell whether she wouldn't get into one of her states down at Big Lil's and wind up sweet-nothinging the bouncer, telling him all about her wayward daughter and how she'd wound up going all the way to Nottingham just to get away from her troubles. Hell, she'd probably give him my full address if he bought her a Bacardi Breezer.'

I gratefully accepted Natalie's life-line. 'Fair dos. I get what you're saying.' I finished the cigarette and ground it out in an ashtray on one of the tables. 'So what do you think I should do? About the pool, I mean?'

'Is that why you called? So I can tell you what to do? So I can do your thinking for you?'

'Kind of, yes,' I admitted.

'Or is it because you want me to come with?'

'I couldn't ask you *that,* Nat. I know just how dangerous it will be and that's why I can't... I'd never... As you say, Jake should be your priority.'

'Jake's not a little baby anymore. He knows something's wrong. He knows if ever anyone – other than you, pal – mentions Leeds I kind of clam up. Get all antsy about everything. And I don't want him growing up thinking that kind of fear is... is *respectable,* or *acceptable...* Oh, I know what I mean, even if you don't. What I maybe mean is I *should* come up there with you. Put all this crap to bed once and for all. Neal?'

I'd stopped listening. Somewhere, a few blocks away, I heard a siren. Nothing new there: sirens were a regular soundtrack to London life. And yet sometimes when I heard them – call it post-traumatic stress disorder, call it my unwillingness to forget a one-time friend – I was dragged back to my past, to the day we fled Leeds. To Natalie's mad dash at the crossroads when she cut out in front of that fleet of emergency vehicles which were thundering down into town from the LGI.

Back then I'd been so concerned with my own safety, and with Nat's too, that I'd barely cared that we got in the way of those ambulances which were on their way to pick up some other poor victim of Leeds, but later, on the motorway, I came to understand the full ramifications of my own selfishness.

And though I had no way of knowing whether the ambulances *actually were* en route to Ads' flat down at Brewery Wharf, chances were that they were. Later still, I'd done some research into exactly how many ambulances were called out on an hourly basis, and I'd decided we would have had to have been very unlucky to have stopped *Ads'* ambulance in particular.

But then again, my life over the past year had been littered with such bitterly poetic ironies, so in my darkest hours I decided our ploughing out into traffic ahead of that ambulance had stopped it getting down to Brewery Wharf in time and Ads had bled out because of our own instincts for self-protection above anything else.

The moment we'd put Leeds behind us – coming off the M621 and entering the M1 – and the skyline sunk out of view in the rear-view, Natalie and I had both let out a barbaric yawp of pent-up emotion and I'd felt freer than I'd done in *beards*. It was as though I'd shed a skin and a new me was emerging. I wound down the window and felt the fresh air on my new, cosier carapace. The Nat clicked on the radio and the tunes sounded better than ever, as though I'd been listening to them underwater for the longest time. Even the M1 motorway looked beautiful.

On a whim I decided I'd put the seal on the deal. I'd say goodbye to the old me in the most definite way possible: I'd toss my Nokia out the window. Let the massive wheels of a ten-ton artic crush it into oblivion. I took one last look at the display, for habit's sake more than anything. And when I did I saw I had one missed call, and I remembered the moment in the changing rooms at the International Pool when my phone had rung, alerting Verity to my presence.

Carl. Carl had called.

There was a voicemail. I shouldn't have listened to it, but in a way I was glad I did. I needed to know we weren't in the clear and that such barbaric yawps, such new-skin feelings, were highly inappropriate. Given the circumstances. Had I not listened to the message, I might have been tempted to return to Leeds in a week, in a month, to get my hands on my money. As it was the message was the fuse and the phone was the detonator and, after I'd listened to it, bridges were well and truly burned.

Carl's voice was frantic. I could barely understand him. And though this was in part due to his broken jaw, that wasn't the whole of it. Something had turned him upside down and inside out and he sounded Lost-er and Boy-ier than I'd ever heard him before. He told me he'd just had a call from Ads. He was trapped on his balcony. Two goons at the glass inside his flat, waiting for him to either jump or come back inside. But one of them took a hammer to the glass – Carl said he heard the smash over the phone line – and then Ads said *na zdrowie...* And then he fell. Or he jumped. Or he was pushed. And I heard his scream. And then the phone cut out. And Neal? I don't know what to do. Call me... please...

My first thought was: that could have happened to me. The Nat had seen SAS guys descending on *my* place at Eastgate too. If I'd have been two minutes slower, if I'd stopped to pull a couple of the framed pictures off the wall, if I'd have stopped for a piss, then the goons would have made me. Chucked me out the window. *The great defenestration of Eastgate.*

My second thought was of Ads. I couldn't picture his beautiful face ruined; his head cracked like an egg from the fall; his body spread-eagled, surrounded by a halo of blood. It couldn't be true. Carl was playing with me. Trying to make me feel guilty. Or maybe Long had put him up to it. Or maybe the police. Maybe they were trying to lure me back in.

My third thought was about the timings, and then I understood if Ads had taken the plunge and if a fellow resident had seen it and called the emergency services, then the ambulances we'd gotten in the way of were... Shit. It didn't bear thinking about. I cursed my miserable self. I felt like cranking open the door, tossing myself out under the artic which was supposed to get my phone.

'Neal?' said Natalie. 'Oh for fuck's sake, *Rob?*'

'Soz, Nat, miles away.' *175 of them, to be precise.*

'Here's what you do. Get yourself to St Pancras. Buy yourself a seat on the next train up to Nottingham. Call me from the train. I'll come meet you at the station and we'll drive up to Leeds.'

'You sure, Nat? I can't – '

'Oh, for fuck's sake, stop making me say fuck. I'm with my son, you know.'

'What are you going to do with Jake? You can't bring him as well.'

'I'll leave him at the commune, don't worry about it.'

Natalie didn't really live in a commune. She just called it that. When she'd first escaped Leeds – with my two K in her pocket and not much else apart from a kid in tow – she'd gone to Nottingham because she had family there, on her dad's side. Not that she'd seen them in a long time, but still. Still, she had gorgeous memories of being down in Nottingham on a real sunny day, down by some canal, with her dad and his brothers, fishing. She'd kept insisting there was no such thing as fish in a canal – they were in rivers and the sea – but her dad and his brothers said it wasn't about catching fish, it was about just being there instead, soaking up some rays and supping some drinks. It was the only time she ever remembered seeing her dad happy.

When she got down to Nottingham, though, she found no trace of her dad (and secretly she'd been hoping he'd be there) and neither did his brothers seem at all enamoured at taking her – and her boy – on. An extra mouth to feed and all that. She told them she had money of her own. She just needed a place to stay was all. But they weren't keen. So she drifted for a month or so, her money gradually frittering away. She stayed in hostels and B and Bs in order to try and keep some back but Jakey was a growing boy and she needed to find somewhere to settle soon or he was in danger of falling behind. He was supposed to be starting school soon.

She whiled away her days at play groups in churches, or in playgrounds in parks, trying to figure out what she should do, because if things kept going as they were, she'd wind up going back to Leeds, tail between her legs, and her mum would never let her hear the end of it. But it was at one of these church play groups she found herself talking to Miriam.

Miriam wasn't The Nat's type. She was a big woman, the size of Nat's mum's house in Leeds, and she made herself even bigger wearing these dazzling African-style clothes which were louder than a night at Europa. Miriam was the most middle-class person Natalie had ever encountered. She *took* (not read) *The Guardian*; she was a vegetarian; she made her own bread; she did all sorts with lentils; she didn't believe in traditional familial structures: instead she'd brought up her daughter India in a shared house in West Bridgford amongst poets, painters, mature students and a couple other mums. The Nat asked her if this meant she was a lesbian and Miriam laughed like a drain. Turned out the pair of them got on like a burning house. They both talked so much, and so quickly, that any differences between them were moot points: they barely listened to what the other was saying *anyway.* So Miriam didn't get offended when Nat called her a lesbian and asked where India's dad was, nor even when she asked whether the shared house was actually a squat, and Natalie wasn't overly bothered when she realised Miriam was trying to make a 'project' of her, trying to mould something she considered beautiful from the base council-estate clay of her.

Turned out, Natalie quite wanted someone to make a project of her because she *did* want a better life. If not for her, then at least for Jake.

Living with Miriam and the rest of the ever-changing miscellany of house guests and residents was only supposed to be a temporary arrangement but gradually Natalie became a permanent fixture. Jakey and India were even faster friends than their mothers had been and the boy loved having plenty of other adults to fuss around him. Some of the other guys in the commune had looked after him when Natalie had returned to Leeds the one and only time, when she'd gone up with the intention of giving me my money back. Miriam had persuaded her that was the right course of action. It was the only way she could really say goodbye to the 'creature' she'd once been when she was younger and a lot less wise. Miriam had also persuaded The Nat to go to night-school. 'Pick any subject you like. See if it agrees with you.' And she'd discovered she liked designing clothes and fashion textiles. She'd progressed from night-school to college and, via a foundation course, into a place at university.

She'd been just starting out, that day she drove me away from Leeds; still growing into her older, wiser self. And I suppose I became her pet project in the same way she'd become Miriam's in the moments which followed my listening to that voicemail message from Carl, and my almost-retreat into blinkered childishness. At first I refused to believe it was true, the thing about Carl. I stuck my fingers in my ears and cried *la-la-la.* And then I took it all so personally. And then I railed against the world. And Natalie tried her damndest to keep the Fiesta on the road while talking me down from my own tall building.

We were just passing Sheffield and I looked out over Meadowhall and the towers and cranes of industry like they were moon bases. I just couldn't comprehend they actually existed. That real people lived, worked and shopped here. That I'd grown up here. That my dad had died here. That my mum was in a home here. I felt vaguely extra-terrestrial and oddly godly, as though the chaos of what I did affected *everyone*, every small ant I could see climbing out their cars in the car park and wandering over to the shopping Mecca. And The Nat was trying to tell me that everything would be okay. We were an hour away now, and as soon as we got to her place she'd fix me a strong drink and then tuck me up in bed and I could sleep for a week if that was what I needed.

And then the radio cut out. Radio Aire wouldn't carry this far. The car filled with static and the static fleshed out and suddenly it was wasps. A whole swarm of them choking up the atmosphere; stinging at my heart, my lungs, my brain. I began swatting at them; waving my arms around madly. And Natalie screamed at me to stop. And then the radio found a new signal, cottoned on to a new station. I don't know which one. And the wasps disappeared. And I slumped in the chair.

The new radio station we'd hit on was broadcasting the news. There was a piece about a demonstration outside a steelworks in Sheffield that we must have just driven past. There was another piece about Sheffield Wednesday signing a new striker. And then, in wider Yorkshire news, there was a piece about an apparent suicide in Leeds. A man, thought to be in his mid-twenties, had plunged to his death off an apartment block in the Brewery Wharf district of the city. He'd sustained multiple injuries and, though treatment had been administered in the ambulance, he'd died shortly before they'd reached hospital. As yet, the authorities weren't releasing the young man's name. They were waiting until they'd informed kith and kin.

Unlike with Carl, I wasn't named next of kin. I never received a call. But of course I knew his name already, and I knew the reason why he'd taken the plunge wasn't, as they stated in later reports, because of pressures of work in his 'high-power' job. Nor was it, as they suggested in even later reports, because of his 'problems with substance abuse'. I didn't even agree with the yet later official finding that it had been suicide.

For it was Ads. The superhero Ads. And Ads would have flown, if he'd wanted to. Even in his suit, even in his no-lens glasses, he never looked like the mild-mannered alter-ego. Ads was always the superhero himself.

He'd been pushed. He'd met his arch nemesis and he'd been pushed.

Somehow, Natalie got me down to Nottingham without my wrestling the car off the road or into oncoming traffic. She took me up to her room and put me to bed, and I stayed there for a week. By the time I emerged, I was a broken man. The guys in the commune tried to help put me back together. Miriam tried to feed me up. One of the poets kept reading me lines about grief and how one got over it. Jakey tried to get me to play football with him in the (overgrown) back garden. Eventually it took the news of the arson attempt on Natalie's mum's place to bring me back, to make me realise there were other people suffering here, not just me.

I stayed for a while, until I could at least pass as a halfway-whole person, at least until the poet showed me his moonlighting skills (he was the computer genius) and wrote me a new identity I could hang my hat on. And then I thought I'd better leave. I'd already polluted their happy atmosphere quite enough. And it was to their eternal credit that everyone in the commune still welcomed the black hole of me back with open arms every time I went up there for a visit.

As Rob Deacon, I told Natalie I'd do as she'd told me, and as Rob Deacon, I journeyed underground through the Hades of London, and with Rob Deacon's credit card I paid for a horrifically expensive rail ticket up to Nottingham. The ticket-wallah told me I should have booked in advance if I wanted to get there cheaper. And I told her I hadn't wanted to go in advance. It was an emergency. How was I supposed to know an emergency situation was going to happen? She shrugged and told me it wasn't her problem. Nothing was ever anyone else's problem in London. That was why so many northerners came down here and walked like they were auditioning to be in the video to The Verve's 'Bittersweet Symphony', banging a shoulder here and there just to announce, *I'm here, you may not look at me, you may not acknowledge me, but I am here.*

And now I was going back up north. Furthest I'd been for six years was Nottingham, and to say Nottingham was north to a true northerner, someone from Sheffield, Leeds,

Hull or Newcastle, say, would be like saying Carlisle was north to a Scotsman.

The train was over-booked and even though I'd paid a premium for my ticket, no seat had been allocated to me. Meant I had to wedge myself behind the narrow train seats and the over-sized baggage which spilled haphazardly out of the luggage compartment. Meant I was forced to bend my legs underneath somebody's guitar case and that my head was propping up a large suitcase which smelled strongly of lavender. I tried to fold a broadsheet newspaper across my chest – something to read to take my mind off Carl, off Ads, off *Leeds* – and ended up with the top half of the paper crushed into my armpit and the bottom half tucked neatly under my chin. I had to somehow use my teeth to turn the pages properly.

It was at this precise moment that the ticket inspector chose to grace the stuffy carriage with his presence. He stepped over me without even noticing that there was a potential fare underneath this mountain of paper and bags. I heaved a sigh of relief, grateful I wouldn't be expected to perform the even more unnatural contortions which would be required to actually reach into my pocket to find my ticket.

Still, maybe this was how I was meant to travel back up north: as though smuggling myself. As though I was dangerous cargo.

I was hardly the prodigal son, and every parent I'd ever had, even those false ones like Mama, were dead now. Hell, even Mrs Deacon was probably no longer on this earth.

She might have been glad of it too. For if she'd have been forced to cramp herself into the luggage rack like fucking *livestock*, as I was, and if she'd have been forced to smell the *livestock*-y smell which permeated the carriage, she'd have said thank you but no. I'm better off where I am.

The source of the problem was the train's only toilet, which had long since given up any hope of flushing away the offending articles. Absent-mindedly, I flapped the pages of the newspaper to give me some air. All the action achieved, however, was to make me even more uncomfortable. It was almost unbearably hot on the train; all of the heaters circulated their stuffy, recycled air – and of course the windows were all painted shut.

Somehow, the evil cradling of the train rocked me into a fitful sleep. I dreamed of Ads like I used to, in the old days, living out the moment of impact as his head hit concrete – smashing like a gourd – over and over again. A section of his jaw punching through his cheek right where his beauty spot was, as though his spot was an 'X' as in old treasure maps, as though it had always been ordained to be the point at which his life would come apart. That scream he made, echoing that of the train's brakes.

And then, in that strange way dreams have of higgledy-piggeldy mixing up narratives so that past, present and future ghosted in at the same time in a snowstorm static of memories and projections, colour and sound, I saw the International Pool falling down, like London Bridge. Fair ladies present and correct as some Fred Dibnah wannabe from the local council plunged down the detonator and the place shook, rattled, and rolled into rubble: a single block of lockers left standing in the midst of the debris and Nathan fucking Long going at it with a tyre-iron, a hoggish look of concentration on his fat face.

And then, Natalie and I, draped around each other in bed. We'd slept together once. It seemed like the right thing to do at the time: the pair of us castaways clinging to each other, to the same life-raft, as we weathered the storm. But the Nat was stronger than I was – always had been. And the morning after, we knew we'd made a terrible mistake. I had to jump out the window and run round the front of the house and let myself in that way before Jakey came in and found us like that and suddenly reckoned he had a mum and a dad. But in my dream we slept together over and over, hotly and fiercely, until we forged new selves from out of the molten mess we'd once been. The bed was like a steelworks, like Sheffield, and we fucked ourselves into a new existence, one in which she wouldn't have to be The Nat anymore and I wouldn't have to be Rob bloody Deacon.

I woke with a start; a terrible pain shot up my leg. Somebody had trodden on me.

'I say! Is there somebody down there?' asked a booming voice from above.

'There is, and you're standing on him,' I said.

'What on earth are you doing down there?' said the best Dale Lightwood impressionist I'd ever seen (better even than Nick Byers when he got in the mood).

'Nowhere to sit,' I muttered.

'Ridiculous! Wait until I've visited the khazi and we'll find you a spot,' said the Lightwood-alike, who then extended his hand through the hoop of a displaced rucksack, bent it under the guitar case and attempted to shake my hand. 'I'm Richard – Dick Coverley. Pleased to meet a fellow northerner.'

He sounded about as northern as the Queen.

'Neal... uh... Rob,' I gasped, trying to escape the unwanted attentions of a huge suitcase which had somehow attached itself to my elbow. Dick politely waited until I'd extricated myself and then half shook my hand, half dragged me to my feet. As I moved, so the foundations of the house of travel bags fell down in an unmanageable heap on the floor.

Dick Coverley stood hands on hips and allowed a broad smile to crack his cheeks. He was an awkward-looking man, all angles and sharp edges.

'What are you smuggling yourself back up north for, Neal? Or would you prefer Rob?'

I smiled. 'That's my name. Neal Robb. And I'm coming up to see my girlfriend.' A large part of me wished she was (fnar, fnar).

'Good lad,' said Coverley. 'She'll be pleased. Now, where's that khazi, then?' He'd already walked through the door marked 'Toilet'. He clearly liked commentating on his own life; had a fondness for letting people know that not only was he capable of finding said khazi, he was proficient enough to walk into it before you could come up with your answer, and qualified enough to unzip his own trousers.

I kicked my heels outside the toilet door, which was slightly ajar. What exactly *was* the correct etiquette for loitering around toilets waiting for strangers? Did a slight whistle make you appear slightly less strange? Did staring at the floor as though you were trying to burn a hole in it through which you could then make your escape make you seem less threatening? How about adopting a blatantly bored expression, as though the only reason you were there, man, was because you fancied standing there? You weren't doing nobody no harm…

Coverley emerged from the toilet looking refreshed and ordered once more. 'Let's see if we can't find you a seat, Neal. Now, where's a seat?'

I stumbled after him down the narrow gap between the rows of seats, wondering why I still spent my whole life following people around.

'Right, Neal, how about this one?' said Coverley, who had started to prod a mean-looking punk on the arm. The punk's legs were stretched across two seats.

'I don't think he's going to wake up… and it's Rob,' I whispered, urging Coverley to move on.

'Yes, yes, I know. What are you telling me your name for?'

'You were calling me Neal,' I said.

Coverley rolled his eyes. 'My friend, if you don't even know your own name, how am I supposed to know it?'

Good question. And how was *I* supposed to know this wasn't another dream?

It appeared that there were, as I'd expected, no additional seats on the carriage. I was about to traipse back up the aisle when Coverley tapped me on the shoulder. 'Well, why not come up to First, with me? Travel in style and luxury? There's a space by me. Free coffee. Free *FT*.'

I nodded. 'All right.'

In First, the seat was like a four-poster bed compared to my previous home in the luggage rack, and yet I still couldn't get comfortable. I felt that mixture of nerves and anticipation which rises up in the stomach of every traveller, every prodigal son, every man with a mission.

I picked up a free copy of the *Financial Times* and Coverley looked very pleased I was a fellow number-cruncher. He looked less pleased I only flicked through the opening pages, paid no attention to current market trends. Eventually I found an Arthur Andersen retrospective which snagged my interest and I settled into reading. The story went into great detail about how a once-proud member of the big five had been brought down (as though by a huntsman's bullet) in the early noughties (and they really were *naughty* times for Andersen). There was of course loads of stuff about the Enron scandal in 2001; the systematic accounting fraud which saw hundreds of billions of dollars of the energy corporation's revenue *sustaining itself* thanks in no small part to its auditors, Andersen. The Powers Committee's assessment was that Andersen did not fulfil its 'professional responsibilities'. In 2002 the company was convicted of obstruction of justice, and though this finding was later reversed the damage was already done. The firm surrendered its licences and ceased to be a going concern later that year.

The retrospective said nothing about how the Leeds branch of the firm had had similar bad eggs and similar scandals. It said nothing about how the ripples of the firm's collapse spread out and hit everyone. It said nothing about how we'd all reached for the sky by missing too many rungs of the ladder. And had our asses handed to us.

But everything was connected, and the cavalier attitudes we'd all been encouraged to display at work had kind of bled into our personal lives, and what happened in the end was, it all came crashing down. Ads, Carl, me.

Was it fate brought Coverley to me on the train? Was it fate caused him to drag me up to First, where I could get my hands on the free copy of the FT*? Did I need that reminder of what we'd been and what we'd done before I returned to the scenes of the (various) crimes?*

The train pulled in at Nottingham and Natalie was waiting on the platform. She saw me stepping out of First and asked me how the journey was, Lord Snooty. I told her it was the worst of my life and she asked if I'd ever thought about how the other half lived.

We fell so easily into conversation she could have *been* my other half. As usual, she talked ten-to-the-dozen, but today I got the impression she was talking so much to mask her nerves. When she thought I wasn't looking, she jammed her hand in her mouth and gnawed on her fingernails (yeah, it looked about as appealing as it sounded) and she seemed kind of fidgety. Kept forgetting stuff. She asked me hadn't I brought any bags and I told her no, she *knew* I was on the hoof, had been ever since Mart told me about the International Pool.

We exited the station and she led me to a short-stay car park. She still owned her old Fiesta. The cuddly toys on the parcel shelf at the back of the car were long gone now and someone – probably little Jakey, who was so hungry to be *big* Jake that I kept wanting to tell him be careful what you wish for; you don't wanna be old like us, kid; you don't want to be in a position where you don't dare take risks; you don't ever want to have to live in the strait-jacket of 'professional responsibilities' – had picked most of the LITTLE MONSTER ON BOARD sticker off the back bumper so it now read simply BOARD, but it was still absolutely recognisably the same car. Plenty more miles on the clock now, sure, and judging by the state of it I had no idea how she'd gotten it through her MOT, but still the same laser-blue Fiesta which had been our getaway car. It was like meeting an old friend and suddenly noticing their grey hairs.

'Christ, Nat. It looks like the only thing holding that thing together is the rust.'

She grinned at my gallows humour. 'And that's why I love it.'

'But they'll still be looking for this car. They had your number plate. That's how they tracked down your mum's place, wasn't it? On account of that was where the car was registered.'

'If *I'm* going, Doris is going.'

Yeah, sure, The Nat had named her car and yeah, sure, it didn't put me off her. Not one bit.

'Furry muff,' I said.

And The Nat shot me a look as though she'd misheard what I'd said and was labouring under the mistaken belief I'd said something insulting about her pink furry steering-wheel cover. *Perish the thought.*

Suddenly the easy back and forth of conversation between us dried up. Suddenly the full weight of what it was we were about to do came crashing down on our shoulders. We kind of *sagged* into the car and then we both sat there a moment, staring through the windshield at nothing.

When The Nat keyed the engine, I noticed her hands were shaking ever so slightly and really I should have offered to drive. But then I looked at my own hands and they twitched and squirmed under my scrutiny and I reckoned I'd have been even less of a safe bet than she was.

We set off, trepidation growing even as Nat edged the Fiesta out her parking space, and coming to the boil as we became snarled up in traffic around the station approach. The uneven thrumming of the car under me; the way I could feel the same loose spring in the seat digging into my thigh; the way my knees grazed against the dashboard: all of them took me back to that day six years ago when things fell apart. I'd spent six years trying to glue the pieces back together and sometimes it felt like I couldn't see the joins and sometimes I could go a whole morning or a whole afternoon without thinking about Adam, the first and the last man. But I could never go a whole night. He always sashayed into my dreams, the ghost of my past.

Maybe it would have been easier had I been able to attend his funeral. Maybe then I could have achieved some closure, as the Yanks like to say. Then I could have said goodbye to him, whispered a few apologies as I scattered the dirt down on his closed coffin. Promised him his death wasn't in vain and that I'd make something of myself in his honour. But I'd been told – nay, *ordered* – to stay away. 'Your coming will only make things worse,' Nick Byers had told me. 'Don't even think about it, even if it seems hard. It would be just too dangerous. Long'll be watching the place like a hawk. He'll be *expecting* you to turn up, and he'll be ready for you. Make no bones about it.'

Byers had been my man on the inside of Leeds. My source, my contact. I called him that first week when I was laid up in bed at The Nat's commune, trying to get some more gen on what exactly had happened to Ads and whether there was anything the media hadn't released yet. And then I called him again a week after, and a week after that. It came to be we'd have a call every fortnight, and before those calls I'd hope and pray *this* would be the call in which he'd tell me the ripples which spread out from my flight had finally ceased and that the coast was clear. But that call had never come. He told me Long's SAS crew still had me down as a marked man: the eternal number one in their Most Wanted list. He told me they still circulated my picture; they still had CCTV rigged so they could watch Ads' grave in case I paid a visit; they still kept tabs on all my old contacts in Leeds. They had eyes everywhere.

And just in case I ever got it into my head Byers was exaggerating the threat, he'd also tell me about some of the ongoing and violent ramifications of my swift departure. For instance: a couple months after I left, I was running low on funds so on the sly I enlisted an estate agent to sell my pad on Eastgate. I wasn't under any illusions I'd get anything like what it was worth, which *should have* meant that, even given the state of the housing market in Leeds, I'd be raking in a stone-cold 10% profit on the place: it was all too cloak and dagger for that, and honestly I think right from the start the agent smelled a rat with my cock-and-bull story about why a certain Rob Deacon happened to be trying to sell a flat which – according to the deeds – was owned by a Mr Neal Grace. But the stereotypical estate agent's greed for deals took over and I *thought* I was onto a winner. That was until Nick Byers told me my estate agent had been put in hospital. Apparently he'd been run over whilst he was walking back to his car (which was parked in the same Long Stay Ads parked his TT).

He sustained terrible injuries. For a while it was touch and go whether he'd survive. They put him in a medically-induced coma, and when they finally brought him round he couldn't remember a single thing that had happened to him. I wondered how much he'd 'remembered' when the SAS goons had gone to see him, and decided it couldn't have been much, otherwise they wouldn't have run him down in the first place.

Then there was the sad, sad case of Tom Green, my former colleague at Andersen. Although it was completely out of character for the most boring man in the world, the given story for why he now walked with a pronounced limp and occasionally, on bad days, had to walk with a crutch was that he'd plunged down a flight of stairs one night when he was absolutely off his head on pills. He was in hospital two months and his rehab went on for two *years.* His physical trainers seemed to think one of the main reasons he couldn't walk properly again was a mental thing: he was still very, very scared.

Then there was Carl. I still didn't know what had happened to Carl but what I did know didn't sound good. His cleaning lady, Liz, reported him missing a month or so after I'd also done my bunk. Apparently she hadn't seen hide nor hair of him for at least two weeks. Oh, a couple of mornings would have been fine. She wouldn't have eyed a batlid about that. She knew Carl was something of a 'man about town'. She knew he had quite a bit of success with the ladies (even if he was somewhat sleazy). But even when she did miss him on her usual three-mornings-a-week schedule, he usually left her a pile of shirts to be ironed. And usually there'd be at least *some sign* that he'd been present in the penthouse at *some point.* He hadn't restocked the fridge with beer. His bed appeared to have been unslept in. She left him a note. *'CALL ME: I'M WORRIED ABOUT YOU,'* it said. It was like something a mum would have left for him, and in a way Liz was yet another stand-in mum in lieu of his real mum over in Spain.

Spain was of course the first port of call for the police investigators. They assumed he'd just taken an impromptu

Jet2 out to Marbella. Gone to stay with his folks a while. After all, they knew about the business with Nathan Long, and they knew it might be the last time he'd get to sun himself for a while. But Carl's mum hadn't seen him, and of course she might have been lying, covering for him, but when a couple Interpol guys paid their bar an off-the-cuff visit there was no sign of him. Nor was there any indication his passport had been used.

So where was he? I didn't like to think it but my first instinct was to think: *lying at the bottom of a canal somewhere.* My second was that he'd found his own 'Rob Deacon', changed his name, and gone into hiding somewhere. Hell, maybe he was in London too. But as time dripped by, I thought this was less and less likely. The thing was, Carl loved Leeds. He loved being a big fish in a small pond. In London, he wouldn't have stood out at all. There was always someone richer, more handsome, and shadier too. I didn't think he'd have been able to stay away, even if there was a bounty on his head.

Nick Byers thought Carl had maybe taken a similar deal to the one he'd been offered. He thought Carl had turned grass and was probably now in some witness-protection scheme, 'probably living it up somewhere off the beaten track, like Norfolk.' If he was, he certainly hadn't told his parents about it. Four years after he went walkabout, in a sudden rash of conscience which came far, far too late, Carl's mum hired a private investigator to look into it. According to Byers, the guy did some digging and managed to turn over some stuff about Long and SAS, but then he was warned off in no uncertain terms. According to Byers the guy called up Carl's mum and told her he was off the case, and when she asked him whether he could recommend anyone else to take his place he told her he didn't hate anyone that much.

I sometimes wondered how Nick Byers got to know so much but whenever I did I decided I didn't want to think on that too much. Because right then he was the nearest thing to having a person I could trust and as soon as I started to doubt him I'd be lost. As it was, I only trusted him with certain things, because what if Long and the SAS men got to *him*? I never told him where I was. Not exactly. And I never told him my new name. I also never told him I was still in touch with Natalie.

Finally, I also kept him in the dark about locker 375 at the International Pool. Back in the early days of our exile, Natalie had asked me why we didn't simply post the locker key back to someone in Leeds – someone we trusted – who could get us the loot? You know, don't tell them what's in the case. Just make out like it's old papers or something.

I told her I'd wondered that myself but the bald fact was I simply didn't trust anyone in Leeds. The only person I spoke to was Byers and that was only out of necessity. Besides, I didn't hate anyone enough to put them right in danger's way. I'd hurt enough folks already. But if *Natalie* knew someone, she could sure suggest a name.

Natalie bit her lip. I could see her mind working. Rachel? Rhys? Her mum? Nope, none of them fit the bill. So we decided, way back when, that the only people we trusted were ourselves and each other, and the only way we were going to get the money back was if we both went together, like we were co-signatories for it.

Nick Byers wasn't my only source of information. Though I wouldn't have dreamed of telling Mart, I scoured the *Yorkshire Post* website on a regular basis (though I'd missed the International Pool story), and in addition, some aspects of the endgame of the piece made it to the national news. There was a TV news feature on Long's arrest then, later, another piece in the wake of his trial. After they sent him down, they interviewed his scared-rabbit-looking lawyer outside court. Long's wife stepped in, spitting fury into the camera. She looked like she was about to punch out the interviewer. And by her side, looking just as mad, was Phoebe. All the while, Feebs stared directly into the camera and it felt like she was searching me out or else casting a spell on me somehow. And sometimes over the years it truly felt as though Phoebe's spell still held. She'd wished me a miserable life; that I'd feel just as trapped, as enclosed, as her dad did. And that pretty much came to pass.

We finally left Nottingham and its rush hour behind us. By the time we hit the M1 it was around half-six and already it was getting dark. It should have brought the old ghosts back. Should have made us even more worried, because all the worst monsters came out after nightfall. But in fact it had the opposite effect. For suddenly we felt less obvious, less *in plain sight.* We would be entering Leeds again under a cloak of darkness, and that was good.

We started talking again, tentatively at first but then with more gusto. Like we meant it. The Nat asked me what I'd missed about Leeds so I told her I missed my rooftop garden; looking out over the skyline of a place I knew very well, even if it was ever-changing. Natalie told me she missed Planet Earth nightclub. Nowhere else on earth, she said, did they have a fully-automated revolving dancefloor. So I upped the ante, told her I missed Ace clothes and the Corn Exchange, and she said, what are you, a mosher? No, what she really missed was Black Prince buses because you could still smoke on them and she missed sunny days in Roundhay Park and she missed the Leeds attitude, you know?

I knew.

As soon as we got into Yorkshire, The Nat flicked through the radio, on the hunt for Radio Aire. She'd missed that too, she said. When she finally found it they were running a 'guess the year' competition. They played a series of hits including 'Lady Marmalade', 'Teenage Dirtbag', Shaggy's 'It Wasn't Me' (which could have been Carl, Ads and my soundtrack back in the day), and a Cool Croc number which was ubiquitous in Leeds during my last summer there.

The Nat said she was sure it was 1999. I told her no way. It was 2001, no doubt. And it felt ever so strange because in a way, for me, it felt as though music had ended in 2001. Film too. Now when I looked back everything from *then* sounded better and it watched better and everything *now* seemed stale, rehashed, boring. In those days we really had lived closer to the sun, and though we'd gotten burnt, and those burns still hurt, for the first time I really missed those days, those halcyon Townhouse-penthouse days in which we were princes.

Barnsley, Wakefield, Morley. I knew every junction on the motorway now, like the lifeline on my palm. Then, rising up out of the gloom, the glittering display of Leeds itself, higher-risen than I remembered it, brighter than I remembered it. And then onto the 621, butterflies fluttering about in my belly, that feeling that I was *coming home* unmistakeable. I believe that feeling was so big, there wasn't even room for fear anymore.

'Shit, look at the place,' said Natalie. 'She scrubs up well, doesn't she, old Leeds?'

Breathlessly, we pointed out new hotels and apartment complexes, new towers and domes. Once upon a time, I'd convinced myself that Leeds would have had the pause button pushed on it, just as I had on me. I thought it would start to resemble the bedroom of a missing child whose parents keep everything exactly the same way just in case that child happens to return. Yeah, I was that solipsistic. But now I saw Leeds had gone on without me. It had gotten bigger and brasher. It was more confident. Here was a Prometheus City which hadn't (yet) had the wax burned off its wings.

'Are we going to go straight there or should we just, you know, see the sights a bit more?' said Natalie.

'No time like the present,' I said. And there wasn't. I'd expected to be haunted by the past when I got back but it wasn't like that at all. Leeds was so *in the moment* you couldn't even consider the past. They'd concreted over it and were dancing on its grave.

Natalie plugged us into the city's complicated new one-way system. Slowly, ever so slowly, we dragged closer to our final destination and our date with destiny. I began to sweat. Checked my pockets for my wallet every other minute. Then pulled it out and checked the locker key was still inside every minute after that. 'Is it getting hot in here or is it just me?' I asked.

Natalie rolled her eyes. 'It's just you. But wind down your window if you like. Get some air. You look a little... green around the gills.'

I cranked down the window. Stuck my head out of it like a dog. After a while I became aware of a fine dust which carried on the breeze, and when I pulled my head back inside the car, I crunched grit between my teeth. But I didn't think anything of it. Of course I didn't. I had a million quid on my mind and my future lay spread out before me in a way it hadn't been before.

Nor did I really think about it when we happened across a sign which read *ROAD AHEAD CLOSED*. The Nat simply reversed then took a different route. As we'd already seen, all kinds of building work was taking place in the city. Maybe they'd simply closed the road while they dug the foundations for a new tower or a new dome.

But the adjacent road was closed too. And the one after that. The grid of this side of Leeds had been effectively shut down. Natalie pulled over. 'I think we'd be better walking,' she said.

So we got out, stretched our aching limbs then headed past the signs. At the end of the street was a tall palisade fence. Another sign which read *GUNION DEMOLITION* was posted to it. Still another read *NO ACCESS: ENTRY PROHIBITED*. We stood there a while, clinging on to the fence and peering through into the darkness. Then I decided we should follow the fence around; surely there'd be a gap in it somewhere.

We completed a full circuit and couldn't find a one. That pissed me off. I wanted my money now. I didn't want to have to climb a fucking fence to get to it. I wanted that case in my hands, then maybe back onto the motorway. Hammer it down to Nottingham then scatter the whole million on the bed. Climb into it with Natalie and forget all about how awkward it was between us that one morning we woke up together after a night before.

Natalie pulled a face which convinced me she'd read my thoughts and I felt the blood rising in my cheeks and I was just about to apologise for being so presumptuous when she got in the first hit. And that hit pretty much floored me.

'I don't think we need to worry about the fence, Neal,' she said. 'It's what's *beyond* the fence we need to worry about.'

I peered through. 'I don't know what you... Oh.'

Beyond the fence was a hulking blank space. The kind which, uploaded to Google Maps Street View, would have looked like it was being censored, like what was *really* there was some kind of military installation or some top secret warehouse in which the government might store lost treasures like the Ark of the Covenant. There was no International Pool. It was simply *gone,* like a David Copperfield magic trick, like aliens had been here before us and zapped the place into the ether.

'We're too late,' sighed Natalie.

'But that's impossible. Mart told me they were demolishing it next week.' I blinked. Ash from the torn-down building had gotten in my eye and told me the truth. *It was possible.* There was some in my mouth, too. Brick dust. I spat it out and the world wobbled. Suddenly I hated Mart – fucking Mart – more than I'd ever hated anyone in my life.

Then I *used* my rage. I threw myself at the fence and then up it. At the top, I caught my trousers on a curl of barbed wire; I tugged it loose. The wire caught on my flesh then, at my ankle, but I didn't even feel the bite. I launched myself over the top and landed, tucking myself into a dusty roll and then coming to a halt on the empty desert beyond the fence.

Security lights flashed on me. I was like an inmate in a prison yard caught trying to make a break for it. But I didn't care. I blinked again, and the frazzle of lights made me believe – truly believe – that in that moment I saw the old International Pool building looming up out of the scabby earth.

Then I heard a shout. A security guard came out of a Portacabin over the way. With him a large, slavering Alsatian which looked as though it might break free of its lead any moment. The security guard himself looked as big as a silverback gorilla – only this silverback was wearing glasses.

Natalie hissed through the fence: '*Neal. Get back over here. Now!*'

I ignored her.

The security guard yelled: 'What the hell are you doing? This is private property!'

I didn't move.

The Alsatian barked. The man did too: 'Get out of here!'

And all I could think of was the lockers. Where were the lockers?

'Where's the lockers?' I yelled back.

The man stopped. 'What you on about, lockers? This is a demolition site. It's dangerous. Now make like a tree and leave, else I'll call five-oh.'

I was still frozen.

'Where are the lockers, from the pool? I had... personal items inside my locker and I need them back. I'm not going anywhere until you tell me where the lockers have been taken.'

The man sneered. 'You've had one too many, son. Ten too many, it looks like. Mind you, Ally here likes the taste of meat after its been marinated in beer.' He was getting closer now. So close I could almost make out the branding on the black bomber jacket he wore. But right then I wasn't worried about physical harm, only the mental pain which was lightning-bolting through me because *my money* wasn't here.

All of this, everything I'd been through, could at least be explained by the money. It was the thing which held the narrative of my life for the past six years together. Without it, I was lost. The original Lost Boy, stuck here in Prometheus City like some never-grown-up Peter Pan. I couldn't bear it. All I wanted to do was flop down on the ground, curl up and let the fucking Alsatian chow down on my useless body.

We were too late. I didn't think it would be possible to go on living with that kind of knowledge beating away like a second heart inside me. I didn't know how I could go on. This was the bottom, the very rocky bottom, and at last I'd reached it. I'd been falling ever since the night the bouncers had beaten seven shades of shit out of those Neanderthal lads and now I'd hit ground zero. The end of the line. Maybe it was a poetic kind of justice for me. Maybe it was just the way of the world. Shit happens, especially to those who bring it on themselves.

The security guy was four feet away from me now. He took off his glasses and polished the lenses. Then he returned them to his face. Then he smiled. There were numerous gaps in that smile which told the tale of a thousand fights. 'Well, well, well,' he said. 'Look-ee what we got here. I know you, boy, don't I?'

I didn't know him. Or maybe I did. Maybe the past six years hadn't been kind to Captain Bouncer. Maybe it didn't matter. All I knew was this guy was SAS – it said so on the ID badge he wore on his shoulder.

'We didn't know this was going to be our lucky day, did we, Ally?' he asked the dog. 'Funny how it happens, ain't it? But we're going to be dining out on steak forevermore. For this is Neal Grace, as I live and breathe. And I'm going to call in my bounty.' He took out his walkie-talkie, lifted it to his face. 'This is the end, kid. Any last words?'

I shrugged. 'Sure, I'm just glad it's over. I'm sick of running away.'

The security guard slapped a paw down on my shoulder. 'Attaboy,' he said. 'Now *stay*, 'til I call this in.' He was about to say something else too, but the words died in his throat. His mouth opened in a wide 'O' and for a moment I wondered what the hell was wrong with him.

Then I heard the almighty crash as a vehicle – a small Ford Fiesta – smashed through the palisade fence like something straight out of a movie. The security guard dived to the side, letting go of the dog's lead. The Alsatian darted off into the night. And then The Nat screeched to a halt right in front of me; the front of the car was all busted up and a section of fence was hanging off the roof. The front bumper was trailing underneath it and the windscreen was cracked. But the engine was still running.

Natalie stuck her head out the window and for a second time, maybe for a second time on this very spot, she yelled at me to get in. And for the second time she became my getaway driver.

II

When the dust settled after our miraculous escape, Natalie gave me hell. What the fuck had I been thinking, just standing there offering myself up to that security guard like I was some sort of human sacrifice? I told her I had no idea, but I did have some history when it came to self-sabotage. Maybe it was that.

She said I'd be lucky if she ever spoke to me again.

I thought the word lucky should never be associated with me anymore. Luck and I never really got along. I mean, what the hell kind of mean luck was it that the council saw fit to demolish the International Pool *ahead of schedule*?

I sat around and sulked about the money for the longest time, until even Natalie's patience snapped and she told me to get over myself. She told me I shouldn't have ever thought about the cash in the locker as my rainy-day money, my just-in-case fund. Life was better if you didn't go round thinking you had a safety net to insulate you from living for today. I didn't believe her, not at first.

Then, a year later, Black Friday came. The *big* crash. Whole of Leeds came crashing down. It too had over-reached and had got burned. It had dreamed too big. And everyone's safety net was gone now. We were all out there alone.

Made me feel a bit better about myself and my luck. Everyone got it wrong, everyone gambled big. Now everyone was paying the price. I called up The Nat to tell her I'd realised I'd been a fool, that we were all up shit creek, no paddle, not just me. She told me the crash didn't happen just to prove to me I wasn't the unluckiest person in the world.

And I got to thinking about the old fella used to come in the Golden Goose. Guy who'd based his whole miserable life on the fact that *this was what he could have won* if only he'd played the game right. And I thought about how *he'd* pushed away everyone he held close – even his dog – because he was so damned pissed off about not walking away with a life-changing amount of money. And I decided I didn't want the same to happen to me.

So what I did was, I went whole hog the other way. Trained it up to Nottingham and got down on one knee. Said I'd like to make an honest woman out of Natalie, and wouldn't I be a great dad to Jakey? She laughed me right back down to London. Said it was the worst idea in the world. Why didn't I set my sights a little lower next time? Enough with the grand gestures; the million quid, the life of crime, the wild escapes from Leeds, the proposal. Just try living *not* like a prince for a while. Just live like normal people do.

I told her I'd try it.

She said good. Maybe I'd finally grown up.

I haven't though. But I have put quite a bit of the *ridiculousness* to one side for a while. And I don't let the Lost Boy madness shine through quite so much. I make out like I'm a fully functioning adult member of society and most people take me at face value.

I suppose that's just how everyone else gets through...?

The End

If you enjoyed *The Lost Boys of Prometheus City*, why not try our other Armley Press titles available from Amazon and through UK bookshops?

Mick McCann: *Coming Out as a Bowie Fan*
ISBN 0-9554699-0-2
Mick McCann: *Nailed*
ISBN 0-9554699-2-9
Mick McCann: *How Leeds Changed the World*
ISBN 0-9554699-3-0
John Lake: *Hot Knife*
ISBN 0-9554699-1-6
John Lake: *Blowback*
ISBN 0-9554699-4-7
John Lake: *Speedbomb*
ISBN 0-9554699-5-4
John Lake: *Amy and the Fox*
ISBN 0-9934811-0-8
Ray Brown: *In All Beginnings*
ISBN 0-9554699-6-1
Samantha Priestley: *Reliability of Rope*
ISBN 0-9554699-8-5
Chris Nickson: *Leeds, the Biography*
ISBN 0-9554699-7-X
Nathan O'Hagan: *The World is (Not) a Cold Dead Place*
ISBN 0-9554699-9-6
David Siddall: *Breaking Even*
ISBN 0-9934811-1-6
K.D. Thomas: *Fogbow and Glory*
ISBN 0-9934811-3-0
Mark Connors:*Stickleback*
ISBN 0-9934811-2-3
M.W. Leeming : *Justice is Served*
ISBN 0-9934811-4-7

Visit *armleypress.com*

www.ingramcontent.com/pod-product-compliance
Lightning Source LLC
Chambersburg PA
CBHW030315200626
46816CB00006BA/1798